In the Midst of Lions

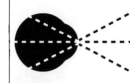

This Large Print Book carries the
Seal of Approval of N.A.V.H.

In the Midst of Lions

SARA MITCHELL

Thorndike Press • Thorndike, Maine

Published in 2000 by arrangement with Bethany House Publishers.

Thorndike Press Large Print Christian Mystery Series.

The tree indicium is a trademark of Thorndike Press.

The text of this Large Print edition is unabridged.
Other aspects of the book may vary from the original edition.

Set in 16 pt. Plantin.

Printed in the United States on permanent paper.

Library of Congress Cataloging-in-Publication Data

Mitchell, Sara.
    In the midst of lions / Sara Mitchell.
        p.   cm.
    Originally published: Minneapolis : Bethany House, 1996.
(Shadowcatchers ; 2)
        ISBN 0-7862-2878-4 (lg. print : hc : alk. paper)
        1. Georgia — Fiction.   2. Large type books.   I. Title.
    PS3563.I823 I5   2000
    813'.54—dc21   00-059957

For Mama and Mom . . .
Even in the midst of life's lions,
the Shepherd's love shines
through you both.

Acknowledgments

While everyone in Thomasville, Georgia, with whom I spoke was helpful, several deserve special appreciation:

C. Tom Hill, Curator, Thomas County Historical Society, for his insights, anecdotes, and wealth of knowledge freely shared;

Pearl Thomas, Librarian, Thomasville Genealogical, History and Fine Arts Library, for her cheerful assistance with the newspapers of the 1890s and other invaluable resources;

Frieda Spangle, who so graciously shared her heritage — the "driving tour" truly made the past come alive!

Contents

Prologue. 11

Part One: Legacy 15

Part Two: Lies. 169

Part Three: Liberty 357

I am in the midst of lions;
I lie among ravenous beasts —
men whose teeth are spears and arrows,
whose tongues are sharp swords.

Psalm 57:4 NIV

Author's Notes

During the 1890s, Thomasville, Georgia, was a thriving winter resort that enjoyed national recognition; I have tried to depict its hotel era as accurately as possible. Thomasville of the 1990s continues to thrive, although the grand hotels and trainloads of passengers are long gone. But the same warm welcome awaits all visitors — and it is still possible to glimpse the town as it was a hundred years ago.

Rose Hill, Adelaide, and many of the businesses, however, are entirely fictional. *All* the characters in this book are fictional and bear no resemblance to anybody, living or dead . . . *especially* the villains!

Prologue

Thomasville, Georgia
October 1892

They were supposed to meet in the last barn at Pastime Racetrack, by the harness room, at three-thirty in the afternoon. At this time of the year, the track would be deserted, which suited him just fine. He didn't know why Soames had insisted on this out-of-the-way spot, unless it was a doublecross of some sort.

He glanced around, irritation rapidly giving way to rage. The upstart! If he thought a lowly stable boss — a *hired hand* — wielded any power, perhaps it was time to teach William Soames a much-needed lesson.

He hid the buggy in the woods beyond the racetrack — no sense in advertising his presence, although it wouldn't make any difference. If anyone ever asked, he'd already prepared two unassailable alibis, depending on what Soames had to say.

The sullen pewter sky promised rain, and damp gusts of wind stirred the branches of the pine trees flanking the dirt lane that led to the stables. There was no sign of life in the office or employees' dwellings, but one of the large sliding barn doors was unlatched. He slipped through, prowling the deserted barn, shuddering in distaste at the dust and straw, the faint musky odor lingering in the air. It was a little before three, plenty of time to prepare for Soames's arrival.

By a quarter past, he was ready. He waited just inside the stall, arms folded across his chest, a pair of heavy horse's hair clippers on the floor beside him, propped against the wall.

"Hey! Anybody here?" Soames's voice echoed hollowly in the deserted barn.

Fearing that the idiot might be indiscreet enough to actually call his name aloud, he stepped into the aisle. "Down here, Mr. Soames. And unless you care to have the watchman and any other passersby party to this . . . meeting, shut your trap and get on down here. I don't like to be kept waiting."

His gaze darting nervously about, Soames sauntered down the aisle, his heavy boots clunking on the wooden floor. "Sorry, Mr. —"

"No names!" he rapped out sharply. "You've been told often enough. If you can't follow the simplest of instructions, your future usefulness . . ."

"That's what we gotta talk about," Soames muttered, twisting a frayed jockey's cap in his hands.

"Make it quick, then." He casually stepped back inside the stall. "I have better things to do than loiter around a stable."

A feral look of cunning flashed through the other man's eyes. "Maybe. Maybe not," he claimed, and cleared his throat. "I been doin' some thinkin'. Them Pinks almost nabbed me the last time." Now Soames paused, blinking rapidly. "I — you said there wouldn't be no trouble."

"What are you trying to say, Mr. Soames?"

"I — I want out. It's too risky." He wiped his face. "I won't tell anyone. You gotta believe me. I just want out," his voice rose.

"Of course you won't tell anyone," he soothed, his tone deceptively calm. "The thought never occurred to me, Mr. Soames." He leaned forward slightly, and his fingers closed over the handle of the clippers. "Thanks for letting me know. Now, scram. It wouldn't do for us to leave together."

Relief and suspicion battled over Soames's irregular features, but he turned with a shrug, cramming the cap back on his head.

The man in the shadows lifted the clippers, and brought the metal end down on the back of Soames's head as hard as he could. The sniveling coward collapsed without a sound.

Out in the aisle a faint noise alerted him — the scraping of a boot? A voice?

He flung the clippers into the straw and stepped into the aisle, every sense alert. A

13

gust of wind from the open barn door whistled through the rafters. Abruptly he froze, sniffing the air, his nose teased by an elusive scent of . . . flowers?

Swiveling, his gaze whipped the length of the barn, searching the empty aisle. A few wisps of loose straw swirled, then settled. Disgusted with himself, he strode out the door, his footsteps firm.

Let the Thomasville authorities chase their tails over this *one.* They'd never solve the murder of Horatio Crump's stupid stable boss. He shut the barn door and headed for the trees. Even the irksome detectives from Pinkerton's National Detective Agency would never unravel this case.

He chuckled. Wouldn't matter if they did — because he'd never go to jail. Never.

PART ONE

♦ ♦ ♦

LEGACY

September–December 1895

1

Atlanta, Georgia
September 1895

Simon Kincaid was irritated. The warm autumn day fairly exploded with color, and for the first time all week, the sky burned a bright clear blue, utterly devoid of clouds. Even the infamous Dixie humidity had abated slightly from its summer saturation point. Simon should have been enjoying the day. He was not.

He ran a finger around his stiff shirt collar and imagined the pleasure of shedding collar *and* tie. Suits definitely were not . . . suitable . . . for tracking humanity's riffraff, those who tended to favor sleazy joints, smelly alleyways, and, here in the South, bug-infested swamps.

Today, however, Simon had come to town for a meeting with Perry Sterns, the assistant manager for the Atlanta branch of Pinkerton's National Detective Agency. A pedantic fussbudget of a man, Sterns was frankly unnerved by Simon, which was why Simon was irritated. Over the past year he had never so much as scowled at the fellow, and today he had even worn the suit, complete with freshly starched collar and cuffs.

I'm frustrated, he acknowledged. *Frustrated, irritated, and . . . restless.* Never in all his years as a Pinkerton operative had he remained undercover for so long, with so little to show for it.

In front of him, the door to a small café opened, and a couple of businessmen emerged, bringing with them a host of tantalizing aromas. As if on cue, Simon's stomach growled. *I must be hungry, too.* Shrugging, he went inside to join the noisy crowd of men jostling one another at the long counter.

Lunch improved his mood, but the delay forced him to hail a hack so he wouldn't be late for his appointment. As he ducked his head to climb inside, a loud yelp from the alley by the café caught his attention.

"Wait here," he told the driver. "Back in a moment."

Scowling, the grizzled man spat a stream of tobacco juice onto the street. "I got better things to do —" he began, then met Simon's eye. "Yessir. Yessir, I'll be here," he nodded, squirming on his seat.

Simon sprinted down the squalid alley, footsteps noiseless, keeping to the shadows. Near the back door of the café, a large man wearing a bloodied butcher's apron delivered a vicious kick to a cowering dog whose

18

high-pitched yelps had first alerted Simon. Grabbing a loose plank from the top of a jumbled stack of citrus crates, Simon splintered the board against the bully's ribs.

"Why, you —" Clutching his side, the man whirled to face Simon, his jowled face purple with rage.

"The dog isn't wearing heavy boots," Simon observed in a remote voice, "so I thought I'd even things up a bit." He shifted, preparing for the attack, almost relishing the prospect.

Behind them the door was flung open and a faceless voice yelled, "Hey, Billy-boy! Get yo' lazy carcass back in here and help peel these taters 'fo the boss peels us!"

"That's your only chance at a reprieve," Simon warned, taking a step closer. "Because the way I feel right now, there won't be anything left for your boss *to* peel."

Billy proved to be a coward as well as a bully. Spitting more curses, he turned and stomped inside, slamming the door behind him.

Simon stood for a moment, breathing deeply, hands clenching and unclenching. Then he walked slowly toward the dog, lying motionless on a heap of garbage. Its eyes were closed, bloody paws dangling. Simon paused a short distance away when the animal stirred and lifted its head, and Simon found himself looking into a pair of dark eyes almost human in the emotion, intelligence — and terror — they conveyed.

"Easy now." He spoke gently, dropping down to balance on the balls of his feet while he studied the injured animal. "I'm not going to hurt you."

The dog whined, its long skinny tail weakly thumping. *Female,* Simon noticed in swift assessment, with smallish head and long, blunt-tipped nose. Short, dark brown hair with white markings on her head, chest, tail, and feet.

"All right, little lady," he murmured, keeping his voice low-pitched and calm, "I need to look you over a bit. How about it?" Slowly he stretched out his hand, but the dog made no move to attack. Instead, her emaciated body quivered, distressed whimpers escaping from her throat, while all the time the liquid eyes gazed at Simon as if waiting for him to strike her.

Something twisted painfully in Simon's chest. She must have been so severely abused, her spirit was virtually destroyed. He waited, kneeling in the stinking garbage — until some of the fear faded from the dog's expression — before stretching his hand, palm down, toward her nose. After a moment, a pink tongue weakly licked his fingers, and her tail thumped once.

"Good girl," he praised her, sliding his hand over her muzzle and scratching behind

20

her ears. "Now, let's see what that bruiser did to you. Maybe I should haul him back out and carve him up for you, hmm? You could use a decent meal, couldn't you, poor little scrap? Easy there — I won't hurt you." He hid the burning anger, hands gentle as he examined her limp body. "Don't worry; *nobody's* going to hurt you, anymore. *Nobody.*"

◆ ◆ ◆

Sheets of rain sluiced through leaden skies, soaking the two men and their mounts as they made their way down the winding path. The muddy track flanked the Flint River several miles south of Albany. In the late afternoon downpour, the horses stumbled and slipped frequently, and the men steadily cursed both rain and the stoic animals.

"How much farther, Abe?" one man called above the driving rain. He shifted in the saddle, wiping his face with a sopping bandana. "This here weather ain't fit for a polecat."

"Quit your bellyachin', Rufus!" Abe yelled back. "We'll be there in a few minutes. Now, don't ask me again!"

Rufus Black muttered an obscenity and hunched his shoulders against a sudden blast of wind. Beneath his slicker he was damp and sticky, and the bone-jarring gait of the horse made his innards cramp. If he weren't being paid a wad for this job, he'd hightail it outta here and let that blowhard Abe Collins see how far he'd get on his own. Stupid bonehead

21

— treating Rufus like he was nothing but a hick Georgia cracker!

Moments later Abe halted, waving Rufus to pull up alongside him. "Down there." He pointed. "See it?"

Rufus squinted, barely able to make out the blurred silhouette of a trestle bridge spanning the swollen river, which was running faster than he'd ever seen it. "River's pretty high," he muttered, swallowing hard. "That's goin' to make things a mite more difficult."

Abe grunted. "You saying you can't do the job?"

"I ain't saying no such thing! But it won't be no cakewalk — and I might be needing a little more for my trouble."

"What you're paid — and whether you're paid at all — makes *me* no nevermind." Abe jerked the reins and kneed his horse. "Come on. This rain ain't letting up none."

A little farther along, they left the path and tied the horses. Then, carrying tools and saddlebags, they carefully made their way to the bridge.

Two hours later they climbed up the bank and over to the stand of trees where they'd left the horses. Though wet to the skin and covered with mud and creosote, both men were smiling with satisfaction.

"Yep, it'll be one fine sight to behold,"

Rufus announced, glancing back at the bridge one last time. "Wonder which train'll do the trick. Too bad we can't stick around fer the fireworks."

"*You* might be fool enough to hang around," Abe drawled as he swung into the saddle, "but I aim to be on the next train outta here."

"They oughtta thank us for this, they ought." Rufus clumsily mounted his horse, then broke into a belly-deep guffaw and slapped his thigh. "This here stretch of line's the sorriest in the state."

He was still chuckling as he followed his companion back down the path and was swallowed by the rain-wet woods.

2

Maymont
In the mountains of north Georgia
September 1895

Elizabeth Granger lined up her five small charges, from eighteen-month-old Thomas to seven-year-old Joan. "All right, lambkins. Everybody hold hands, remember?" she instructed. "We'll visit the stables one last time to say good-bye to all your grandmama's horses. But we must stay together."

She waited quietly while Horatio III and Lamar squabbled over who would go first, making faces at each other until four-year-old Jessica inserted her sturdy body between them, grabbing each brother's hand in a death grip. Joan, the eldest Crump daughter, held onto Thomas, keeping her solemn brown eyes fastened on Elizabeth. Joan didn't like horses. Elizabeth, on the other hand, loved horses as much as she had grown to love the Crump children. She had spent the past year working with the small girl, trying to help her feel comfortable around the big animals. Her approach was always patient, gently coaxing, and Joan had come to trust Elizabeth enough to risk an occasional visit to her father's stables at home in Thomasville, as well as the stables here. Yesterday, small fingers trembling, she had even fed a carrot to Mercutio, the placid old coach horse who could barely summon the energy to nibble the treat.

Elizabeth leaned down to rumple Joan's curls. "Would you like to feed Mercutio another carrot today? Maybe an apple?" Immediate pandemonium erupted as the other children demanded the same privilege.

With the blend of firm tolerance and good-natured humor that had secured her the position of paid companion fifteen months earlier, Elizabeth shepherded Horatio Crump's five children down the sweeping gravel drive. At first, there had been grumblings that the children didn't really need a "companion" — for months, both their mammy and the tutor had treated Elizabeth like an unwanted stepchild. Elizabeth, all too familiar with rejection and hostility, simply tried to make herself useful but unobtrusive. At least the childen's adoration was unrestrained, and eventually the entire Crump staff had come to accept Elizabeth as a permanent addition to the household.

A soft breeze laden with woodsmoke and autumn leaves tickled her nose and feathered wisps of her fine brown hair about her forehead. Overhead, the mid-morning sun blazed in a bright, enamel blue sky, burning the last bit of frost. All around her, draped in muted tones of gold and rust, loomed the gentle peaks of the ancient Blue Ridge Mountains. A lone hawk swooped silently down to perch in the top branches of the trees beyond the stables. *Alone, but free,* Elizabeth thought. She could almost envy the hawk. Wistfully she returned her attention to more practical matters. The day was beautiful, but they would spend most of it preparing for the long train ride home, so they'd best enjoy these next few hours.

Every September the Crumps joined Mr. Crump's mother at Maymont, her summer estate in the mountains of north Georgia, to watch the leaves turn. A tall, patrician woman, Georgina Crump's impeccable manners did not completely disguise an autocratic disposition.

Always mindful of her own tenuous status within the household, Elizabeth was careful to remain in the background, seldom speaking to the older woman after a quiet greeting. The five children worshiped their grandmother, however, and clamored for her attention.

Despite her objections to "the smelly beasts," as Georgina Crump referred to the horses, she also knew of her grandchildren's fondness for them and had reluctantly granted permission to make this farewell visit to the stables.

Mr. Watts flashed Elizabeth a gap-toothed grin as her five charges tiptoed in a miniature chain down the barn's central aisle. "You sure got those younguns trained," he observed. "The madam told me just the other day she don't know how Mr. Crump's family managed before you come."

He tugged out a bulging burlap tote and turned toward the children, either missing or ignoring Elizabeth's look of discomfort. "Now, gather round, and I'll hand out these here apples."

"Remember how we taught you to hold them on the palms of your hands," Elizabeth added, scooping little Thomas up into her arms.

"Down!" he demanded.

"He wants down," Lamar interpreted for his little brother. "He saw Billy Pritchard petting the horses one time, and he wants to do it, too."

Elizabeth gave a firm shake of her head. "Billy's mama wouldn't let him run about the stables, either." But the truth was she wasn't at all sure that Maisie Pritchard kept a tight rein on her brood of four. In fact, from what she had observed in Thomasville on the occasions Maisie had brought her children over to play with the five little Crumps, it was her youngest, Billy, who most often needed rescuing from some imminent disaster.

As Elizabeth struggled to contain the squirming Thomas, she realized for the first time that the good-natured baby was growing into a headstrong toddler — much like Billy Pritchard. . . .

"Here, now, Miss 'Lizbeth." Mr. Watts started forward. "That sprout's way too heavy for a little lady like yourself. Let me tote him fer awhile, why don't you?"

"Elizabeth is stronger than she looks." Joan edged over shyly, her hand reaching for Elizabeth's free one. "You should have seen her yesterday, helping Grandmother's cook knead eight loaves of bread, even though Cook told her she wasn't s'posed to be in the kitchen. Elizabeth can do *anything*." She glanced up, her eyes worshipful. "I wish Mama was like her."

Elizabeth squeezed the child's hand. "Hush, darling. Your mother loves you very much, and it would hurt her to hear you talk like that." Forcing a smile, she reached down to hug the abashed Joan while the other children clustered around, chattering like magpies.

"Even if you *do* look sad *most* of the time, Elizabeth, you *always* smile when we come to the stable, 'cuz you told us you loved horses best, after us."

" 'Lizbeth, come over here. I want to feed the big black horse. You *said* I could. . . ."

"Why do horses' ears move? I wish *my* ears could move like that."

Once again, the childish babble pulled Elizabeth back from the dangerous precipice of the past. She set about filling their last day at Maymont with happy memories, along with a few bittersweet ones of her own.

An hour later, she asked a trusted groom to escort the children back to the house. After they had trooped reluctantly out, she turned to another grinning stableboy, who approached with a saddled horse. "Thanks, Joey." She stroked the bay's questing nose. "Big Red is one of my favorites."

Joey's grin filled his face. "I do know that, Miss 'Lizbeth. I warmed 'im up real good for you, so don't you worry none. He's rarin' to go."

The field behind the barn beckoned, and the minute Joey closed the gate, Elizabeth gathered the reins and squeezed Red's sides. He leaped into a gallop, and Elizabeth laughed aloud as they flew across the meadow. "Fly like an eagle," she urged the straining animal. "Fly!"

Her spirit soared as they raced around the perimeter of the field. Sights and sounds spun and mingled in a kaleidoscope of color and, for a few precious moments, Elizabeth was free.

Ten minutes later she urged the horse to a walk, and after one head toss and two tail swishes, Red complied. Elizabeth leaned forward to pat the glistening neck. "I know, I know. You'd have made a wonderful racehorse. It's too bad, but I guess you'll have to accept your lot in life, just as I must. If Mr. Crump were at all inclined to flat racing, I might find a way to bring you to his attention. But I'm afraid, dear one, you'd make a dreadful trotter, and that's all Mr. Crump cares to own right now."

They plodded along in silence for a while. For the past fifteen months, Elizabeth's "lot in life" had forced her to live a lie. "What do *you* think I should do, Red?" she asked, the corners of her mouth tilting when one of the animal's ears politely swiveled backward. "Would you be willing to share a bit of horse sense with me? No? Well, that's pretty smart of you, I admit. Right now, my life is about as tangled as a box full of bridles . . . no matter how hard I try to arrange it otherwise."

She wished she felt comfortable speaking with someone — other than a horse. Someone she could confide in — someone she could *trust*, here on earth, as she trusted God. Her throat tightened as old grief dimmed the glow of the morning. It was six years now. . . . Grandpapa had been gone six whole years. Elizabeth had never known her grandmother . . . *or* her mother. Or the two older brothers whose fates remained a mystery. Nor even the father whose selfishness and greed had destroyed his family. What Elizabeth *did* know was that human relationships were fragile and never to be trusted.

In the woods next to the field, a flock of crows took flight, swooping up into the sky, shattering the stillness of the morning with their indignant caws. Red shied sideways, but Elizabeth controlled the eruption of movement, soothing the animal with her voice and hands. *Back to the unpleasant surprises of life,* she thought, turning Red's head toward the barn. "We have to go. . . ." She lifted her head toward the sky, blinking back the threat of tears. "We have to go back now, Red."

As she left the stable for the last time, she slipped a red-faced Mr. Watts a stack of clean white handkerchiefs tied together with a ribbon. "I'll never forget your kindness," she whispered. "May God keep you."

Before she reached the house, Elizabeth carefully shook out her rumpled blouse and divided skirt, finger-combed her windblown chestnut hair and clipped it back with a tortoiseshell clasp. Outwardly composed again, she spent the next hours helping Josephine Crump finish packing for the all-night trip home to Thomasville.

Flushed and distracted, Josephine gratefully accepted Elizabeth's aid; she had never enjoyed traveling, and this trip would be especially harrowing. She was sending the children ahead with Elizabeth and Tilda, the

31

children's old mammy; Josephine would follow the next day with her husband Horatio and her mother-in-law.

Two days earlier, Horatio had gone to Atlanta to meet with a businessman. "A Mr. Avery Paxton," Mrs. Crump told Elizabeth. "Apparently the man is trying to compete with Mr. Crump, who as I told you is extremely . . . ah . . . *discomposed* about the matter. I thought . . ." She stopped, blushing more like a young girl than a plump matron who had borne five children.

"I'm sure he *would* feel better if you were here when he returns." Elizabeth fastened the straps on the last suitcase and straightened. "Tilda will be coming with us, remember. Please don't worry. We'll be fine."

"You *are* a treasure, Elizabeth," the other woman murmured, coming round to give her a hug. When Elizabeth stiffened, Josephine sighed and dropped her arm. "I'm sorry, dear. I forgot how uncomfortable that makes you. I wish you'd . . ." she paused, head tilted. "Someday, perhaps you'll trust me enough to tell me what causes the sadness in your lovely blue eyes."

When I tell you my real name, you'll know, Elizabeth thought, feeling more traitorous than Brutus in *Julius Caesar*. Or Judas Iscariot in the Bible. The very last thing Josephine Crump would want to do *that* day would be to put her arm around Elizabeth.

32

$\blacklozenge \quad \blacklozenge \quad \blacklozenge$

A little past ten that night, the Horatio Crump household, minus Horatio and Josephine, boarded the train. Elizabeth and the children occupied the Crumps' private car, with the rest of the staff scattered throughout the other coaches. They should be home by suppertime the following evening, Elizabeth promised the children, if the weather held. She knew Mr. Crump had purchased the ailing Rabun Gap Line the previous year, which allowed the Crumps to ride on their own lines all the way to Albany. Unfortunately South Georgia Central owned the notorious road from Albany to Thomasville — a bumpy, painfully slow piece of track which Mr. Crump planned to improve, once it was owned by the Crumps.

Clouds darkened the night sky less than an hour down the track, and by the time they left Atlanta, rain was splattering the windows with increasing intensity. Overhead, light from the elaborate gas chandeliers glowed softly, creating a snug cocoon of warmth and security. One by one the children, lulled by the rain and the rhythmic motion of the swaying car, drifted off to sleep.

Finally free of responsibilities, Elizabeth dismissed the children's mammy, then retired to an upholstered chair in the observation room, at the back of the luxurious Pullman Palace car. Pensive, full of troubled questions, she opened her traveling bag and tugged out a much-folded slip of paper from a hidden compartment in its depths. Three names were written there: *Rattray, Graham,* and *Crump.*

Two of those individuals, Rattray and Crump, had good reason to hate the third, Charles Graham. A liar and a cheat. A man who had buried a quarter of a million dollars' worth of Yankee gold — and told his two partners that the Yankees had stolen it. A man who happened to be Elizabeth's *father.* He had betrayed not only his business associates but his own family. Charles Graham might have been dead for nearly twenty-five years, but the wind he had sown with his perfidy had reaped the whirlwind, sweeping his daughter into its wake.

For many minutes Elizabeth stared at the paper as if it were a cobra poised to strike. She had discovered the list of names a little over two years ago, when she had gone to meet a man at Pastime Stables — and had instead overheard his murder. Fear had initially been her motivation for assuming a different name when she returned to south Georgia . . . but shame was perpetuating the lie.

At length Elizabeth thrust the paper deep inside the hidden compartment, snapped the lid shut, and turned her head toward the rain-streaked window.

3

Atlanta

Simon sauntered into Sterns's pristine office while the clerk who held the door turned his head aside, his face a grimace of disgust.

"Good heavens, what *is* that odor, Mr. Kincaid?" Perry Sterns stood, glaring at Simon as if he had committed an unforgiveable breach of etiquette.

"I was sidetracked for a little while." Simon dropped down into a chair opposite the assistant superintendent's desk.

"In one of the city's sewers, it appears," Sterns observed, holding a handkerchief to his nose. "Couldn't you at least — never mind. . . ." The dapper man shook his head and stuffed the handkerchief back into his pocket. "At least this time you're . . . ah . . . more appropriately attired." He cleared his throat, a flush tinting the pale cheeks. "You wished to discuss the situation down south, I believe."

Simon relaxed and tried to wipe his face free of a fresh surge of annoyance. "In the fourteen months since I was ordered to Georgia to investigate the charges against Crump Systems, we've only been able to secure enough prima facie evidence to convict what amounts to a handful of hired underlings — not any of the kingpins." He looked down at his fingers and began absently cleaning dried blood from the nails. Then his gaze lifted to Sterns. "And no evidence against either of the Crump brothers."

The manager stiffened. "Mr. Kincaid, I must remind you — again — that the Crump family is one of the oldest and most highly respected in the state. Beyond that, they have retained Pinkerton's services on numerous occasions, which makes your investigation extremely awkward. The superintendent, as you know —"

"Has promised his full cooperation," Simon snapped. "Where is he, anyway? Perhaps it would be better if I spoke with him directly."

"He's in a meeting with the Bankers Association." Sterns's voice was stiff. "I'm afraid you're stuck with me, Mr. Kincaid."

He's not the criminal, Simon reminded himself. *Quit treating him like one.* He sat forward, letting his arms dangle while he studied the offended manager. It was one thing to stalk a two-bit hoodlum or threaten to beat up a bully, but though he didn't particularly like Perry Sterns, the man *was* his superior. And Simon didn't really *want* to intimidate him.

36

He just wasn't good with decent people, it seemed. The thought was depressing. *I don't belong here. Most likely, I'll never . . . belong . . . anywhere.*

"Mr. Sterns," he offered now, lowering his gaze. He had learned that direct eye contact always seemed to make the man nervous. "What I propose is another undercover operation — but I'll need a backup, one who is completely unknown to the locals. Did Mr. Jenkins empower you with that level of authority in his absence?"

"You must know he did not." There was a brief, uncomfortable pause before Sterns continued, "However, as you have proven to be every bit as resourceful as Superintendent Hostler in Richmond promised, Mr. Jenkins did indicate that I was not to . . . ah . . . refuse any reasonable request." He swallowed hard, his gaze darting to Simon's, then sliding away. "*Reasonable* request, Mr. Kincaid."

"Hmph." Simon slouched down in the chair, idly stroking the armrests. "Would a plan to infiltrate Horace Crump's estate in Thomasville by posing as a horse trainer constitute 'reasonable'? Rumor has it that Horatio's not real happy with the current man."

Sterns stood his ground this time. "Such a proposal would have to have approval from levels above both myself *and* Mr. Jenkins. I think you know that, Mr. Kincaid."

The corner of Simon's mouth quirked, and some of his tension at last melted away. "I do," he admitted. Abruptly he rose. "Tell me, do you have a dog by any chance?"

"A . . . dog?" Sterns repeated, flabbergasted. "You mean, as a pet? Well, not at the moment, no. We used to — that is, my wife and I owned a fox terrier. But he died last year." He looked across at Simon, his bewildered expression so comical Simon almost smiled. Almost, but not quite.

"I rescued a dog," Simon explained, thinking of the pathetic mutt he'd bribed a young boy to care for while he met with Perry Sterns. "She could use a good home."

"And you thought *I* would provide a good home?" Sterns's cheeks flushed again as a look of relief gradually replaced the stiff awkwardness. "I . . . appreciate the vote of confidence — in that matter, at any rate — Mr. Kincaid. Um . . . what kind of dog?"

Simon raked a hand through his unruly hair. "I'm not sure. She's fairly large, with very unusual markings. Actually, she's unlike any other dog I've ever seen —" he broke off, feeling suddenly ridiculous. "I'll come back in the morning. Tell the superintendent that if he wants to solve the problem of extortion and train sabotage in southwest Georgia, I'll need permission to pursue the plan I mentioned. And . . . let me know if you'll take the dog." He turned and headed out the door, ig-

38

noring the manager's faint bleat of protest.

The clerk glared, his long nose quivering in disgust. Simon almost smiled again, but the urge faded between breaths and was gone before he reached the office door.

Simon Kincaid never smiled anymore. He thought he'd probably forgotten how. There was little reason to smile in a sick world where evil triumphed and goodness cowered, where murderers slaughtered the innocent, and bullies abused the weak and helpless. Years ago — a lifetime it seemed — when he was young — Simon stopped the thought before it formed.

He could not change the past. He could only accept reality: the Almighty had turned His back on a depraved humanity, and Simon couldn't blame Him. He didn't blame God for turning His back on Simon Kincaid, either.

That gloomy refrain accompanied him down the steps, where he was met by a young boy whose eyes were wide and worried.

"I can't make her wake up," he explained in a hurried, breathless voice. "She puked a lot, then she jes' keeled over an' I couldn't get her to drink or eat any of the food you give me. I'm sorry, mister. I done the best I could. Uh . . . you're still goin' to pay me, ain't ya?"

4

Atlanta

". . . And according to the barkeep, he was three sheets to the wind at the time, so all the talk about a bridge collapsing might turn out to be the ramblings of a drunken fool." Sterns finished, glancing across the desk at Simon. "But the super from South Georgia Central called us. He was afraid to take the chance."

"Especially when your ailing company is about to be bought out from under you by the Crumps," Simon clarified, his voice soft. "I've noticed that companies the Crumps want to add to their collection seem to suffer from mysterious accidents and unforeseen tragedies — until they're purchased, that is."

Sterns shifted uncomfortably. "Find proof, if you can," was all he said. "Proof, Mr. Kincaid, that will hold up in a court of law."

Simon studied the other man for a moment. "Proof doesn't always guarantee prosecution, especially down here, where family honor is about all these people have left. . . ." He paused. "But you can be sure I *will* make it a point to learn the truth."

◆ ◆ ◆

By the next afternoon Simon was in Albany, where he risked a quick visit to the Flint River Bar and Billiards to have a chat with the barkeep. Surly and suspicious, the uncooperative man offered little additional information. Simon finally leaned forward, planting both hands on the high counter. His eyes were gritty from lack of sleep, and he was as suspicious of the barkeep as the barkeep was of him. "If I find out something later that you could have told me now — and didn't — I'll be back," he promised.

The hardened keep gaped at him a moment, then reached beneath the counter. Simon's hand shot out and grabbed his arm. "I wouldn't advise it." He applied just enough pressure to make his point, his gaze locked with that of the now sweating barkeep. After a prolonged moment the muscles protesting Simon's vise-like grip slackened, the man wisely deciding it wouldn't be a good idea to draw a blackjack . . . or a gun. Simon released his arm. "I'll be back," he repeated in an ominous tone. He left without a backward glance.

Outside, a wizened colored man clutching a broom darted across the alley from the shadows. "I can tell you where they went," he whispered, as Simon was about to mount his horse.

Simon turned. "Where *who* went?"

41

The old darky shook his head. "Follow the track 'long the river," he hissed. "The nawth side." Before Simon could question him further, he scuttled back inside.

A weight as palpable as a heavy stone lodged in Simon's throat — a bad sign. That tense, choking sensation usually spelled trouble. He wheeled the horse toward the depot and set his jaw.

"A train just left 'bout twenty minutes ago," the ticket agent drawled, indifferent to Simon's urgency. "Been three others before today and as many yesterday. Ain't heared a word 'bout the bridge being out. Somebody fed you a slug, mister."

Simon didn't bother to argue. After remounting, he headed down the path that followed the river. It was a dismal, rain-drenched day, the humidity thick enough to stir with a spoon. Due to the rain, the river was running abnormally high, its mud-colored water churning.

He smelled the smoke and heard the screams long before he broke out of the trees. So did his horse.

Simon pulled the snorting, half-rearing animal to a halt and dismounted, his gaze riveted on the nightmarish scene. The trestle bridge had collapsed, dumping the caboose and several passenger cars of the ill-fated South Georgia Central into the turbulent Flint River. Smoke and crackling flames from the burning cars billowed skyward; the air reverberated with screams and shouts and rushing water. He yanked off his coat and kicked free of his boots, then tore off down the wet, slippery path at a dead run.

Shouting and pointing, men aimlessly dashed up and down both sides of the river. Others stood immobilized, mouths slack, arms dangling. A brakeman and one of the conductors struggled chest deep in the swift water, trying to reach the smashed cars. Trapped passengers were screaming, bloodied hands clawing at the broken windows. Those few who had miraculously escaped now floundered in the deadly currents of the seething river.

Simon momentarily closed his eyes. Then he leaped down the muddy, rock-strewn bank and snagged the arm of a dripping man who was staring transfixed at the scene. "Help put out the fire in that other car!" he snapped. "If we don't kill those flames before they spread, those passengers will die as well."

"My wife . . ." The man tore his eyes from the incinerator of the slowly submerging car. "My wife . . ."

Simon's hand shot out and gripped the man's shoulder in a mute gesture of sympathy. Then he turned and ran along the bank, gesturing toward the other car as he yelled to the crowd of onlookers. Galvanized by his

43

commanding voice, several men jumped to obey his directions. Simon was about to plow into the river when he felt a tug on his arm. Turning, he looked into the blackened, sweat-streaked face of the engineer.

"Stand back!" the man shouted above the roar of water and flames, pointing upward. "That car . . . it's going . . ."

Simon's gaze followed the shaking finger, and he sucked in his breath. A green-and-gold Pullman Palace car now teetered on the edge of the tracks, scant yards from the yawning gap over the river. It was one of the more elaborate Crump system cars, a plush palace number with a clerestory roof and gold embossed lettering on the sides.

As they watched, a fractured crosstie gave way with a loud crack, and the car lurched downward. Without the support of the rails, its rear wheels twisted sideways. For the space of a dozen heartbeats the car rocked back and forth, then stilled.

Simon and the engineer started forward — and froze. The figure of a small boy had appeared in the window at the front of the car, his face pressed against the glass.

"Grab some men," Simon ordered the engineer, his eyes glued to the child. "Some ropes, too, if you can find them. Bring them and the men to the opposite side of the river, beyond that last car. I'll go after the boy." He ran along the bank, and fifty yards down, plunged into the dark swirling water.

When he emerged, dripping and winded, on the other side, he paused to search out the small boy — and saw that two more children had appeared at the window. Simon shouted, waving both arms to attract their attention. *Why wasn't anybody else helping?* He clambered up the embankment, but a loose stone near the top pitched him to his knees. When he regained his balance, his gaze flew back to the window, and his jaw dropped. A young woman was now standing behind the three children. Simon bit his cheek against a groan.

The young woman had taken charge, however, the motion of her hands swift but efficient as she set about breaking a window, then cleared away the glass with the curtain. One by one, with her help, the children climbed up, then out.

They just might make it, Simon thought exultantly. All three children, sobbing and frightened, tumbled onto the tracks, then scampered to safety. But the young woman, instead of following, disappeared from view.

"No!" Simon yelled. "No! Get out! Don't —" Then he spotted the bobbing heads of two *more* children, near the opposite end of the car, and understood why she had retraced her steps down the aisle of the car.

Breathing hard, Simon made his way to the small figures on the track — two little boys and a girl. Dropping down beside them, his arms automatically enfolded the smallest. "Shh. It's all right. . . ."

"Please," choked out the girl, a curly-haired moppet of about seven. "Help her save —" The words died in her throat as her gaze swung past Simon's shoulder, and the terror-glazed brown eyes dilated with fresh horror.

5

Simon turned, lifting the smaller boy, and watched helplessly as the palace car tilted farther, then, with a screeching of metal and a splintering of wood, hurtled downward into the river. "God . . . *why?*" he muttered, sweeping all three children into his arms to shield them from the sight.

"Stay here," he ordered. Then he was running, half-sliding down the steep embankment.

The car had not crashed onto the other coach cars. Instead, it had plunged straight down into the churning, debris-strewn water. Simon enjoyed a second's relief as he reached the bank and found the young woman, miraculously still alive, struggling to hold aloft a toddler. But seeing the water rising in the wrecked car, he threw himself into the river, swimming with furious, determined strokes.

Somehow, in spite of her long skirt and petticoats, the girl managed to lever both herself and the baby through a window. When Simon reached her side, he wrapped one arm tightly about her waist, treading water with the other.

At his touch, she jerked, head whipping around in astonishment. Dark blue eyes stared into Simon's glittering green ones. "Take Thomas," she stated, her voice hoarse but devoid of fear. "I have to go back for Jessica."

Simon peered beyond her into the dark car. Water already half-filled the once luxurious interior. He didn't waste time arguing. "I'll be back as soon as I can." He tucked the limp baby close beneath his chin.

Gratitude flashed through the dark blue eyes before she wriggled back through the window and disappeared once more.

Moments later, willing hands reached for the baby. "Is —" Simon rasped.

A bearded fellow with a large beaked nose was leaning over the still form. Gnarled, work-roughened hands began to rub the back and fragile limbs. "Little shaver's still breathing. Has a bruise above his eye . . . but I think he'll make it — hey! You're not going back out there, are you?"

Simon barely heard the protest. He dived back into the water, all his energy focused on saving a young woman with fearless blue eyes and a steady voice. But by the time he reached the window of the palace car, it was already partially submerged. If his life had been different, Simon thought, he would be praying to God for help — and believing the request would be honored.

Instead, he took a deep breath and tried to squeeze through the window. It was no use — he was too broad through the shoulders.

He scanned the darkened interior, his probing gaze catching a flash of movement. "Here!" he called, waving his arm through the window. "Down here!"

He heard a tiny sob, followed by a low, soothing murmur, then the sound of splashing. Simon strained to hold onto the rapidly submerging window, while with his free arm he shoved aside some floating debris.

"I'm here . . ." The soft, cultured voice, still unbelievably calm, sounded inches away. "This is Jessica. She's four, and very scared, but I've promised her that everything will be . . . fine."

The hesitation was slight but Simon heard it. "Everything will be just fine," he affirmed, his voice deep, resonating with as much strength and reassurance as he could muster. "I've got you now, Jessica." He caught a tiny arm and gently squeezed. "I've got you."

"Let go of me, sugar-diddle," the woman urged. "Go to the nice man. I'll be right behind you."

Jessica sobbed once more, then Simon tugged her through the window. Tucking her close against his body, he bent over the small head and brushed a kiss on her cold cheek. "It's all right. Close your eyes and hold on tight." As he kicked free of the car, he called back, "Careful now — just hold on. It's sinking fast, but I'll be back to help you."

"Take care of Jessica."

He made it to the shore without incident and gently forced the clinging arms to free him. "Don't be afraid," he repeated. "This man took care of your little brother, and he'll take care of you while I fetch your —" he hesitated, then handed the child over.

"It's too late for *her,* I'm afraid," the bearded man muttered under his breath.

Simon looked up, and a spasm twisted his insides: there was nothing of the palace car in view but the dome of the ceiling. No sign at all of the courageous young woman who had given her life to save five children.

"I won't let her die like that!" he ground out. "Not without trying." He whirled, staggered, then waded back into the water, ignoring the calls and the cries that it was too late. *Don't you die on me!* he ordered the valiant young woman.

His arms and shoulders ached, and a roaring to rival the flames filled his head as he swam once more toward the fast-sinking car. Twenty yards away he paused, treading water, searching frantically. "Where are you?" he yelled, shoving aside a smoldering cushion. Fierce anger flooded his body, refueling his flagging energy. "Answer me!" he roared.

Incredibly, she did. "Over here. . . ."

Simon searched the seething currents, and

50

finally spotted a hand, weakly waving, then a drenched head. But even as he took a deep breath, a cascade of bubbles burst to the surface as the palace car continued to sink. Arm over arm, Simon plowed through the water, his gaze pinned to the woman, willing her to hang on, hang on. He was still thirty feet away when — with a singular look of acceptance that would haunt him the rest of his life — her head began to slip beneath the surface.

Lungs burning, Simon reached her just as she went under. His groping hands snagged her trapped body, and in a final burst of desperation, he managed to pull her free of the window. "Easy. . . ." he gasped in her ear. "You're safe now. All the children are safe. Just rest."

Close up, her face was colorless, the closed eyelids almost translucent. Wet hair plastered her skull and streamed down her back. Simon held her while they both regained their breath. Her bones felt as small and delicate as a newborn foal's. A needle of intense feeling pierced all the way through to his soul. *Where had she found the strength?*

She coughed a little, moved her head. "I . . . can swim." Her arms fluttered, barely moving. Deep blue eyes blinked, trying to focus. Simon lost himself in those eyes, the same rich, depthless hue of an October sky in late afternoon. Her blue-tinged lips moved, and he tore his gaze away to listen. Amaz-

51

ingly, she was trying to smile.

"Thank you," she whispered.

"You're thanking *me?* Why? You're the heroine of the day. . . ."

The smile faded. "No," she protested, so hoarse and low Simon could barely make out the word. ". . . nothing special . . . about me." She blinked once, winced, then with a defeated little sigh, her eyelids drooped and her body went limp.

Simon swam with his unconscious burden to the safety of the shore and other waiting arms. He handed her over with reluctance, his ears buzzing from shock and the excited babble around him. All he could really hear, however, was a small, shaky voice and its poignant denial of self-worth.

Something deep inside Simon had responded to that haunting assessment. It mirrored exactly the black hole where his own soul had shriveled and died, many years before that hot autumn day in south Georgia.

6

Adelaide
Thomasville
October 1895

Exhausted, Elizabeth trudged across the gently sloping back lawn. Her destination was an old pine bench she had discovered months earlier, near one of the paddocks. For the past three days the Crump household — beset by chaos, crying, and confusion — had resembled the train wreck she and the children had miraculously survived.

Josephine Crump was sedated, under a doctor's care; Tilda had perished in the crash, along with half a dozen of the other household servants and Horatio's horse trainer, Mr. Clarke. Elizabeth had seen Horatio only twice in the past thirty-six hours. Tall and gaunt, his voice roughened with fatigue, he had tried to thank her, only to break down and hurriedly leave the room. The second time, he had begged her to look after his children until his wife recovered. So to Elizabeth had fallen the difficult task of caring for five bewildered children who now treated her more like their mother than a cheerful companion.

She reached the sagging bench, worn smooth from age, and gratefully collapsed. A couple of the coach horses trotted over to the paddock fence, ears pricked. "Not right now," Elizabeth told them. "I'm too tired." Too tired, too overwhelmed, too . . . swamped with memories.

In truth, Elizabeth's memories were more sensory than visual — wrenching screams, crying children, explosions, rushing water. Because Horatio and Georgina seemed to need to hear the details, she had attempted to recount everything to them. But either the shock or God's merciful hand had overlaid the tragedy with a thick, amnestic mist, and her account remained sketchy. Except for the man.

Memories of the mysterious rescuer hovered in Elizabeth's thoughts, waking and sleeping. Piercing green eyes. A deep voice filled with reassurance — and a feeling of security she had never known. *Who is he? Whom did You send, Lord?* The man had disappeared from the scene before Elizabeth regained consciousness, and in the confusion nobody had even thought to ask his name or where he lived. He had simply vanished . . . like a guardian angel swept back up to heaven.

Elizabeth stood, wincing as abused muscles protested. For once, the unseasonably hot October sun felt good as it burned down on her unprotected head. She ambled over to rub the velvet noses waiting to be patted, poking over the fence. A slow smile tugged at the corners of her mouth, her thoughts still on the "guardian angel" who had saved her life, and that of Thomas and Jessica.

"I wonder how he would feel, being compared to an angel," she speculated aloud to Barney, one of the horses. He snorted as if in reply, butting his head against her hand. "You're right," she said. "I doubt somehow that he'd appreciate it. But, Barney . . . I've never felt so — so *safe,* even though I thought I was going to die." She remembered the sensation of strong arms closing around her, so firmly and securely that — for the first time in her life — she had completely relinquished control.

You're safe now, he had promised her. *Just rest.*

In the distance someone called her name, and with a weary sigh Elizabeth turned back toward the house. She might never again see the green-eyed man who had risked his life for her and the children, but she would never forget him. And she would offer a prayer in his behalf every day for the rest of her life.

◆ ◆ ◆

Atlanta

Three days after the Flint River bridge collapsed, George Jenkins, Pinkerton's Atlanta

55

superintendent, held a meeting in his office. When Simon arrived, a little past four o'clock on a windy Friday, the room was crowded with men. One of the faces was almost as familiar as his own and, seeing it, relief cascaded over Simon in a floodtide.

"Alex!" Striding forward, he clasped the hand of one of the few men in the world he considered his friend. "Marriage agrees with you, pal."

"Aye, that it does." Blue eyes crinkling, Alexander MacKay surveyed Simon, mouth turned up in a broad smile beneath his bushy moustache. "And Eve warned me that I'd best be prepared for a tongue-lashing if I don't bring you round for supper before we leave for Thomasville."

"Done." Simon swiveled to face the superintendent, a white-haired man with full matching beard. The man may have resembled a jovial grandfather, Simon mused, but he was well aware that the affable manner and unhurried Southern drawl disguised an incisive brain. "It's arranged, then?"

"After the disaster in Albany, it was agreed by both Principals that the risk justified the reward." Jenkins paused, studying his fingernails for a moment before meeting Simon's narrowed gaze. "There remains, however, disagreement among all those involved as to whether or not Horatio Crump should be apprised of our plan. It *was* his family who al-

56

most perished in the crash, and Mr. Sterns has already been contacted by the Crumps to retain the Agency's services for an investigation into the accident."

Simon took his time before replying. There was irony here. Was the sabotage a deliberate attempt to mislead . . . or a near-fatal flaw in someone's calculation? "It's the Crumps who have been trying to take over the South Georgia Central," he finally pointed out. "I think, Mr. Jenkins, that it would be highly imprudent to reveal my identity to *any* of the Crump family. The fact that the Crumps' private family car happened to be part of the train might be coincidence — or it might be a case of bad timing. Several other trains made it across earlier in the day, as you may recall."

A vivid memory surfaced: terrified, childish arms clinging like a limpet; deep blue eyes without a trace of fear . . . Simon shook his head to clear his brain. "We . . . ah . . . we'd best play our cards close to our chest, sir. Send an operative to Albany to investigate openly — but keep *me* undercover."

"I agree," Alex put in, his Scottish brogue warning Simon that Alex's temper had been ignited. "Otherwise, you're asking Mr. Kincaid to bare his throat to the lion, as it were."

"May I remind both you gentlemen that Horatio Crump, and his father before him, have retained Pinkerton's for years?"

57

"Until three days ago, only as guards," Simon shot back, his voice steely. "Not as criminal investigators." He glanced at Alex, whose grim expression and look of surprise told Simon he hadn't known that. "In the last seven years, four private detectives have been hired for small jobs relating to minor criminal activities, but they were *not* Pinkerton men. I can't answer for you, but I find myself wondering what Crump might be trying to hide, Mr. Jenkins." He glanced around the room at each man present, noting varying expressions of surprise, dismay, and anger. "It's fairly easy to hire an incompetent detective or one eager to have his palm greased. But Pinkerton operatives can't be bought — or bamboozled. And Crump knows it."

"Then he knows more than either the Principals and I do," Jenkins murmured, looking suddenly weary, and every one of his sixty years. "No organization is free of human vice, Mr. Kincaid. I should think you, of all people, would know that. Even Pinkerton's National Detective Agency has its share of skeletons." He glanced at Perry Sterns, who looked, Simon thought, as if he'd swallowed a green persimmon. "Were you aware of the information Operative Kincaid just shared?"

The deputy flushed, avoiding Simon's eye. "No. I was not," he said. Then he took a deep breath. "But in light of this revelation, I would have to agree with Mr. Kincaid's argument to remain unknown to Mr. Crump. It's too dangerous otherwise." He finally glanced at Simon, then looked away. "We almost lost two men last year. . . ."

Alex, who had leaned back in his chair, was studying Simon with a look of subtle compassion that made him vastly uncomfortable. "It would be a shame to risk another operative just to placate the sensibilities of a client of dubious loyalty," Alex observed. He stood, clapping Simon on the back before turning to the super. "Don't you agree, now?"

"I'll notify everyone." Jenkins tugged out his watch. "We'll see to the details immediately. An operative will proceed openly to Albany, and arrangements for coded communication with you will be made. In the interim, Mr. MacKay, *you* may continue your present investigations here until an identity can be constructed for you in Thomasville."

He turned to Simon. "I've corresponded with William Pinkerton. Mr. Pinkerton assures me that, before he convinced you to become an undercover agent, you were one of the best trainers ever to work in his racing stables. But it *has* been a number of years, Mr. Kincaid, so may I suggest you sharpen your skills in the fine art of training trotters? The season down there starts the first of December, which doesn't give us a lot of time."

♦ ♦ ♦

The short note was delivered by special

59

messenger, directly into the trembling hand of a man who already knew that, no matter what they wanted him to do this time, he'd have to do it. But this time, he would hedge his bets and sell information to Crump as well.

That decision made, Rufus Black read, then burned the message exactly as he'd been told. Confidence and strength flooded back, and with it a restless energy. He jumped to his feet, prowling the bare room of the flophouse where he'd stayed for the past week. Avery Paxton was nothing but a Yankee blowhard who was fixing to learn that there was a lot more to power than waving equal amounts of greenbacks and threats.

Without *him* — without Rufus's skill and knowledge — bloated moneybags like Avery Paxton and Horatio Crump had all the zip of a spent cartridge. Rufus rubbed his hands together, chuckling as he imagined what they were going to demand of him as a test of his loyalty.

Reckon he'd have to do somebody in? The prospect gave him pause, but only briefly. He'd heard that the death toll from the collapse of the bridge had risen to forty-seven. That wasn't so bad, he told himself. There were a sight too many folks in the world anyways.

Yep, if they needed somebody knocked off — Rufus Black could get the job done right.

If Paxton was half as smart as he pretended to be, he'd dump ol' Abe mighty fast and stick with Rufus.

He quit his pacing, and a smile spread across his face. Now *that* would be the ticket — getting rid of Abe! It'd serve him right, too, Rufus decided, grabbing his hat and stomping out the door.

It'd sure teach Abe not to call Rufus a dirty redneck again.

7

Alexander MacKay gave Simon a sidelong assessment as the buggy made its way down Edgewood Avenue, toward the house that Alex and Eve had purchased the month before. "You're looking . . . especially lethal, my friend. Has it been so bad down here, then?"

"Yes . . . and no." Simon was moodily surveying the street. Alex had never seen him looking so grim. So . . . alone. "I'd forgotten what it's like to be the loser in a war," Simon continued after a moment. "These people had everything stripped from them — homes, possessions, dignity . . . pride. I find myself wanting to excuse even the lowest panhandler in the gutter, because I know . . ." His voice trailed off in futility.

Alex tugged out a chamois pouch and dumped some irregular pieces of fragrant cedar wood into his hand — puzzle pieces carved by his grandfather. "Tell me about the Crumps," he suggested, his fingers busy with the wood. "I've read Jenkins's reports, and talked with Perry Sterns, but I'd rather hear from you." He glanced across at Simon, wondering if he would ever know the tormenting secrets that darkened the man's soul.

"Tell you about the Crumps. . . ." Simon stretched, crossing his legs and lacing his hands behind his head. "Horatio Crump, Jr., is the quintessential railroad baron, though the system actually was started by his father, after the War. He died back in the seventies. Horatio's mother ran things for a while, I understand . . . at least until the eldest son was old enough to take over. Horatio, Jr., has been running things for the past fifteen years, though their questionable *modus operandi* of acquiring railroads has only surfaced in the past several years." He paused, looking thoughtful. "There's also a younger son, James. So far he's been more involved with other family . . . acquistions — lumber, turpentine, a couple of orchards. You name it, and the Crumps have a piece of it. I haven't pursued James since the Agency was hired to investigate the railroad angle. But I wonder. . . ."

"Is the mother deceased?"

"No. She's apparently become an eccentric recluse who stays holed up on the original family plantation eleven months out of the year. The place is about five miles south of Thomasville. Rose Hill, they call it. Used to be some kind of showplace before the War.

"Most of the locals don't even remember what the woman looks like, though, from the little I gleaned, they think the family can do

63

no wrong. About ten years ago, Horatio, Jr., built a place nearer town, near a racetrack, I believe. He's obsessed with horses. But from what I've heard, he's the only one in the family who is. James is a widower."

Alex paused in the middle of fitting a puzzle piece to glance up. "And where does *he* live?"

"I'm not sure. I'll be able to find out more after I'm established as Simon Kincaid, horse trainer."

Alex slanted him a sidelong look. "Um . . . I'd better warn you that Eve is trying to inveigle herself along. For some reason, she seems to think I can't muddle through without her."

He was teasing, of course, for there was no way Alex would allow his wife to place herself in jeopardy, and Eve knew it. Simon, however, leveled a cool stare in his direction that would have sent any other man diving under the seat. "I trust you'll disabuse her of the notion?"

Ach, but he'd forgotten what a dour sobersides the man could be. Alex elbowed him, and winked. "Nay, my friend. I'm going to leave that pleasant little chore to *you!*"

♦ ♦ ♦

When Simon and Alexander MacKay arrived at the MacKays' new home, the door opened and Alex's wife, Eve, flew down the steps and into her husband's waiting arms.

Brown eyes alight with joy, red hair swirling in untidy strands about her face, she bore little resemblance to the young woman Simon had met a year earlier.

He froze on the porch, feeling suddenly awkward. "Hello, Mrs. MacKay. You're looking . . . well."

Rosy from Alex's hearty kiss, Eve twisted about, still in her husband's embrace. "It's wonderful to see you, Mr. Kincaid. And since I was being stalked by a deranged killer the last time we met, I should hope my appearance *had* improved!"

She smiled at Simon, whose assignment for several months one winter had been as shadow and unseen guardian of the irrepressible young woman who had subsequently become Alexander's wife. Simon remembered well the pain in her eyes, the brave defiance of constant fear leaching her face of the color and life she now radiated.

Both Alex and Eve, Simon realized with uncomfortable insight, had not only persevered in spite of life's cruelty; they continued to nourish their naïve faith in a loving God. Simon wondered when that fragile happiness would be shattered. Life, he had learned, was seldom kind. And neither was God.

After helping himself to another kiss, Alex murmured, "The lass is as opinionated as ever, isn't she now?"

The warmth and indulgence toward his

glowing wife was so palpable that Simon turned away.

After supper Simon and Alex secluded themselves in the study. Somehow Simon wasn't surprised when Eve appeared moments later with a tray of hot cocoa and cookies. She set the tray on a table and calmly began to pour, her demeanor as intractable as it was placid.

"If all the meaningful looks you two have exchanged the past hour concern Avery Paxton, I might be able to help," she announced just as Alex lifted his cup to his mouth.

Simon studied the steam swirling up out of his own cup until Alex quit sputtering. *Independence is definitely to be preferred over the stranglehold of the marital relationship,* he decided.

"Eve . . ." Alex warned, still coughing.

"I've been doing a good bit of work at the Young Men's Library Association — they've opened a section for women now, you know. One hears all sorts of useful tidbits. . . ."

"Eve, lass." Alex's voice rose in volume now, the brogue more pronounced.

Simon continued to examine a dollop of cream floating on the surface of his cocoa, and waited.

"Like the textile mill up in Dalton, recently purchased by a very short, fussy Yankee whose last name is Mr. P-something." Eve calmly sat down and plonked her elbows on her knees, gazing at her stone-faced husband with all the innocence of a purring cat next to a birdcage.

Simon's mouth barely twitched. He'd best be careful not to voice the feline analogy; Eve had earned a bachelor's degree in ornithology and had published two books on birds. She was *not* fond of cats.

Alex laid his mug aside and leaned toward his wife. "Lass, you may share whatever information you've unearthed — and include the names of all the people you *think* you were *subtly* interrogating — then I want you to —" He caught himself just before his voice crescendoed to a roar.

"To lock myself in the bedroom?" Eve tartly suggested, brown eyes flashing.

Alex shot Simon a single glance. On cue, Simon rose. "I'll take a look out back," he called over his shoulder as he casually sauntered from the room.

♦ ♦ ♦

Alex joined him a quarter of an hour later. For several moments he and Simon gazed at the star-studded night.

"Nobody's lurking in your backyard," Simon observed after a while, "though I'd recommend you have the woods cleared of all that underbrush and maybe cut down some of the trees."

"Hmph. Little chance of that. Eve wants to keep a natural habitat for the birds."

"She still knows how to set you off, doesn't she?"

"Aye, like a torch to kindling." Alex chewed on his bushy moustache a moment before Simon glimpsed a hint of his smile in the light of the golden autumn moon. "What makes it so difficult is that she never means to provoke it . . . doesn't *want* to provoke it, but" — he turned to face Simon, propping his elbows on the back porch rail — "she ends up erupting, which, to my eternal frustration, I find . . . stimulating." He heaved a sigh. "To quench all that life and emotion, after what she endured last year . . ."

"You're letting her interfere with your investigation," Simon returned, his voice flat, devoid of feeling. "Again. Alex —"

"She won't interfere when I'm down in Thomasville with you, Sim."

Simon faced him down, and his utter implacability gradually prevailed over Alex's flashfire temper. But only temporarily. "Blast it, man!" Alex finally exploded, jerking around to slam his palms against the rail. "I trust you with my life! Two years ago I trusted you to guard the woman I love *more* than my life! Can't you scrape up a shred of feeling to appreciate my dilemma and try trusting *me* for a change? Eve won't be a hindrance, I tell you! Or is my word not good

68

enough, either?"

His friend's rebuke stung, even though Simon knew it was justified. "Your trust in me is misplaced," he muttered, each word burning his throat like hot ground glass. He'd known for years that he didn't deserve the friendship of a godly man like Alexander MacKay. "Beyond that, conditions down there are volatile, and the criminal mind capable of murdering innocent train passengers isn't going to care if your wife stumbles onto the scene." He stared into the stygian darkness, muscles bunched, throat tight. "In our job, a man worrying over a woman will end up dead." He paused, adding with cold finality, "I won't be a party to anyone's death, man *or* woman." Then he muttered beneath his breath, "Never *again*."

The silence that followed was thick. When Alex didn't respond, Simon balled his hands into fists. "I'll be going. I'll leave word with Jenkins to send a different operative to Thomasville." He took two steps before Alex halted him with a single word.

"Simon."

Slowly Simon turned, keeping his expression blank.

"I ken what you're doing, lad . . . but it won't work," Alex murmured, the rumbling burr now soothing as a balm. "You've never shared any of the demons hounding you, my friend, and the last thing I'd want to do is to add to your burdens by prying." He stepped up to Simon and threw one arm about his shoulders — a quick, hard hug, over before Simon could react. "I know you've little trust for anyone or anything — but that doesn't change my own trust in you. I'm sorry for what I said, Sim. My temper — ach! But I suppose that's my own particular thorn. I never mean for it to prick the people I care about — but as you see, I fall a wee bit shy of perfection." He grinned in the darkness, and his hand came back to squeeze Simon's shoulder. "We're all of us flawed creatures, Sim. Go gentler with yourself, now, won't you?"

"Tell Eve goodnight for me. Supper was the best I've enjoyed in months." Without looking back, Simon took the porch steps two at a time, and cut around the side of the house, merging into the shadows as if he belonged there.

8

Rufus Black sauntered into the smoking lounge of the raucous vaudeville house, bowler tipped to the back of his head, hair slick with pomade. He hadn't wanted to leave the variety show — one of the dancers had given him the eye. But prissy ol' Paxton had made it plain that Rufus was to meet him in the gentlemen's parlor. Grumbling, Rufus made his way over to an empty table, sat down, and spent the next moments chewing on a good Havana, watching the entrance with a wary eye.

At five minutes before eleven, an uneasy muttering rippled through the crowd of smokers. Rufus gulped, swallowing a mouthful of cigar smoke. In the doorway stood the biggest, meanest looking Chinaman he'd ever seen, and the man was staring through slitted eyes, straight at Rufus. Coughing and sputtering, Rufus watched while the Chinaman lumbered forward in a queer rolling gait, oblivious to the gawking crowd.

Two feet away, he stopped and folded his arms across his expansive chest. "Come."

Rufus glanced around, humiliation burning in his craw. Everyone was staring at *him*

71

now, their smirks and speculation undisguised. "Why don't you tell Mr. Pa—" He broke off, alarm flaring when the Chinaman seemed to swell even larger. In that instant Rufus remembered that Mr. Paxton had been mighty insistent about never having his name spoken aloud.

He threw down the ragged cigar. "Oh, all right — move out of the way, then, and lead me to him," he snarled, wanting to have the scene over and done with. Paxton was a pompous little tin god — him with his pigtailed, yellow-skinned flunky — treating Rufus like he was some rube straight from the cornfield.

Rufus had thrust back his shoulders back and started to swagger past Paxton's bodyguard when the Chinaman's ham-sized fist closed over the back of his shirt collar, lifted him a good two feet off the floor, and carried him through the silent crowd, out the door. At the edge of the street, next to a closed carriage, Rufus was dropped like a bale of moldy cotton.

He leaped to his feet, wildly swinging his fists. "You got no cause to treat me like this. I oughtta —"

Avery Paxton climbed out of the carriage. His lips curled into a sneer and his gaze swept over Rufus with a superiority that made Rufus itch to plant a haymaker smack in the middle of that sneer. "Fang . . ." Paxton murmured, and like a trained gorilla, the big lug reached for Rufus.

Rufus scrambled backward. "He touches me again, and I'm through. You keep that filthy coolie away from me or I'll —" He choked back the threat and glared at Paxton, who stood there in his fancy striped suit and white cravat, complete with cane and gloves, looking like some dandified stiff from England or something.

"You'll what, Mr. Black? Report me to the authorities?" He tugged out an elaborate gold watch and opened the lid. "I wouldn't recommend that. Wo Fang here is rather particular, you see, about my health and well-being. Should anything unpleasant happen to me, well . . ." The veiled threat trailed off. He snapped the lid of his watch shut and tucked it back in his vest pocket.

"Incidentally, Wo Fang is many things, but he is no coolie. He's not even Chinese, Mr. Black. He's Japanese — a trained Sumo wrestler — and I suggest you watch your mouth in the future. Now that we understand each other — we *do* understand each other?"

Sweating, Rufus jerked his head up and down in agreement.

"I thought as much. Good. Now, it is my heart's desire, my cherished dream, to build a home for myself. Something that will appropriately reflect my taste, my power" — he rubbed his hands together in anticipation —

"my fortune. Something like Mr. Vander-bilt's new residence in North Carolina. Biltmore, I believe he calls it. Yes, that's what I'll have one day, and it will even be larger, grander than his Biltmore."

He paused, and at the look in the older man's eye, Rufus blanched. Should he bolt for it?

"Unfortunately," Paxton continued, "to establish my empire, it is imperative that I acquire supremacy over the railroads here in the South, as Jay Gould and Jim Fisk did in the North." A look of naked fury flared in the backs of his eyes, but disappeared so rapidly that Rufus blinked. "It should have been *mine*. . . ." Then he smiled. "But I have discovered that the South is a fertile field, ripe for the picking. All I need, Mr. Black, are a couple more lines — specifically all the north-south routes from Richmond to Thomasville, via the western corridor."

Rufus stared. "The Crumps will never sell," he blurted, "no matter what you want me to do."

"That would be most unfortunate . . . for both of us." Paxton arched an eyebrow, and Wo Fang moved to stand directly behind Rufus. "I trust your narrow-minded focus will change, particularly as you figure prominently in plans that will persuade them to do exactly that." His voice dropped, and the flat Yankee twang grated on Rufus's frazzled

74

nerves. "According to my sources, the Crumps' five children miraculously survived the crash, largely due to the heroic efforts of their female companion."

Rufus felt as if an elephant instead of a rabbit had just stomped across his grave. "I don't think . . ." he began, but a warning hand brushed the back of his neck again, and he almost choked on the bile that rose in his throat.

"Mr. Black, your final chance to redeem yourself in my eyes will be to arrange for the Crump children to become more . . . vulnerable, so that Horatio Crump will be more easily persuaded to negotiate. If the very devoted companion was out of the picture — permanently . . ." His gaze lifted, the narrowed eyes boring into Rufus's. "Need I say more?"

Feeling sick, Rufus shook his head.

Paxton nodded in satisfaction, and Wo Fang stepped back. "You have exactly one month," Paxton finished, shrugging into a full-length cape that his bodyguard draped over his bony shoulders. "One other thing." He lifted the cane, its point poised a hand's breadth from Rufus's nose. "See to your assignment in any fashion you please, but you will not — *ever* — inflict upon me the details."

He gestured to the giant Oriental, and the absurd-looking pair turned back toward the carriage. "I'll be in touch," Paxton called through the window. His flunky slammed the door, clambered up beside the driver, and the buggy rumbled off down the street.

9

Thomasville
November 1895

"Whoa, there, Mosby!" Elizabeth laughed at the mettlesome gray stallion whose halter she firmly held. "You big baby! You have your shoes checked every week, so you know this doesn't hurt." She gave the glossy neck a reassuring pat.

"You be careful, Miss 'Lizbeth," the blacksmith warned as he lifted Mosby's left hind foot to inspect the hoof. "Las' time, he took a piece o' Jefferson's arm, he did. Don't know why Mr. Crump gotta have me check the shoes of these hosses so often," he grumbled half under his breath. "You bein' such a little mite, it makes my ol' heart near bust these suspenders, every time I see you coming with this snake-mean ol' hoss." He glanced up at Elizabeth, his eyes wide. "What you reckon Miz Crump would say if I has to call Doc Arbuckle over here to patch you up — and the missus barely out of bed after nigh losing all them younguns?"

Elizabeth's smile faded. "I'll be careful,

Ezra. I don't want to worry Mrs. Crump any more than you want to fetch the doctor." Mosby tossed his head, and she automatically stilled the animal's agitated movements. A sleekly muscled standardbred, Mosby's official name was Gray Ghost, even though his temperament seemed more volcanic than ethereal. To Elizabeth, he was splendid. "Mosby is one of Mr. Crump's favorite trotters. I have no intention of risking his neck *or* my own."

"You hear 'bout the new trainer he's hired for the season?" The blacksmith straightened, spitting a stream of tobacco juice into a battered spittoon. "I heared the feller's arriving this afternoon."

Elizabeth scratched beneath Mosby's forelock; she wouldn't look at Ezra. "Jefferson told me about him yesterday." She turned to one of the Crump stableboys who had accompanied her to the blacksmith, gesturing for him to take the momentarily calm stallion. "Willy, I have to run an errand. If he starts acting up, Ezra will help you put him in the stall. I'll be back as soon as I can."

Tools clanging, Ezra followed her to the entrance of the smithy. "I s'pect you'll still be able to ride," he ventured kindly. "Don't look so down in the mouth, Miss 'Lizbeth."

Elizabeth summoned a smile. "I'm sorry, Ezra. I suppose I have been a . . . trifle spoiled, haven't I?" She had been treated

78

with nothing but kindness and respect by the Crumps. They had allowed her access to the stables after learning of her love for — and skill with — horses. Mr. Crump especially had begun to rely on that skill these past weeks, due to the loss of his stable manager and trainer, Mr. Clarke, in the train crash.

The Crumps trusted her. A fresh wave of guilt swelled, choking off Elizabeth's breath. *Soon.* She *had* to find some answers soon. Her conscience would not allow her to continue living a life of deception. "Perhaps the new trainer will be so busy with Mr. Crump's trotters, he won't even notice when I'm around." She took a deep breath. "Have you heard whether Mr. Crump hired a new manager, or will the trainer assume those responsibilities like Mr. Clarke?"

Ezra shook his head. "You'll have to talk with Mr. Crump."

"Oh, I wouldn't do that." Elizabeth felt inside a hidden pocket in her cloak, found the paper-wrapped twists of horehound candy Ezra loved, and thrust them out. "Here. I forgot these last time. Now, I need to scat. I'll be back in less than an hour."

The November day was unseasonably cool, the tang of smoke mingling with that of impending rain. Elizabeth glanced at the sky, calculating how long she had to get Mosby tucked safely in his own stall at Adelaide. He detested rain. Smiling a little, she hurried down the crowded walk. Mosby detested being wet, period. Washing him down after a workout required the combined efforts of half a dozen stableboys as well as Jefferson, the wiry colored man who had been acting as stable boss since the crash. The new trainer would have his work cut out for him with Mosby alone.

The familiar sensation of dread froze the smile on Elizabeth's face. She would have to be very careful to remain in the background until she could prove her usefulness to the new man. The horses liked her, and everyone at the stable trusted her around them. Both Mr. Crump and his widowed brother, James, had watched her ride, and approval had been granted for Elizabeth to have that privilege whenever her duties allowed.

A shiver, which had little to do with the rising wind, trickled down her spine. She didn't like to think about James Crump, the handsome, enigmatic man whose presence in his brother's home delighted his nieces and nephews — but whose insolent gaze left Elizabeth feeling . . . restless. James's wife had died of influenza barely a year after their marriage. That had been over two years ago, and Elizabeth didn't understand why he still chose to live with his brother, nor did she know how he filled his days. She simply avoided James as much as possible and asked no questions.

She hurried inside the post office, nodding to two elderly ladies. The day before, James had told her a letter was waiting for her — the first she had received in almost a year. He hadn't pursued the matter, but his curiosity had been as palpable as a touch. Elizabeth's hands began to perspire inside her gloves, and her heart pounded as she peered through the little glass door and spotted the white envelope.

Outside, the sky darkened abruptly, and a fiercesome wind lashed the flag in front of the post office so that it cracked like a whip.

"Looks like a nasty one coming," observed a weather-beaten farmer, holding the door for Elizabeth as she left.

Stifling her frustration, she stuffed the envelope inside her pocket. The letter would have to wait until she was back at Adelaide. Of course, then she would have to spend some time with the children . . . and reassure Mrs. Crump again that all five of them were *fine*, that Pansy, their new mammy, was more than capable of handling them. The tide of time-consuming tasks was endless. It would likely be bedtime before Elizabeth could see if the letter from a distant cousin provided any clues to the location of the gold her father had stolen.

Elizabeth's pace slowed. She still hadn't found Mr. Rattray, but through a bizarre twist of circumstances, she now not only knew the Crumps — she was *employed* by the son of one of the men her father had betrayed! Many times over the past year, she had been tempted to confess, but somehow a propitious occasion never arose. How could she explain her unwitting part in William Soames's death? How would the Crumps react when they learned she was the daughter of Charles Graham? The question festered in Elizabeth's soul. They might never forgive her deception, even if she did manage to recover the gold and restore to the Crumps their portion.

Because of her father, and in spite of her avowed innocence concerning Mr. Soames, Elizabeth might find herself in jail — for murder.

◆ ◆ ◆

James Crump poured himself a liberal splash of Kentucky bourbon and tossed it down, his gaze on the drawn portieres on either side of the library doorway. He'd heard the butler greet Elizabeth Granger, so he knew she had returned. He also knew she would have to pass by the library on her way upstairs. James set his glass on the table and intercepted her as she drew even with the door. "I see you made it home just before the rain, Miss Granger," he said, sweeping the dismayed young woman a mocking bow.

"Yes. I did." Her tone was circumspect,

her gaze discreetly lowered.

She *never* faced him directly, he thought, frustrated and angry, though he was careful to keep his expression bland. He had observed that confrontations made Elizabeth uneasy, to the point that she ran like a rabbit when faced with displays of temper. With *adult* displays, James amended. None of his nieces' and nephews' childish scrapes and tantrums ever ruffled her composure or the poise she wore as naturally as some women wore perfume. Elusive, elegant, she could have graced the head table of any plantation in the county, yet for some reason she held the position of a household menial. Strange.

And she avoided James as if he were a garden slug. "Yes," he stated deliberately now, watching her, "everyone knows how . . . *accommodating* . . . you are."

Her head lifted, blue eyes dark, unrevealing — unfathomable as the Gulf. She twisted her hands together, though her well-modulated voice betrayed no nervousness. "If you'll excuse me, I need to go to the children."

Not this time, James decided. She might enjoy playing cat and mouse with him, but it was past time she learned the price of thwarting James Crump. He stepped back, gesturing for her to precede him into the library. "I have something to discuss with you first."

She hesitated, then swept past him, so

close he caught a whiff of violets, along with the distinct odor of horses. "Ah . . . you've been at the stables again. As well as the post office?"

She turned, and James glimpsed the brief flash of outrage in her eyes before she brought herself under control. *It won't be long now.* Very shortly Miss Elizabeth Granger would be more compliant — not so aloof and disdainful. He studied her, moving his gaze over her in a deliberately insulting fashion. Before he was through, she'd be on her knees, begging.

"What did you need to discuss?" she asked, stepping behind one of the matching wingbacks, as if to barricade herself.

James poured himself another shot of whiskey. "My brother is still in Atlanta," he drawled, toasting Elizabeth with his glass, "leaving to me the dubious pleasure of welcoming the new trainer . . ." He paused, then finished very softly, "And me with the even more dubious task of warning you away from the stables." He watched the color drain from her face. "For myself, I don't care. I'm like my mother when it comes to horses — messy, smelly, troublesome lot, if you ask me. But I do know how much they mean to *you.*"

His voice dropped, became almost caressing. "Now, this trainer's supposed to be a big cheese my brother claims has driven for some of the best stables in the country. He won't want a slip of a girl interfering with his regimen. On the other hand, *I* might be willing to intercede for you." He took a step closer to the wingback. "An appropriate show of gratitude on your part isn't too much to expect for my trouble, is it?" He laid one hand on the back of the chair.

Elizabeth moved to the other chair. "I'll wait for Mr. Horatio to return, and discuss the matter with him. They're *his* horses, not yours *or* the trainer's."

The little chit! Taking me to task as if . . . as if she were my mother! Raw violence, quickly masked, flared.

But Elizabeth was watching him closely and stiffened, her expression wary. *Good. She deserves to be afraid,* James decided abruptly, blocking her only avenue of retreat by stepping between the two chairs. "The trainer arrives within the hour, Miss Granger. You'll discuss it with *me,* here and now."

He waited, his frustration mounting. She appeared as dainty, as delicate as a wildflower he could crush beneath his boot; he had never understood how she managed to consistently defy him with such self-possession. It was past time to teach her a lesson about the realities of power and position. About what it meant to defy the Crump family. To defy *him.*

"My brother and his wife might have hired you last year," he said, all but purring now, "and you might have done a superb job of making yourself indispensable. But, my dear Miss Granger — *Elizabeth* — you are *not* indispensable. More significantly, you're not a Crump. What would happen, do you suppose, if something occurred to, say, sully your lily white reputation? In this neck of the woods, reputation is everything."

He stepped closer, crowding her in a blatant display of power, until she was hemmed in by bookcases — and by James. "And your reputation," he finished in a sibilant whisper, "depends on *me*."

"Excuse me, Master James," the butler intoned from the library door, "Mr. Simon Kincaid is here — the trainer Mr. Horatio hired, suh. Shall I show him to the parlor?"

◆ ◆ ◆

Simon studied his surroundings while he waited for the butler to announce him. "Adelaide," they called the multi-gabled, sprawling mansion with its hodgepodge of architectural styles. He had steeled himself to dislike the place on sight. And yet, he couldn't bring himself to do so. "Adelaide." An absurd name — unless you were familiar with both Horatio Crump, Jr., and the harness racing world. Simon's mouth twisted sourly. Adelaide had been a famous trotter, back in the eighties — a small but tenacious filly who had consistently bested larger horses with even larger reputations.

86

"Adelaide," he had learned in the past year, also happened to be the name of Josephine Crump's mother.

He ran a finger around the stiff shirt cuffs, struggling to maintain his contempt for a man who named his home for a horse . . . and his wife's *mother*, of all things. He tried not to admire the inviting hallway, decorated in shades of golden browns and rich blues, and adorned with vases of autumn flowers, whose spicy fragrance mingled with the enticing aromas of beeswax and lemon oil. After almost two years, Simon was finally here, in the lion's den. But instead of hating the place on sight, along with its owner, he found himself *admiring* it. Only a decade old, already Adelaide exuded a look of permanence, dignity, and quiet wealth. Everything, in fact, that Simon himself once might have inherited from the man he'd called his father. . . .

The butler approached, his unlined black face expressionless but for the speculation gleaming in the chocolate eyes. "Mister James will see you now, in the library," he instructed, a note Simon couldn't quite interpret underlying the soft drawl. "Master Horatio was unable to meet you. Mister James is his brother."

Simon walked into the room as the butler stood aside. Tension swirled in the air, dark and intense. Simon's gaze marked the careless good looks of the tall man with slicked, wheat-colored hair, his posture radiating an arrogant authority. He might be anywhere between twenty-five and thirty-five. Dissipation from too much alcohol had already loosened the flesh over his cheekbones, and Simon had a feeling that the unhealthy flush was as much from brandy as from temper. So . . . this was James Crump.

His erstwhile host shifted slightly, revealing behind him a slight young woman clad in a demure hat and navy serge jacket. She was standing, statue-still, back against the floor-to-ceiling bookcases lining the wall. Crump's expression was savagely triumphant; the woman's, placid as the surface of a calm lake . . . except for the eyes.

Even if he hadn't known, Simon would have recognized her instantly. He watched puzzlement, then dawning recognition flare across her expressive features.

"Mr. Kincaid." Oblivious to this silent interchange, James approached Simon, his arm outstretched. "Sorry Horatio was called away on business. He's the one who's obsessed with horses and the man you'll primarily answer to. I'm his younger brother James, and will help as much as I can. . . ." He glanced over his shoulder, then back at Simon. "Ah . . . allow me to introduce Elizabeth Granger, companion to my brother's children. I've been trying —"

Noting at last the sudden tension, James

88

narrowed his gaze. "Say, have the two of you already met?"

Hmm, Simon thought as he watched Elizabeth's pale face flush with what might have been embarrassment — or anger. "As a matter of fact, we *have* met, albeit not formally," he inserted smoothly. "Though I'm surprised that Miss Granger remembers."

"We . . . the children and I . . . never knew your name," she whispered, "to thank you."

Crump whirled, and Simon intercepted a fleeting glimpse of suspicion. "You know this man?" James asked, advancing toward the young woman. "Why haven't you said anything?"

She avoided his gaze, Simon noticed, all his senses alert, humming. Instead, she stood there, eyes fastened on Simon like a pilgrim's to a shrine. "The Crumps posted a reward, trying to find you."

"And now, here I am." Simon kept his voice polite, nonchalant, all the while gauging every angry breath James Crump took — and storing every bit of information in the vault of his brain. The man was *not* pleased to learn that Simon and Elizabeth had met. Why? "I happened to be passing through Albany a couple weeks ago," he told Crump. "I was able to help Miss Granger with the children during the unfortunate train incident, but she deserves all the praise."

"Without you —" she began, but James

89

Crump's hand slashed downward in a gesture that silenced Elizabeth instantly.

"How . . . interesting that the two of you know each other." He smiled at Simon, who wasn't fooled. Neither, Simon suspected, was the woman.

"Excuse me," she murmured. "I've just returned from town and must see to the children." She walked — no, fled, Simon concluded — to the door and disappeared.

He raised a sardonic brow as he studied Crump's reddening ears and the muscle twitching at one corner of his mouth. *Something* was going on between these two, and Simon was vaguely disconcerted by a sense of bitter regret. So much courage, such selflessness — but like everyone else, Elizabeth Granger's feet were fashioned of clay. It was a wonder God had created man in His image in the first place, since the race — after Adam — had done nothing but disappoint its Maker.

"You'll have to forgive our Miss Granger," Crump offered. His indulgent tone belied the anger in his eyes. "She's so consumed with her duties to my brother's children that she often forgets her place, not to mention her manners. I'd planned to have her show you around the stables, as she's something of a horse lover herself. And since you . . . know each other . . ."

Simon shrugged. "I'd rather explore the stables on my own, anyway," he returned.

"I'm sure someone there can answer most of my questions." On the other hand, he doubted very much whether James Crump *or* Elizabeth Granger would care overmuch for the questions he would have put to each of *them*.

10

To avoid being recognized in town, Rufus jumped train a couple of miles out, when the engineer slowed to a near crawl for some reason. The ride had been slow and bumpy, with tedious stops and neck-wrenching starts.

He slogged through several miles of swamp and choking woods, keeping a wary eye on the angry-looking clouds overhead. He then followed the wide, sand-packed boulevard circling Thomasville. Whenever he heard voices, he ducked back to hide in the undergrowth, cursing the Yankee blue bloods with their fancy horses and buggies. Crump's place, he'd been told, was so easy to find that even a simpleton would be able to follow the directions. Rufus scowled, aimed a vicious kick at a rock, and sent it flying into the weeds. One of these days, he swore to himself, he'd prove he wasn't just another brainless bumpkin to be kicked around like a dog.

The rain started an hour later. Creeping among the weaving pines, pellets of rain stinging his eyes, the queasiness rose up in his throat again. Ding-dang it! Why'd Paxton have to order him to kill a *female?* Why not that blabbermouth Abe — or old Horatio himself?

Killing females . . . well . . . t'weren't *respectable*. 'Course there was women and even a couple of younguns in that wreck — but that was no fault of his. A blast of wind near blew his hat clean off his head, and by the time he finally reached the lane leading to Horatio Crump's fancy house, Rufus was wet, cold, and hornet mad. He was also past caring whether the companion was female, old, *and* crippled. He just wanted to get it over with, take whatever money and valuables he could grab, and then make Avery Paxton regret the day he was born.

He'd do in the companion, fill the croaker sack he'd stuffed inside his shirt, hike back to the tracks, and be halfway to Albany before dawn.

◆ ◆ ◆

" '. . . are closed and lambs are sleeping; lullaby, oh, lullaby! Sleep, my baby, fall a-sleeping, lullaby, oh, lullaby!' " Elizabeth closed the book of rhymes, her gaze moving over the five sleepy faces gathered around the rocker. "Into bed with all of you now," she murmured, lifting an already dozing Thomas into her arms.

" 'Lizbeth, will you carry me, too?" Jessica lifted her arms.

"She's already carrying Thomas," little Horatio, called Ho-Boy, pointed out around

93

a wide yawn. "Besides, you're too big."

"Am not. She carried me on the train, and Thomas, too." Jessica's bottom lip trembled, and she wrapped her arms around Elizabeth's knees, burrowing her head in the folds of her skirts.

"Take my hand," Joan intervened, giving Elizabeth a drowsy smile. "Lamar, you take my other one."

Elizabeth smiled gratefully at the little girl, whose recovery from the frightful crash had been more prolonged than the others. But Joan seldom mentioned the accident anymore and was quick to divert any discussion or re-living of the episode. She still hadn't met Simon Kincaid, so did not know that the man who had saved them was their father's new trainer.

Earlier, after supper, Josephine had drawn Elizabeth aside to warn her not to bring up the matter. Mr. Kincaid was adamant — he'd threatened to leave if further mention were made of compensation for his heroic rescue. Already distracted herself, Elizabeth merely nodded agreement. Now, after tucking in the last child, she tiptoed down the upstairs hall, frowning a little. Would Joan recognize their rescuer, as *she* had?

Elizabeth left her bedroom door open a crack and went over to the radiator to warm her hands. Outside, the sound of a steady downpour helped to calm her nerves, jangled since that afternoon. Simon Kincaid: Horatio's new trainer — and Elizabeth's unknown "guardian angel." Thoughts of those piercing green eyes had intruded all evening, along with her rising concern over James's less than subtle threats.

Strangely unsettled, Elizabeth pondered both her wary fascination for Simon Kincaid and her growing fear of James. If she were prudent, she would make an effort to avoid *both* men. Sighing, she stood by the heater, listening to the falling rain while she tried to decide how best to deal with the situation.

If only Grandpapa were still alive. . . . He was the only person who had ever loved Elizabeth, whose counsel she had trusted, even though her grandfather had sent her away when she was thirteen years old. Memories surfaced, pouring over her like the rain, drowning out the present. *He thought she needed to live among gentlewomen, to better learn how to become a lady. He wanted what was best for her. . . .*

"But why didn't you try to find me, Grandpapa?" a seventeen-year old Elizabeth had asked, over and over, during those last anguished weeks of her maternal grandfather's life. "You sent me away. I never heard from you, not once. All these years, I waited and dreamed. . . . You were the only one who ever loved me, and you sent me away."

His hand, blue-veined and skeletal, crept

95

across the bedcovers to rest over her clenched fist. "I did what I thought was best," he whispered. "Perhaps I was wrong. People make mistakes, Elizabeth. But . . . God does not . . . ever." He coughed. "Don't you forget that, child. Don't ever forget that you can depend on God" — the fragile chest rose and fell with his labored breathing — "even when you can't depend on anyone else."

The rasping sound made Elizabeth flinch. Silently she poured a teaspoonful of medicine, then held his head so he could swallow. "Grandpapa —"

"Promise me." His hand clamped down on hers with surprising strength. "Promise me you'll never be bitter, that you won't let your family or your circumstances defeat you. . . . Elizabeth, you're one of His lambs . . . He'll never let you go. . . ." He began coughing again, and the handkerchief Elizabeth held against his lips came away stained with red.

A whistling wind rattled the shutters, and Elizabeth blinked, returning to the present. She tugged out a clean handkerchief and wiped her eyes. Tomorrow, she decided, removing her hairpins, tomorrow she would ask Mrs. Crump to help Pansy mind the children a few hours so she could run into town and find out how much a ticket to Ochlocknee cost. Fifteen miles north of Thomasville, the small town mentioned in her cousin's letter might yield some information. Besides, she would welcome a brief respite from her duties at Adelaide, if only for the day.

Separating her hair into three sections, Elizabeth began to plait the long strands into a braid, her jumbled thoughts leap-frogging from her father's perfidy, to Simon Kincaid and the shock of his appearance as the new trainer, to James. James, she abruptly recalled, had been not so much shocked, as *angry*. For some reason, he wanted to maneuver her into an untenable position, not only with Mr. Kincaid — but with her status in the Crump family household.

Elizabeth winced. She was painfully familiar with such a scenario. First, the jealousy over an unwanted intruder, followed by irritation and slights and innuendos. Next, shouting matches behind closed doors — and sometimes in Elizabeth's presence. Finally, a hastily stuffed carpetbag and spurious explanations of how she would be better off elsewhere. Even now, the sight of a carpetbag sitting by a door squeezed her heart.

But why would James perceive her as a threat? Unless he had somehow discovered her real name.

Outside, the wind picked up, lashing rain against the windows in a frenzied burst, and Elizabeth closed the drapes, her eye falling on the toy animal propped in the middle of her bed. She scooped up the fuzzy lamb, lost in the past once more. Her grandfather had given her the toy when she was only four. Fashioned from real sheep's wool, the now bedraggled lamb had been both favored toy and needed security. Elizabeth had kept it with her ever since.

"Whenever you feel lost and alone," Grandpapa had told her, "I want you to remember that the Lord is like a Shepherd, caring for His sheep. He will always protect you, Elizabeth, because you're a beloved member of His flock."

Sighing, Elizabeth patted the toy, then placed it carefully aside. With profound reluctance she picked up the envelope, hidden inside the lace pocket of one of the many decorative pillows scattered across the bed. It had been months since she had written a letter of inquiry to a woman she barely remembered, but the tentative thread had yielded the second verifiable clue to the location of the money. *Think about the progress you've made,* she ordered herself sternly. *Concentrate on this second clue, instead of the nightmarish memories of discovering the first clue. Don't think about Mr. Soames. Don't —*

Her lecture was interrupted by a pounding on the bedroom door. Through the panels Elizabeth could hear Dora's frantic voice calling her name. Elizabeth hurried across to open the door for the upstairs maid. "Dora, what's wrong? One of the children? Mrs. Crump?"

"No, ma'am." Dora gave Elizabeth's bedtime attire a harried glance. "Luther was roused by Jefferson, an' Jefferson begged him to fetch you. Something's spooked the horses — mos' likely this storm — and they need some help down to the barn. It ain't fitting, Miss 'Lizbeth, but Miz Crump says you'd best go, seeing as how Mr. Horatio's away, an' Mr. Clarke killed in that train wreck, an' the new trainer barely arrived. Ain't nobody else knows them critters like you. . . ."

Elizabeth was already in a flurry of motion, and five minutes later, she ran lightly downstairs, where Jefferson waited in a fever of impatience. "Best put on a slicker, Miss 'Lizbeth," he urged her. "It's a reg'lar gully washer out there. I hates to bother you, but —"

She waved his apology aside. "I'd have been *more* bothered if you *hadn't*."

11

Even over the roar of the rain, Elizabeth could hear the distressed neighs, the thud of hooves beating against the stalls. "Mosby?" she called above the din.

"Mr. Kincaid's with him. It's these two new ones Mr. Horatio bought last month that's causin' all the trouble."

Elizabeth nodded and turned down the aisle where the two stallions were stabled at opposite ends of the row. A clutch of white-eyed stablehands huddled together, outside the stalls. "Abraham, try whistling like you do when you clean his stall," she ordered, pitching her voice above the ear-splitting screams of the stallions. "Eddie, you join him. The rest of you see to the other horses. They're restless and agitated, but if you talk to them, they'll calm down."

"The new trainer said —"

"Mr. Kincaid doesn't know these animals yet," Elizabeth interrupted. "He'll have his hands full with Mosby, and the best way to help him is to settle these other two."

Her air of quiet authority quickly dispelled the hesitancy in their manner, and they moved to obey. Elizabeth spared scant seconds wondering at their reluctance before she turned toward the bay stallion who had just splintered one of the slats in his stable door. She walked slowly over, her gaze never leaving the panicked animal. "Easy, now," she crooned. "There's nothing to be afraid of, but you're going to hurt yourself if you don't stop that thrashing about."

It seemed an eternity before the stallion began to respond. Her heartbeat drummed a rhythm to match the pouring rain, while the snorting and pawing and agitated whinneying assaulted her ears. But at last the animal remained on four legs, blowing and tossing his head while his gaze focused on Elizabeth. She kept talking, though her voice was growing hoarse from the strain.

"Hand me a carrot or an apple," she murmured to Jefferson without taking her eyes from Sir Peabody. A moment later a carrot was slipped into her palm. She stepped forward, stopped, then slowly lifted the carrot into the stallion's line of sight.

Five minutes later peace had been restored.

Weaving from fatigue, Elizabeth slowly made her way back down the aisle. Conscious now of her damp and bedraggled appearance, she wanted only to slip back to the house, unnoticed. Jefferson had just told her with admiration plain in his eyes how the new trainer had "the touch." Elizabeth swallowed hard. Mr. Kincaid might have needed her assistance, but she was ill prepared for an encounter with him right now, when she was exhausted, untidy — and uninvited.

"Don't reckon even you could have kept old Mosby from tearing the place apart," Jefferson continued, not realizing the impact of his words on her vulnerable spirit. "Too bad Mr. Horatio didn't have Mr. Kincaid the last couple o' seasons. It's a pleasure to work with a man who knows what he's about. Why, he even —"

"Jefferson."

The resonant male voice triggered Elizabeth's defenses, but she wasn't truly alarmed until she turned around to face the new trainer and confronted, head on, the look in his glittering green eyes — a powerful blend of admiration and ire.

Simon studied the disheveled young woman in front of him. Part of him was riled because the stableboys had disobeyed his orders; another part of him grudgingly acknowledged Elizabeth Granger's ability to subdue the high-strung horses with a skill to rival his own.

But the tightness in his throat warned him to tread carefully. He glanced down the aisle, where a half dozen stableboys were trying to overhear them without appearing to do so. "I gave specific orders that nobody be disturbed at the main house."

Miss Granger's gaze followed his. "They were thinking of the horses, Mr. Kincaid." Her manner was dignified in spite of the damp tendrils of hair trailing free of her braid and the hurriedly donned shirtwaist and skirt beneath a shapeless mackintosh. "It was obvious that you wouldn't be able to handle all of them without help. . . ." She paused, searching his face, and Simon wondered at her poorly concealed anxiety. "Please don't blame the stablehands for disobeying you," she repeated. "It won't happen again. They think you're —" One hand fluttered upward, then dropped. "They think you have 'the touch.' "

" 'The touch,' " Simon repeated. His thoughts spun backward in time almost a quarter of a century, to the big strapping rancher who had told Simon much the same thing. "Some have a way with people," he'd said. "And some have a way with animals." He'd grinned and slapped Simon on the back. "And then there's those as are blessed with both. But be warned, my boy — some blessings turn out to be more of a curse." *And they had. They had.*

"Mr. Kincaid?"

The quiet inflection brought Simon back from his musings. "I've been told I'm good at my job," he admitted. "So perhaps, in the future, you'll leave me to do it." He watched her anxiety fade to embarrassment and . . . pain?

"I understand, Mr. Kincaid." She turned and began walking away, shoulders slumped.

Feeling as if he'd swatted a homeless kitten, Simon ran a hand through his tousled hair, but just as he started to call her back, Miss Granger turned around. "Did . . . ah . . . did Jefferson warn you about Mosby's dislike of water?"

"Yes, he did." Simon watched her closely, every muscle alert, poised. Her manner had swung from an air of confident authority to sheepish diffidence and back again in the span of a heartbeat — and he wanted to know why. Had she belatedly realized that dashing outside in the middle of the night — at the height of a storm — was not only reckless but potentially dangerous? *Or has she come for another reason altogether?*

Yet this was also the young woman who had almost died in her effort to save five children. The young woman who had denied that she was anybody "important." Frustrated because he neither understood nor trusted Elizabeth Granger, he stepped closer, looming over her. When he spoke, a hard edge tinged the words. "Now *you* tell *me* why they fetched you. Regardless of your skill and his proclaimed indifference, it is James Crump's job to oversee problems down here at the stables in his brother's absence. You're the children's companion, as I understand it, and under the circumstances, you have no business here. It's obvious you've a certain affinity for horses, but at this moment that's beside the point."

He pinned her with the hard green glare that had sent more than one quaking individual running for cover. "In the future, Miss Granger, try to restrain your heroic impulses, no matter how urgent you may perceive a situation to be." He hesitated, disturbed by her stricken expression. His voice softened. "Horses are unpredictable at best. I don't want you to be hurt, especially when your intent was only to help." *Or was it?* He could not afford to overlook a lurking suspicion where Miss Elizabeth Granger was concerned.

"Yes, of course. I understand. I — the last thing I'd want would be to get in the way." She darted a quick glance around, then produced an empty smile. "You'll need to reassure the stablehands. I think they might be a little afraid of you."

She turned and made her way out of the barn, leaving Simon with the same uncomfortable sensation he'd experienced that afternoon when she'd fled the library. *Elizabeth Granger is not only afraid of James Crump. She's afraid of me, too.*

Simon's hands curled into fists. He felt

trapped, exposed — dangerous. There was nothing he could do about Miss Granger's fear; it was imperative that he hold every person in the Crump household under suspicion until he was convinced of their innocence. It was the only way an undercover operative could stay alive.

It was also the only way he could find out who had spooked the horses because one thing was clear — it hadn't been the storm.

When Simon had come running toward the stables, roused by the first trumpeting neigh, he'd caught a glimpse of a dark figure disappearing around the end of the barn. But by the time Simon reached the spot, the pounding rain had already obliterated any footprints and hidden the sinister figure from view.

◆ ◆ ◆

Rufus huddled in a clump of rhododendron, some fifty yards from the main house. He was wet to the skin, though the blasted rain had finally let up an hour earlier. He was also cold, still shivering from the near disaster at the barn when he'd tried to sneak through to snitch some vittles, and his belly was cramped with hunger and uncertainty.

Dawn was only a few hours away. Even if he managed to slip into the house and do the job, he'd still have a pretty far piece to travel in order to hop aboard a northbound freight without risking detection. But hanging around this place wasn't his idea of a safe way to spend a day, either. Stifling yet another sneeze, he muttered an expletive, then peered through the dripping shrubbery at the dark house, lit only by a hanging lamp over the front entrance.

There were sure to be a lot of folks lurking about, even at this hour. Now just wasn't the time, ding-dang it! He'd have to hole up in the woods and try again tonight. Rufus swore under his breath as he made his way backward, squirming on his belly like a snake. Why'd it have to be a *woman?*

♦ ♦ ♦

Josephine Crump summoned Elizabeth after breakfast. Her brow puckered with concern, she waved Elizabeth toward the family parlor. "Tell me about last night, when you went flying out the door to the stables. I was asleep when you returned." There was no censure in the gentle voice, but Elizabeth flushed.

"Mr. Kincaid wasn't pleased," she admitted, unable to meet Josephine's clear gaze. "I hope I haven't caused any trouble for Mr. Horatio with him because of this. . . ."

"Well, it might not have been very wise from Mr. Kincaid's perspective, but we all know how you feel about the horses. Here, my dear — let me pour you a cup of café au lait. You're looking a bit peaked this morning." She paused, the thread of anxiety returning. "The children . . . ?"

"Are fine. I'll be collecting them after lunch. I read some of their favorite poems, and everyone went right to sleep." Elizabeth risked a swift sidelong peek. "Would you like to keep them with you this afternoon?"

Tears gathered at the corners of the gray eyes. Josephine dabbed at them with her handkerchief, her smile rueful but sad. "I . . . would, yes. You explained that my . . . emotional state has nothing to do with them?"

"They understand more than you realize." Elizabeth reached out her hand, yanked it back, then — unable to bear the woman's pain — briefly brushed her fingers over the lace cuffs of Josephine's morning gown. "They know you love them so much that it's taking you longer than the rest of us to recover from almost losing them."

"Elizabeth, my dear, what would I do without you?"

Lord, dear Lord, I cannot continue like this. "You'd manage as beautifully as you did before we met." Elizabeth bit her lip. "Children need the love of their parents, Mrs. Crump, far more than they do that of a transient companion."

"I wish you wouldn't belittle yourself. You're not merely a 'transient companion'! Why, even Mother Crump commented to me this past summer how good you were for her grandchildren." Her mouth curved in a watery smile. "You might not realize it, but coming from Georgina Crump, that's high praise indeed. Do you know she always refers to them as *her* grandchildren — never *our* children? Family has always come first with Mr. Crump's mother."

The plump features fell as Josephine picked at the tatting on her lace handkerchief. "It took years for her to accept Horatio's marriage to a woman whose wealth was only second-generation. So, you see, for her to make that observation about you is" — she paused, looking up, a mischievous glint drying her tears — "is practically like an endorsement from President Cleveland himself. Or perhaps, Queen Victoria?"

The image of Georgina Crump's sharp, aristocratic features and regal bearing came to mind. "I'll remember. Mrs. Crump?" Elizabeth took a deep breath.

"Yes, dear? What is it? Why, Elizabeth, you're trembling!"

"I'm sorry — it's nothing, really," she began uncertainly. "I just wondered when you were expecting Mr. Crump to return. I wanted to ask permission to watch Mr. Kincaid work with the horses. Not every day, of course," she amended hastily. "Just every so often . . . whenever it wouldn't be an inconvenience. . . ." She took a sip of the cream-rich drink to avoid Mrs. Crump's thoughtful perusal.

"Seems to me the person you'd need to ask would be Mr. Kincaid. I'm surprised you didn't ask him last night, while you were down at the stables."

Well, she should have known that was coming. "I'll talk to him, of course, but since we're both employed by Mr. Crump, I thought . . ." Elizabeth's voice trailed off in a sigh.

"You don't want to be an imposition. I declare, my dear, I don't know what we're going to do with you!" She set her own cup down and contemplated a moment, then lifted her head, eyes dancing. "I have a delightful solution! Luther told me Mr. Kincaid planned to take several of the horses over for a few trial heats at the track today if the weather cleared. Why don't you hitch up the children's cart and drive them over to watch? It would be a fine outing!"

Unbidden, the vision sprang to mind: a dark stall . . . a lifeless body sprawled in blood-soaked straw. . . . Elizabeth drew a steadying breath. "That *is* a good idea," she murmured, hating the lie. Hating even more the necessity compelling her to carry it out. She rose. "I'll make the arrangements." At the entrance to the parlor, she paused. "Why don't you come along, Mrs. Crump?"

The older woman brightened. "Now, why didn't I think of that? We'll have to take the family carriage, of course, but —" Her face

110

crumpled in dismay. "Oh, dear — I forgot! I'm going along with Maisie Pritchard to visit her grandmother this afternoon. Poor Mrs. Coates has taken a turn for the worse, I'm afraid, and since the dear woman has been such a good neighbor all these years, I told Maisie that I'd come with her. I'm sorry, my dear. Perhaps, next week?"

"Next week it is, then. I'm sorry about Mrs. Coates. She's in her eighties now, isn't she?"

"Yes, and so healthy, until last winter. Elizabeth?"

"Ma'am?"

"You . . . will be careful? Don't drive the cart too fast, and make sure Joan holds Thomas's hand. And —"

"Don't worry. I'll take good care of them," Elizabeth promised, aching with pity for the mother whose ferocious love for her children was corroded by her crippling fear for their well-being.

◆ ◆ ◆

The ripple of laughter woke him with a start of panic. Were them brats playing in the woods? What if they stumbled over his hiding place?

Rufus dived over the fallen log where he'd been napping, scrambled to his feet, and hid behind the trunk of a massive oak. Sweat beaded his brow, and he waited, frozen in a crouch, his gaze darting about the undergrowth.

Moments later, less than thirty yards away, he spotted the dappled pony pulling a wicker cart laden with the Crump children. The paid companion was driving the cart. If any of them glanced his way, they'd spot him like a flushed partridge. He hadn't realized last night, in the dark and drizzle, that one of the estate paths was cut so close to the spot he'd chosen to bed down.

Unmoving, fear and hatred burning his empty belly, he glimpsed the pale oval of the companion's face, the gentle curve of a smile on her lips as she listened to the children, her hands firm and competent on the reins.

This was all her fault! If she hadn't saved all them brats, he wouldn't be down here now, risking his neck for a hoity-toity who was too big for his fancy britches. It was all *her* fault.

The cart trundled around a bend, though he could still hear the children, and he stayed where he was until long after the sound of their childish babble died away. Then he slid down at the base of the tree and stared at his hands. *Tonight,* he promised the dainty companion. *You won't be smiling after tonight.*

12

Pastime Racetrack
Thomasville

Simon had forgotten the joy of working with horses.

He nodded to Jefferson, who released his hold on the head of a young filly they'd been schooling for the past hour. "She's looking good," Simon affirmed as he gathered the lines and settled his body into the low seat of the sulky. "All right, sweetheart, let's see how you like the track when Jefferson isn't trotting along beside you."

Meadowlark was still a little sluggish, he thought a minute later, as they approached the first turn. But her ears were pricked forward, and she trotted strongly without breaking stride. By the start of the racing season, Simon figured she'd make adequate odds. He lifted his face into the wind, inhaling the pungent fragrance of pine and magnolia, reveling in the tug of the lines and the rhythmic one-two beat of the filly's hooves on the dirt-and-sand track. The power and freedom of being out in the open. Of working with horses again. *I've missed this. I've really missed this.*

Meadowlark trotted past the viewing stands, and from the corner of his eye, Simon caught a flurry of motion — the Crump children, with Elizabeth Granger. Meadowlark didn't deviate from her steady pace, and Simon grunted in satisfaction. It was a good thing he'd decided to leave the blinkers in place. Seconds later he pulled to a halt beside Jefferson, who was fairly dancing in glee, leathery face creased in a grin.

"Sho' looked good, Mister Kincaid. As steady and purty as if she'd been born in them traces."

"She does have good instincts, but we'll have to try her without the blinkers before we'll be able to judge her performance accurately." Simon hopped out of the sulky, then nodded toward the stands. "Looks like we have an audience."

"Yassuh. The children enjoy watching, and Miss Elizabeth does, too." The stableman chuckled. "I expect she'd as soon be out *here,* though, instead of sittin' in them bleachers minding the younguns."

Simon quirked a brow before turning back to the filly. "Let's try Mosby now, then the stallion you told me keeps trying to kick when he's in harness. Sir Peabody, isn't it? The wind's as calm as it's going to get. If Mosby's going to act up, I'd just as soon not have a crowd witnessing the event."

114

"Best warn you, Mr. Kincaid, them stands'll fill up more as the season commences. People hereabouts act like it's the real thing instead of only training." Jefferson ran ahead to warn the pair of stableboys who had helped bring the trotters down from Adelaide.

Simon spent a few minutes patting and praising the filly, though his mind was more on the young woman and her charges sitting in the stands. He'd been delicately probing for more information on Elizabeth Granger since early that morning, but had only turned up a few useful tidbits about her skill with both horses and children. With *anything*, Simon was told, that she put her hand to. Always smiling, always pleasant — more like a gracious lady than a children's companion, except she never put on airs. But nobody knew where she hailed from or if she had any kinfolk left. She had returned with the Crumps from an excursion to the coast a little over eighteen months earlier, and had been at Adelaide ever since.

Either none of the stablehands knew anything of her background, or they were keeping their mouths shut about it. Loyalty to Elizabeth, Simon wondered — or fear of reprisal? All he knew about this mysterious young woman was what he'd gleaned in the Agency files from his two predecessors — and what he'd learned about her that day in the river. None of that sparse recital, however, explained the essence of her personality. But then, what difference did that make?

Simon secured the long reins, then began leading the filly toward the barn. Even more frustrating was the unanswerable question: why did he *care?*

He wasn't really surprised when the children tumbled from the stands and ran toward him. Nor was he surprised when Elizabeth called them to an immediate halt, lined them up, then made them all hold hands.

Taking his cue from her, Simon advanced to meet them outside the entrance to the barn. "Miss Granger." He inclined his head in a polite nod.

"Mr. Kincaid." Her answering smile was uncertain. "The children would like to know if they may pet Meadowlark. She's usually pretty even-tempered, and I thought —"

"They can pet her for one minute — but that's it. Here, hold her for me." He waited until Elizabeth obeyed, then hunkered down, at eye level with the five children. Faces alight with expectation, they gazed at Simon with barely restrained excitement, except for the oldest girl, whose face wore a puzzled frown. "I want all of you to listen to me very closely," Simon began, waiting until all five pairs of eyes were trained on his. "You're being very good, and because you are, I'll allow you to tell Meadowlark what a good job *she's* done today. But then you'll have to go back to the stands and stay there."

"I want to pet *all* the horses."

"Me, too."

Simon lifted one stern brow, and after a second, silence reigned. "I imagine all of you have lessons," he observed, reaching out to lightly tweak the button nose of the youngest boy, the toddler whose sturdy body and wind-rosy cheeks defied Simon's last image of him. "Except this little one here. Am I right?"

Reluctantly they nodded.

"Well, right now the horses are having lessons, and they need to concentrate on what I tell them, just as you need to concentrate on your studies. When you come here to see them, they think it's time to play instead of work."

"Can we play with the horses *after* they have their lessons?"

"Ho-Boy," Elizabeth broke in, "don't pester Mr. Kincaid, or we might not be able to watch at all."

The boy pursed his lips in a pout, but when he looked back at Simon, he offered no further argument. Simon tousled his hair and tugged his cap down over his eyes. "We'll see," he temporized, standing up, watching with Elizabeth while the children patted Meadowlark.

"I've seen you somewhere before," the oldest girl suddenly blurted out.

Joan — that was her name, Simon remembered.

Soft brown eyes widened, and she clapped her hand over her mouth. Her horrified gaze flew to Elizabeth, then back to Simon. "I didn't mean to be rude," she whispered.

"It's all right." Simon took the reins from Elizabeth. "You weren't rude. But you do need to return to the bleachers with Miss Granger now. I have work to do." He headed toward the barn without looking back, though he could hear Joan talking earnestly to Elizabeth, followed by the high-pitched voices of the others.

"I know I've seen him before, Elizabeth . . . I just can't remember where. Was he angry, do you think? He looks very stern."

"He looks like a pirate!"

"Does not. Pirates have eyepatches and a moustache. Mr. Kincaid doesn't even have a moustache!"

"His eyes are the color of my favorite marbles. 'Lizbeth, did you see his eyes?"

" 'Lizbeth, does he scare you? You look all funny, like you did that other time we came here to watch the horses when Mr. Clarke was Father's trainer. I didn't like him."

Simon reached the barn, handed Meadowlark over to the grinning stableboys, then strode down the aisle toward Mosby's stall. He had to force his mind to the task at hand.

For now, he was a trainer. But he couldn't afford to forget the primary reason he was here — as a Pinkerton operative. Still, those children, so full of life, of innocence . . .

The vaguely wistful yearnings evaporated, yet for the rest of the afternoon, in spite of the exhiliration of working the horses, it was Elizabeth Granger — serene and secretive — who challenged his discipline more.

Something one of the smaller girls had said — Jessica, wasn't it? — niggled at Simon like a mosquito. He asked Jefferson about it after everyone else had left to take all the horses but Mosby back to Adelaide. Elizabeth and the children had also departed, and Simon took advantage of the rare opportunity. "Did Miss Granger bring the children here last season?"

"Well, not at first," Jefferson supplied amiably. "Miss Joan, see, used to be afeared of horses, and Miss 'Lizbeth weren't going to leave one youngun behind, so she worked with Miss Joan most of the winter. Funny, now that I think on it. The couple o' times Miss 'Lizabeth *did* bring them younguns here, she stayed clear o' the barn. Not a'tall like she does back home." He spoke sharply to Mosby, who was baring his teeth, then turned back to Simon. "Fact is, she'd ask me to take the younguns inside so they could pat the horses, whilst she stayed over yonder in the stands."

119

He shook his head still again. "I wonder . . . no. She's been here a spell, but she still probably ain't heared about what happened here at Pastime. Mr. Crump — he don't like nobody to talk about it, neither, so I don't reckon Miss 'Lizbeth has cause to be skittish about *that*."

"About what?" Simon asked, fighting irritation.

"Oh, several years back, ol' Mr. Soames got hisself kilt down here, in that last stall near the door. Head bashed in with a pair o' clippers. He was Mr. Horatio's stable boss, but nobody cared for him much."

Several years? About the time Pinkerton's started an active investigation of the Crumps? William Soames had been one of the men the Agency had hoped to investigate.

His interest piqued, Simon finished buckling Mosby back into the harness. "Why was that?" he asked very casually.

After an uncomfortable pause, Jefferson cleared his throat, then stared down at his feet. "Well . . . he had squinty eyes, for one thing. Always got the feeling his mouth said one thing, but his heart said another. And he liked to put on airs, just 'cause he knowed how to read and write."

Simon decided to have Alex re-open the file on William Soames. "Was the murderer ever apprehended?"

"Nope. The old watchman who found the

body swore on a stack o' Bibles he'd seen a female running off into the woods, but nobody ever found nothin'. That old feller was mostly blind anyway. There weren't nothin' in Soames's pockets, and nobody come forward to claim the body. Mr. Crump had to pay for the burial an' all. I'd near forgot the whole thing, till you started asking 'bout Miss 'Lizbeth."

He hooked his thumbs inside his suspenders and spat into the straw. "You must have noticed she's got a steadier head than most females, and I ain't never seen her rattled. But I was watching, when you was down talking with them children this afternoon, and I got to tell you, Miss 'Lizbeth kept eyein' this here barn as if she thought it might be about to fall on top of her. It don't make no sense, Mr. Kincaid. No sense a'tall."

13

Thomasville

James Crump swung by the depot in time to meet Horatio's train. As was his habit, he had been out to Rose Hill for the weekly visit to their mother, a virtual recluse on the vast family plantation for over twenty years now. The "visits" were nothing so much as thinly disguised inquisitions, to his way of thinking, but his mother expected to be kept informed despite her chosen isolation — and the inconvenience to her sons.

James brought the carriage to a standstill, then struck a match on the heel of his boot and lit a cigar. He leaned back in his seat, puffing while he waited for the train. Mother might refuse to venture beyond the garden wall, but James knew better than to make an observation on her lifestyle.

Moments later a whistle shrieked. James straightened, waiting until the Crump Crown Flyer pulled to a clanging halt in a cloud of steam, Horatio's flagship car directly in front of James. Presently Horatio disembarked, followed by a porter, who carried the luggage.

"You look grim, brother," James observed, tapping cigar ash on the door. "Apparently your latest talk with Paxton was less than successful."

Horatio removed his derby and rubbed his temples. The late afternoon sun glistened on his balding head and emphasized the deep lines of weariness in his sallow face. "Paxton's a pretentious, conceited Yankee, bloated on his self-importance," he muttered.

"My, my, all that?" James shifted to one side to allow his brother room, then turned the carriage toward home. "So he still isn't willing to negotiate?"

"Not an inch. Just sat there like a smug little toad and warned me that if we don't sell, 'unfortunate incidents' even worse than the accident in Albany on the South Georgia Central this past summer could plague all *our* lines."

"He said that, did he?" James scowled. With a quick flick of his wrist, his cigar sailed into the street. "The little worm's playing a dangerous game, but he isn't going to win this one," he finished under his breath.

"How's Mother?"

"Enjoying the fine weather. She's been out in the garden a lot, terrifying the grounds staff. Mother and her flowers — you and your horses. . . ." James shook his head. "She'll be interested in what you've learned, I'm sure, but I can pass the information along for you. You look whipped, big brother, if you don't mind my saying so. Since you've a family at home, eagerly awaiting your return, why don't I run back over to see Mother again first thing in the morning?"

Horatio sank back against the seat, closing his eyes. A tall, gaunt man, he had always possessed a passive manner that had irked James from the time they were young boys. "You should have let me handle Paxton," James growled.

"It's my place as head of Crump Systems," Horatio reminded him. "The responsibility falls on my shoulders." He opened his eyes and stared at his younger brother. "James, Paxton has someone feeding him information about us. He knows too many details, especially about our negotiations with South Georgia Central. And he wasn't a bit shy about rubbing my face in it." He loosened his tie and sighed. "Blasted little blowhard. It's just as well you weren't there." He smiled fondly at James. "You might have been tempted to light into him with your fists, I'm afraid. You always were something of a hot pepper."

James forced himself to return the smile. "It probably would have been more effective than trying to negotiate. I don't know why you bothered in the first place."

He stared out the window, thinking hard.

124

So Paxton had a stool pigeon in their camp, did he? And he was arrogant enough to think they couldn't figure out who it might be. Glancing across at his big brother, James stifled a burgeoning rage. No wonder the carpetbagger was so confident, since he'd only been dealing with Horatio Crump, Jr. If *he* — James — had gone to Atlanta instead of Horatio, not only would he have discovered the identity of the traitor, he also would have sent Paxton back north — in pieces.

James swore to himself. Mother insisted that, for the sake of the family, Horatio remain under the illusion that he was the controlling power behind the Crump System. Soon, everyone would know differently. *Soon.* He nudged his brother with the toe of his boot. "Horatio?"

The older man lifted his head. "What is it?"

"There's a possibility that we can't afford to overlook." James paused, then added slowly, as with great reluctance. "I . . . hesitate to bring it up, but . . ."

"I'm not sure I like the sound of this." Horatio groaned, but he sat up a little straighter. "What possibility is that?"

"Paxton's been dogging us for almost a year now, hasn't he? But have you ever wondered why he chose *us?* Why not go after Flagler, on the eastern seaboard, or one of the big lines up North? Somebody has to have been feeding him information for a long time

— maybe even longer than a year. Long enough and with damaging enough facts to convince him he could be successful. . . ."

James took a deep breath, stared across the aisle at his brother, then away, as if he couldn't bear to look him in the face. "Horatio, exactly how much do we really know about Elizabeth Granger?"

♦ ♦ ♦

The courier pedaled his bicycle down the hard-packed dirt road as fast as his aching legs could churn. Inside his gray worsted uniform, he was sweating, even though the November day was brisk. He was late, and he knew it. He also knew tardiness was grounds for far more than a tongue-lashing.

Maybe the letter in his courier pouch would divert the wrath of his employer.

Moments later he reached the huge wrought iron gates. Breathing hard, he glanced fearfully about for the dogs as he pedaled up the long drive, then hurried up the steps to the front entrance, where a stone-faced butler held the door open.

"You're late. You better go in immediately."

The courier scuttled down the hall to the small room that had been turned into an office. He handed across the envelope, keeping his eyes lowered as he had been taught from the first day he started work here, some six years earlier.

"You're late, Matthew."

"I — I know. The train . . . it was delayed."

He locked his knees to keep them from shaking

126

and forced his posture to remain rigidly upright. "I got here fast as I could."

"In the future, telegraph me from the station if you expect to be late by even five minutes. That way I won't . . . worry. I don't like worrying, Matthew, especially over employees upon whom I depend to keep me informed."

"You can depend on me —" he began, then clamped his lips together, swallowing hard.

"We'll see . . . won't we?"

Matthew watched in silence while his employer slit open the envelope, then read the contents. "So. Avery Paxton was responsible for that wreck . . . with the help of a man who works for me. What do you think should be done about this, Matthew?"

The courier's head jerked up, then down, while he scrabbled frantically for something to say. "I . . . I don't know."

"No, I'm sure you don't." The soft response, uttered in that cold, cultured voice, froze the sweat on his brow. "But I know what to do. Afterwards, perhaps Mr. Paxton will be convinced to pursue his dream empire somewhere else. If not . . ." There was another, longer pause. Then, "Leave me now, Matthew. Oh — one more thing. If you're ever late again without letting me know, may I suggest you cultivate a proper relationship with the Almighty."

Matthew was halfway back to town before he was able to draw a deep breath.

14

Adelaide
Thomasville
Late November

Elizabeth returned from the train station just before dark; she had secured a timetable, so all she had to do now was arrange the day for her trip to Ochlocknee. The morning had dawned brassy and humid. By the time Elizabeth turned the cart back down the drive leading to Adelaide, a dull ache throbbed at the base of her skull. She massaged her neck and allowed Barney, the amiable old coach horse, his lead, since he could find his way home blindfolded.

A flock of Canadian geese honked overhead, and off somewhere in town, a factory whistle blew. Elizabeth suppressed a stab of longing. She had grown to love Thomasville, and the prospect of leaving saddened her. That she *would* leave — sooner or later — was inevitable. Since her birth in Milledgeville twenty-six years ago, she had lived in a score of homes, in almost as many towns, from Georgia to New York. And always, *always*, she had been told to move on.

As the horse clip-clopped down the street, Elizabeth's thoughts returned to her cousin's letter, which had led to this trip to the depot. She had read it so many times in the past few days, every word was inscribed in her brain: "I remember very little about the incident, for I was but a child of eight at the time," the now middle-aged woman had written Elizabeth in a rambling and somewhat priggish style. "My sister and I used to hide beneath the stairs, the better to spy on our elders, shameful creatures that we were! From the perspective of adulthood, I've been able to form a bitterly sad conclusion as regards your father, however.

"It would seem, my dear Elizabeth, that he engaged in a liason with a young woman who was not his wife. . . ."

My father . . . a liar, a thief — and now, it seems, an adulterer as well. Without guidance, Barney turned down the drive to Adelaide. Elizabeth barely noticed.

According to her cousin's sister, Elizabeth's father and the young woman had rendezvoused at some pre-arranged place in Ochlocknee, and it was Elizabeth's theory that perhaps her father had hidden the gold somewhere in the area where he was conducting his . . . affair. Her cousin hadn't known the identity of the young woman, and Elizabeth didn't care to know. Adultery was a grievous enough sin — only one of many

129

committed by a selfish man who hadn't cared a fig about anything but satisfying his own desires.

All Elizabeth could hope to do was to find the gold and make partial restitution to the Crumps and, eventually, the Rattrays. *But would it be enough?*

Elizabeth left the stables and started toward the main house, where the children swarmed over her in an exuberent tide. Joan and Jessica wanted to show her the new dolls their father had brought them from Atlanta, while the boys begged her to play baseball with *their* new bats and gloves.

"Pansy can't pitch as well as you can," Lamar announced, disgusted.

"Mama's having a tea party with Joan and me." Jessica shoved her way in front to tug on Elizabeth's sleeve. "You have to play with *us!*"

"Miss 'Lizbeth, Jefferson says if you can spare a few minutes befo' supper, he needs a word with you," Pansy put in, waving her arms to shoo the children away. Beneath the neatly bound turban, her face glistened with perspiration. "Lawd, but this day's been hot enough to fry a whole chicken! Not at all like November. Come along, now, sweet peas, and leave Miss 'Lizbeth alone 'cause" — she cast a worried glance in Elizabeth's direction — "she's plumb wrung out like a dishrag!"

Unfortunately, the remainder of the afternoon disappeared before Elizabeth found out what Jefferson wanted with her.

At a little past eight-thirty, she had just tiptoed out of the last sleeping child's bedroom when yet another message arrived. This one requested that she meet Mr. Kincaid at his quarters to discuss a matter of some urgency. Urgency? In his *quarters?*

Elizabeth read the note through twice, then studied the stablehand who had brought it. "Willy, did Mr. Kincaid give this to you himself?"

"No, ma'am. I got it from Snaps, who said it was important and had to be delivered directly to you, jest as soon as the children were tucked away for the night." Willy searched her face, looking anxious. "I 'specs Mr. Kincaid knows you'd need to see to 'em first, Miss 'Lizbeth, but can we go now? That's one gentleman I sure don't want burning me with that green fire of his!"

Elizabeth knew exactly how Willy felt. And yet, other emotions teased the corners of her mind every time she thought of Mr. Kincaid — anticipation, challenge, security . . . fear.

Hastily she folded the note and stuffed it inside her pocket. "Run on back, Willy. I'll tell Mrs. Crump and be only a step or two behind you."

Josephine had already fallen asleep. Horatio's door was closed, and no light showed through at the bottom. Stifling her uneasiness, Elizabeth wrapped a shawl about her shoulders and slipped out the kitchen door. She fought an inward battle all the way down the dark path leading to the neat frame bungalow where the trainers always lived. Three years ago, the last time she had allowed her mule-headed determination to supercede prudence, she had had to flee for her life.

Fiddly-foot! she scolded herself, opening the gate. *Stop expecting to stumble over a corpse every time you approach a stable!* She marched up the path, her gaze on the shadowed contours of the cottage and the dark bulk of the barn beyond. Years earlier, someone had planted shrubs all around the foundation; over time they'd grown wild and untamed, imprisoning the walls behind a dense thicket. Elizabeth swallowed hard as she approached the front door. It was very dark here, she realized. Prickles blossomed up and down her arms and the back of her neck.

Something . . . wasn't right.

Without pausing to think, she whirled and ran, propelled by an instinct for survival honed from childhood. She dashed for the stables, a stone's throw from the bungalow, skidding to a breathless halt just before the sliding doors. The horses. She couldn't go bursting inside like a squawking hen, or the horses would panic. *Where was everyone?*

Slowly, deliberately, she willed her racing heartbeat to slow down. Drawing a deep breath, she glanced about and took a tentative step forward. From the corner of her eye, a dark shadow reared up from behind some stacked bales of hay.

"And what do you think *you're* doing?" Simon Kincaid's level voice demanded.

Elizabeth bit back a shriek. "Mr. Kincaid! You startled me out of my wits! Oh — behind you — !"

Another dark shape swelled from behind the corner of the barn. The trainer whirled, but was too late to counter his attacker. Hands thrust uselessly out to help, Elizabeth stumbled backward as Simon Kincaid was hurled to the ground beneath a flying tackle.

"No!" She lurched forward, grabbed the attacker's arm, and dug her fingers into a sinewy wrist. A suffocating blast of foul breath and sour body odor almost gagged her.

Mr. Kincaid twisted beneath the assailant and managed to free a hand. But it was too late. In spite of Elizabeth's frantic effort, the attacker lifted a deadly blackjack and brought it down toward the trainer's unprotected neck.

"No!" Elizabeth shouted again as he tore his arm free of her clutching fingers. She grabbed a fistful of coarse, greasy hair and yanked as hard as she could. "Jefferson! Snaps! Help!"

Mr. Kincaid collapsed without a sound. Elizabeth leaped aside, her terrified gaze on the ruffian. He turned from the sprawled body at his feet and lifted the cosh again — only this time he was aiming for Elizabeth. In the muggy, starless November night, she glimpsed only a pair of glittering eyes.

"You little she-wolf," he snarled, and lunged for her.

"Mr. Kincaid! Miss 'Lizbeth!" Jefferson erupted from the barn, along with several wild-eyed stableboys.

The attacker cursed, then fled across the stableyard toward the cover of the woods on the other side of the pasture. Elizabeth dashed after him, her only thought to keep him in sight so she could direct the others, all of whom had clustered around the fallen trainer. She barely heard Jefferson's urgent shout.

The attacker scrambled over the pasture fence, fell, and glanced over his shoulder as he stumbled to his feet. Elizabeth ran up to the fence, breathing hard, straining to see his face. Fifty yards behind, one of the stableboys waved his hands and shouted, but she couldn't make out what he was saying.

Too late, she realized the danger.

With another foul oath, the man suddenly reached over the fence. Grimy hands closed about Elizabeth's forearms, yanked her completely off her feet, and dragged her over with him. She kicked and struggled, opened her mouth to scream, just before something hard

134

slammed against her temple. Pain exploded in her head, and the world went black.

♦ ♦ ♦

"Easy. It's okay. Miss Granger — Elizabeth. You're safe. Lie still. I'm not going to hurt you."

The voice was soothing, reassuring. The hands holding her weren't bruising her in a vicious grip. Instead, they were strong, firm, supportive. Elizabeth grew still, the pain in her head blinding as she struggled to focus on that voice.

"That's it . . . easy does it. You're safe. Try to relax and open your eyes, Elizabeth. You've been hurt, and I need you to open your eyes."

Water. So much water . . . Fire — the train! The car was going to crash into the river! She had to save — "The children!" She struggled weakly, trying to propel the dead weight of her arms to action. "Have to save . . . children. . . ."

"No, no. The children are safe, Elizabeth. Shh . . . You saved the children. And now *you're* safe."

That voice. She knew that voice. It had reached her above the screams, above the roaring of the flames and the spewing, churning water. She remembered green eyes, burning a message of courage into her soul. It had been the look in those eyes, that deep commanding voice that had rekindled her deter-

135

mination to save the children, to live. Now he was telling her to — to . . . what? He wanted her to do something else. Confusion swirled in her head, and she moaned.

"That's it. You're coming around now. Open your eyes for me, Elizabeth."

Feeling as if she were fighting her way up through a choking vat of cane syrup, Elizabeth lifted weighted lids. Her vision swam alarmingly, then stilled, and she blinked, wincing from a bright light. She tried to turn her head aside and gasped with pain. The light disappeared, and her world faded to soft tones of luminous gray and brown. She blinked again, and a man's face loomed above her. Memory exploded with the suddenness of the blow that had knocked her cold. But Simon was *here,* not unconscious on the ground. Confused, Elizabeth shrank back, still dazed.

"I'm not going to hurt you," the trainer soothed, and his voice drove away the last remnants of unconsciousness. He turned away momentarily, retrieved a cold, damp cloth, and applied it to her forehead. "It's fortunate you have a hard head — at least in the literal sense."

The rebuke, though subtle, found its mark. "I . . . shouldn't have chased him." She stirred, searching the impassive face. "He struck you, too! I tried to stop him."

He laid two fingers over her lips. "Relax.

136

You blunted his aim enough that I was only stunned." The corners of his eyes crinkled slightly. "I've also been told that I, too, have a hard head."

At that moment a knock sounded on the door. "Don't move," Mr. Kincaid ordered Elizabeth. He returned a moment later. "I've assured Jefferson that you'll be all right. He'll inform the others." He looked down, assessing her with a frown. "I don't think the household should be notified yet. The incident would alarm Mrs. Crump, and I understand she's only now recovering from the accident this past summer."

"I — no. You're right, of course." Still muddled, a spate of involuntary apologies tumbled forth. "I don't want to worry anyone. I'm fine, truly. It was my own recklessness, and nobody else should have to pay —"

"Shh. Here, now. Rest easy." His frown deepened, rendering an even more intimidating cast to the harsh planes of his clean-shaven face.

Suddenly aware of her surroundings — an old couch in Mr. Kincaid's quarters — Elizabeth tried to rise. "I shouldn't be here. . . ." He pressed her firmly back against the cushions. "I'm fine. I must go. I'm fine," she repeated.

But in spite of her resolve, her voice wavered.

15

Simon leaned forward and passed the damp cloth over her mouth, then held it to the ugly bruise purpling her forehead, just above her left eye. If the blow had been a finger's breadth over, Elizabeth Granger would be dead.

He studied her frantic expression and abruptly decided that a neutral discussion would work better than a denunciation of her colossal stupidity. Chasing after an armed footpad! The little idiot. How could she charge an unknown assailant one minute — yet lie here watching him as if half-expecting a blow the next? "I'll take you back up to the house as soon as I'm convinced you're sentient," he told her, adopting as non-threatening a tone as he could muster, given his anger.

"I . . . just have a little headache. I can make it to the house by myself."

Simon ignored her protests, instead easing her a little higher, deftly propping a pillow behind her neck and shoulders. His action obviously embarrassed and disconcerted her, but at least she didn't shrink from his touch. For the moment, at least. Her conflicting responses toward Simon flicked him on the raw. "Stop looking at me as though *I'm* about to bash your head," he muttered.

"I'll be needed back at the house. Please."

Simon pressed the heels of his hands to his own aching head and took a deep breath. Either the girl was afraid of what he might discover — or she was still, for some indefinable reason, afraid of him. The fleeting image of a helpless, injured dog lying in an alley flashed through his brain. *Take it slow and easy, man. Stop acting the bully, or you'll never learn anything about Elizabeth Granger.*

"I need you to answer a few questions," he began in a milder tone, dragging over a pressed-back chair and sitting down. "Humor me, all right, and rest a few more moments. I promise not to browbeat, or yell, or badger —"

She relaxed visibly. But if Simon hadn't been watching her so closely, he would have missed her rueful expression. "You haven't done any of that," she responded. "Trust me — I know. I also know you seem to spend a lot of time rescuing me. If I didn't know any better, I'd believe . . ." She searched his face, and her voice trailed off, the thought unspoken. "What was it you wanted to know?"

More than you're willing to tell, I'd wager, Simon suspected. "For starters, what were you doing down at the barn this time of night? Were you meeting someone?"

She gazed up at him stupidly. "Well, of

139

course . . . only you weren't at your house."

He would have been, had he not caught sight of the intruder when he opened a window to get a breath of fresh air. And this time he would have caught the blighter, too — except Elizabeth Granger had materialized like a big-eyed wraith, effectively catching him off guard. Simon kept his face and voice blank. "I know where I was — and wasn't. Whom were you meeting, Miss Granger?"

"What do you mean? You sent me a note." She paused, the momentary guilelessness evaporating. "You didn't request an urgent meeting at your house, did you? I wondered at the time, but I came because I —" She hesitated again and turned her head, wincing.

"Because — ?" Simon leaned forward.

"Never mind. You didn't send the note." Her hand moved, fumbled along her side. "Wait — I have it here somewhere."

Simon gave her plenty of time, part of him even admiring her skillful charade. "You've lost the note," he observed blandly. "What a surprise."

Her gaze jerked back to his. "Mr. Kincaid, if you speak to the stablehand named Snaps, he can verify the note's existence, as will Willy, who delivered it to me at the house. Why would I lie about it?"

"I don't know. Why *would* you?"

She went rigid. In the light of the single table lamp, the deepening bruise rebuked Simon with the force of a slap. He'd best watch himself. A barrage of questions — from a man who was supposed to be a horse trainer — was definitely out of place. And yet . . .

"You don't believe me, do you?" Elizabeth asked, almost as if she'd read his mind.

"I'm responsible for the safety and well-being of a dozen expensive blooded trotters, not to mention a handful of pleasure and coach horses. When strangers sneak around my stable, I want to know why."

"But I'm not a stranger."

"Perhaps not. But the man who coshed us was certainly a stranger to me." He kept his expression impassive. "How about you, Elizabeth Granger? Was that man a stranger to you — or did the two of you arrange a meeting under the pretext of a non-existent note from me?" *After which, your traitorous companion bashed your head and tossed you to the wolves to avoid capture?*

Simon quashed the stirring embers of rage. Rage — and unexplained guilt. Why did he feel as if he were stalking a helpless lamb, staked out with no hope of redemption?

Her fingers picked restlessly at the afghan he'd placed around her after he'd laid her unconscious body on the davenport. "I'd never seen that man before, either. Willy and Snaps told me the note was from you." Now her voice was flat, lifeless. "You don't know me, and you have no reason to believe me, but I would never do anything to hurt the horses. They're —" She stared up at the ceiling with a fixed, unblinking stare. "I don't understand."

Finally she looked at Simon again, and he drew in his breath at her expression. "I think . . . I'm afraid that someone is trying to teach me a lesson." She closed her eyes.

A hard, authoritative knock rattled the door. Simon strode across the room — angry, and more confused than ever. He yanked open the door to confront a scowling James Crump.

"One of the grooms fetched me. What's going on here?" His gaze moved from Simon to the room beyond. "Elizabeth — Miss Granger!" His face hardened in contempt.

"Don't say anything you'll regret later," Simon inserted smoothly. "She was attacked and knocked cold outside, at the edge of the paddock. The stablehands alerted me, and I brought her here to avoid alarming Mrs. Crump." There was no point in admitting that he had been bumfuzzled at the time, suffering from a blow of his own. He stepped back. "Ask her yourself — and while you're about it, have a look at the side of her head." Crump started across the floor, but Simon moved to block his way, his intent clear. "She's been viciously abused *once* tonight. . . ."

James whipped around. "Don't you presume to lecture *me!*" He shoved Simon aside

142

and reached Elizabeth in three long strides. "Did *he* do this to you?" he ground out, his back to Simon. Then, "Kincaid! Fetch a couple of boys and a lantern. I'm taking Miss Granger back to the main house."

Simon stood without moving, hands jammed deep inside his pockets, restrained only by the role he was committed to play out. As far as Crump was concerned, Simon was a mere underling, and unless Simon wanted to risk ruining the entire operation, he would have to behave like a meek, spineless . . . *obsequious* trainer.

Without a word he turned and stepped outside, shutting the door with exaggerated softness. He didn't immediately go to the barn. Instead, he melted into the bushes flanking the house, crept around to the side window, and inched upward until he could look into the parlor.

James's back was to Simon, and partially obstructed his view of Elizabeth, but with the window still open a good three inches, he hoped to be able to hear everything that was said. Simon pressed forward, holding his breath, as James leaned over Elizabeth and began to speak in a low tone, but the words were too soft for Simon to hear.

He wasn't sure he needed to.

The pair of them looked like nothing so much as a pair of lovebirds who had finally managed to find their nest.

16

December 3, 1895

Alex MacKay watched Simon prowl the small hotel room in Thomasville like a big, restless cat. "You say the two stablehands only *assumed* the note was from you?"

"Snaps found it on the floor in my office at the stable. He can't read, so he took it to Willy. Willy's not much better, but he recognized Elizabeth's name on the outside."

"Sim, give my poor neck a reprieve and sit down, will you?" He hooked a chair leg with his foot and dragged it out. "Here. Rest your legs in a fine chair from 'the best *second*-class hotel in America.' " He smiled, stroking his moustache. "There was a sign at the front desk when I checked in. Too bad you have to sneak in the back, but —"

"I've seen the sign," Simon interrupted. "Alex — I don't like the feel of this. Have you had any luck finding out more about Elizabeth Granger?"

"I've only been here two days, lad. I may be one of the best — but even the . . . ah . . . *real* MacKay needs more than a couple of days."

He leaned back against the iron bedstead and stretched out his legs on the counterpane.

"I'm in no mood for levity, Alex."

"Shochel me tongue!" Alex sat up and swung his feet to the floor, fixing his restive friend with a commanding stare of his own. "Settle down, lad, and help me think, then. So far, the only 'proof' of Elizabeth Granger's involvement is flimsy and circumstantial."

"The bruise on the back of my head tells me otherwise," Simon shot back in the clipped, emotionless syllables that warned Alex he'd best tread a wee bit more lightly. "I still don't know if the culprit's the same one I spotted before. The only useful information I could gather from the stable staff was that he had light-colored hair and his chest was even with the top railing of the paddock fence."

Simon dropped down onto the scarred captain's chair and moodily contemplated Alex. "I don't know if he was out to sabotage the horses, or whether he was meeting Elizabeth, James — both of them, or *neither* of them." He pounded the chair arm with his balled fist. "I do know I haven't spoken with Elizabeth in four days. She hasn't come down to the stables in all that time, which worries the entire staff. It's not like her, they swear up and down, and they're all afraid the blow to her head was worse than I let on."

"Could it have been?"

There was a pause. "I checked her over after I brought her to my quarters. Her breathing was regular, no skin broken, and though light seemed to hurt her eyes, both pupils responded equally. Once she was fully conscious, she was lucid in spite of the pain." He took a deep breath, the expression in his green eyes as stormy as Alex had ever seen. "Except 'lucid' doesn't begin to describe Elizabeth Granger. She's more complex than a Chinese puzzle, and —"

"And what?" Alex prodded Simon, who sat staring off into space.

"She's still . . . afraid of me, and I don't know why. But there's nothing I can do about that right now, no matter how much I —" He broke off again, then finished, his tone short, "She made a statement that I discounted at the time, but now . . . I'm beginning to wonder. Something about someone teaching her a lesson. . . ." He ran a hand through his hair, worrying it until the thick layers reminded Alex of a shaggy wolfhound. "Then Crump burst in, throwing his weight around." Simon glanced at Alex. "I wanted to wring his neck."

"I wonder if he knows how close he came to meeting his Maker." Simon sent him another black look, and Alex shrugged. Simon wouldn't unleash his deadly brand of violence on a friend. But Alex also knew when to change the subject. "Want to hear about

Horatio Crump's meeting with Avery Paxton?"

Simon nodded.

"It didn't go well. We've had an operative shadow Paxton since Eve's tip about his purchase of a mill in Dalton. She's minded her own business since," he put in hastily. At Simon's nod, Alex continued, relieved, "The operative told Superintendent Jenkins that Horatio sailed into the building with his usual aplomb, smiling at everyone. But three hours later, he slunk out like a whipped dog."

"Paxton's going after the Crump System," Simon concluded.

" 'Fraid so," Alex agreed and reached for his chamois pouch on the table by his bed, dumping out the puzzle pieces. "And that means we're trying to corner a whole pride of lions, instead of only one apiece." He fitted one piece of fragrant cedar into another. "You with the Crumps, me with Avery Paxton." He cocked his head to one side, soberly contemplating his friend. "Watch your back, lad."

Simon looked grim. "I always do."

◆ ◆ ◆

Atlanta

Avery Paxton drummed his fingers on the leather-topped desk. "I want you to find out what happened to Rufus Black," he snapped, glaring at Wo Fang.

147

Standing with folded arms in front of Avery, the imperturbable bodyguard shook his head. "In Thomasville, I would too clearly stand out. Everyone would know — and you would lose an important advantage."

"I don't care if the Crumps *do* know I'm around." Avery picked up a letter opener and hurled it across the room. "That horse-faced clod should have reported back here three days ago. How *dare* he defy me?"

Fang calmly walked across the room, picked up the letter opener, and rang for Amos, Avery's butler. "You think this man will betray you, as Mr. Leoni did?"

Avery glared at Wo Fang, his rage so great that for a moment he almost ordered his bodyguard to leave. No one had mentioned Shiv's name in the year since he'd defied Avery to go after the Sheridan girl on his own. Everyone from the lowest scullery maid to his top associates knew that any reference — however oblique — to Joe Leoni would result in instant dismissal — or worse. Everyone . . . except Wo Fang.

Avery's hand dropped to a paperweight, and his fingers closed around the smooth marble. He continued glaring at Wo Fang, wordlessly daring him to move out of the way. Stolid and unblinking, the giant wrestler stared back, black gaze calm as a fishpond. After a minute Avery relaxed, and his mouth stretched into a playful grin. "What would you have done if I'd thrown it at you?" he asked, good humor restored.

"I would have permitted it to strike me. The pain would not be pleasant, but the action would relieve your frustration." He bowed. "I live only to please the man who saved my life."

"Don't start all that mawkish Oriental clap-trap again, Fang," Avery growled, though he craved the almost-worshipful attention. Abruptly he came around the desk and walked over to his bodyguard. "I want to go to Thomasville and find out what happened to Rufus Black," he repeated more quietly. "If the Crumps find out I'm in town, what difference will it make? I'll have to recruit another spy after you . . . ah . . . take care of Black, anyway." He rubbed his palms together. "Besides, we've got the Crumps just about where we want them. I predict that within another month, the South Georgia Central will be mine. *Mine,* Fang. The Crumps are going to *crumple.*"

With that, he threw back his head and began to laugh.

17

Adelaide
Thomasville

Even the mild-mannered Horatio insisted that Elizabeth stay inside the house, at least until he was satisfied with the results of the sheriff's investigation. "Since the panic of '93, times have been bad," he'd confessed to her the morning after the attack. "People are desperate. We've had run-ins with thieves and vagrants before, though they've never stooped so low as to attack a helpless woman." For some strange reason, she noticed, his manner was polite, but withdrawn.

"From what the stablehands told me, Miss Granger was far from helpless," James drawled, languishing on a floral chaise lounge in the morning room. He appeared bored, but elegant, the insolent gleam in his eye reminding Elizabeth that he had carried her in his arms, in spite of her protests.

Elizabeth had refused to stay in bed, although she was beginning to wonder if the blow to her head *had* rendered more damage than a mere bruise and a headache. Horatio wouldn't meet her gaze, and his entire manner made Elizabeth very uneasy. She returned James's patronizing survey with a cool look of indifference. Beneath her skirt and petticoats, unfortunately, her knees wobbled. She never intended to be that close to James Crump again.

"You've not had an easy time of it recently, Miss Granger," Horatio next remarked. "When you've fully recovered, we'll have to reward you in some manner. Perhaps another day off? More time to spend at the stables?" A note of constraint, bordering on hostility, underlay the normally friendly drawl.

James lazily rose. "Anything to keep you here," he finished. "We certainly don't want you to feel compelled to flee, now, do we?"

♦ ♦ ♦

Even after four days, Elizabeth still shuddered at the memory of that interview.

"Elizabeth? Dear — are you *sure* you should be up?"

Josephine's concerned voice broke into Elizabeth's reverie, and she started, blinking. "I'm sorry," she murmured. "I was woolgathering, I'm afraid. But I'm quite well, Mrs. Crump. Really, I am." Moments earlier Elizabeth had delivered the four older children to the tutor for the morning, then relinquished little Thomas into Pansy's capable hands. Though she had been up and about for three days now, everyone — except

Horatio and James — continued to treat her as if she had suffered a grievous injury.

"I shouldn't have asked you to help me clean this old desk," Josephine fretted. "The must and dust alone gives one a frightful headache. I just thought . . ." Her hands fluttered, and she sighed. "You're so *organized,* and since I'd promised to give James his father's old desk months ago, this seemed a good opportunity, with you needing to stay indoors for another day or two."

"I don't mind," Elizabeth said quietly. In fact, she'd been elated when Josephine asked. For Elizabeth, the opportunity was tinged with an ulterior motive, making her actions devious, dishonest, and dishonorable. *And desperate. Don't forget that one, Elizabeth.*

"Here," she said to Josephine, pointing to the right side of the huge kneehole desk. "Why don't you start going through the drawers on this side, and I'll start on the other. With any luck, we should be through before dinner."

Josephine at last managed a smile. "Or at least until the children search you out and drag you away."

"They'll be dragging *both* of us away," Elizabeth corrected.

They worked in companionable silence for quite some time, until Elizabeth sat back on her heels with a groan, massaging the aching muscles of her back. "Your father-in-law was

152

a pack rat, wasn't he?" she observed. "Didn't he throw *anything* away?"

"I never knew the gentleman, but apparently not." Josephine collapsed into a huge oak office chair. "From the little I've heard over the years, he was supposed to have been something of a tyrant. I suppose that's why Mother Crump is —" She broke off, covering her mouth with a plump hand.

Elizabeth smiled at the belated display of conscience, then stretched her arm to search the back of a hidden drawer she'd discovered. It was the third such cubbyhole, and she'd lost her anticipation of discovery two drawers earlier. "Don't worry," she said over her shoulder. "If it helps, even the servants I talked to agree that they wouldn't want to cross your mother-in-law."

"She never made *you* feel like a servant, did she?"

"I never gave her an opportunity to treat me in any manner at all," Elizabeth murmured. Her fingertips touched crumpled paper, and she tugged.

From the landing below, Dora called up the attic stairs, "Miz Crump! Yoo-hoo! The tutor wants a word with you, ma'am!"

Josephine heaved herself to her feet with a grunt. "Coming, Dora." She glanced down at Elizabeth. "Gracious, child! You're covered with dust. Why don't you come along, too? There's no need for you to stay up here all by yourself."

"I'll be along in a minute, just as soon as I finish this drawer."

Josephine smiled down at her, shook her head, and hurried off, skirts swishing about her feet.

With a hard yank, Elizabeth managed to free the scrap of paper from the back of the drawer, pulling it out as Josephine descended the creaking attic stairs. Carefully she smoothed the page, but the edges were blackened and crumbled into her hands. Why would anyone want to keep a half-burned note? Frowning, Elizabeth read the remaining words:

— more time? I am afraid, dear Charles, of what the future . . . please meet —

The next legible word that leaped out at Elizabeth was the name of the town. . . .

Ochlocknee, beneath the chestnut tree at Mrs. H's boardinghouse. My love for you . . . desperate, dear Charles. If only you could . . .

Again, fire had consumed the pitiful words. Elizabeth read on:

. . . don't care what they say. I am forever yours, Helene.

154

After a time Elizabeth carefully folded the note, her fingers black with soot. She picked up an old envelope from a pile of papers to be discarded, tucked the note inside, and slipped the envelope into the pocket of the apron she had borrowed from the house-keeper.

Charles — her father's first name.

Helene — the name of James's and Horatio's sister, who had died in childbirth over twenty years earlier.

Elizabeth groaned inwardly. *God help me. . . .*

18

"I trust you've learned something."

"Would I have come if I hadn't?"

"Don't be fresh. Now, tell me everything you know."

"She worked as a bookkeeper at the Jekyll Island Resort Hotel from '93 until she was hired as —"

"I'm aware of her current status. I want to know her history before she came to the hotel."

"The manager said he would send a copy of the letter of recommendation from her last employer. She was an assistant bookkeeper for Graverly Racing Stables, in New York."

"I . . . see." Long fingers stroked the glistening stem of a freshly cut floribunda. "That would explain the obsession with horses, perhaps, but not a possible connection to Paxton. You've found nothing that could connect her with him?"

"Is it absolutely necessary to establish such a connection? Since the possibility of exposure exists, we've initiated appropriate steps, especially after that mess a couple of years ago with Pinkerton's. We don't need them nosing around again. To my way of thinking, any information we might glean from the girl becomes sec-

ondary to her removal. "

"*I'll decide if — and when — she's outlived her usefulness.* " *A lengthy pause ensued.* "*Speaking of that . . . I am not pleased about the incident at the stables.* " *The voice turned wintry.* "*Whatever you're doing behind my back shall be disengaged at once, or you can rest assured Pinkerton's National Detective Agency will be only one of many worse problems on our doorstep.* "

"*It won't happen again.* "

"*Of course it won't.* " *They exchanged looks.* "*Next week, then? The usual time?* "

"*I'll telegraph, or send a message, if plans change.* "

19

December 8, 1895

At twilight, Simon was making his final notes on the day's training. He doublechecked the list of grooms assigned to the horses, then shoved back from the desk in the room designated as the trainer's office. In the past few weeks he had expended untold hours attempting to organize the place; the task, he concluded, was hopeless. And he *detested* wasting valuable time in an attempt to *help* the very man he was trying to convict of sabotage, extortion . . . and murder. Rising, he took two steps and flung open the door, then sat back down, worrying his hair with his hands.

A moment later Jefferson poked his head through the open doorway. " 'Night, Mr. Kincaid. Mosby's finally settled down, like you said he would."

"He sure is a temperamental old plug." Simon stood, relieved, stretching the kinks from his neck and shoulders. He loathed sitting in an office, pushing a pen. "How's McKinley's hoof?"

"Doin' just fine. But you going to tell Mr.

Horatio he won't be ready for the track for nigh onto two more weeks?"

"I'll tell him." Horatio might be a pleasant, non-assertive type, but he also bordered on being neurotic about the health of his horses. Simon had fought several skirmishes over some of the man's more compulsive habits, such as having the animals' shoes checked by the blacksmith every week.

"Oh — Miss 'Lizbeth's out in the large paddock, having herself a ride. It's about time, I say."

Simon lifted a brow. "I don't know that a week is enough time for her recovery. Besides, it's almost dark. Horses spook more easily at night."

"Strawberry don't spook."

"*All* horses can be startled. Even Strawberry." He walked out of the office, past Jefferson. "See you in the morning." He was aware of the groom staring after him, but he didn't look back.

He watched from the shadows, grudgingly admiring Elizabeth Granger's easy seat in the saddle, her obvious skill. There was a lot about this mysterious young woman he didn't trust, but her ability with horses was not one of them.

Simon waited until she pulled up to the mounting block, then stepped forward. "You ride very well."

159

Strawberry nickered a friendly greeting, but Elizabeth jumped as if Simon had flicked her with a buggy whip. "Mr. Kincaid!" She turned to pat the roan, keeping her face averted. "You have a habit of appearing out of nowhere, it seems."

"I've been watching you for a quarter of an hour. Strawberry knew I was around, even if you didn't."

Even in the gathering darkness, Simon saw her tense. "Should I have asked your permission to ride in the paddock? Mr. Crump agreed, and I confess that after being cooped up in the house for a week, I was so eager I didn't stop to ask you. . . ."

"I train Mr. Crump's trotters. Jefferson manages the rest of the horses for me. Does quite well at it, too. Who is allowed to ride for pleasure — and where — is not my concern. If Jefferson and Horatio Crump care so little for your neck, why should I?" He tossed off the remark lightly, then noticed the sudden slump of Elizabeth Granger's shoulders. Hadn't Alex warned him many times that he had yet to master the fine art of teasing?

"Oh, then I'll not trouble you further." Elizabeth gathered the reins and stepped down off the mounting block. On the ground, the top of her head barely reached his shoulder. "Good evening, Mr. Kincaid."

There was nothing but remote politeness in her voice, but Simon's senses were as keen

160

as any hunting animal's. He watched her lead Strawberry into the barn, disgusted with himself. *Idiot!* he berated himself, an angry accusation that echoed down through thirty years. As if it were yesterday, he could hear his father's angry voice: *You've about as much feeling as a shark . . . you always go for blood. Why can't you think of someone else for a change? If it weren't for your mother and me, you'd be back East, probably slaving in a coal mine or a sweat shop somewhere. We gave you everything, and what have you given us in return but misery and grief?*

Ten minutes later Simon followed Elizabeth into the barn, walking soundlessly down the aisle until he came to Strawberry's stall. Elizabeth was brushing the marks of the saddle away, a grooming kit in the straw next to the stall door. Without a word, Simon picked up another brush and moved to the horse's opposite flank.

"I suppose I owe you an apology," he said after a while. "I didn't mean to be rude."

"It's all right, Mr. Kincaid. I should have told you I was going to ride, but Jefferson said you were working in your office and that he'd rather face a rabid hound dog than interrupt you when the door's closed."

Simon glanced across Strawberry's back, into the pale oval of Elizabeth's solemn face. He was relieved to see that the bruise marring her left temple had faded a little. Her mouth might be curved in the semblance of a smile at his apology, but she radiated uneasiness all the same. If he wanted answers, he was going to have to do more than frighten her off with his lamentable lack of sensitivity.

"I detest paperwork," he admitted, casting about for some neutral topic.

Her entire face lit with unexpected humor, catching Simon completely off guard. "Perhaps I'd better not confess how much *I* enjoy it," she murmured, the slight smile growing.

They groomed on in silence, until Simon sensed that Elizabeth was finally relaxing. He studied her while they worked, watching the expert motions of her hands, the graceful sway of her body as she lost herself in the ritual. Simon would have staked his professional reputation as an undercover operative that though Elizabeth Granger might be involved in any number of criminal acts, she would never be party to harming the horses. Or the children.

So what was *her relationship with James?*

"I never thanked you for saving my life, and the children's . . . that day in the river."

Simon finished cleaning Strawberry's left hind hoof, then straightened before he answered. "As a matter of fact, you did. Several times, in fact."

"I don't remember."

"I'm not surprised. I'd forget the whole experience if I could." He reached for another

162

hoof. "The children seem to be all right now. I believe the oldest girl — Joan, isn't it? — might have remembered me."

Elizabeth nodded. "I explained to her that you hadn't mentioned the incident because you didn't want to bring up unpleasant memories. She understood that. Jessica and Ho-Boy — little Horatio — suffered nightmares for a week or two, but they're all right now. They all regard the episode as an exciting adventure." She seemed to hesitate, then confessed, "Joan and I decided you were our personal guardian angel, especially after you turned up here, working for Mr. Crump."

Decidedly uncomfortable, Simon frowned at her. "I'm no angel, Miss Granger."

She shrugged, waving the comb she'd been using on Strawberry's mane. "Angels take many forms, to my way of thinking, Mr. Kincaid. Sometimes even human. If the Lord wishes to use as His instrument a dark, dangerous man who more resembles a fierce pirate than a respectable horse trainer, who am I to object? The children are safe now, aren't they?"

"Through your efforts, and perhaps mine in some small measure," he conceded. "*God* had nothing to do with it, Miss Granger. He has little use for man's idiocies and wanton cruelty to his fellow man, and rightly so." He snatched the comb from her hand, and with one fluid motion, swept up the grooming kit and dropped all the tools inside. "I'll put this away while you fasten on his blanket."

Again. She was doing it again. Elizabeth Granger was getting under his skin, and Simon didn't like it one bit. Hardening his resolve, he stored the supplies, then stalked back down the aisle, intercepting Elizabeth as she was latching Strawberry's stall door. "I'd like to talk with you a few moments, Miss Granger."

"What have I done now?" Her voice was guarded.

Feeling as surly as a caged cat, Simon gestured for her to precede him. "Why must you always assume you've done something wrong?" he demanded curtly. "Are you trying to hide something? Most people who accept culpability so readily are usually suffering from a guilty conscience."

Her step faltered, and even in the fitful light of the naked bulb hanging above them, he could see her face drain of life and color. "I'm . . . not hiding anything," she whispered, but her eyes, her voice told him she was lying. "At least, not that I can help."

A whippoorwill called its haunting refrain, the notes mingling in the frosty evening air with the faint sound of a harmonica, coming from the direction of the servants' quarters. Simon halted outside the barn, but didn't speak. In the past he'd found that a threatening silence often achieved swifter results than physical intimidation.

On the other hand, he'd never tried this method on a slip of a girl who possessed a baffling predilection for mentally retreating behind a wall, impenetrable even by an operative nicknamed "Smoke." She was doing it right now, Simon realized. Standing there with the aloof remoteness of a stone statue. "You *are* hiding something." He paused, then added almost casually, "I've been wondering what kind of hold James Crump has over you." *It probably isn't carnal. Family is far too important for him to seduce the companion of his brother's children . . . yet.* He pinned her in a searching, pitiless gaze. "But he does have some kind of hold over you, doesn't he, Miss Granger? He desires your . . . company?"

The pose wavered, her lips forming the word *yes*. But it took her two tries. Once again Simon was caught off guard, this time by her obvious revulsion. Whatever familiarity existed between Elizabeth and James had doubtless been fostered solely by James.

After all these years, Simon should know that appearances did not always reflect personal feelings. *You're slipping, Kincaid.* He had to admit that right now, his attitude toward Elizabeth Granger was due in large part to the grating visual image of her docile body in James's arms the night he had carried her from Simon's quarters. "Have you told any-

165

one?" he asked, slowly.

She shook her head. "Whom would I tell? James would deny it, and of course his word would be believed over mine." Her tone betrayed no bitterness, only resignation. "It would upset Mrs. Crump as well as the children, and I'd have to leave that much sooner."

Simon pounced on that revealing statement. "You're leaving, then?"

"I . . . probably so. Yes." She turned and fixed her gaze on something in the distance, as if she were looking into the maw of hell itself. "When the time comes . . . they'll not want me anywhere near them . . . or the children."

At last her eyes met Simon's. "Lately, I've sensed a . . . distance, especially from Horatio, almost *disapproval,* and I suspect James is the reason. Horatio wouldn't question anything his brother tells him. I wish I could . . ." Her voice dropped, and Simon watched her finger a necklace fastened about her throat. "James Crump will continue to discredit me as long as I spurn his advances, and he's free to spread with impunity whatever lies he fancies."

She looked over Simon's shoulder, her expression full of pain, of yearning — of that baffling *acceptance.* "It's ironic, and probably what I deserve" — her gaze swung back to Simon — "but I promise you, Mr. Kincaid, that

166

I have *never* done anything to encourage him."

Simon wanted to believe her. Badly. And that desire, coupled with the poignant memory of her heroic efforts after the train wreck, undermined the harsh discipline of a lifetime. "If you need help . . . at any time . . . send for me." His hand lifted — of its own accord, it seemed — and his fingertips brushed against the fading bruise. "Next time, Miss Granger . . . wait for me instead of going into battle on your own."

She blinked as if surfacing from a laudanum-induced sleep. "Mr. Kincaid, I'm used to being on my own. I can take care of myself." She bit her lip. "But thank you for the offer."

"It wasn't an offer," Simon returned, adamant. "It was more in the way of an order. And while we're at it — don't wander about the grounds by yourself after sunset. It's not safe."

"*Living* isn't safe, Mr. Kincaid. I had learned that lesson by the time I was five." She began twisting the fingers of her glove. Then she stared straight into his face. "You don't act at all like a horse trainer."

And after that unsettling pronouncement, Elizabeth Granger glided down the path, disappearing around the end of the barn. The sound of her steps faded into the night, and with a muttered imprecation directed at himself, Simon sprinted after her. Only *his* foot-steps made no sound, and he drifted through the heavily wooded grounds behind the house like a trail of smoke.

PART TWO

Lies

December 1895

20

Atlanta
December 15, 1895

Eve Sheridan MacKay darted from the ladies'
entrance of the Young Men's Library Association on Marietta Street to the buggy parked at
the curb. The December wind was raw, and
she'd spied a drifting snowflake or two earlier
on her way to the livery to fetch the horse and
buggy. Shivering, she leaped into the phaeton,
then turned to glance outside.

She scanned the street, then the sidewalk
on the other side. The man was still there, his
bulky figure propped against a lamppost. He
looked as if he'd been huddled there for quite
some time — at least two hours, she calcu-
lated, ever since she'd hitched the horse outside the library. He turned his head away just
as she rolled down the curtain and covered
the side window.

Eve shuddered with a sickening chill that
had nothing to do with the inclement
weather. That man had been *watching* her;
she was sure of it, having lived through the
nightmare of being stalked the previous year

by one of Avery Paxton's hired thugs. Lifting her chin in fierce determination, she picked up the reins and headed off down the street. At the corner she had to wait for a passing trolley, and took that opportunity to lean forward to peek around the curtain, back down the block.

The man leaning against the lamppost had disappeared.

♦ ♦ ♦

". . . and I couldn't determine his hair color because he was wearing a dark stocking cap pulled down over his ears, along with the muffler. Is he an operative?" Eve finished, watching Mr. Jenkins's impassive face.

The Atlanta superintendent contemplated his chest, and Eve listened to the quiet ticking of his desk clock for a full minute before he finally responded. "No, Mrs. MacKay. That does not describe any of my operatives." He looked up, scratching a heavy eyebrow with one finger. "You're convinced he wasn't merely enjoying a smoke or a spot of fresh air while he waited for someone?"

"He wasn't smoking, and it was too cold to be enjoying the fresh air. All the other pedestrians were rushing down the walk as fast as they could to get *indoors*." Eve's heart thudded uncomfortably. "Mr. Jenkins, Avery Paxton couldn't have discovered me again, could he? And before you try to fob off an evasive answer on me, I'll tell you that I already know he's moved himself and his filthy band of associates down here to Atlanta."

"And how would you know that?"

"I have my sources," Eve informed him sweetly, brown eyes flashing. "And it was *not* my husband!"

"Mrs. MacKay, if Avery Paxton has found you, from what Operative MacKay tells *me,* I'll put a man on the case right away." He peered over the top of his spectacles. "Have you done anything, gone anywhere that would reveal your identity to Mr. Paxton?"

Eve studied a jagged hole she had ripped in one of her gloves. "Well . . . not since I overheard that remark I told Mr. MacKay about. And I . . . might have asked a question or two at another meeting — though I wouldn't think either Mr. Paxton or his associates would be involved with members of the Atlanta Ornithology Society."

She pulled on a loose thread dangling from the hole in her glove. It lengthened by several inches. "That's been over a month now, and I haven't even mentioned his name since. I've been busy working on another book, and the only outing I recall where I would possibly have been 'exposed' was last week, when I visited the Cyclorama in Grant Park. I'd been feeding the pigeons, and — oh."

"Yes?"

"A man came up to ask if I had the time. He — he remarked on the color of my hair, but he was so polite, I wasn't offended."

The superintendent thoughtfully perused Eve's red hair, now mussed from the wind, unruly tendrils slipping beneath her hat. "Harumph. Your hair *is* remarkable, though no gentleman would offer an opinion to a strange lady. I take it you were . . . alone?"

Eve gave a little sigh. She had been married to a Pinkerton operative for six months now and had learned something about reading their expressions. *I think I'm in trouble again, Lord.* "Yes, I was alone. I thought I was safe now. The park was full of sightseers — and I was not the only unaccompanied lady."

"I'm aware of the changing times, Mrs. MacKay." He cleared his throat. "Ah . . . but you *will* accept an escort home?"

"Yes. Thank you." She stood. "Would Mr. MacKay be endangered if I wrote to him?"

"I'll see that your husband is contacted, Mrs. MacKay." There was a pause. "He'll be more disturbed if he feels he can't trust you to take proper precautions — at least until I have a chance to talk with the police commissioner." Jenkins allowed a little smile. "I'm telling you more than is prudent for any other civilian, and you know it. So return the favor, Mrs. MacKay, and restrict your independent ways for the time being."

Disgruntled, Eve jabbed the pins holding her hat in place securely, then held out her hand. "I suppose," she conceded, "that I've

174

gathered enough research to do most of my work at home. For a few days, at any rate."

The superintendent did not hide his relief. He took Eve's hand briefly, then released it. "By the way, Mrs. Jenkins purchased a copy of your *Birds of the New Testament*. She found your commentary extremely insightful and would enjoy discussing the book with you. Perhaps — ?"

Eve felt the color storming all the way up to her hairline. "Th-thank you," she managed to stammer. She would *never* become used to the broadening interest in her work, although she knew that when her third book was published in the fall, Alexander would doubtless behave with even greater indignity. With the publication of *Birds Of The New Testament*, he had visited every book shop in the city of Richmond, where they'd married, and had "persuaded" the booksellers to purchase and prominently display copies in their stores.

She shivered again, this time from an aching loneliness. Then she smiled a good-bye, promised she would wait for a free operative to ride home with her, and tried not to think about how much she missed her husband. Or about her ever-increasing fear for his safety.

♦ ♦ ♦

Thomasville

It was a wet, chill night, though far milder than any December eve in Scotland, or even

175

the wooded hills of the Virginia Piedmont where Alex had grown up. Alert to his surroundings as he sauntered down Jackson Street, he chewed over the information he needed to pass along to Simon at the bowling alley where they were to meet, several blocks from the Stuart Hotel.

When he arrived, the bowling alley was crowded, full of smokers. The constant noise of the rolling ball, the clatter of falling pins, the resultant shouts or groans, gave Alex an instant headache. He was half-heartedly watching the pin boys scramble behind the barrier to dodge a wildly thrown ball when Simon's voice spoke next to his ear. Without a word, Alex rose and followed him outside.

"Both Horatio and James Crump visit their mother out at the family plantation every week," Alex began, his voice barely above a murmur. They were deep in the shadows, but neither man could risk exposure. "The security out there is obsessive, even for an eccentric recluse." He shook his head. "Georgina Crump actually paid to have both private telegraph *and* telephone lines installed. She also employs an entire regiment of couriers."

"Interesting. You think the brothers might be orchestrating things from there, using Rose Hill as a screen?"

"It's possible." Alex contemplated the ground for a protracted moment, then raised his head. "Do you have any idea how difficult it's going to be to secure a conviction, no matter how incontrovertible the evidence? The Crumps pull a lot of weight down here, Sim."

"Which they don't mind throwing around."

"Even Horatio?" Alex countered mildly. "From what I've learned from my queries thus far, Horatio's a veritable saint of a man. Donates large sums to a local church and several other philanthropic organizations. Is active in the formation of some new country club a couple of miles from Adelaide, and don't forget he's an alderman. So far, lad, I've yet to uncover even a hint of scandal. Even the man Jenkins sent to investigate the crash in Albany warned that public sentiment falls almost without exception on the side of the Crumps."

Simon folded his arms across his chest. "Maybe you haven't talked to the right people. But then, *they* keep disappearing — or dying."

Alex grimaced, listening with mounting concern as his friend's deep baritone rumbled on.

"Two years ago the Crumps bought a lumber company for a song, after producing 'evidence' that the owner was embezzling funds from his own company. The owner was indicted, but disappeared before he was to have begun serving time. Summer a year ago, the

Crumps purchased a bankrupt railroad whose chairman swore to me that he'd been blackmailed — by the Crumps."

Alex straightened. "Did you — ?"

"The chairman committed suicide a week after I talked with him. I was to have met with him the next day, to get his written deposition. It would appear that his fear . . . of the Crumps! . . . was too much for him. Then there's Horatio's old stable manager William Soames — the one I asked you to dig up more info on? What I never told you is that the Atlanta office had given me his name as a possible stool pigeon, based on information they'd received from another operative. What *they* didn't know was that he'd been murdered."

"Fall of '92, your note said. I still haven't had an opportunity to dig, but I will now. You also said the murderer was never caught?"

"No. According to Jefferson, there were no clues, no motive, and little interest. The man was not popular." Simon uncrossed his arms, glancing across at Alex. "Still think the Crumps are candidates for sainthood?"

Alex lifted his hands in a mock gesture of surrender. "I concede. I'll do all I can. Um . . . Sim? I found out a bit about Elizabeth Granger." Even in the near total darkness, he could feel the tension coiling about the big man. "The Crumps happened onto her *apparently* quite by accident, when they were vacationing over at the Jekyll Island Resort Hotel where she was employed as a book-keeper. I gather Elizabeth was on the beach when one of the Crump children drifted out to sea in a small raft. I don't know the details, but the parents were so impressed with her resourceful rescue that they hired her as companion on the spot, no matter that the children already had a full-time mammy and a tutor."

"So . . . what else? What are you having trouble telling me, Alex?"

Alex felt in his pocket for the puzzle pieces. "I persuaded a clerk at the hotel to send me a list of the guests for the time period Elizabeth Granger was supposed to have been working there. It arrived on the 4:40. One of Paxton's associates — a slimy politician named Cletus Street — spent a month at the hotel six weeks after Miss Granger arrived. And — before she came to Georgia, word is she'd been living somewhere in New York City."

He studied Simon for a moment, concluding it was safe to go on. "According to one source, she also knows how to operate a telegraph key. That would provide her the means of instant communication anywhere in the country . . . including Rose Hill . . . should she be so inclined." Seeing Simon's mutinous expression, Alex rushed ahead. "Local gossip has her pegged as a genteel lady from a good family, whose fortune was lost in the

War. On the other hand, she could just be a fine actress. Either way, the lass is getting to you, isn't she? Sim, I wonder if —"

"Nothing will interfere with this investigation. And Elizabeth Granger means nothing to me beyond her connection with the Crumps."

Simon's tone was flat, hard, utterly devoid of expression, and even though the two men were friends, Alex instinctively backed up a step. *What have we here, now, Lord?* What lesson was being carefully orchestrated in behalf of his stubborn fellow operative? Alex prayed that it wouldn't be as painful a lesson as the one *he'd* had to learn. "Aye . . . well, it's your call, laddie. I'm only here to back you up."

"You're more than a backup, and you know it, Alex." Now Simon sounded impatient. "Don't feed me that Scottish brogue. And don't go weaving fanciful notions about a young woman who stumbled onto an easy ride with a rich family and now is in over her head." He dropped his hand to clap Alex on the shoulder. "Sorry, pal. It's just that . . . after I rescued her last summer, I suppose I wanted so badly for her to be what she appeared to be that day."

"There was a time when all the evidence painted Eve as one of Paxton's limmers, remember? Don't worry, my friend. You'll do what's right."

Simon's answering look was bleak. "What

if I don't agree with what is right?"

◆ ◆ ◆

Metcalfe, Georgia
December 16, 1895

For several days Rufus stacked and sorted lumber with only half a mind on his work. On the afternoon of the sixth day, he overheard the news that Horatio and his missus would be attending a Christmas ball at the Piney Woods Hotel that very evening.

It was the best chance he was likely to get, Rufus decided. "See you in the morning, Mr. Skinner," he tossed out, not being so stupid as to say anything to alert his employer. Of course, if he was smart, ol' Skinner would keep his trap shut, because if he didn't . . . well, Rufus knew what he'd have to do about *that.*

At a little past midnight, he crept up to a pair of French doors at the back of the house. He wore his heavy work gloves, and after watching for nigh onto thirty minutes, concealed by some shrubbery, he slipped across the veranda, then broke one of the panes. The tinkling of the shattering glass made only a faint sound. But what difference did it make? 'Tweren't nobody home, and all the servants would be sound asleep.

Rufus didn't risk turning on any lamps, and the cold white light of a crescent moon shone brightly enough to guide him across a carpet as thick as a bed of moss. He spared a couple of minutes to poke about, excited at the assortment of geegaws he spied. Those would most likely fetch enough to take him out of the state of Georgia altogether.

Maybe he'd head West, where a lot of displaced Southerners had found a new home and no interfering Yankees to stick their greedy noses in everybody's business. Rufus chuckled quietly to himself, his mouth watering with anticipation. As soon as he took care of the woman, he'd —

"Take one more step, and I'll blow a hole in the back of your head."

A flare of light exploded in the darkened room. "Now turn around, slowly. Hey — wait a minute! I *know* you. . . ."

21

James strode across the room, his gaze moving over the defiant man whose baleful eyes followed the motion of the revolver in his hand. "Thought you'd break in while everyone is out but the hired help and the brats, did you? Too bad for you I didn't feel like attending another Christmas party."

He stopped several feet away. "I *do* know you," he repeated, though he was muzzy from brandy. "You work for us at" — he thought hard, struggling to put a name, a place to the pock-marked face, fringed with lank, stringy hair — "the sawmill in Metcalfe! You're one of Hank Skinner's foremen. Well, well, biting the hand that feeds us, are we?"

"You gonna flap your gums all night, mister, or you gonna use that pistol?"

James stepped forward with a smirk. "Perhaps some of both," he murmured and calmly cocked the trigger. "Now what are you doing here? Is robbery your game?"

The intruder shook his head, then blurted, "Yeah! Robbery . . ."

"You're a lousy liar, but about what I'd expect from poor white trash. Ah-ah . . . I wouldn't suggest you show your cracker temper to me," he warned as the man advanced a step, head lowered like a bull. "My finger's liable to slip — and it would be a shame to bury you in the compost pile without even knowing your name." He slapped the man's cheeks, hard enough to sting. "Talk! Or I'll have you strung from the nearest tree here and now."

"Name's Rufus Black," he mumbled in a sullen voice, glaring at James. "An' I might have some other information" — he blinked rapidly, looking as crafty and vicious as a trapped weasel — "information 'bout Avery Paxton."

James straightened, his brandy-induced boredom vanishing. "What do you know about Paxton?"

Rufus Black clamped his jaw, staring straight ahead.

James considered his options, then with a shrug lowered the gun and dropped into a plush lounge chair. "Talk," he repeated, "and it better be worth listening to, because my trigger finger's still pretty itchy. Besides, I don't care for no-account trash cluttering up the parlor of my brother's home."

"Paxton paid me," Rufus muttered, still defiant, "to take care of the companion."

" 'The companion?' Elizabeth Granger, you mean?"

"I reckon. She the female who looks after

them five younguns?"

Slowly James nodded, his mind whirling. "And why were you paid to . . . ah . . . 'take care of' Miss Granger? Does Paxton know her?"

"That ain't none o' my business. All I know is he wants her out of the way." The narrow eyes darted about the room. "I was going to do the job, but I swear it weren't nothin' to do with you, Mr. Crump."

The cur was still lying, but James didn't particularly care. He pondered for a while, then his smile erupted into a laugh. He waved the revolver at the dumbstruck Rufus Black. "I think it might have something to do with *me*," he announced. "In fact, I can predict that you and I are going to reach an agreement of sorts concerning Miss Granger, not to mention your own future." Keeping the gun trained on the other man, he stood, then walked across the room and switched off the lamp. "Let's go. There's someone we need to see, before we . . . agree on terms, shall we say?"

◆ ◆ ◆

Elizabeth tossed and turned — for hours, it seemed — before she gave up and turned on the floor lamp by her bed. The house was silent — a pervasive, ominous silence that scored her senses like a patch of briars. It was nothing but a reflection of her own feelings of guilt, she knew, magnified by the anticipation of certain grief, but the knowledge offered little comfort.

She drew up her knees beneath the quilt and hugged them, her gaze traveling about the comfortable bedroom. "Will I ever have a home of my own, Lord?" she whispered, just to ease the pressure of silence. "Will You ever send someone I can care for, who will care for *me*?"

Blindly she felt for the little lamb, which had fallen to the floor in her restless tossing. She retrieved it, shoved the covers back, then padded across the chilly floor and picked up a half-finished sampler. She had never particularly enjoyed needlework, but had persevered until she could now execute exquisite stitches, thanks to Aunt Marie. Elizabeth had lived with the maiden aunt for two years, and the martinet of a woman had refused to feed Elizabeth supper if her work was less than perfect. Thankfully, Grandpapa's lawyer had found her three months past her eighth birthday, and for the next five blissful years, Elizabeth had learned what it meant to be loved — by her grandfather . . . and by God. But then . . .

"You don't always make it easy for Your sheep, do You?" she murmured, settling into the chair and spreading a shawl over her knees. "Of course, that was never one of Your promises." She tucked the stuffed lamb at her side, and for several quiet moments her fingers deftly plied the needle. "Sometimes, I wonder if even *You* tire of these rambling thoughts of mine." Smiling a little, Elizabeth was about to continue her droll soliloquy when she heard a noise.

Alerted by the distant sound, she paused, listening. Cold prickles raced down her spine, and her heart began to race. Had that been voices outside . . . or tree branches scraping the house? Or someone . . . ?

From the hallway outside her room came the plaintive sound of a meow, followed by a marmalade-colored paw batting beneath the door. "Sam . . ." Elizabeth exhaled in relief, retrieved the family cat, and brought him back with her to the chair. "What's the matter? Did you get shooed out of Lamar and Ho-Boy's room?"

Purring contentedly, the plump tom kneaded her shoulder, then settled in her lap and curled up into a warm, furry ball. Silence settled once again, except for the rumbling comfort of the purring cat.

With a wry headshake over her lurid imaginings, Elizabeth went back to work on the sampler. "I thought you might be someone breaking into the house, Sam, or, well . . . if you must know, I was afraid it might be James." Elizabeth sighed, dropping the sampler to run her fingers through Sam's soft fur. "You don't like James, either, so don't just lie here like you haven't a care in the world. I've seen you skedaddle behind the draperies when he enters a room."

The rumbling purr intensified and, finally relaxing, Elizabeth picked up the sampler once again, studying the neat stitches. It was to be a pair of cuddly lambs, of course, frolicking on either side of one of Elizabeth's favorite Bible verses. Oh, for the innocence of frolicking lambs! Or even a pet cat. . . .

Tomorrow, Elizabeth pondered while she worked. Tomorrow was her day off, and she couldn't delay the matter any longer. She *had* to go to Ochlocknee, to try to find the boardinghouse of a Mrs. H— the one where perhaps an old chestnut tree still grew. If successful, within days she would at last be able to reveal her real name.

Elizabeth worked on the sampler well into the night, knowing she had little time left. Even Josephine had withdrawn now, though she was too kind-hearted to openly confront Elizabeth. Instead, she found it "convenient" to keep the children with her, instead of send them off with their companion. How ironic, Elizabeth mused, that it turn out to be *false* rumors of her character that would end her employment, rather than the revelation of her true surname.

At a little past two, she told Sam good night. "Enjoy your nocturnal ramblings," she whispered, opening the bedroom door and shooing out the cat. "But remember, do *not*

bring me any more dead mouse offerings."
At least the cat didn't care who her father
was.

Weaving from fatigue, Elizabeth picked up
her unfinished sampler and looked again at
her last few stitches, adjusting the tension on
one stitch before she climbed into bed. She
had completed four samplers. This one
would make the fifth. Years from now, would
the children look at them and remember —
or would they be cast aside, along with memories
of a childhood companion named Elizabeth?

◆ ◆ ◆

The next morning Snaps drove her to the
station. "You sure look peaked, Miss
'Lizbeth," he commented. " 'Specially on
such a fine day. Yo' head ain't still bothering
you, is it?"

Touched by his concern, Elizabeth smiled.
"I'm fine, Snaps. I . . . just have a lot on my
mind today."

"You sure you don't want me to pick you
up this evening? Mister Kincaid ain't going to
like the notion o' you finding your own way to
home."

"Mr. Kincaid doesn't have anything to say
about it," Elizabeth retorted. Her hands
gripped the boxed lunch Josephine had insisted
she carry. "I'll rent a buggy from Mr.
Ainsworth."

"Waste o' good money, if you asks me,"

189

Snaps grumbled beneath his breath, but he didn't argue.

Forty minutes later Elizabeth was seated by the window in a crowded day coach. The train started with a jerk and pulled away from the platform. Idly she watched the milling people at the station, eyeing — a little wistfully — the stream of wealthy northern families and visitors, with their lively, expectant faces and their luggage piled high with gaily wrapped Christmas gifts.

One man stood off to the side of the crowd, all alone, which was the only reason her gaze remained on him since there was nothing else remarkable about him. He wore a flat cap instead of a bowler or homburg and was stroking a thick, brown moustache while he scanned the passenger cars. His gaze and Elizabeth's crossed, and she saw that his eyes were blue.

The station disappeared from view, and Elizabeth settled back in the seat with a sigh. By evening — a mere handful of hours from now — her life as Elizabeth Granger might almost be over. An uneasy premonition stirred, deep inside.

For some reason, Simon Kincaid's image sprang to mind. Elizabeth shivered again. Now *there* was a man who would not take kindly to deception. Several times over the past week, she had been tempted to confide her dreadful secret, but something had always stopped the confession — doubtless, the subconscious fear of his reaction. She had known both the gentleness of his touch and the ruthlessness of his mind . . . and she didn't know which unnerved her more.

The entire journey to Ochlocknee, Elizabeth pondered a host of bewildering emotions, foremost among them the pain of never seeing Simon Kincaid again.

◆ ◆ ◆

Albany, Georgia

It was a crisp sunny morning, lacking the sharp bite of the bitter Chicago winters he had known. Wo Fang did not deviate from his steady path down the street, even though the cruel stares and finger-pointing never failed to sting. He knew his uncommon appearance would always set him apart from others. He accepted the prejudice here in the South the way he had accepted the same prejudice he had found in California and in Chicago, where Avery Paxton had saved his life. Like animals, he knew, humans tended to stick with their own kind; anyone different was perceived as a threat. Even in the various Chinatowns scattered across the country, Wo Fang had been ostracized. He wasn't Chinese, and though lumped together with that community by all round-eyes, he had never been a part of it.

Here, in this small Southern town, Wo

Fang knew he was about as different as an exotic peacock in the midst of a flock of ravens. He watched several negro women clap their hands over their mouths, then scuttle inside a dry goods store to avoid any contact with the pig-tailed giant in his blue kimono. A young boy riding a bicycle wavered, then collided with a man crossing the street. Wo Fang's expression never altered, nor did the measured beat of his footsteps. He walked with the same rolling cadence he'd learned as a boy, studying under an ancient but wise master, high in the mountains of northern Japan.

Today Wo Fang's destination was a certain pharmacy on the corner a block farther down. When he arrived, the belligerant clerk tried to refuse him entrance. Wo Fang folded his arms across his chest and subjected the watery-eyed man to a single unswerving stare. The man bolted into the store and out of sight through a door at the back.

Several customers shifted uncomfortably, whispering as Wo Fang walked up to the man sitting at the soda fountain. He was slurping a lemonade, but looked up as Fang approached. His eyes widened, and he scrambled to his feet, plunging his hand inside his loose-fitting coat.

Fang's hand shot out. "No." He twisted the arm of the man named Collins, whom he had been sent to apprehend, then hauled him to his feet. "You will come with me. Quietly."

The authoritative tone was unmistakable.

The coward's face suffused with color, then paled, while his gaze darted about like a rodent searching for an escape hole. None of the other customers, however, stepped forward to issue a challenge. Shoulders slumped, Collins allowed Wo Fang to usher him out the door.

In their wake, a disbelieving silence froze all movement in the store. Wo Fang barely noticed. He had an unpleasant task to accomplish for the man to whom he owed his life. To whom he had promised unflagging loyalty — regardless of his personal distaste for a particular task.

"W-where we goin'?" Collins asked, stumbling as he was propelled down the street.

"*Where* you are going is of no significance," Fang murmured. "What happens to you after you arrive there will be between you and your Christian God."

22

Thomasville

Alex leaped aboard the last car as it rolled past, waving his ticket at the irate conductor. He submitted to the stern lecture about disregarding station rules and personal safety, meekly apologized, then proceeded down the aisles of three day coaches, a diner, a parlor car, and a through sleeper until he reached the coach where Elizabeth Granger was seated.

It had been a near disastrous mistake, that — letting their gazes meet as if he were a raw recruit. Simon would be right to flay him to the bone. Alex shook his head and sat down some twelve rows behind Elizabeth.

The young woman was something of an enigma. Reports on her indicated that she was resourceful, self-sufficient, independent. Highly regarded by everyone who had dealings with her. Close up, she appeared as dainty and fragile as a newborn fawn, smaller even than his Eve, with great tragic eyes.

Those eyes. They filled her face, darker blue than his, full of — what? Alex turned over in his mind the memory of Elizabeth's expression, struggling for an accurate description — one that could be included, say, in the Pinkerton Rogues' Gallery file cards. Was it pain? Peace? Resolution? Acceptance? *Ach!* He made her sound like a fanciful cross between saint and martyr. No wonder Sim was in a lather!

Alex dug into his pocket for the puzzle and spent several moments mulling over everything Simon had told him about the Crump children's companion who — according to all the friendly townsfolk in Thomasville — could all but walk on water.

Simon claimed James Crump wielded some kind of control over her — but he had yet to learn the nature of it. As for Elizabeth herself, she was — depending on Sim's mood whenever he met with Alex — wary as a wounded badger, a gifted actress but a terrible liar, and the most confusing woman Simon had ever met. She was also almost as apprehensive of Simon as she was of James. "And no, I've not bullied her nor threatened her, Alex, so get that look off your face," he'd growled earlier that morning, in the predawn hours when they'd met on the edge of town.

" 'Tis the fierce look on your face that worries me, lad," Alex had retorted, rolling his r's as his brogue thickened. "If you glare at Elizabeth Granger like that, small wonder the lass is afraid of you."

"She's taking the first train to Ochlocknee,

in about three hours. I want you to follow her, Alex. I can't leave, obviously, and we need to know if she's meeting someone there."

Now, as the train lurched and groaned at a snail's pace down the track, Alex slouched in the miserable seat and half-closed his eyes, studying the back of Elizabeth Granger's head, much the way he had eyed a certain red-haired lass one night on a train to Richmond. Paxton had led Pinkerton's on a merry chase these past several years, but as far as Alex was concerned, using his Eve as bait had sealed the man's fate — no matter *how* many years it took to put him away for good.

Ahead of him, Elizabeth stared out the window without moving, giving Alex an unimpeded view of her pensive profile. Her short little nose, unsmiling mouth, and milk-white cheek might strike him as poignant — but he valued Simon far too highly to discount the girl as an innocent dupe when she very well could be a conniving little actress in league with the powers of darkness. Still, he better understood now why his friend was so ambivalent about the girl. That wasn't a surprise to Alex, either. He'd known Simon Kincaid for years, had known that for some reason the big lug was unable to credit mankind with any nobility, nor the Lord with any motive other than merciless justice.

Perhaps we can prove him wrong, eh? Will

196

You help me, Lord?

The train clattered across the Ochlocknee River, and in his spirit, Alex heard a serene response. *Don't I always?*

◆ ◆ ◆

At a little past eight that evening, Alex walked into the hotel. The friendly clerk handed him several letters, along with a hand-delivered message. "A boy left it an hour ago," he replied in answer to Alex's query.

Disquiet growing, Alex mounted the hotel stairs three at a time, his long legs eating the distance down the hall to his room. Once inside, he swiftly checked to make sure nobody had searched the room in his absence, then ripped open the envelope sealed with its special seal. Instructions from Jenkins were firm: Alex and Simon would have no direct contact with the operative assigned to investigate the Albany crash for the Crumps. But the superintendent was no fool and, in emergencies, Sam Traynor could send a coded letter sealed with a mark that was impossible to duplicate.

The message was brief — but chilling: *Shipment arrived unexpectedly here yesterday. Regret to inform you some goods damaged beyond repair. Will contact proper authorities here as well as home company, but felt compelled to bring this development to your attention.*

Translated, this told Alex that Paxton had arrived without warning in Albany — and

197

that someone had already died because of it. Probably the slack-jawed lout who put Simon on the trail to Albany in the first place.

Alex ripped open the letter with an Atlanta postmark. As expected, it was an alert from Jenkins that Paxton had left the hotel where he was staying while his mansion northeast of town was being completed, accompanied by the large Oriental who had replaced Shiv as his bodyguard. An operative had trailed them as far as the depot. Alex scanned the rest of the letter impatiently, until the final paragraph: *An unknown man has been spotted following Mrs. MacKay. . . .*

He crushed the paper in one fist, then smoothed it out to finish reading. Jenkins, as well as the Commissioner, assumed the shadow was a Paxton associate, but thus far he had not surfaced again after an initial sighting on Marietta Street. "I realize the difficulty of your position, Mr. MacKay," the letter concluded, "but urge you most strongly to trust that your wife is being protected with every means available. Mr. Kincaid, on the other hand, has no one there to turn to in dire emergency except you, which makes it imperative that you continue your pose as the land agent for a midwestern millionaire, investigating sites for a winter residence. You have far more freedom of movement than Mr. Kincaid. But you *must* maintain your alias. Do not, under any circumstances, make inquiries about Avery Paxton. I will keep you apprised daily."

For a long time Alex stood at the window, staring vacantly out over the bustling street. He saw nothing but Eve's uplifted face. Her brown eyes — unlike Elizabeth Granger's blue ones — were filled with love and trust. In his mind Alex watched them darken with disbelief and raw terror. *God . . . help me.* He *had* to return to Atlanta. He couldn't allow her to go through another year like the last one. *Dear God, that You should allow her to endure this again!*

He sensed more than felt the steadying, sustaining Presence enfolding him, calming his racing heart. With a ragged sigh Alex turned from the window to drop down onto the edge of the bed. He bowed his head, asking forgiveness, praying for courage.

He was composing his response to Jenkins, thirty minutes later, when a knock sounded at the door.

◆ ◆ ◆

Simmering with ill-concealed rage, James paced the study. "You're asking for trouble," he repeated for the third time, earning a frigid look of displeasure from his mother. "Let me handle it, Mother. I've done so in the past — and you haven't complained."

"You will not speak to me in that tone of voice, James," she said, her tapered white fingers tightening on the arms of a delicate

199

Hepplewhite rocker. "You know better. Must I remind you again that it's your *brother's* name on the letterhead? Have you discussed this with him? I thought not."

"I am not six years old, Mother." He whipped around, muttering a curse beneath his breath. He might be pushing thirty, but when she glared down her nose at him like that, she could make him feel as if he were six. And he loathed it. "Rufus Black has proven he's neither trustworthy nor loyal. Horatio would agree to that much, don't you think?" He modulated his tone in time to soften the sarcasm his mother despised. "I *still* think we can use Black to rid ourselves of Paxton once and for all."

Georgina picked up a framed photograph on the table by her chair. It was one of many likenesses of James's dead sister, Helene, and he wished he dared destroy every single one of them.

"We will see to Paxton — but we will not involve Elizabeth Granger," his mother decreed in the peremptory tone James hated almost as much as her patronizing one. "She may not be a Crump, but her devotion to my grandchildren has been unstinting. Don't forget she saved their lives, almost losing her own — which proves to me beyond a doubt that she feels more than a casual loyalty to this family." She rose, and lamplight glinted on the pearl-and-diamond-studded brooch fastened at her throat. "What we will do, my son, is to find a way to *guarantee* that loyalty."

James could think of several ways he would enjoy securing Elizabeth Granger's "loyalty," but he kept his mouth shut. "And Rufus?"

His mother's thin lips curved in the barest suggestion of a smile. "Can he write?"

"I doubt it."

"Then we'll help him. We'll dictate a letter to Sheriff Calhoun. In this letter, Rufus will enumerate everything Avery Paxton has paid him to do while in his employ. I'll have Lamar Briggs out to witness that the statement was made without coercion." She flashed a look of steel at James, who growled beneath his breath again, but held his peace. "Lamar will then notorize this document. He's been our family legal counsel for thirty years, and there is no question of *his* loyalty. As for Rufus, a week or so in jail — for his protection, of course — should be sufficient for our purposes."

She paused, then finished in a soft drawl punctuated with an unmistakable bite, "And it will teach him not to trespass at my son's home." After ringing for a servant, she sat down at her davenport desk, opened a side drawer, and picked up a fountain pen, ignoring James as though he had already taken his leave.

"Very well, Mother." James had learned when to argue with his mother — and when

201

to wait. What she didn't know would not lose him any sleep. "I'll take care of it."

"Of course you will. Be sure to tell Horatio."

"I always do."

And he would. He *always* told Horatio what both he and their mother wanted to hear. That left James free to carry out his *own* plans . . . which meant discreetly "arranging" for Rufus Black's temporary escape from the city jail.

♦ ♦ ♦

Simon waited until after Elizabeth had paid the driver of the rented hack before stepping forward. "Did you have a . . . productive trip?"

She stiffened, but answered readily enough. "Actually . . . not really. Why are you here?"

"I left orders to have one of the stableboys meet you. Which of them is going to be looking for a new position in the morning?"

Her head lifted, and beneath the brim of her felt hat, the deep blue eyes flashed a warning. "I explained last night why I didn't want to be met. And I'll point out — again — that you've no right to dictate what I do or don't do. Threatening to dismiss a stablehand is nothing but blackmail." The cool voice didn't give an inch. "In the morning I'll talk with Mr. Crump and —"

"Horatio . . . or James?" Simon inserted,

202

keeping his voice deceptively soft. If Elizabeth correctly assessed his real mood, she'd run like a scalded cat.

"James Crump has no more to say about what I do than you." Her hands moved restlessly over the handle of a small picnic basket. "I was hired by Mr. and Mrs. *Horatio* Crump. Just as you were. Now, if you'll excuse me, I'll go inside. May I suggest that *you* go train trotters, and leave me to *my* duties, Mr. Kincaid?"

Simon went very still, and something in his expression must have betrayed him. Elizabeth's head flew up, and her wide-eyed gaze reminded him of a small animal immobilized in the steel teeth of a trap. Simon lifted his hand and was not surprised when she flinched. Anger dissolved, and at that moment, he almost hated himself.

His half-formed suspicions regarding Elizabeth's involvement with the Crumps were not yet proven. If he couldn't discipline his unruly emotions around her, he'd best stay out of her way altogether, or they'd *both* suffer.

He touched the brim of his cap in a little salute without commenting on her telling movement. "I'll do that, Miss Granger. I'll do just that."

Simon swiveled on his heel and headed for the barn, with every step berating himself for his baffling lack of control around Elizabeth

Granger. The last time he had allowed emotions to rule his behavior, someone had died, and it had been Simon's fault. Would he never learn?

For two hours he prowled the pine woods surrounding Adelaide, blending with the forest and the night so completely not even a herd of deer grazing in a frost-tipped meadow noticed his passage. When he padded quietly back to the barn a little before midnight, everything was peaceful.

So why were the muscles in his throat so tight that every breath twanged a silent warning?

23

Elizabeth was reluctant to face Josephine the next morning, but there was no help for that. At a little past nine, Dora knocked on the playroom door where Elizabeth was reading to the children. "Miz Crump wants to see you in the library. She asks you to come now. I'll take the babies to Pansy."

"I'm not a baby," Ho-Boy piped up.

"Me neither," chimed in Lamar, looking mulish.

The four youngest began jumping up and down, and with a rueful smile, Elizabeth glanced at Joan, then the others. "Do you see Joan jumping about like a cricket? Do you see her bleating like a sulky lamb? Now tell me, if you please, who's *behaving* like a baby — and who isn't?"

Dora gathered the chastened children and shepherded them out of the room, teeth flashing in her smiling black face. Elizabeth followed more slowly.

For over a week now, Josephine had avoided spending time alone with her. And today was no different: Horatio stood in front of the fireplace, hands clasped behind his back. And only seconds after Elizabeth arrived, James strode into the room.

"Good morning, Miss Granger." Unfailingly polite, Horatio's deep baritone held a reserve that alerted Elizabeth even more than the knowing gleam in James's eye.

"You look pale today," he murmured. "Perhaps your outing yesterday was too taxing for you after the Tragic Incident?"

Elizabeth ignored James's remark, nodded to Horatio, and walked over to Josephine, who was sitting on one of the settees flanking the hearth. Her plump hands worried the yarn she was working into a needlepoint chair cover. "Is something wrong?"

The question, delivered in Elizabeth's soft voice, prompted a flood of color and a distressed glance from Josephine's suddenly brimming eyes. Horatio walked over and laid a hand on his wife's shoulder.

"It's Mrs. Coates," he explained. "She's near the end, we're afraid, and her granddaughter's here, needing to borrow the cart to take her children over to see their great-grandmother, perhaps for the last time. Mrs. Crump thought it would be . . . ah . . . a kindness if you drove the cart back to town with Maisie."

Mertis Coates's property formed the western border of Adelaide, but Maisie now lived in town with her husband and their four children. She was a pleasant enough young woman, but her manner toward Elizabeth had always been touched with condescension.

"I — certainly," Elizabeth replied, sensing the heavy undercurrent, almost audible in the stillness of the room. She glanced from Josephine to Horatio.

James came and stood so close to Elizabeth she could feel the heat of his body and smell the hair pomade that always made her queasy. "The cart will be around shortly. Maisie's waiting in the parlor." He examined Elizabeth as if he were the cat, maneuvering a field mouse into a blind corner.

Elizabeth inched backwards, but she found herself trapped by Josephine and the settee. The corner of James's mouth kicked up in a sardonic grin, and he turned to Josephine. "I'd offer to accompany them as well, but I've an appointment with George Jackson at the Club, and must be off immediately." He kissed Josephine's cheek, nodded to Horatio, and left the room.

"I'll be quite all right," Elizabeth promised, relaxing somewhat. "It's not unpleasant today — I'll walk home. It won't be any trouble at all."

Thirty minutes later she met a distraught Maisie out front. Elizabeth thanked the stablehand and climbed into the seat. Turning to Maisie, she summoned a comforting smile for the red-eyed mother of four, whose slight stature more resembled Elizabeth's than Josephine's more matronly curves.

"I don't know why they wanted *you* to come," Maisie fretted, moving over to make room for Elizabeth. "It's just a *pony* cart, for mercy's sake." She jiggled the reins impatiently, and with a jerk they started down the drive.

Elizabeth had been wondering the same thing while she hurriedly fetched her warm cloak for the ride. "I'm sure Mr. and Mrs. Crump thought you might appreciate some company," she murmured. "Or that you might be too distressed to drive the cart yourself."

"I'm perfectly capable of managing. That's what I told James when *he* suggested you tag along, for all the good it's done. *I'm* not a shrinking violet who collapses like wet sugar in the face of any tragedy." She darted Elizabeth a glittering look. "And I certainly don't need the hired help offering meaningless platitudes."

"That's fortunate, since you haven't been offered any," Elizabeth responded politely. "If you really prefer to be left alone, I'll get out now and walk back to the house." Torn between pity and hurt, she was nonetheless taken aback when Maisie hauled back on the reins so abruptly the placid pony snorted and tossed his head, backing in the traces.

"I *do* prefer it!" Maisie snapped. "And you can tell James I said so!" She glared straight ahead, but Elizabeth glimpsed the tears pooling in her eyes, then slipping over.

"I *am* sorry . . . about your grandmother, I mean," she said, feeling helpless as she climbed down.

Maisie lifted the whip. She swiveled her head, looking down at Elizabeth with a look of contrition. "I'm sorry, too," she choked out. She cracked the whip and the cart leaped forward.

Elizabeth watched until they rounded the first corner on the long winding drive, then turned with a sigh and trudged back toward the house.

◆ ◆ ◆

Rufus heard the sound of hoofbeats approaching and knelt down behind the thick bushes, balancing the hunting rifle James Crump had supplied against his shoulder. *About time,* he grumbled to himself. This piece of calico had been naught but trouble, but even if he still shied away from shooting her down like a flushed quail . . . it beat the tar out of city jail. Besides, Mr. James had promised to pay him a hundred dollars.

He swallowed hard, wishing he could spit. He weren't enjoying it none, though — and Crump had even warned him there might be more than one, ding-dang it. What Rufus did about that was his own business, however, since the rifle held only one bullet. Rufus couldn't afford to miss, this time. He steadied the rifle. Sure would've been easier if he'd managed to get it done when the gal was asleep in her bedroom.

Poor little pigeon. 'Twixt Paxton and James Crump, she never stood a chance.

The pony came into sight, then the huddled figure. There was only the one, but he shrugged that development aside. The driver was female, with brown hair. Small. Driving a wicker cart no one else ever drove. Just like he'd been told. He closed one eye, sighted through the crosshairs, and fired.

The sound reverberated through the woods, but since it was hunting season he knew nobody would be alarmed. Everyone herabouts was used to hearing the sound of gunfire. They'd call the companion's death a tragic accident. The pony hadn't even broken stride, but kept right on trotting down the lane, even though its driver had slumped sideways. As Rufus lowered the rifle and crept out of the shrubbery, he saw the body fall backwards into the cart.

He loped off into the deepest part of the woods, where he'd hidden his horse. James Crump was there, waiting.

"Is it done?"

"Yeah. It's done." Rufus shifted uncomfortably, eyeing the revolver in Crump's hand. "Now what?"

"Why, now you return to jail, Mr. Black — until I have use for you again." An oily smile that made Rufus start to sweat spread across his face. "And if I were you, I'd be careful about what I talked about. Not to mention *who*."

♦ ♦ ♦

Atlanta

Eve Sheridan planned her moves with the same meticulous care with which she conducted her research. Tight-lipped, guilty but unrepentant, she made arrangements to take a southbound night train to Thomasville. Her decision had occupied hours of prayer, tears, and indecision, but she could no longer deny her growing conviction: If she did not go to Alexander, he would jeopardize his job, Simon's life as well his own — and return to Atlanta to protect Eve from Avery Paxton. She *knew* it as surely as she knew her own face.

Carrying a single carpetbag, she slipped out the back door of the house to elude the friendly young patrolman on this beat. Her beacon-bright red hair was smashed beneath a powdered gray wig, and she wore a pair of Franklin spectacles she'd purchased from Woolworth's. The dowdy traveling costume had been bartered from the coal man. Several throw pillows pinned beneath the skirts provided misleading weight, but Eve decided the cane added the final ingenious touch. *Watch out, Sarah Bernhardt,* she thought triumphantly, limping down the street toward the trolley stop.

Just before she boarded the train, Eve posted a note of explanation to Mr. Jenkins. By suppertime she was stowed in a private sleeping compartment. When she disembarked shortly before noon the next day, the arthritic old lady had been replaced by a dignified gray-haired matron in old-fashioned widow's weeds. A courteous station agent secured her a hack, and thirty minutes later, she presented herself to the clerk at the desk of the Stuart Hotel.

Rather than risk exposing Alexander, she booked another room through the month of January. After putting away her belongings, she spent the better part of the afternoon pretending to write letters in the hotel's rotunda, which happily faced the street and afforded Eve a clear view without compromising her own security.

When Alexander finally walked through the door a little before three, Eve could scarcely restrain herself from throwing caution to the wind and running to him. *He looks exhausted.* Exhausted, grim, and pursued by demons. Fighting tears, Eve managed to stuff her writing materials inside her reticule in time to follow him up the stairs, only to discover that his room was one floor below hers. After he was safely inside, Eve hurried down the hall.

With no one in sight, she knocked firmly, then stood back, hands gripped convulsively around her bag. The door opened.

"Yes?" He paused, then added in a softer voice, "I'm afraid you have the wrong — madam!"

Eve darted past, ducked behind her husband, and pushed the door shut. "Alexander . . ."

For an excruciatingly long moment he gaped down at her. Then, her voice breaking over his name, Eve tore off the spectacles and wig, and threw herself into his arms.

"Eve?" He held her by her shoulders, dangling her at arm's length, his blue eyes searching, sweeping over her in dawning comprehension. *"Eve!"* he shouted and hauled her close, then kissed her breathless. "What have you done, my lass . . . darlin' . . . I should have known . . . you shouldn't be here. . . ."

Laughing and crying, tears rolling down her face, Eve allowed herself to be swept along in the rising tide of emotion. At last he lifted her in his arms and carried her over to an upholstered chair and sat down, still holding her close.

Caging her face in his hands, he tilted it toward his own. "I can't deny that I'm . . . over-

213

joyed by your presence," he murmured, his mouth smiling beneath the moustache. "But you've thrown a rare spanner in the works, my love. What am I to do with you?"

"I've come to help," Eve announced bravely, though inside she was quaking. "I wrote a letter to Mr. Jenkins, so he won't worry. I've booked a room on the third floor, and you can see what a dab hand I am at disguises —"

"I ought to . . ." Alexander leaned over to whisper in her ear.

Relief choking her, Eve lifted her hands to smooth the lines furrowing her husband's forehead. "I know you should," she whispered back. "But you won't. I love you, Alexander MacKay." Her voice caught, and she repeated it. "I love you — and I knew that if I didn't come to you, you would come to me . . . and it would tear you apart. I don't ever want to place you in that position again, having to choose between your vocation and me. One time was too many."

"Lass . . . you cannot stay here. It's too dangerous." His hands closed over hers and he lifted her fingers to his mouth. "Eve, Avery Paxton is in Albany, with his new bodyguard. One man has been killed already, probably one of the saboteurs from the Albany crash in October."

A shudder rippled through Eve, and Alex held her closer. "I'm safer here, with you, regardless of where that despicable little Napoleon may be," she pleaded. "Alexander, think! Not even Simon was able to protect me from Dante Gambrielli *or* Joe Leoni, and you've assured me Simon's the best." She hid her face in his shirtfront. "I trust God with my *heavenly* security, Alexander," she went on, "but I-I'm afraid I trust *you* more with my safekeeping here on earth. . . ."

For a long time Alexander held her in silence, one hand absently stroking her hair. Beneath her ear his heart beat in a steady, even rhythm, but when he finally spoke, resignation — and warning — shrouded the words. "That's no' the way it should be, lass, and we both know it. But God help me — I canna let you go. I won't be minding asking the *Lord's* forgiveness . . . but *Simon* will be an entirely different matter altogether."

24

Thomasville

Simon seethed with quiet fury. He'd been working the trotters at Pastime with Jefferson and a couple of helpers, when the news of the accidental shooting death of a local woman out at Adelaide reached them. Nobody had immediately come forward to admit it, the deputy sheriff had reported, but likely some trigger-happy greenhorn had paid a dreadful price for his inexperience. Needless to say the Crumps were horrified and were offering to help in every way they could.

It took all of Simon's self-control to respond as a mildly concerned horse trainer instead of an undercover Pinkerton operative. He managed to express appropriate shock, promised to cooperate with the authorities and to notify Horatio or James Crump immediately if he heard anything that would help identify the guilty party. But it wasn't until late the following afternoon before he could contrive an opportunity to pay the sheriff a visit.

An hour after his arrival, Simon left the

county courthouse. He *must* contact Alexander. *Immediately.*

During his conversation with the sheriff, Simon had skillfully extracted information about the dead Maisie Pritchard: early thirties, brownish hair, slight build. . . . "Married, too, she was . . . and with four young children." The sheriff had waxed maudlin as to the fate of the motherless babes. But Simon's blood froze when the sheriff described Maisie as "a slip of a woman who looked more of a girl than a woman full grown, with a passel of little ones."

"Tragic," Simon agreed, adding casually, "Well, I best be back to my duties. It's a shame, isn't it, that she didn't stand out in some way to alert the hunter. If she'd had red or light-colored hair, or had worn a brightly colored hat or clothing . . ."

The sheriff nodded glumly. "Yep. Might've helped. But most folk from hereabouts leave all the fancy bright-colored silks and satins to the northern visitors." He hooked his thumbs in his striped vest. "It's a shame, it is, the whole blamed mess."

A small woman with brown hair, wearing nondescript clothing, driving the children's pony cart on Crump land . . .

What if this was not an accidental death — but a botched attempt to murder Elizabeth Granger? A hired killer, needing the safety of concealment, would have been too far away to verify the correct identity of a target with no outstanding features. He would probably depend on prearranged information. And that meant more than one conspirator was involved.

But why Elizabeth? After two years in Georgia, Simon was convinced of the Crumps' guilt, even if Alex and the Atlanta office were not. He was determined, now more than ever, to scrounge sufficient evidence to unearth the truth — especially the truth regarding Elizabeth Granger.

After a four-block detour, he managed to slip in a side door of the Stuart without being recognized. He found a secluded spot in the hotel rotunda, penned a note, and as soon as the lobby emptied, he climbed the stairs. Good. No guests strolling about up here, either. No maids or bellhops loitering about the halls. At Alex's door he casually dropped the note to the floor and started to nudge it through the crack with his toe. But at that moment, he heard the sound of voices coming from inside the room.

Simon put his boot on top of the note and his ear to the door, listening. The words were not distinguishable — but one of those voices was female. A number of explanations occurred to Simon, but one in particular filled him with a sensation of impending doom. *Eve.* Unpredictable, headstrong Eve Sheridan MacKay.

Simon retrieved the note, slipped back down the hall, and was on the street seconds later.

He rode back to Adelaide at a hard canter, his mood vile. *Alex, you're a fool, man,* he raged to the absent operative. *And I'm a bigger one, for not calling your hand immediately.*

"Are all the horses back?" Simon tossed the reins to Snaps as he strode into the barn. "Where's Jefferson?"

"In the feed room, measuring out grain. Uh . . . Mister Kincaid?"

"Yes?"

"They — they's asking for you, up to the main house."

"Who's asking for me?"

"Well . . . I reckon Mr. Horatio, for one — though Jefferson done told me Mr. James was picking at his brain, too. 'Bout Miss Maisie?"

Simon grunted. "I'll go on up there. Have you been soaking Clover's hoof every hour?"

"Yessir. Looks a lot better."

"Well, keep it up until the evening feeding, then we'll try her in the small paddock. And don't forget to check Meadowlark's mouth to see if it's still too sore for the bit."

"Yessir. Uh . . . Mr. Kincaid?"

Simon whipped around. "*Now* what?"

Snaps began stuttering.

"What is it?" Simon repeated, deliberately softening his voice. "Come on, Snaps — quit acting like I'm about to come after you with a horseshoe."

Snaps relaxed and flashed a sheepish grin. "I sure wouldn't be happy if you *was* to come after me, Mr. Kincaid, horseshoe or not . . . 'specially after the way you lit into that sorry excuse for a boy last week for feeding Sir Peabody a double ration of oats!" He slapped his britches and chuckled. "Never raised your voice, even, but I bet he ain't quit runnin' yet!"

"Snaps . . ."

"Yessir, Mr. Kincaid." The crooked grin abruptly faded. "Uh . . . boss?" The stablehand shuffled his feet, looking uncomfortable. "Uh . . . I wanted to — to warn you," he mumbled after darting a quick look around.

Simon went very still. "Warn me?"

"Mr. Horatio . . . well . . . he got to questioning Miss Elizabeth, and whatever she said lit a fire under Mr. James, so I heared. Then Mr. James and Mr. Horatio got into it, and now the butler done told me they's liable to grill you, too."

The corner of Simon's mouth twitched. "Don't worry," he promised Snaps. "I can take care of myself."

"Yessir, I reckon you can."

Simon approached the house from the

back, passing silently through the kitchen and down the servants' hallway. He could hear James's angry voice all the way, attacking Elizabeth as if she were a recalcitrant lackey. The strange, irrational tugging of emotion gathered momentum: Simon couldn't spare the time to analyze, much less question, his decision. Regardless of the consequences, regardless of her innocence or guilt, he would protect Elizabeth Granger. He had saved her life, and in some indefinable way, the act had irrevocably bound them in spite of logic, circumstances, or common sense.

He heard Elizabeth's quiet reply, instantly swallowed up in another diatribe from James. Simon's eyes narrowed. Elizabeth might be in league with either or both Crumps, but she was not their equal. For a moment longer, he stood outside the entrance to the library, listening.

". . . specifically *told* you to go with her! She might still be alive if you'd been there. Now Josephine's taken to her bed again, Horatio's in town trying to placate Maisie's husband — and you stand there, the picture of misunderstood innocence! Perhaps I —" He broke off as Simon stepped noiselessly into the room. "What the — ! Get out of here until you're summoned!"

"As I understand it, I *was* summoned." Simon strolled across the room, placing himself between James and Elizabeth. He spared her a brief but comprehensive look, then turned to James and folded his arms over his chest. "According to Sheriff Calhoun, the death has been ruled accidental. You're treating Miss Granger as though you suspected her of deliberately arranging for Mrs. Pritchard's untimely demise."

"My motives are none of your business." James took a menacing step toward Simon. "Get out!" he repeated.

Simon didn't move. "I don't think so."

"Mr. Kincaid, please. It's all right. . . ." Elizabeth's voice was thin, taut.

James reared his head like a fractious stallion. His gaze swiveled from Simon to Elizabeth, and the handsome features flattened into viciousness. "I should have guessed. The two of you —"

"I don't think you want to finish that thought," Simon interrupted, his arms uncoiling, stance shifting slightly. Behind him, he heard the rustle of fabric, followed by Elizabeth's barely audible murmur. "Miss Granger, would you excuse us, please? I'd like a word with Mr. Crump."

"Stay here!" James rapped out. "*I'll* tell you when you're dismissed!"

Elizabeth ignored him. Wraith-like, she vanished from the room without a sound. James cursed, then whipped around to face Simon. "You're fired! If you're not off this property within the hour, I'll have you *thrown off!*"

For an endless moment Simon stood unmoving, muscles bunched beneath his jacket. The back of his neck tingled with a raw killing rage — one he hadn't felt in all his years as a Pinkerton operative. A red mist swam before his eyes. Then, inexplicably, over the roaring in his brain, a voice — or was it the rushing sound of his pulse? — pulled him back from the edge. As if nudged by unseen hands, Simon backed one step, then another, and his arms dropped to his sides. A feathering sensation brushed along his spine, the back of his head, almost as if someone had touched him.

He took a deep breath. "You can't fire me," he murmured, surprised by the huskiness of his voice. "Your brother hired me, and I don't think he'll support your . . . wish." James's flushed cheeks had paled. He was glaring at Simon, his eyes wild, almost glassy. "One of the stableboys told me you and Horatio wanted to see me," Simon continued matter-of-factly. He looped his thumbs over his belt and took a long breath. The urge to throttle James continued to subside. "If now isn't convenient, I'll leave, and you can send for me later."

James lifted one hand in a jerky gesture of dismissal. "Later," he muttered. "We'll talk later." He moved to the nearby sideboard and reached for a crystal decanter.

Simon headed for the door.

"Kincaid!"

He stopped.

"Stay away from Miss Granger, or you'll find yourself in more trouble than you bargained for."

The empty threat warranted no response. At the back door, Simon paused. The faint aroma of spring violets lingered in the hallway, but with an instinct he had learned to trust, Simon knew Elizabeth had escaped into the woods, not upstairs to her room. He opened the door and stepped outside. Then he broke into a run.

25

Unthinking, Elizabeth fled down the flagstone path, her only instinct to hide. She dashed into the cover of the woods, her mind a confused jumble of incoherent prayers — and disbelief.

Why?

James Crump, youngest son of one of the most respected families in the state, wanted to ruin her . . . destroy her. She had seen it in his face, heard it in his voice. It didn't make sense. She had tried so hard to keep to herself, to avoid any kind of confrontation — a lifetime of painfully learned behavior. And still, still she hadn't deterred him from alienating her from the rest of his family. Turning them against her. After all, they were Crumps, and she . . . a penniless nobody.

Or perhaps she was no longer a "nobody." Had he somehow discovered her last name? If so, she would have to leave immediately. She would never be able to explain her motives, make amends.

Like wild birds trapped in a small cage, the irrational thoughts beat in ever tighter circles. She sank to the cool, damp earth beneath a large pine, leaned back against the rough bark, and buried her face in her knees.

Behind her a twig snapped. Elizabeth's head jerked up.

"Hello there," Simon Kincaid said from behind the tree. He tossed aside two pieces of a dead branch.

She rose, her movements stiff, hands clumsy as she brushed dead leaves and earth from her skirt. She studied the dark-haired man towering over her, then glanced at the broken twig. Back at the house, Mr. Kincaid had intervened in her behalf. She didn't understand him; had, on several occasions, been frankly intimidated by him. But for some reason she felt . . . safe? . . . whenever he was with her.

"Mr. Kincaid."

"Miss Granger," he returned, duplicating her level tone. "I apologize for frightening you."

"I wasn't frightened." She half smiled. "You startled me, is all. But thank you for . . . warning me of your presence." She gestured to the broken twig.

"Then why are you trembling?" He bent and retrieved a pinecone and idly traced the prickly scales with his thumb. The discerning green eyes moved over her face, subtly assessing. "Hmm . . . your cheeks are — shall we say — less than rosy?"

"Mr. Kincaid, are you trying to embarrass me . . . to divert my attention perhaps?"

His thumb paused a fraction. "Is it working?"

Was he *teasing* her? "I — yes. *No!*" She covered her now flaming cheeks with both hands. "Why did you follow me? I thought James —" She choked back the words, a tingle racing along her limbs at Mr. Kincaid's expression. Stepping back, she bumped into the tree, and his hand shot out to steady her.

"Careful. I'm not going to hurt you, Miss Granger. You don't have to bolt again." He paused. "And I'm certainly not going to browbeat you. Actually, I tracked you down to make sure you were all right."

He released her elbow and stepped back. Elizabeth stared down at her arm, marveling that she could still feel the warmth and strength of his clasp. "Thank you. I'll be better after a while. It's just that scenes like the one in the library . . . well, I do my best to avoid them. But I didn't have a choice this time. I mean — of course, one always has a choice," she rattled on. "But I wasn't expecting to be blamed for it, you see. And he wouldn't give me a chance to explain."

"Blamed for what?" Mr. Kincaid asked, an ominous frown creasing his brow.

"Maisie Pritchard's death." Feeling suddenly cold, Elizabeth rubbed her arms. "I . . . they had asked me to accompany her back to town. Only Maisie wanted to be alone . . . Mr. Kincaid? Why are you looking at me like

227

that?" *He agrees with the Crumps. That's why he appeared in the library. He believes I should have stayed with Maisie, too.*

"Don't you understand? You might have been killed as well, you little idiot!"

Elizabeth gaped at him. "Oh. I . . . hadn't thought of that." She set her chin obstinately. "And I'm *not* an idiot."

The hard, uncompromising line of his mouth softened. "Then perhaps you could enlighten me as to what you *are*, Miss Granger. You puzzle me, you see — and I don't like puzzles. For instance" — he stepped closer — "could you explain what's going on between you and James Crump? He certainly has no right to treat you as he did in the library . . . unless you have feelings for him, or —"

"What difference could it possibly make to you?" Elizabeth asked, bewildered by Simon Kincaid's inquisition. "Oh, never mind. I think I see. James is just as puzzled because you and I had met before . . . when you saved my life, I mean. I think James is afraid you'll interfere, so he'll doubtless try to interrogate you as well." She suppressed another shudder. "It's my fault, I'm afraid. Because he wants to discredit me — in any manner possible — he doesn't care if you're caught in the middle."

"That's all about as clear as swamp water," Mr. Kincaid muttered. He kicked the pinecone he'd dropped. "Every time I'm with you, this happens." He shook his head. "It makes little sense for James to hound you so savagely merely because you spurn unwelcome advances . . . unless —" He narrowed his gaze.

"I won't even dignify that with a response. I told you . . . in the stable, and you even tried to — to *bully* me into coming to you if I needed help." Elizabeth bit her lip, then blurted, "I thought you finally believed me, but it's plain you don't."

"I don't know what to believe any longer," he shot back wearily. "Look . . . I'm sorry."

"No . . . *I'm* sorry." Elizabeth flushed, feeling awkward and unaccountably near tears. "You've rescued me so many times now that it's embarrassing. I haven't even thanked you for this last episode, with James." She closed her eyes, then opened them and looked away, into the serene stillness of the forest. "If I just *understood*," she whispered.

"If you'll tell me what it is you don't understand, I might be able to help," Mr. Kincaid offered quietly.

Elizabeth was astounded. For some reason, Simon Kincaid didn't trust her, and yet he wasn't casting her aside. Never, in all her twenty-six years, had anyone offered to help her understand *anything*. She shrugged helplessly, struggling to keep her voice even. "James . . . M-Maisie . . . even you. Why would you want to help a stranger, one who's brought you nothing but trouble? Why is James trying to ruin my reputation by making me feel that I'm somehow responsible for Maisie's death? If he's found out who I —" She snapped her mouth shut with a gasp. She couldn't tell Simon Kincaid about her father. Not yet. He didn't know her, didn't trust her. And, God help her — she couldn't afford to trust *him.*

Even now, his probing gaze was burning into her, and though she told herself she was not afraid of Simon Kincaid, she couldn't bear for him to look at her with disgust and disillusionment. *Please . . . don't let him look at me like James does. . . .*

"Found out who you . . . what?" Simon asked, and his voice was as soft, as deadly, as the sting of a scorpion.

♦ ♦ ♦

Avery Paxton signed his name with a flourish at the front desk of the Piney Woods Hotel. He nodded to the clerk, and strolled back across the lobby while Wo Fang attended to the luggage. Though the management had been disconcerted by the appearance of his personal bodyguard, Avery gave them high marks for not demanding that the Oriental be housed elsewhere. Avery had purchased outright the last hotel whose proprietor had made the mistake of insulting Wo Fang. Within ten days, the four-story structure had

230

been razed, its employees jobless.

Avery wandered down the broad piazza of the Piney Woods, admiring the graceful lines of the architecture with its projecting towers at either end. Across the railroad tracks in front of the hotel, an attractive wooded park beckoned.

"Are you ready to retire to your rooms, Mr. Paxton? The bellhop has already taken the luggage up."

Avery disregarded the query and waved his cigar toward the park. "They call that 'Yankee Paradise,' Wo Fang. Imagine that. I find the attitude here in Thomasville most refreshing compared to that in Atlanta."

"You would still find it difficult to build your kingdom here," Wo Fang warned. "The Crumps established *their* dynasty over half a century ago."

Avery leveled a chilling stare on the unperturbed giant. "If I wish it, it will be so."

Wo Fang bowed. "Your room, sir? Would you prefer that dinner be sent up there, where you can scheme in privacy?"

"I begin to regret sparing your life."

"Yes, Mr. Paxton."

A train rolled past the hotel in a cloud of billowing steam, blocking the view of the park. Avery turned away, crushing the cigar into a stand. His mellow mood vanished. "Find Horatio Crump. Find out where he lives. Tell him we will meet here, at the hotel, and that if he refuses my final terms, he can expect unfortunate accidents, *soon*. First, with his stupid horses. Then, his family. And the next time, there won't be a companion around to save his children."

"What about his railroads, sir? His other businesses? I understand the Crumps own an orchard on the edge of town, a sawmill in Metcalfe, and several others within an hour's drive."

The low musical voice with its singsong cadence bore no trace of disrespect, and the round moon face maintained the same expression it had since Avery first laid eyes on the gigantic Sumo wrestler. Wo Fang had learned to speak his precise English from a Catholic priest, but Avery was beginning to wonder if his infuriating servant had picked up a few other irritating notions from the papist as well.

He stopped a few yards from the Otis elevator in the hotel and spoke under his breath, "I plan to take over their railroads and any other businesses that would help establish my reputation. I don't care what happens to the *Crumps,* but destroying something I plan to own would be cutting off my nose to spite my face."

"Pardon? That American idiom is not one with which I am familiar."

The elevator doors opened and the operator nodded to Avery. "Going up?"

"One moment." Avery looked up at Wo Fang. "If you wanted chicken for dinner, would you poison the chicken?"

"Ah." He nodded in comprehension and followed Avery into the elevator, where they stood in silence until they reached the second floor.

Avery tipped the delighted elevator operator, then turned to Wo Fang, who was smiling an enigmatic smile. "Stop looking at me like that!" Avery ordered.

Wo Fang merely gestured for Avery to precede him down the hall. "Your rooms are halfway down, on the right, Mr. Paxton. And Mr. Paxton?"

"What?"

"You might remember . . . I do not eat the flesh of the chicken, or poultry of any kind."

Devil take his Oriental eyes! He was speaking in those confounded riddles again! "If I order you to eat chicken, eat chicken you will! You owe me your life. Don't forget *that,* Fang."

An obsequious bow. Then, "Yessir, Mr. Paxton."

26

Rose Hill
December 20, 1895

Distracted, Georgina Crump dismssed the messenger boy with an impatient wave of her hand. So. Avery Paxton, that abominable carpetbagger, was in Thomasville. Tapping the note against her palm, Georgina strode down the hall, her silk morning gown rustling, heels clicking impatiently on the parquet flooring. Checked into Piney Woods with a monstrous Oriental man as his personal servant, demanding that a five-course dinner be served in his suite.

What was Curtis Bellamy thinking? Georgina would have to arrange a talk with the manager. She turned down another hall, the one leading to the messengers' quarters. "Jacob," she demanded, her cold gaze raking the ragtail assemblage of uniformed messengers who had hurriedly stiffened to respectful attention, "fetch Mr. James at once. He should be in town — try Mrs. Scott's on Jackson Street or the Randall House."

Georgina had telephoned Horatio immediately, so he should already be on his way, even though she'd interrupted their evening meal. James, regrettably, was more difficult to track down, in spite of her repeated injunctions that he remain accessible at all times.

She turned to leave, then paused. "At least two of you are dressed improperly, and all of you know better than to lounge about like a pack of shiftless fieldhands between assignments. Don't let it happen again."

Two hours later Horatio arrived. "Mother, I don't know why this couldn't have waited until morning. Paxton has brought himself to our camp, after all, which places *him* at the disadvantage — not us."

"Any man with the gall to check into Piney Woods as though he were one of the Vanderbilts doubtless considers himself invincible." Georgina laid aside the report she'd been reading, and over her reading glasses, fixed her eldest son with a censorious glare. "Good *heavens*, Horatio! You could have at least worn a tie."

"Mother, it's almost ten o'clock. For almost two days now, I've been dealing with Maisie Pritchard's death — her entire family, as well as Josephine, who's taken to her bed."

Georgina sniffed. "You should have married Elsie Young, as your father and I wished."

Unruffled, Horatio gratefully settled into the wingback in front of the fire and lifted his feet onto the footstool. "Elsie died in child-birth less than two years after she married, Mother. And look what happened to that poor creature you forced on James. Josephine is my wife, and you know you care for her. Her emotional constitution might be a trifle . . . unstable . . . at times — but she *has* blessed you with five healthy grandchildren."

"What about Mertis Coates? Still in a coma?" Then she waved an impatient hand. "Never mind. What took you so long? I telephoned over two hours ago."

"Oh . . . James has had a wild hair about Simon Kincaid, my new trainer, and I felt compelled to talk with the man. He's good, highly respected, even admired by other trainers, as well as the stableboys. In fact, I've had several friends approach me with mock threats to steal him away, after the season." He frowned, his gaze on the dancing flames. "I'll have to confess that I do find him personally somewhat forbidding, perhaps a trifle too independent — but he is careful never to overstep his authority, or usurp —"

"Horatio!" Georgina interrupted, exasperated. "Forget your horses and some boor of no consequence." She rose, agitated, and paced the sitting room. "Oh, where *is* your brother? We must decide what to do about Avery Paxton tonight. Immediately."

"You plan to have him evicted from Piney Woods? I doubt Bellamy would accommodate even us, for a wealthy guest who's done nothing to deserve being thrown out on his ear."

"If I make the request, it will be granted." She dropped at last into the chair opposite her eldest son, wondering how on earth she and Mr. Crump could have ever produced such an unpretentious child. Her gaze unconsciously sought the huge family portrait over the fireplace. Helene would have been fifty years old this January.

Georgina's hand formed a cold white fist. At least she had had her revenge for Helene's death — for the monstrous betrayal by Charles Graham. She had never discovered what happened to his squalling brat of a daughter — but there would never be any heirs to bear the infamous Graham name through his *sons*.

Now Avery Paxton would also discover what happened to those who threatened the Crump family.

Gathering control about her like a shield, Georgina walked over to a grouping of paintings on the far wall. Behind the Winslow Homer landscape was a safe. Georgina unlocked it, withdrew a sheet of paper, then sat down once more. "I don't think it will be necessary to have Avery Paxton evicted, so you can wipe that troubled look from your face."

She held up the sheet of paper. "I am, however, going to see to it that he is arrested —

and held without bail — for extortion, sabotage . . . and murder." She settled back in her chair, a thin smile of anticipation spreading. "When James arrives, we'll discuss the details."

27

Pastime Racetrack
December 21, 1895

"Looking forward to the heats this weekend."

Simon finished his conversation with another local trainer and strode toward the barn. A blustering wind tousled his hair and rattled several loose slats of the fence rail around the track.

He ducked inside the barn, yelling for Snaps to harness Pretty Boy. They needed to run all six of Horatio's trotters today, in spite of Simon's inability to concentrate fully on the task at hand. Scowling, he reminded himself forcefully that his primary job as an undercover operative was a *necessity* — he was only *posing* as a horse trainer. *That's right, Kincaid. You let Horatio's horses show poorly, and he'll sack your sorry carcass . . . which will lose you your cover as* well *as your real job.*

Muttering to himself, Simon waited impatiently for Snaps to bring Pretty Boy out; moments later he was on the track, and the old magic worked its way into his spirit, relaxing and reviving. He rounded the bend and came abreast of the viewing stand, his gaze automatically searching the crowd. She wasn't there.

His hands momentarily tightened on the reins; Pretty Boy resisted — and broke stride.

"It wasn't his fault," he told a concerned Jefferson after pulling up beside the head groomsman. "It was mine. Don't worry. He'll be fine this weekend." Unless Simon allowed Elizabeth Granger to continue disrupting his concentration, that is.

She had tiptoed into the barn at Adelaide early that morning while he was on breakfast rounds with Jefferson, mute as a church mouse, those great, dark blue eyes following his every move. Simon had quickly realized that she was waiting for an opportune time to approach him, but even after Jefferson left, she hesitated. Less than five minutes after her appearance, she fumbled her way through yet another apology for disturbing his rounds, then flitted out the door. Simon hadn't seen her since.

What had she wanted to tell him?

"Bring Mosby out, before the wind picks up," he ordered Jefferson, more curtly than he'd intended. Before the week was out, he and Elizabeth Granger would have a meeting of minds — and this time, Simon would not allow her to retreat, physically *or* mentally.

He was still in a black mood when he met Alex late that night for their thrice-weekly

240

rendezvous. After a brief discussion of the possibility that Maisie Pritchard's accidental death could have been a failed attempt to kill Elizabeth, Simon tackled the issue of Eve. For the first time since their confrontation on the MacKays' back porch the previous autumn, he faced the possibility that Alexander's judgment might be impaired due to his feelings for his wife.

Regardless of duty, common sense, or reality, Alex would protect Eve.

". . . even though her presence here is unauthorized, dangerous for us all, and could seriously compromise the resolution of the case?" Simon glanced around the shadowy graveyard where they'd met. The cold, silent tombstones seemed to mock their heated exchange.

"I won't allow it," Alex returned. "Simon . . . understand this. I love her. God knows I don't deserve such a fine woman, but for whatever reason, He chose to give her to *me*." His blue eyes blazed in the darkness. "As He did, I'll keep her safe, Sim. Even from *you*."

"I wouldn't hurt your Eve, Alexander."

"Ach, man! The trouble is, you *could!* You may have earned your moniker 'Smoke' due to your uncanny powers of shadowing — but I've known you long enough to beware of the man behind the smoke. You're dangerous to her, my friend" — Alex leaned back against the high brick wall of a family burial plot, his

241

pointing finger barely discernible — "not because of what you'd *do* to her — but because you can't *understand* her feelings or her faith. You won't accept God's love, so you can't understand its manifestation in the marriage relationship. You think God is only a God of wrath. Of unforgiving justice and unrelenting vengeance."

"And you've been itching to tell me otherwise for years, haven't you?" Simon retorted. "Tell me this, then — didn't He warn mankind that vengeance belongs to Him alone? Or do you want to remind me again how He manifests His infinite love and compassion by allowing monsters like Paxton and the Crumps — like Dante Gambrielli and Joe Leoni — to maul their victims . . . and get away with it?"

Goaded and defensive, already raw from his own conflicting feelings for Elizabeth, Simon finally unleashed a deep-seated rage. "Don't preach to me again of a loving God, Alexander! I know better. God is like the wealthy, childless couple who purchased me off a hellish orphan train when I was six. They adopted me as their son, promised me security and love, treated me as their own — as long as I lived up to their demands. When I finally rebelled, they turned their backs."

"Sim . . . I never knew. I —"

Once begun, the words spilled out in a painful torrent. "I wasn't easy to raise, I'll grant you that . . . restless, headstrong. But whatever I put my mind to, I mastered — horses, crops, schooling . . . My . . . *parents* . . . thanked God for their good fortune and demanded more. Because I thought I owed them my life, I tried to live up to their expectations." He looked down at his hands, clenched so tightly around a fragment of old brick that he crushed it to powder. "God," he whispered the word — a hoarse, tortured prayer. "You might not believe it, Alex, but at one time God *was* my anchor, my hope. I used to ride out to a finger-wide brook, in this tiny valley a couple hours from the spread. There was a cottonwood growing there . . . mountains on all sides . . . endless expanse of sky. I'd lie underneath that cottonwood, and . . . I'd talk to Him."

"What happened, Sim?" Alex finally asked.

Simon felt the choking sensation spread, and a muscle jumped in his cheek. "The man I called 'Father.' His demands grew more and more irrational. At sixteen, I was helping him breed and train horses for ranches and racetracks all over the country, but I was also expected to handle all the accounts as well as the household servants and make arrangements for all the guests they loved to entertain. I had to learn, he told me. And I had to *earn* the name of 'Kincaid.' He'd yell at me, and when I lost my temper — as hot-headed teenagers do — he'd hit me. Tell me I was an ungrateful orphan brat . . . and a whole lot worse. Of course, I never hit back. I . . . couldn't. He was . . . he was supposed to be . . . my father. . . ."

"I understand. Go on."

Simon flexed his shoulders, ran a hand around the back of his collar. "One day I ran away. Spent a year with a crowd of cutthroats and outlaws who made the Jameses and Younger boys look like tame tabby cats in comparison." He stared bleakly across at Alex's dark silhouette. "I knew what I was doing was wrong . . . terrible sins . . . but I was angry. Confused, hurt — but mostly angry."

Alex slid down the rough wall and sat on a stump, arms propped on his knees, head resting against the bricks, as relaxed as an old man dozing in the sunshine. "I understand. Then . . . ?"

"My . . . father . . . came after me." Even after all these years, the memory burned like acid.

For several moments there was silence. The earlier rain had blown over, and now the washed-out moon shone fitfully among tattered shreds of departing clouds. A gust of wind sent droplets from the drenched tree branches above them splattering onto the stones. Only one other man knew the story . . . Adam Moreaux.

Strange, he'd never realized until now how much Alex and the man called "Panther" resembled each other in their unshakable faith in a loving God. Perhaps that explained the compulsion to unburden himself to Alex now.

Simon braced himself, and finished it. "My father found where we were holed up, in a stinking makeshift camp high in the Colorado mountains. He rode in — alone. The only reason he wasn't shot on sight by the lookout was because" — he tried to speak calmly, cleanly, but the expression on Alex's face, illuminated by the moon, almost unmanned him — "because *I* was that lookout, and I recognized him. I stopped him before he was seen by the others. We argued. He told me what a disappointment I was, that I had shamed him and his wife, that they regretted ever taking me into their home. I was no longer their son. He told me God would punish me for the terrible sins I had committed. Then he mounted his horse and turned to leave. . . ."

Simon swung around, unable to face Alex, and stared sightlessly around the shrouded graveyard. "A couple of the gang rode up then. They wanted to know why I hadn't taken care of the outsider. I told them he was my father, that he was leaving and wouldn't be back. But they didn't care."

"You don't have to finish it. I can guess the rest." Alex rose, laying his hand on Simon's shoulder. "Don't do this to yourself, lad."

245

"I could have stopped them," Simon persisted hoarsely. "I saw them go for their guns — I should have stopped them. But I was so angry, so hurt. So full of shame and guilt that I —" he broke off, his voice agonized, "I should have let them kill me, too!"

He pulled away, tearing free of Alex. "You want to know what happened next?" Eyes glittering, Simon snatched up a loose stone and hurled it across the cemetery. "I pulled my own gun and shot both of *them*. Then I mounted my father's horse and rode out."

He turned back around, breathing hard. "God doesn't have anything to offer a man like me but justice. Not love. Not mercy. I committed murder, Alex. *Murder.* Deliberately, in cold blood. I broke not only man's laws, but God's."

"What do you think *they* would have done next?" Alex shot back. "What would they have done, knowing you were the only witness to your father's murder?"

Simon couldn't answer. "It doesn't matter," he finally muttered. "I still committed murder."

"In self-defense, Simon. I *know* you — stop torturing yourself. Regardless of your feelings at the time, you killed them in self-defense. *God* forgave you long ago. All you need to do is forgive yourself."

"Do you think I haven't *tried?*"

"I think," Alex said, rising and stretching,

then fixing Simon with an unswerving blue stare, "that you've locked up your soul in a prison, one that's robbed you of joy, of love, of laughter. You've punished yourself enough, my friend, far more than the deed deserves." He hesitated, then added roughly, "Tell me — was what happened to me last year a sin *I'll* be having to carry about to my grave?"

Simon felt as if he'd been punched in the ribs. "Alex, that has nothing to do —"

"It has everything to do with you!" Alex roared, his infamous temper flaring. "Ach, man, you've a head as thick as quarry granite! As far as I'm concerned, you rid the earth of two spawns of the devil who would have met an unsavory end regardless of who pulled the trigger. Newspaper stories and dime novels about the West are naught but hogwash. We both know what it's really like out there, and twenty years ago, it was even worse."

He leaned closer and practically shook a fist in Simon's face. "Why do you think Pinkerton's established a Denver office back in the eighties?" He shook his head. "What happened to you — 'tis all in the past. Over and done with. Let it go, Sim. Let it go." He narrowed his gaze. "Look at it this way: If you hadn't killed those two blackguards, where would Elizabeth Granger be today? Tell me that, now."

Simon sank against the stone wall. Alexander was right, and he knew it. In his head, he had accepted long ago that Jake and Percy would have gunned him down as mercilessly as they had his father. And Elizabeth was alive because Simon had saved her life one hot October day.

But had he saved a courageous young woman caught in the middle — or a deceitful schemer whose perfidy rivaled that of Jake and Percy?

28

The funeral service was over. Eyes shadowed, Elizabeth walked slowly toward the line of buggies waiting at the Methodist church. Her heart ached for Mr. Pritchard and the children. Especially the children, with their blank faces, as doleful and dreary as their black mourning clothes.

There was little conversation as the crowd dispersed, though speculation over Maisie Pritchard's tragic death hovered as thick as swamp mist. A step ahead of Elizabeth, Horatio walked with Josephine. The plump woman was leaning heavily on her husband's arm while she mopped her eyes with her handkerchief. James had slipped out of the service early, and Elizabeth wondered where he might have gone. For the past three days she had waited for him to corner her, to elaborate on his threats, but he had ignored her completely — an ominous sign, Elizabeth suspected.

Josephine, too, was avoiding her as much as possible, and Horatio's cold formality told Elizabeth that James had spread his poison well. Even the servants were whispering behind their hands. *Lucifer, spinning his webs of deceit.* If she couldn't find the embezzled gold soon, she would never have the opportunity to restore honor to her family name. All those years of scrimping and saving and searching — risking her life! — would be for nothing.

"Elizabeth."

She looked up. Horatio stood waiting, his expression somber beneath the black top hat. He had already handed Josephine into the family carriage. Elizabeth's heart lurched. "Yes?"

"Would you mind . . . ah . . . taking the rest of the day off? I'll send one of the boys back for you, or you can rent a buggy again if you prefer." He paused, and it appeared to Elizabeth as if his gaunt face had taken on the color of clay. "Perhaps . . . ah . . . you'd rather spend the rest of the day out at the racetrack, since Pansy is minding the children." The words were stiff, almost strangled.

Now she knew. First, James implicated her in Maisie's death; now, as she had feared, he was fostering the rumor that she and Mr. Kincaid were carrying on an illicit relationship. *Just like my father . . .*

Elizabeth drew herself up proudly. She *had* deliberately deceived them about her true identity, perhaps, but she was innocent of whatever accusations James had made, and she refused to cower like a whipped child. Not this time. "Thank you. I believe I'll do just that. I haven't been to the stables *or* the track for a week now. I've missed seeing the horses."

There was a subtle emphasis on the final word that Horatio didn't miss. A red band stained his cheeks and the narrow bridge of his nose. Elizabeth opened a plain black parasol. "Please tell Mrs. Crump I'll be home before the children's supper."

"Very well." He touched his hat, then climbed into the carriage.

Elizabeth watched them leave. A dwindling group of mourners meandered past her, unnoticed, their slow footsteps scattering piles of dead leaves. Overhead, a gray afternoon sky shimmered with a harsh glare that hurt her eyes, even beneath the shelter of the parasol. *Get on with it, Elizabeth.* It wasn't as if she had never been shunned before, and nothing would be gained by standing here like a lamppost.

She followed the departing line of buggies, with every step questioning her impetuous decision. How would she be able to go to Pastime Stables without the children's presence as a buffer? A little past the corner of Broad and Jackson, her step faltered, and she stopped completely. The parasol listed to one side as Elizabeth stared unseeingly at the window display in Jerger's Jewelers.

"Are you all right, my dear?"

Startled, she looked up into the veiled face

251

of a woman wearing dowdy widow's weeds a decade out of fashion. But the voice was kind, and Elizabeth mustered a rueful smile. "I'm quite well, thank you." She carefully closed the parasol and hooked it over her arm.

The widow hesitated, and Elizabeth thought she heard her mutter some foreign phrase beneath her breath. A black veil obscured her features, but Elizabeth sensed that her polite answer had not satisfied the widow. "I'm staying at the Stuart . . . for the winter," she announced abruptly. "Perhaps —"

"Oh, I'll be leaving Thomasville before long," Elizabeth admitted, wanting only to escape. "I —" She lifted her hand, uncertain how to proceed in the face of such unexpected kindness.

"I'm sorry. It was rude of me to intrude upon your privacy. I — my husband tells . . . I mean my husband *used to tell* me I'm much too impulsive. But you appeared . . . upset, and I thought perhaps I could help." She studied Elizabeth's dull black gown.

Feeling awkward in the ugly, ill-fitting dress Josephine had instructed Dora to loan her, Elizabeth backed away. "Few people involve themselves in a stranger's troubles," she said. "It usually doesn't prove a very wise course for anyone."

An oxen-drawn dray clattered by, and two men emerged from the hardware store, arguing good-naturedly about the price of sweet potatoes. They nodded to Elizabeth and the persistent widow, and Elizabeth seized the opportunity to escape down the street.

The widow did not pursue her, but Elizabeth could feel the other woman's gaze upon her retreating figure. Though it had been a bewildering encounter, she had managed to put it out of her mind — along with Maisie's funeral — by the time she reached the road leading to the stables.

Don't be a henwit. Buck up, and pretend this is just another walk, to — to the track in New York, where you first grew to love harness racing. All the way down Broad, across the tracks, past Yankee Paradise Park, Elizabeth lectured herself, but her stern admonition sank no farther than her cold nose. By the time the barn roof rose above the trees, she could barely force her reluctant feet down the familiar path. *Think of the horses,* she ordered herself even more fiercely. *Think of the crowds, the stablehands who'll be swarming about the stables. Think of all the other trainers and owners. Don't think of that poor man's body, or the blood. . . .*

Think of Simon Kincaid.

Elizabeth stopped dead in her tracks. Even though she had told Horatio she planned to observe the horses, she had realized on the walk over here that this would, in fact, be an opportunity to warn the trainer. She had tried to tell Mr. Kincaid early one morning, after the cook made a comment about "the two of you carryin' on right under poor Miz Crump's nose." But when he had studied her in that alert, expectant manner of his, as if he could pry every secret from her heart, Elizabeth had lost courage.

He still might blame her, but she had to make an effort to counter James's lies.

"Miss 'Lizbeth? That be you?"

At the sound of a familiar voice, Elizabeth looked up in surprise. The stablehand, bareback and feet dangling, was astride one of Mr. Crump's pleasure horses. "Hello, Snaps."

"I was just headin' back to the stables to fetch Mr. Kincaid an overdraw bit. You comin' on down to watch? They's busy today, what with the first heat an' all —" He broke off, looking puzzled. "Why you walking, Miss 'Lizbeth?"

She ignored the question. "Are you expecting a big crowd today?"

"Lawdy, yes! I think every single body from Albany to Tallahassee's heared 'bout Mr. Crump's new trainer, with his magic touch. And yesterday ol' Mosby had a 2:06 lap that near 'bout had Jefferson dancing on top of the barn. I reckon Mr. Crump'll be mighty pleased tomorrow." He peered down at Elizabeth, the flashing grin faltering. "Miss 'Lizbeth? You feeling poorly? You look 'bout as spent as a wet match."

"I'm fine," Elizabeth repeated, stifling a sigh. "Snaps?"

"Yes'm?"

"Have you . . . has anyone at the stable . . ." She faltered, then blurted, "Is there any talk about my relationship with the Crumps? Or . . . or Mr. Kincaid . . . that you're willing to share?"

Snaps fumbled with the reins, unable to look Elizabeth in the eye.

"It's all right. Forget I asked, Snaps. I can see it's made you uncomfortable."

"None of us for real believe what they's saying," he burst out suddenly. "None of us. But, Miss 'Lizbeth, you be careful. Mr. Kincaid, well . . . he be . . ."

"I know." She patted the horse's neck. "But thank you for the warning. Now, you better go before you draw Mr. Kincaid's wrath on *your* head."

Snaps glanced down at her, the warm chocolate eyes alive with knowledge and with pity. Then he kicked the horse into a canter and disappeared in a swirl of dust and thudding hoofbeats.

29

Simon was speaking with a trainer from Boston when he caught sight of Elizabeth. Clad in a sober black gown, she was walking along the edge of the dried grass surrounding the track. Why, he wondered absently, was she on foot today?

He continued to monitor her progress while he listened with only half an ear to Rupert Slade expound on some new hoof oil. There was something about her gait and the way she clutched her parasol as if it were a weapon. Simon frowned. She must have come here directly from the funeral service.

"You know the lady?" Slade inquired, his gaze following Simon's.

"She's companion to Crump's five children," Simon answered.

"Dainty piece of goods, isn't she? Mite young to be a widow, I would have thought."

Irritation — and something else — rippled just beneath the surface of Simon's skin. "Age has little to do with it. At any rate, she's not married. A local woman was buried today, and people in these parts still show respect for customs and manners."

The subtle censure was lost on Rupert Slade. "The one all the coloreds are muttering about? Shot dead to rights on Crump's property?"

Simon slowly turned to face the other man, whose skill with horses was overlaid by a coarse insensitivity toward humans. "There's talk, none of which concerns me. Or you."

Slade ignored the terse warning tone. "Way I hear it, some fool mistook her for a deer, and feelings among the locals are running pretty hot." His glance moved back to Elizabeth, who by now had reached the stands. "Maybe I'll have you introduce me to the dainty peach there. My wife stayed behind this year, and it gets a tad lonely at my lodgings, come evening."

Simon straightened to his full height. Casually he lifted the whip from the sulky seat and just as casually rapped his open palm with the stock. "I think not." He paused. "In fact, I think both Mr. Crump and I would take exception to any attention you visited upon Miss Granger."

After a moment Slade's mouth twitched, then exploded in a nervous laugh. "Whatever you say, chum. Whatever you say." Moving jerkily, he backed away, lifted a meaty hand to touch the brim of his homburg, and disappeared inside the barn.

"Mr. Kincaid?" One of the younger stable-boys darted up to his side. "Jefferson told me

257

to fetch you. Moonbeam's thrown a shoe."

Simon tossed the whip back into the sulky and followed the colored boy, for the moment laying aside all thought of Elizabeth Granger.

She was still there two hours later, he noted as the sulky rounded the track several paces behind three other trotters. Sitting by herself on the far side of the stands, apart from the dwindling crowd of onlookers. Simon brought his colt to a ragged halt on the side of the rail opposite the other trotters. Sir Peabody tended to bite, and still resisted pulling the sulky. Simon leaped, catlike, to the ground, wiping speckles of sand from his face and hair.

"Still a pesky firecracker, ain't he?" Jefferson observed, trotting up to them. His normally smiling black face wore a ferocious scowl, and he glared at the sweating colt. "What you plan on telling Mr. Horatio?"

Simon tugged off his gloves and tossed them over the traces. "I've been working with this animal almost a month now, and he's little improved." He stepped over to inspect Sir Peabody's withers. Even that small movement sent ripples of tension quivering through the sleek flanks, and Simon stifled a real stab of regret. "He's not ready to race, and I doubt he ever *will* be. Some horses are born with a wild streak that's impossible to

258

tame, much less discipline into a marketable racing animal." He stepped back, his gaze returning to the stands.

"I'll take him on back into the barn, then. Ah . . . I reckon Miss 'Lizbeth wouldn't mind if you took a notion to chat."

Simon squinted at his wily assistant. Jefferson stared back, not budging an inch. "Oh, all right," Simon growled. "I'll go over *there.* Maybe one day *someone* will tell me why she's so skittish about approaching the stables here." He stalked off, more irritated with himself than he was with Jefferson.

He wanted to see Elizabeth, not because she was a vital piece in the complex puzzle he was determined to solve, but because he simply couldn't stay away.

She met him halfway. The color black, Simon decided, did not suit Elizabeth. It rendered her fine porcelain skin a ghostly chalk white. For the first time he noticed a tiny scattering of faint scars, probably from smallpox or measles, dotting her high cheekbones. Dark circles smudged the fine skin beneath her eyes. "Are you all right?" he demanded in a curt voice, then could have kicked himself for the peremptory tone. *If James had been baiting her, or spreading more of his crafty innuendos . . .*

Elizabeth appeared taken aback, but she didn't retreat. "I'm not ill, if that's what you mean," she said. Her aplomb both surprised and, illogically, pleased Simon. She lifted a hand, flicking the brim of her neat felt hat. "I . . ." she hesitated, seeming at a loss for words. "I . . . need to warn you about something," she finally admitted, faint color seeping into her cheeks. "I tried . . . the other morning, in the barn, but . . ." She made a face.

"Ah." Simon studied her, then offered casually, "You're referring to James Crump's smear campaign to destroy your reputation — and mine?"

"How did you —" Bewilderment and uncertainty chased across her delicate features. She glanced around, but with the heats over, the crowd had melted away. The blue eyes blinked once, then narrowed as the mask slid firmly into place again. "I've remarked before that, for a horse trainer, you notice a lot more than one would expect."

"Mm. Perhaps . . . but then, for a children's companion, you *accomplish* a lot more than one would expect."

For a single breath the mask slipped again, revealing a stark desperation that tempted Simon to gather her into his arms on the spot. Then she smiled a heartbreaking smile. "I have to," she replied very simply.

Simon studied her for a moment. "So do I," he said at last, breaking the long silence. "Now that we've established that fact, tell me what disturbs you about the stables here so

260

much that you avoid them to the point of absurdity."

"Wh-at?"

Simon idly leaned down to pluck a drifting scrap of paper from the ground. Left on its own, even something so small could spook a high-strung horse and cause incalculable damage. He straightened, regarding Elizabeth closely. "One of those things I've 'noticed' is your reluctance to approach the stables here. Yet at Adelaide, you'd probably *live* in them if given half a chance. And that strikes me as . . . odd."

He folded the piece of paper — an advertising circular — and stuffed it in his pocket. "Pastime keeps its stables just as clean, so it can't be the odor and mess. Now, I understand there *was* a murder committed here three years ago. . . ." He paused once more to observe her carefully. If anything, her pallor was more pronounced. "But since you weren't even living in the vicinity at the time that certainly doesn't — Miss Granger?" Seeing her composure falter, he stepped forwad to grasp her elbow. "Are you *sure* you're not ill?"

"I'm . . . quite sure." She tried to smile, a pitiful effort. Even her lips were colorless, and the deep blue eyes reflected the blank horror of shock.

Frowning, Simon steadied her until she recovered. His thoughts raced, and he made a mental note to ask Alex what he had turned up concerning the William Soames murder. "I'm taking you home," he announced, firmly enough to stifle all objections. "And on the way, we're going to have a talk — you and I — Miss Granger."

"I was hoping for the opportunity," Elizabeth responded, surprising him yet again. "But the horses —"

"We're finished for the day. Jefferson can handle the rest. You walked here, didn't you? Yes, I saw you. Why didn't the Crumps drop you off on their way home?"

"That's one of the reasons I wanted to talk to you," Elizabeth confessed, her voice subdued. "I think . . . I believe if it weren't for the children, they'd dismiss me tonight. First, James convinced them that Maisie's death was my fault, you see. I could handle that because *I* know it's not true. But it's not just Maisie. I'm not even sure it's the rumors about . . . the two of us. There's . . . something else" — she hesitated, then tacked on uncertainly — "I *think*. Of course, people distance themselves from you when they know you're going to be leaving soon." She glanced up, then away, looking in that moment young and unguarded, as vulnerable as a child.

Simon fought a losing battle with himself. "Come along," he ordered. "I drove the phaeton over today, so there's room for us both. It's beyond the stables. Will you walk, or shall

I bring it over here?"

She lifted her chin. "I'll come with you."

"You realize, of course, that my driving you home will only reinforce the rumor James is spreading?"

"I know. But I can't think what else to do. It would be best to resign and quietly leave." She hesitated again. "But I won't." The look of desperation hovered, then faded. "Not yet. I can't."

"We'll talk about it on the way home."

30

Simon waited until they were halfway to Adelaide, then pulled the buggy to a halt, set the brake, and secured the reins.

"What if someone comes by?"

He shrugged indifferently. For the first time he had Elizabeth Granger alone, and he planned to make the most of it. "We won't be long. Besides, last I heard, it was no crime for a man to escort a young woman to her home."

Elizabeth looked at him, her gaze open. "Adelaide isn't my home, but when you put it like that . . ." She sat back with a little sigh, lifting her hands to smooth wisps of windblown hair.

Though bleak and colorless, the December afternoon was mild, with only a light breeze stirring the Spanish moss dangling from the trees on either side of the lane. Deep within the woods, a squirrel scolded, and beneath the bushes across the road, a brown thrasher searched for food. Into the peaceful stillness, Elizabeth's husky murmur blended as seamlessly as sunlight moving through the trees — in sharp contrast with her words.

"First, I apologize for the trouble James has caused you," she began. "He's . . . not a pleasant man, and his arrogance is difficult to swallow gracefully." She tried for a feeble smile.

Simon propped his boots on the dash rail and shifted so that he could better watch her face. *Conniving criminal or hapless victim? Which is she?* He was fast reaching the point that, for him, it didn't matter. "You've been here how long? A year? Two? Will anyone actually *believe* all the rumors?"

"*You've* been here long enough to know the answer to that." She paused. "If the Crumps say it, then it must be true. That doesn't mean the people here are gullible, any more than it means the Crumps are all good, all bad, or all powerful. But they've invested *everything* in this community over the years. Money, time . . . influence. Josephine let slip once that they have actually purchased dying businesses for inflated prices, just to salvage the owners' pride."

Simon couldn't suppress the snort of disbelief.

"Well, you asked. I'm only trying to explain," Elizabeth defended, her voice stiff. "It was that generosity of spirit that led to the creation of *my* position as the children's companion. Well . . . and perhaps their gratitude. . . ."

"Truly noble, I'm sure," Simon murmured sarcastically.

Color seeped across her skin. "You misunderstand. I'm not so much whitewashing their faults as I am acknowledging their virtues. Even weeds serve a purpose in God's kingdom, Mr. Kincaid. The Crump family has its skeletons — their ugly and ignoble traits. But that doesn't render them beyond hope of redemption."

Remember your role, Simon reminded himself, and barely managed to keep his mouth shut.

"I never realized, until it was too late," Elizabeth finished, "what a formidable task I'd set for myself."

"What task might that be?" Simon asked softly. "Reforming James?"

Elizabeth stiffened. "Of course not!" She wriggled on the seat. "Um . . . Mr. Kincaid? I'd . . . rather not talk about that part of it, not just yet. Just my talking with you this way could very well provoke your dismissal as well. I wouldn't want to cause you any more trouble."

It's way too late for that, little one, Simon thought. "You won't cause more trouble than I can get myself out of," he promised dryly. *At least, I hope not.*

"Yes . . . well, I'd noticed that about you, too."

For several moments they sat listening to the thrasher scrabbling in the leaves. Simon

266

curbed his impatience, knowing by now that Elizabeth would never respond to bullying. Beyond that — and far worse, to his way of thinking — was her defense of the Crumps. He wanted to shake her, shield her, share everything with her. Instead, he sat beside her, fighting with himself, and waited. If he could have trusted that a response would be proffered, he would even have prayed for wisdom.

"Have you always been a horse trainer?" Elizabeth's gentle voice squelched that faint stirring. She slanted him a curious look.

Unnoticed, the thrasher flew off. "No, I haven't. Why do you ask?"

"That day — the day of the wreck . . ." Her voice trailed away as she stared at her lap, the horse, the sky, and finally Simon's loosened ascot beneath his chin. "I told you once that I thought of you as a sort of fiercesome guardian angel. I know you're uncomfortable with that perception, but" — she spread her hands helplessly, and tried another smile — "here I am again, intruding on your life, asking your advice, in spite of knowing how you feel about me."

"I'm relieved *one* of us knows," Simon muttered. He studied her bent head, the sleek brown hair wound into a dignified coil at the nape of her neck, the fine wisps softening her brow. "I do recall pointing out that I'm no angel, Miss Granger, but why don't you just come right out and ask me what it is you want, instead of tiptoeing about the issue? I'm no James Crump, either, and I've told you more than once I'm willing to help."

"I learned very early not to ask anyone for anything, Mr. Kincaid. People, I find, are neither dependable nor trustworthy." Her mouth curled at one corner. "Even the Crumps."

"Cynical, but an accurate observation, Miss Granger. One I wouldn't have expected after your glowing testimony in their behalf." His gaze flicked over the thin gold chain around her neck with the tiny lamb dangling amidst the black serge of her jacket. "Much less someone whose only jewelry consists of likenesses of sheep and whose faith in a loving God is both naïve and misguided." Still raw from his recent confessional and impatient with Elizabeth's hesitance, Simon's response was perhaps more caustic than he intended. "The concept of God as the Good Shepherd no longer applies in a society where men like James Crump are free to devour helpless lambs such as yourself."

"I wasn't looking for a theological debate, Mr. Kincaid." She swallowed. "My childhood was neither happy nor secure, and the only way I survived at all was through my assurance that God *is* the Good Shepherd."

Simon snorted again. The blasted girl sounded like Alexander, with her infernal assertions and dogged refusal to accept God's true nature. "That being the case, then you won't need me, after all." His hand moved to release the brake. "Shall I deliver you to James? You can explain to *him* how a loving God is protecting you."

Elizabeth made no response. Simon's hand dropped back as he eyed the motionless woman. She was staring ahead, her carriage erect — resigned, remote, alone. A chill of self-disgust feathered down his spine. "Stop it!" he ordered, twisting around so fast the violent motion startled the horse. Elizabeth didn't flinch, but Simon sensed her inward shrinking as if he were inside her skin. *Right. So you're nothing like James Crump, are you, man?*

"Miss Granger. Elizabeth . . . I'm not going to throw you to the lions." He gentled his voice with difficulty, forced his clenched fists to relax, then set his jaw.

All right, then. He'd bared his soul once in the past week. He could bare it again, here, with this difficult, mysterious woman. He needed her to trust him. Needed . . . *her* . . . even more than he needed to protect himself. He wasn't prepared to admit why he felt this way. He only knew he would do *anything* to reach the woman whose self-imposed barricade was even more impregnable than his own. "Listen to me. I had a miserable childhood myself, living with a couple who mea-

269

sured my worth in terms of what I could do for them. Not for who I was, not for what I —"

His throat closed over the words. *No more.* He couldn't say any more. First, Alexander; now, Elizabeth. Two more different individuals he'd never met, yet both of them, in the space of twenty-four hours, had succeeded in challenging him to the very core. He took a deep breath, glancing across at Elizabeth. At least his words *had* jarred her back from that infuriating "other world" to which she frequently retreated. He wondered sourly if she had even heard his pathetic confession. "Sorry. I . . . felt defensive. I have a friend who views God much like you. He and I debated the issue recently. I reacted poorly then, too."

"I understand. You're right, though. I shouldn't inflict my views on you or anyone else." She produced a travesty of a smile, still looking straight ahead. "We'd better move along. It's growing late."

Simon sat back and folded his arms. "No."

The single syllable provoked a response, as he had intended. Her head swiveled, and confused blue eyes searched his face. She bit her lip, and in a movement he'd come to recognize, began fiddling with her glove. "Should I walk home, then?"

"Don't be absurd."

"You want to claw me some more? I'm not

270

bloodied enough yet to suit you?"

Simon's dark mood lightened at last. Good. He hadn't vanquished her spirit entirely, after all. If he were very careful, perhaps he could eventually teach her to trust him enough to — *what was he thinking?* He was an undercover operative, as highly trained and ruthless as a bloodhound. This . . . this unfamiliar tenderness, this obsessive *yearning* for the kind of relationship Alex shared with Eve could never be for Simon. He opened his mouth, then clamped it shut. He didn't know what to say. *Splendid, Kincaid.* He finally had the girl alone, ripe for interrogation, and he didn't know how to proceed, other than to spout off like a callow youth — or a sinner at a Catholic confessional!

Suddenly the horse's head lifted, its ears twitching backwards. Simon froze as he belatedly picked up the same sound. Someone was approaching, and the staccato beat of hoofs betrayed speed and urgency. He twisted around to look down the lane.

Countenance grim, Alexander MacKay flew toward them at a hard gallop, coattails flapping wildly behind. He reined the horse to the left as he drew abreast of the buggy, glancing down as he passed. Then he hauled back on the reins so forcefully the horse reared, front hooves slashing the air.

For a moment his gaze rested on Elizabeth,

then his eye met Simon's. "I beg your pardon," he said, the courteous tone belying the lathered condition of his horse and his own windblown appearance. He lifted his cap to Elizabeth. "Mr. Kincaid, is it not? I've watched you work at Pastime, and have concluded you've a fine hand with horseflesh. Mr. Crump, I imagine, is grateful."

"Haven't had any complaints." Simon sat back and waited, his pulse racing in alarm. *Get on with it, Alex!*

"I've just come from town," his fellow operative continued, the brogue thickening. "It seems there's a wee bit of excitement at the Piney Woods." His eyes blazed. "The judge has issued an arrest warrant for one of the guests."

"Maisie Pritchard's murderer?" Simon queried, frowning a little. Why was Alex in such an all-fired hurry? He wouldn't be racing out to Adelaide, risking both their covers, to deliver that particular piece of information.

But Alex was shaking his head. "No." Only the horse's restless sidestepping and swishing tail betrayed the man's tautly reined temper. "They've arrested one . . . Avery Paxton, as the perpetrator and mastermind of the sabotaged bridge over the Flint River, which caused the deaths of forty-nine train passengers this past October."

31

"Everything is proceeding as planned, in spite of the regrettable but fortunately temporary mishap at the jail. I knew I could depend on you."

"Remember that the next time we have a slight disagreement."

"I was not aware of any disagreements, however slight." The icy tone was laced with warning. *"Or is there something you're keeping from me?"*

"Would I keep anything from you?"

For several moments a throbbing silence filled the air.

"Until recently, that question would not even have arisen." The voice changed, became brisk, demanding once again. *"I've heard the rumors concerning the Crump children's companion. Innuendos and insupportable claims, of which denial only breeds further doubt, are contemptible. I want them stopped —"* This time the pause was short, but significant. *"Unless, of course, they are true."*

"Are you asking me to find out if they are?"

"I'm telling you to squelch them . . . if they are not."

The sound of a grandfather clock tolling the

273

hour rang out, and not until the ponderous chimes faded did a response come. "I promise to do whatever is necessary. By the way — I understand that one of the bids for the South Georgia Central has recently been withdrawn. Do you think the Crump System will finally succeed in its quest to control the lines in the western corridor of the state?"

A dry chuckle was the response. "I think it quite likely. Yes, I do think it quite likely."

Chairs scraped, and footsteps echoed on the polished hardwood floorboards. "Until next week, then."

"Until next week. Oh — one other matter. A minor one."

"Yes?"

"The horse trainer . . . Kincaid?"

"Ah, yes . . . Simon Kincaid. He must be dealt with. I can —"

"Do nothing until we discuss it." The swift reprimand was sharp. "Much as you might enjoy it, violence must be controlled, and carefully timed, for maximum benefit."

"All right . . . all right. You make your point, as always." He halted abruptly, his voice accusing. "You know something! I can see it in your face. What is it?"

"Not much. He's been spotted on two different occasions in town, speaking to an unknown man who's staying at the Stuart. I've someone working it, but" — the incomplete sentence hovered in the silence — "until we know who he is, you'll

274

have to wait. As for the companion —"

"The girl is . . . more intelligent than I thought. Also stubborn, even dogmatic. She could be trouble . . . if there's anything to those rumors about her and Kincaid, of course."

"You've been angling for her removal for weeks now. I've told you, we'll do this my way, in the timely fashion that I choose. Now . . . do we understand each other?"

"Perfectly." With a humorless half-laugh, he swiveled on his heel. At the door he turned back. "I understand you, all right, and one day you'll know more about me. And you will listen to me!"

They'd learn, the lot of them. One day — soon — they'd all *learn.*

32

A little before midnight, Eve crept up the stairs to Alexander's room, diligently avoiding the creaking boards. He was waiting for her lightly tapped signal. The door opened immediately, and he yanked her into the room, then into his arms.

"I feel so . . . daring," Eve confessed breathlessly when she could finally speak.

Alexander dropped a last kiss on her nose, then reluctantly set her aside. "Ach, lass, but do you ken what I'm feeling?"

Even after all these months, she still blushed. "I do love you, Alexander Mac-Kay." She hesitated, chewing her lip. "Will you be able to come home soon, do you think? Now that Avery's been arrested?" She looked up into her husband's face, but the dim light of the single lamp he had switched on concealed all but the dark outline of his moustache and the firm, unyielding angle of his jaw. "We could share our first Christmas in our new home . . . together. There's no longer any danger," she persisted, but her husband's silence was unnerving. "Is there? Alexander?"

He cupped her face in his hands. "Lass . . . don't do this. You must know I can't leave yet."

"But I thought . . ." She picked up Alexander's puzzle and toyed with the wooden pieces, trying to sound as calm as he did. "I do realize you'd want to satisfy yourself that Avery is securely jailed, with no bail allowed." One of the puzzle pieces clicked into place. Delighted, Eve held it up with a triumphant smile.

Alexander did not return her smile. Disquiet building, Eve laid the puzzle aside. "You told me that he's more slippery than a boiled egg, and you'd even considered sleeping outside his cell if it wouldn't blow your cover. You told me —"

Suddenly Alexander's fingers were pressing against her lips, stilling the flow of words. With difficulty Eve swallowed a lump in her throat. Cold waves of dread chilled her skin.

"Eve," he spoke gently, "Mr. Jenkins knows how I feel about Paxton." His fingers moved to stroke her cheek, her throat. "Especially after what he cost you and your family. But he also knows how much Simon needs me." A look of wry irony flitted briefly across his face. "What I haven't told you is that it seems there's an outstanding warrant, in Denver, from 1890, when friend Paxton was arrested for forgery, if you can believe it. The Denver office is sending an operative Simon recommended to escort Paxton back there to trial. I've asked Mr. Jenkins if I might go along to make sure the little eel doesn't slip away again. But if I don't go to Denver, I'll have to remain here, to guard Simon's back."

For a brief moment Eve glimpsed his agonizing tug of war — and ducked her head in shame.

When Alexander spoke again, his voice was a heart-catching blend of understanding and tenderness. "Eve . . . this is something I have to do, not because it's a personal vendetta — but because it's my job." His hands closed over her shoulders and pulled her back against him, holding her close.

Safe. She wanted to feel safe, Eve thought, choking back tears. She wanted her *husband* to be safe. But she also wanted to free him so that he could do what he felt was right. Alexander deserved that much — and more — from the woman he had freed both from earthly danger and spiritual oppression.

Alexander continued to rock her back and forth in his arms, while his low voice with its entrancing hint of Scottish brogue murmured in her ear. "Perhaps *job* is too prosaic a word for how I feel, especially with this case. It's more of a need to see justice done at last.

I've been chasing Avery Paxton's shadow for over six years now. I . . . *need* to do this, Eve. There's so much evil in this world, lass, and I guess I somehow feel that God has called me to do what I can, in His name, to protect those who are threatened by that evil."

His breath gusted in a puff of laughter. "I know, and you know, that Pinkerton's National Detective Agency was founded by a shrewd, stubborn Scot who wanted nothing to do with Almighty God. And over the years there have been more than a few cases in which the Lord's providence doubtless would not have rested upon either the villain *or* the Agency. Nonetheless, this is where God placed me, to serve as best I can." His hands tightened on hers. "But lass — my heart, my love — the Agency pales to mist compared to my need for you." Eve felt his lips brush her temple, and his fingers began kneading the tense muscles in her neck and shoulders. "Yet I canna live with my conscience, my Lord, or" — he turned her back around to face him, and his eyes burned into her very soul — "the woman I love more than my life, if I dinna try to do what I know is *right*."

"I understand, Alexander." She stood on tiptoe to brush a trembling kiss at the corner of his mouth. "I can't pretend I like it, because we'll be separated again. But I *do* understand." She hugged him, then moved

279

away, determinedly brightening her tone. "If you do go to Denver, I'll stay here in Thomasville and become Simon's contact. Since everybody here knows me as 'poor Mrs. Sheridan,' I can move about as freely as you. It's the most logical solution to protect Simon until you return."

Alexander closed his eyes and whispered an inaudible phrase which Eve, after a cautious peek at his face, decided was best left untranslated from the Gaelic. He collapsed onto the bed, and for a few moments sat without moving, contemplating his hands, dangling loosely between his legs.

When he finally did look up, goosebumps blossomed on Eve's forearms. "Alexander?" she began, belatedly remembering her husband's obsession with her safety. "With Paxton out of the way at last, there's no risk to me. I told you, I've been careful . . . everyone thinks I'm Mrs. Sheridan, recently widowed —" The words fluttered to a stop.

"Wo Fang." He took one step toward her, blue eyes sizzling, his entire body poised as if he were about to pounce.

"I — beg your pardon?"

"Rufus Black." He advanced another step.

"Alexander, you're making me very uneasy."

"Horatio Crump. James Crump." Eve found herself backing away, but Alexander followed, each step reflecting the same deliberate, ominous beat of his words.

"A greasy blond thug, whereabouts unknown, who wields a vicious blackjack. A trigger-happy gunman, still at large. Two known people — dead."

He stalked Eve until she bumped into the wall. "You've made your point!" she snapped. "Stop baiting me, Alexander." She tried to dart past him, but in a motion so swift her breath caught, Alexander's palms slammed against the wall on either side of her head, and she was trapped.

"You do like to leap into the fire, don't you, lass?" He stared down at her, so close that with each word, his breath stirred red tendrils of hair springing about her temple and forehead.

"Alexander . . ." She couldn't help the quavery, almost frightened note in her voice, even though she was so angry she wanted to kick the shins of her over-protective Scottish warrior of a husband. Still, he *was* right . . . and, with a muffled sob, she threw herself against his chest. "I'm sorry. I guess I wasn't thinking." She rubbed her watering eyes against the soft linen of his shirt. "Will you forgive me?"

"Ach . . ." His arms enfolded her in a crushing embrace. She felt his hand burrowing into her hair, felt pins tumbling to the floor as he urged her head back. His expression was stark. "I love you," he said hoarsely.

281

"I think I'd die if anything happened to you. . . ."

Eve barely had time to whisper back her love before his mouth descended to hers, and then no words were necessary.

33

Elizabeth pulled up in front of the Chicago Candy Company, then turned to the five eager children squirming behind her in the cart. "Now, remember what your mother told you. Christmas is coming, so only two peppermints each, and *only* if you behave —"

"Uncle James says we can do whatever we want to 'cuz we're Crumps," Lamar interrupted, his belligerent tone and childish arrogance mirroring his uncle's attitude.

Elizabeth stepped down and secured the lead line to the hitching post in front of the confectioner's store. "Does that mean you can . . . let's see, now" — she glanced around, then fixed an eye on her five charges — "that you can run out in the middle of Broad Street and play a game of hopscotch?"

" 'Course not! There's too many horses and buggies!" Lamar shot back.

"And bicycles!" Jessica shouted, bouncing up and down in the seat, prompting Thomas to parrot both phrase and action. "We'd be runned down."

"I don't want to play in the street," Ho-Boy began thoughtfully. "If we got hurt, Mama would cry again."

"Hmm." Elizabeth nodded as she began helping the children alight. "But you're Crumps. Don't you think all the horses and buggies and bicycles would stop or go around you?" She arched a brow and reached for Lamar, who refused to take her hand and instead jumped to the ground on his own. His thin face and the light gray eyes, so like his uncle's, reflected both suspicion and doubt.

"Some of them might not be able to," he admitted, staring at the busy street. He considered the matter a moment longer. "Was Uncle James telling a fib?"

At that moment Elizabeth's eye caught on the vaguely familiar figure of a man, propped against a hitching post on the other side of the street. Their gazes met, and he straightened, touching the brim of his bowler. With a jerking motion of his chin, he strolled across the walk to stand in front of Levy's Mercantile, then turned back to Elizabeth — and casually beckoned.

Her breath caught as the memory clicked into place. Benjamin Dawes! What was *he* doing in Thomasville? She hadn't seen the private detective in — was it three years now? — since he'd stomped out of the boardinghouse in Valdosta, where Elizabeth had been staying at the time. It had been Mr. Dawes who'd located William Soames, but when Mr. Soames would agree to meet only with Elizabeth — alone — the detective had refused to work for her any longer. She hadn't seen him since, had assumed, in fact, that he'd gone back to Savannah, where she had first secured his services.

Elizabeth's heart skipped a beat. Perhaps he had discovered more information! Perhaps —

"Elizabeth?" Joan's small hand tugged at her wrist, and Elizabeth belatedly realized she was standing by the cart, as still as a cigar store Indian. "Maybe Uncle James was teasing Lamar."

For a moment Elizabeth was blank. "I — yes, that must be it." She plucked a squirming Thomas from the cart, holding him fast with absentminded skill. "Joan, do you think your mother would mind very much if I treated all of you to ice cream floats at Mr. Hopper's soda fountain, instead of going to the candy store? You may even twirl on the stools if he gives his permission."

A chorus of enthusiastic agreement arose at the prospect, and five minutes later, the children were happily slurping. Elizabeth begged permission from the soda jerk to run a quick errand across the street. "Any way I can help the Crumps, you let me know," he promised, though he carefully avoided Elizabeth's eye.

Last time she'd brought the children in, the young man had smiled, even flirted with her, his manner more than friendly. Elizabeth walled off the burgeoning oppression and hurried across the street.

"Knew you'd seen me," Mr. Dawes grunted when she joined him.

He hadn't changed a bit in the past three years. His rumpled clothing would shame a scarecrow, and the sparse growth of facial hair failed to soften the line of his sharp chin. The gravel-pit drawl still mocked with every word. "Smart move, dumping the kids. Let's go inside, else half the town'll go flapping their gums."

As irascible as ever, too. Elizabeth obediently ducked inside Levy's, her uneasiness growing. "Why should there be any gossip?"

He shrugged, looking her up and down. "Beats me. You seem to have landed on your feet all right . . . considering. Ah . . . I take it Mr. Soames passed along the information you needed?" He fiddled with the faded brim of his hat. "Too bad someone had to go and bash in the back of poor Willy's head. Someone who didn't want him rattling family skeletons, maybe?"

Shaken but not surprised, Elizabeth studied the detective a moment, wondering why he had waited almost three years to question her about that awful day. Down the next aisle, two elderly ladies were fingering a bolt of yard goods in a calico print, while near the back, a clerk showed a selection of neckties to a well-dressed man whose back was turned to Elizabeth and Mr. Dawes.

She took a deep breath, stalling. "That's all in the past, Mr. Dawes. I fail to see what would interest you after all this time."

"We'll just have to see, then, won't we?" He leaned closer. "You're in *another* spot of trouble now — Miss *Granger,* is it? Word hereabouts is that you've been carrying on with Horatio Crump's new trainer. There's even some friendly wagers as to how soon you'll be out on your" — he paused, his bold gaze deliberately raking her figure — "on your own."

"Mr. Dawes, I was hoping you had discovered some useful information for me, which is the *only* reason I acknowledged you in the first place." She picked up a fringed shawl at random, holding it up as if considering making a purchase. "Since you haven't, I must get back. I left five children unattended across the street." A five-year old Lamar could manipulate more skillfully than this unprincipled man. Why hadn't she seen him for what he was three years ago?

She refolded the shawl and turned to him. "You want to blackmail me, don't you? It doesn't matter that we both know I had nothing to do with Mr. Soames's death."

Mr. Dawes was unimpressed by her plain speaking. "The thought occurred to me. But seeing as how you still haven't found the gold, how about if we take up where we left off three years ago instead? Only this time, we'll be *partners*. I'm betting you *did* find those names you were hunting, else you'd not still be hanging round this place, much less toadying to the Crumps under an assumed name."

"What makes you think I haven't found the gold?"

He snorted, scratching his armpit, his gaze turning derisive. "You don't have the gumption to lie *that* good, girlie. I read you real good three years ago, when you were nothing but a big-eyed chit who thought God was always on the side of the virtuous. All full of noble plans, you were, about restoring honor to your family's name. So earnest I had all I could do to keep from laughing in your face. You and I might both know you wouldn't kill an old man, but if you don't care for the rumors percolating about you and that horse man of Crump's . . . wait and see what happens when the word *murder* is tossed in." He waited for the space of two heartbeats. "Especially after the death of a woman who might be alive today if *you'd* been driving that pony cart."

Elizabeth whirled and marched toward the door.

Mr. Dawes reached it first. "You managed to worm your way in with the Crumps through those five brats, but your little nest is about to fall out of the tree," he whispered. "Way I figure it, if you had found that gold, then tried to explain, you'd *still* be out on your ear. Maybe even in prison. Ever see what happens to female prisoners, Miss *Graham?* No? Well, you either climb down off your high horse and deal with me, here and now, or you might just find out. You're not the only one who's been rubbing elbows with the big shots the past few years. . . ."

His coarse words and manner burned beneath her skin, but Elizabeth managed a confident smile. "I'm willing to take my chances!" She pushed past him, through the door and onto the pavement.

"Now that ought to be interesting, with James Crump feeling about you the way he does." The persistent detective followed her across the sidewalk. "Come to think of it, I wonder what the horse trainer will have to say, not to mention all the good folk of Thomasville here. Shall we find out? Why don't I come across the steet with you right now and tell those five children how good it was to run into my old friend Elizabeth *Graham,* whose family used to own most of the land from the Crumps' north border all the way to Albany? Whose mother died in an asylum, crazy as a loon with grief. Not only was her dear husband a liar and a thief, seems he was also carrying on with another woman, right under her nose. You look shocked, Elizabeth. It's common knowledge around these parts — if you know who to talk to and where to look."

He snapped his fingers. "Say, I almost forgot the best part. Maybe you *did* kill William Soames, since it was your thirteen-year-old brother who pulled out a gun one day and —"

"You've made your point." In her mind Elizabeth retreated to a green hillside, where she sat at the feet of the Shepherd, while all around grazed a herd of peaceful sheep. *How do lambs really feel, facing the wide-open jaws of a ravaging wolf?* Right now, all she could feel was a sensation of cold spreading through her limbs, numbing her heart, her ability to do anything other than passively accept. In that moment, she despised herself more than she did Benjamin Dawes. "What do you want me to do?"

The corner of his mouth twitched in satisfaction. His eyes glistened. "Meet me at four o'clock, at" — a sly grin spread — "at Pastime Racetrack. The grandstand will be deserted by then. I'll wait at the top of the bleachers, on the east end. Four o'clock. And, Elizabeth . . . don't keep me waiting."

Dawes sauntered down the street, whistling between his teeth, while a spasm of panic rocked Elizabeth from head to toe. For a moment she was afraid she would be sick on the sidewalk.

Behind her, the two elderly women

emerged with their purchases. One of them glanced sharply at Elizabeth. She managed a weak smile, and they strolled off down the walk.

Which was worse? she thought. A marauding wolf like James Crump . . . or a sly rat like Benjamin Dawes? *There, Elizabeth. Think of Mr. Dawes as nothing more than a beady-eyed rat who skulks in alleys and sewers. He's not a wolf. He's a rat. Even a helpless lamb can run from a rat.*

On the other hand, a woman who stood on the sidewalk woolgathering instead of facing consequences was doubtless no better than — than her mother, who had abandoned her infant daughter and retreated from life, until death released her from her self-imposed prison.

As Elizabeth threaded her way between the crush of buggies, bicycles, and horses to cross the street, she at last faced a bitter reality. Over the years she had allowed her shame — and her pride — to distort her motives and her sense of right and wrong. Changing her name three years ago had seemed the safest course at the time, not so much because she was afraid for her life — but because deceiving the Crumps had also seemed . . . prudent. God Himself had providentially placed her at the Jekyll Island Resort Hotel so she could carry out her mission. Or so she had thought at the time.

Today, Elizabeth acknowledged the depth of her folly. She had been wrong . . . and her miscalculation might very well cost her her life.

◆ ◆ ◆

Alex watched Eve carefully arrange the wig to cover her mass of vivid red curls, his gaze brooding. He didn't know which he hated more: the fact that his wife was masquerading as a widow — or the fact that she was enjoying it immensely. Now she was staring at the mirror over the washstand in his room at the Stuart, lips pursed as she tilted her head first one way, then the other.

"Do you think I'll look like this when I really am older, Alexander? Hopefully I won't be wearing widow's weeds, of course, but — Alexander? You're glaring again." She rose and came over to hug him. "Can you feel the hole you burned in my back?"

Alex obediently put his arms around his wife and began stroking her shoulder, but his movements were perfunctory, and Eve was too attuned to his moods to be deceived. She leaned back, looked up into his face. "Alexander . . . are you worrying over Avery Paxton still — or is it Simon?"

"Some of both," he admitted, and dropped a kiss on her nose. "I'm also a bit . . . boggled . . . that my impulsive wife is enjoying playing at the game of undercover work far too much."

"I'm not playing!" He had to smile at her indignation, but the guilty flush betrayed the accuracy of his observation. "Well . . . all right, perhaps I am enjoying it more than I should, but I have helped, haven't I?"

Alexander had never been able to resist her when those great brown doe-eyes looked at him with such uncertainty. For all her seeming confidence, his Eve harbored deep pools of insecurity. "Aye, love. In spite of wearing me down with worry, you have been of help, especially where Elizabeth is concerned."

"Oh — that reminds me. I saw her while I was out a while ago. She looked a little peculiar, but she was talking to a disheveled little man who —"

Alex grabbed her shoulders so forcefully Eve winced. Instantly he softened his grip, but his words burst forth, betraying his alarm. "Where? When? Did you overhear anything? Lass — tell me now, and quickly."

"Alexander, what is it?" She bit her lip. "I suppose I should have told you as soon as I came in. But so many people speak to her, and I don't know any of them . . . though I try to describe them to you. . . ."

The muffled words reeked of apology. Alex curbed his temper with an effort. She lifted her head. "Today, I *did* notice that more people avoided her. Mrs. Endicott — that's who I was with in Levy's Mercantile — told me that Josephine is so mortified by it all that

Horatio's going to —"

"Eve! Tell me about the man."

"Oh. Well, Elizabeth came into the store with him, and they stood there talking for several moments. He was wearing a wrinkled suit, soiled bowtie, held a bowler in his hands. Narrow face, scraggly beard, and no moustache. Beady eyes. Elizabeth looked at a paisley shawl, but she didn't buy anything. Then they left. Alexander, what's wrong?"

He held her close, thanking God for his wife's powers of observation. Then he gently put her aside. "I have to find Simon, lass. I want you to stay here, in the hotel, until I return. Eve? Promise me?"

She searched his face, but after an endless moment, lifted a soft hand to his cheek. "All right, Alexander." Her voice was full of love, of understanding. "I'll wait for you to tell me what you can, when you can."

Alex closed his eyes, shoulders sagging in relief. Then he kissed her hard, once, and turned to go. "Don't let anyone see you leave my room, remember."

"Yes, Alexander. Of course."

He barely heard, his mind already focused on his unpleasant task. Not only must he locate Simon discreetly, and soon — but he must warn him that Elizabeth might be in cahoots with the Crumps, after all.

The previous afternoon, when Alex had been nosing around Rose Hill — Georgina

Crump's plantation — a man driving a one-horse gig had pulled up at the front door of the main house and had disappeared inside. Alex had hung around. An hour later, when the man left, Alex had been able to fix his image firmly in mind.

His appearance matched perfectly the man Eve had just described.

34

Adelaide

Simon was working a filly on the longe line in the large paddock when Elizabeth slipped up to the fence. Silent as one of the posts, she watched him, and after a nod of acknowledgment, Simon continued putting the sorrel through her paces — until he caught a glimpse of Elizabeth's stricken face.

He brought Meadowlark to a halt, unclipped the line, then released her inside the paddock. "What's the matter?" he asked sharply, striding across the ring. His gaze moved over Elizabeth in a comprehensive sweep. Frowning, he coiled the longe line around the post and ducked beneath the rails.

Still she stood there, looking aloof, regal — and terrified. Her ungloved hands were clenched so tightly the knuckles protruded in sharp relief.

By now, Simon knew what to do. Propping himself against the fence, he crossed his ankles, and waited.

"I . . . you said I could —" she faltered,

and closed her eyes.

Patient as a stalking cougar, he merely inclined his head.

"I didn't know if you meant —"

"I meant it," he finally interrupted, straightening. "Miss Granger . . . Elizabeth . . . we're going to stroll over to that old pine bench under the trees there. Collect your thoughts, then we'll talk." He took her arm, freshly astonished by her refined elegance and the fragility of her diminutive frame. "Easy . . ." His hold tightened when she stumbled, and the elusive fragrance of violets wafted to his nostrils.

They sat down on the crude bench, and Simon turned to Elizabeth. In the early afternoon light, her skin appeared gray. Beads of perspiration dampened her temples and upper lip. Above the pristine collar of her shirtwaist, the pulse in her throat fluttered visibly.

Simon could no more restrain the impulse than he could have ignored the cries of the injured dog in the alley behind that restaurant. "Elizabeth." He plucked one small fist from her lap and held it between both his hands. Her fingers were cold, clammy. "This is getting to be a habit," he observed mildly.

Her lashes blinked once as she looked up at him. "I shouldn't have come," she whispered. "But I didn't know what else to do. Where to turn. Even when I was thirteen, and Grandpapa sent me away, I —" She clamped her lips together and drew a deep, shuddering breath.

After a moment or two, Simon lightly squeezed her hand, then ran his thumb over the mottled knuckles. "What has James done to you this time?" he prompted.

He was completely baffled when she laughed. Her free hand trapped the sound almost immediately, but Simon realized that, for all her self-possession, Elizabeth Granger was dangerously near collapse. "It's all right," he soothed her, gentling her as he would a frightened horse. "I won't let him hurt you, Elizabeth. Trust me." Further comforting words abruptly caught in his throat. *If Elizabeth had broken the law, he was honor bound to see justice done.*

Unbidden, a subconscious prayer erupted from the deep, long-neglected sanctuary of his spirit. *God . . . help me. Please.*

Still distraught, Elizabeth remained oblivious to his turmoil. "I don't know why," she began haltingly, "but for some reason I *do* trust you, Mr. Kincaid. At least, I think I do." The soft words seared Simon like a branding iron. "I've never trusted anyone before, you see, other than my grandfather. Even then, it wasn't the same. . . ." Beneath his hand her fingers jerked, then stilled. "But ever since you saved my life — that day in the river — it seems you've always been here, when I . . . when I needed you — someone — the most."

"It won't amount to much if you still won't tell me what devils are hounding you now," he returned, his tone a shade rougher than necessary.

She sighed, shook her head wearily. "I'm sorry. There's nothing more frustrating than a babbling female, is there?"

His brows shot up, and he actually felt the muscles in his jaw relaxing. *She's recovered. Thank . . . God.* "How about one who speaks in riddles and conundrums?"

"One who weeps every hour on the hour?" Her stiff, chilled fingers stirred, warming to life.

"One who never does what she's told," Simon countered. "Or never does it *when* she's told to."

"Mr. Kincaid, it has occurred to me more than once that *you* can be even *more* frustrating." She almost smiled, then seemed to realize for the first time that Simon was holding her hand. "Oh! You . . . we're —" Delicate rose pinked her cheeks.

"Yes," Simon confirmed. "But don't worry. Meadowlark over there promised not to tell."

Elizabeth tugged at her hand, and Simon released it. Shakily she smoothed down her skirts, patted her hair, touched the delicate locket. "Mr. Kincaid, I do believe you're one of the most understanding, perceptive people I've ever known."

"Since I did save your life, and we've held hands . . . do you think you might call me 'Simon'?"

The blush deepened. "All right — *Simon*. How can I thank you for —"

"Now don't go hanging that halo over my head."

This time her smile was completely natural. "I wouldn't dream of it. I'll let the Lord supply your halo and wings." She took a final deep breath, shifted a little, and lifted her chin. "In fact, what I'm about to tell you now is liable to make you quite angry." The smile vanished, and for the blink of an eye, desperation clouded her features again. "I'll understand if you refuse to involve yourself further."

"Elizabeth. It's time. No more evasion." His voice, still soft, was laced with warning.

"Very well. My name isn't Granger. It's *Graham*. Elizabeth Graham. . . ." She paused, then plunged ahead. "A little over thirty years ago — right before the War ended — my father sold some cotton to the Yankees. Six months or so after Appomattox, he told his two partners that the Yankees had refused to pay the $250,000 in gold they promised, that it was a doublecross — nothing more than they should have expected from — well, from Yankees. Only it wasn't the *Yankees* who had reneged — it was my father. He stole the gold and buried it, but nobody

300

knows where. Everyone believed his story until he . . . died five years later, and a receipt for the gold was discovered among his papers. . . ."

Simon didn't move, didn't speak. Many explanations for Elizabeth's complex personality had been racing through his brain, but hiding behind a false surname had *not* numbered among them. He waited for her to finish.

"I — our family was devastated by the scandal. I was only a year old and never knew either of my parents, or my . . . brothers. I was sent to live with relatives and passed around like some stray animal." Her gaze wandered to Meadowlark, cantering playfully about the paddock. "I found out about my father six years ago . . . from my grandfather. He made me promise to finish my schooling, and I did. But I also vowed that one day I would find that gold, no matter how long it took. You see, I want to restore the rightful portion to my father's two partners — or their families — to try and right a thirty-year wrong."

The blue eyes darkened and her voice dropped to a hoarse whisper. "One of those partners was Horatio Crump, Sr."

"No wonder you changed your name," Simon muttered, stunned. He studied her upturned face, the deep pools of her eyes full of shadows and secrets. Secrets, Simon realized furiously, that could get him killed. If he did his job as an operative, he'd put as much distance between himself and Elizabeth Granger — *Graham* as possible. And quick!

Better yet, he mused, twisting the knife in his belly further, he could turn her over to the Crumps and expose her in a last-ditch effort to ingratiate himself. *That would do it, Smoke — finish her off. Blow into her life and out again . . . like everybody else.* What could matter more than securing incontrovertible proof that the Crumps were a nest of pit vipers in need of extermination? What was one more not-so-innocent victim?

Without warning, Elizabeth stood. "I knew you'd be angry." She gathered her skirts and fled toward the woods.

Simon caught up in three swift, silent strides, blocking her way. She was forced to stop, or run right into him. "No, you don't," he growled. He opened his mouth with the intention of breaking her, of battering down *all* of those infernal protective walls with the merciless detachment for which he was famous. Instead, surprising even himself, he reached out, drew her into his arms, and covered her mouth with his own.

At his touch, Elizabeth had gone rigid, still except for the sound of her fractured breaths and her skittering pulse. But when he kissed her, she exploded in a flurry of thrashing arms and desperate twisting and turning.

There were any number of ways Simon

could have effectively subdued her, but in the last span of seconds, he had learned something about himself that illuminated his soul for all eternity. Jerking his head aside to avoid the worst of her blows, he let her struggle in impotent fury until, with an exhausted shudder, she went limp.

"I'm not going to hurt you, Elizabeth," he promised, his throat aching. "I'm not going to hurt you."

"Then let me go!"

"I can't do that."

The last of the fight drained from her body. Simon tucked her closer and pressed a conciliatory kiss to her forehead. He drew back a little to explain, but before he opened his mouth, Elizabeth began to speak.

"I'm sorry . . . I'll leave." The husky contralto voice was now stripped of life. "Just don't be angry at me. Don't . . . yell. Don't —"

He gently covered her mouth with his palm. "Be still. Hush, Elizabeth, and just be still. I won't shout at you." He paused, head spinning with confusion — and resolution. His gaze burned into hers. "But I can't promise not to kiss you again. Will that make you run away, too?"

She blinked once, twice, and the choking sensation in his throat eased as awareness washed into her eyes. Awareness, bewilderment — and the unexpected flash of humor that never failed to surprise him.

"I don't know," she whispered. Then, in a nearly normal voice, she confessed, "I bit the first boy who tried to kiss me . . . when I was twelve. And I slapped the only man —"

"Well, you didn't bite me. Do you want to slap me?" Simon dropped his arms, stepped back, and spread his hands. "Go ahead. I deserve it." What he really deserved was to be drawn and quartered. He watched her, the strange feeling expanding inside his chest, painful, exhilirating . . . uncontrollable. "But don't run. Don't run from me again, Elizabeth."

She searched his face. "Why did you kiss me?"

He answered her honestly. "Because I couldn't help myself."

"But . . . you were angry. You felt deceived, betrayed. You *were* angry — I could see it in your face."

So much for hiding his feelings. There was only one other person on the face of the earth to whom Simon had ever felt this nakedly exposed. "I can't deny that," he agreed, very quietly. "But when you were in my arms — all I wanted to do was hold you and kiss you."

He hesitated. Then, his gaze steady on Elizabeth, he allowed another human being to glimpse the inside of his soul for the first time since he was seventeen years old. "When I saved your life, that day in the river —

something happened. You'd probably call it God. Once, I would have agreed. I don't know anymore. But whatever it is, it keeps growing stronger. We're bound in some way, Elizabeth Granger or Graham or whoever you are." He lapsed into silence, then extended his right hand — palm up — toward her. "Take my hand, Elizabeth. Whatever happens, I promise to keep you safe."

He stood there, each heartbeat a hammer blow of pain, until her hand fluttered at her side, then slowly lifted. It hung, suspended in midair, as if she were debating whether to reach out — or run. Simon couldn't tear his eyes away from her hand. But when she spoke, that tantalizing thread of humor tugged his gaze back to her face. "If I do," she asked, "will that mean I'm granting permission for you to kiss me again?"

"What would you do if I said yes?"

For a moment fear turned the blue eyes the color of spilled ink. Then she exhaled in a tremulous puff — and placed her hand in Simon's.

35

Thomasville

Wo Fang climbed the steps leading to the Thomasville jail. It took several moments to persuade the authorities to let him in, but even the burly guards and deputies were no match for Wo Fang's determination.

"What took you so long?" Mr. Paxton exploded the instant Wo Fang appeared.

The giant Oriental dropped his gaze to the floor to avoid gaping at the sight of his employer. His favorite suit, tailored by a London haberdasher, was creased and rumpled; his silk cravat dangled inside his soiled shirt, from which the collar was missing. There was no sign of his diamond stickpin, his pocket watch, or the tiger's-eye ring.

"Get me out of here, Fang!" he screamed. "I don't care what you have to do! Just get me out of here!" He shook the cell door in frenzied rage.

Wo Fang kept his head discreetly lowered. "I regret to say that will not be possible, Mr. Paxton. I have been informed that you are to be held without bail."

"Impossible! You're lying, you worthless coolie!"

Wo Fang inwardly winced. "A thousand apologies, Mr. Paxton, but I regret very much that there is little I can do."

"You're fired! Go on, get out of here! Go back to that rat-infested sweatshop where I found you! Get out of my sight. I don't ever want to see you again!"

He paused, panting, and Wo Fang risked one swift upward glance. His employer's tirade had brought the other prisoners to their feet, and an ominous rumble began, punctuated by the banging of bars. He stepped up to Paxton's cell, carefully concealing all trace of emotion. "There is a Pinkerton operative on the way from Denver, with orders to take you back there. Even if I could secure your release from this jail — you would not be able to escape —" He paused. "Perhaps, if you agreed to negotiate with the Crumps? It is *their* influence, after all, that is keeping you here."

"I'll see them — and you — in the blackest pit of hell before I bow and scrape to *anyone!*" He swiveled on his heel, his back to Wo Fang. "I told you to go away. Your presence offends me."

"Very well. I have arranged with the hotel to deliver your meals, and —"

"I don't want *you* to arrange anything, ever again. You're fired, Wo Fang. Remove yourself from my sight, permanently. If you do

307

not . . ." The unfinished threat hovered between them. He whirled back around, pressed his face against the bars, eyes glazed with hatred, and hissed, "I'll see to it that not only the police but the *Pinks* as well find out who murdered Abe Collins."

Wo Fang bowed deeply. "Then I will not trouble you again." In the past year his employer had threatened to fire him many times. This time, there was no question that Mr. Paxton would no longer require his services.

He left the jail with dignity, with each step feeling as if links from a heavy chain were falling away from his feet. Outside, he lifted his face, breathing deeply of the fresh air. A colorless sky and thin winter sunlight did nothing to dim the lightness spreading within. Released at last from the burden of an onerous debt, he was free to walk whatever road he chose.

Wo Fang reflected as he strolled along the street. He would petition whatever gods there might be for an opportunity to live a more worthy life. Father Mullaney would have explained it as the yearning for redemption. For reconciliation with his Creator. Wo Fang had never understood the concept of a single personal God, but in serving Avery Paxton, he *had* come to know the subtle entrapment of serving evil, as well as its inevitable destruction.

His path eventually brought him to the

park across the street from the Piney Woods Hotel. *Yankee Paradise*, Mr. Paxton had called it. Ignoring the doubletakes and gaping stares, Wo Fang made his way along the crowded, yet peaceful, paths.

Every culture created its own version of "Paradise," he had learned. Though this dignified stretch of land was inhabited primarily by Caucasians and coloreds, he found himself hoping that there would be a small secluded spot where a lonely Japanese warrior could at last seek his *own* paradise. A place where he could decide how best to atone for the criminal acts he had committed out of obligation and duty.

♦ ♦ ♦

Adelaide

Elizabeth stood at her bedroom window, watching Josephine playing with the children on the back lawn below. They were engaged in a lively game of croquet, their joy in their mother's presence almost painful to behold.

Earlier, Josephine, her plump face clouded with concern, had been waiting when Elizabeth and the children returned from Thomasville. "I'll take them now," she had told Elizabeth. "It's past time for the children to rely on their mother again, don't you agree?"

Only Joan had hung back. "Elizabeth doesn't feel well," she announced, slipping her hand inside Elizabeth's. "She wouldn't eat *any* ice cream, and she didn't say a word all the way home."

Josephine's face had flushed a deep red. "Then the best way to help her is to allow her to rest, alone in her bedroom. Come along, Joan."

Elizabeth wondered now what would have happened if she *had* retired to her bedroom, instead of slipping out the kitchen door to seek out Mr. Kincaid. Lost in thought, she rested her forehead against the cool satin drapes. The memory of his touch, his *kiss*, enfolded her as softly as the drapery. She felt . . . restless, as though she were standing on a precipice, with Simon at her back. His arms were outstretched — to keep her from falling . . . or to push her over the edge?

A lonely meow floated across the room and, seconds later, Sam wandered in from the open door to the window where Elizabeth stood daydreaming. Loudly purring, he stropped himself against her skirts, then rubbed his face on the toe of one house slipper.

"I know how you feel, you spoiled old pussycat, you." Elizabeth leaned over and scooped up the animal, cuddling him like a baby. "Life can be pretty lonely, can't it? Especially when your loved ones are ignoring you. And yet . . ." *Simon.*

"Simon." She tried the name aloud, rubbing her cheek against Sam's fur, hearing the rasping purr in her ear. Hearing in her heart the sound of Simon's deep voice and the intoxicating undercurrent of humor when he'd asked her to call him by his Christian name. "Simon . . ."

There had been no smile on his face. "What do you think, Sam?" she murmured, remembering. "The more I chew on it, the more I realize that I've not seen him smile at all." She wondered why, but Sam, boneless and contented, offered little insight into the enigma of the man who consumed an alarming portion of Elizabeth's thoughts.

On the lawn below, Lamar screeched a loud protest, and Ho-Boy shouted back. Elizabeth glanced down, her heart lurching. Josephine admonished her two sons with loving firmness, cuddled a whimpering Thomas, and offered a conspiratorial smile to Joan and Jessica. *They don't need me anymore, do they, Lord? Neither Josephine nor the children.*

She turned away from the window, the random thoughts flitting through her aching head like a swarm of fireflies. The Crumps. Her father and the gold. Benjamin Dawes. And brighter than all the others — Simon. *Simon.*

Why did her heart leap whenever she saw him? Why did she feel so safe when she was with him, in spite of the aura of danger that always swirled about him? *We're bound,* he

311

had told her. *When I saved your life, that day in the river — something happened. You'd probably call it God.*

"You can see that I'm confused, Lord," she confessed aloud. "But I can't help it." She could still feel the powerful surge of roiling emotions Simon had imparted in the single kiss — passion, anger, an aching tenderness, a yearning so poignant it . . . burned all the way to her soul.

But could she really trust him?

"I'll take care of Benjamin Dawes," he had promised an hour ago, his voice and face hard and unyielding as Georgia clay. "At four o'clock, he'll have his meeting — but it will be with *me* instead of you. You stay here, preferably hidden away in your room where you'll be safe. I'll" — he'd hesitated, then added dryly — "I'll put the fear of God into Mr. Benjamin Dawes."

Still holding the now dozing cat, Elizabeth dropped down into the chair, kicked off her slippers, and tucked her feet beneath her, then settled Sam in her lap. Simon had muttered something else, something about his "being good at instilling fear, at least." Elizabeth leaned her head against the back of the chair and closed her eyes, one hand idly stroking Sam's twitching tail.

Simon . . . He had sounded so . . . miserable — an intense, dangerous man, trapped by the dark side of his personality. It was as if he were blind to his own tenderness, and Elizabeth realized in surprise how much she wanted to help him discover it.

The musical clock on the bureau began to play. Elizabeth sat up, heaving a sigh. Five o'clock. Way past time for sitting about as if she had nothing better to do than dream foolish dreams. "Sorry, lovey. Naptime's over." She deposited a groggy Sam on the rug, shaking her head when the amiable beast stuck out a graceful hind leg and began to wash.

"Very well. Go ahead. Indulge in your evening ablutions while I pack." She stood, stretched, then began the tedious process of packing her possessions. Regardless of her feelings toward Simon or his toward her, Elizabeth was under no illusion as to how matters stood with the *Crumps*. Doubtless her notice of dismissal would be left folded and tucked beneath her dinner plate, so averse to her presence had they become. At least Sam still enjoyed her company, although she knew he wouldn't notice once she was gone.

With the wages she had accumulated in the past year, she could afford to stay in a boardinghouse in Ochlocknee, perhaps even until spring. Her excursion there earlier had yielded nothing concerning "Mrs. H's" boardinghouse, and large chestnut trees abounded. The gold could be buried under any one of them . . . or none of them. Nonetheless, the town was still the best clue Elizabeth had unearthed, so she might as well hang her hat there for a while. As for the *rest* of her life . . .

She squelched thoughts of the future and the frightening uncertainty of her emotions. With a rueful smile, she quoted to herself Jesus' admonition to His followers — one about daily troubles and struggles and the evil thereof — and fixed firmly in her mind the image of peaceful sheep guarded by a watchful, loving Shepherd.

36

Pastime Racetrack

At four o'clock, shadows were already lengthening, and a light breeze had chilled the mild December afternoon. Simon dismounted several hundred yards from the grandstand where Elizabeth was to meet Benjamin Dawes and slipped into the woods behind the racetrack.

A lone horse had been tied on the eastern side of the stands. Simon easily picked out the figure of a man, perched at the top of the bleachers, under the eaves. If Dawes had been a halfway respectable detective instead of a blackmailing slug, he'd know better than to smoke when arranging a clandestine meeting.

Simon pulled the brim of his hat lower, took several calming breaths, then held out his black-gloved hands. The tremor had finally subsided, leaving in its place a deep, coiled violence, ruthlessly controlled. He blocked all thoughts, all memories of Elizabeth from his mind. It was the only way he'd be able to verify the truth of Alexander's claim.

An hour earlier, the other operative had intercepted Simon at one of their checkpoint sites; Simon knew the news would be bad, because the farthermost corner of the Episcopal churchyard was one of the few places they left only *written* messages. Face-to-face meetings were held elsewhere, under cover of darkness.

"What's up?" Simon asked, automatically scanning their surroundings. "I don't have much time."

"This won't take long — but you're not going to like it, lad." Beneath the moustache, Alex's mouth was a thin slash.

"I didn't think I would."

"Simon . . . Eve spotted Elizabeth earlier today, talking to a man."

"She talks to half the population of Thomasville, a lot of them male," Simon retorted, his voice clipped. "Alex, you know my feelings about your wife playing at —"

"*This* man was at Rose Hill for over an hour yesterday afternoon. I was out there, scouting around, and Eve's description of the man with Elizabeth matched this bloke to a T. Simon . . ." He lifted his hand, then let it drop. "I thought you needed to know as soon as possible," he finished lamely. "Simon . . . it doesn't have to mean —"

"I'll find out for myself what it means," he interrupted shortly. "I'm meeting the man at Pastime at four. Elizabeth claims he's a private detective she hired three years ago."

Beneath the trees, Simon flexed his shoulders and neck, then stepped into the stubbly field behind the grandstand. Regardless of what Dawes planned for Elizabeth, it was his connection with the Crumps that *must* command Simon's full attention. The greasy flatfoot had just become Pinkerton's best lead in two years, and Simon wasn't about to waste the opportunity.

Elizabeth . . . .

Dawes didn't spot Simon until he was halfway up the bleachers. The other man stiffened, threw aside his smoldering cigar, and wiped a hand over his mouth. Ten paces from the top, Simon saw a flicker of recognition in Dawes's countenance, and spared a mental shrug of regret. Anonymity had been a long shot anyway.

He didn't stop until they were at eye level. "Benjamin Dawes?"

Flat brown eyes surveyed him in silence. "So. All the rumors about the two of you are true, after all."

"Are you Benjamin Dawes?" Simon repeated with the exact inflection he'd used the first time. He took one step closer.

"What's it to you?" The man glanced down, took one shuffling step sideways, then glared at Simon. "All right . . . so I'm Dawes." Abruptly he swore, the weasel face flooding with color. "She told you, didn't she? And like a fool, you fell for her tragic eyes and tale of woe."

Simon folded his arms across his chest to keep from wrapping them around Benjamin Dawes's throat. Something must have warned the sputtering detective, for his tactic and voice abruptly changed. "Listen to me — Kincaid, isn't it? She's lying to you. Her whole family is rotten with lies, treachery, and deceit."

Simon didn't move. He merely lifted an eyebrow — and waited.

"Whatever she told you about me and her — don't believe it. She's trying to save her skin." The whining voice dropped lower. "She spins a good yarn, I'll give her that. Had me going for a while, 'til I learned she doesn't know the meaning of the word *truth*." He leaned forward. "For instance, I'd wager she *hasn't* told you she's about to be sacked, has she? And I bet she hasn't told you her real name, or that her old man was a no-good, cheating scoundrel."

"She told me," Simon inserted with deadly lack of emphasis, "that you were trying to blackmail her."

Dawes snorted. "Doesn't surprise me at all. I'm the only one who knows all her dirty secrets. But I wasn't after blackmail, Kincaid. I'd be slitting my own throat professionally. I'm a private detective — did she mention that? She hired me three years ago."

318

"She told me."

"Did she mention . . . why she hired me?"

Simon didn't respond.

Looking miffed, Dawes shrugged, stuffing his hands in his pockets. "Look . . . I don't know what's going on between the two of you, but you look to be a solid enough fellow, so I'll be straight with you. Sort of feel like it's my Christian duty and all. She . . . ah . . . hired me — then she fired me, so I reckon I'm not violating any rules." He paused again, plainly waiting for some kind of reaction from Simon.

After a moment, Simon dropped down onto one of the bleachers, pulled out his penknife, and began to clean his nails with the blade.

Dawes broke in less than a minute. "All right, you —" He called Simon a name which, under normal circumstances, would have earned swift retribution, but Simon's eyelids didn't so much as flicker.

"I don't know what game you're playing here, but don't think you can intimidate me. If you're smart, you'll drop that conniving bit of goods, then try to keep yourself in the Crumps' good graces. If you don't, you'll be out on your ear, same as *her*. She's trying to pull a doublecross, just like her old man. And if you're dumb enough to believe her lies, getting sacked'll be the least of your worries, seeing as how you'll likely end up like William Soames."

Simon froze. "William Soames?" he repeated carefully. Every drop of blood seemed to crystallize. Until that moment, he'd ignored most of Benjamin Dawes's vitriolic spewing, because he'd as soon trust a *Crump* as to trust this sleazy character. But now. . . . "What do you know about William Soames?"

Their gazes met. Dawes gaped, then scuttled backward. "Keep your mitts off me!" he snarled.

"I wouldn't dirty my hands with the likes of you." Simon stood in a single fluid motion, jamming his hands in his pockets. If he didn't, he might be tempted to pitch Dawes over the railing. "Soames?" he prompted with silky menace, his patience at an end.

"Miss . . . uh . . . Gra—"

"I know her last name. Use it."

Dawes grabbed hold of the top rail, his expression riddled with sullenness and fear. "She met him here, three years ago, in the stable. I arranged it, but the old codger was a wily fox — wouldn't give me the time of day. So Miss . . . Graham . . . came alone. And Soames wound up dead."

A look of malicious satisfaction shot through Dawes's eyes when Simon could not conceal his shock. "Be careful, Kincaid. I'm not saying she did the deed herself, mind you — but then, maybe she *did*." He smiled a crocodile smile, revealing uneven yellow teeth.

"After all, her thirteen-year-old brother didn't have a problem putting a bullet through their old man. Shot him right through the heart, he did, just because he was playing pat-a-cake with another woman right under his wife's nose. Who'd have thought it, eh?"

Stone-faced, Simon waited. "Are you finished?" he finally inquired.

Dawes nodded warily.

Simon's gaze never left the other man. "Good. Now *you* listen to *me*. If I catch you within a city block of Elizabeth *Granger*, I'll assume you're tired of the way you look. And if I hear that you even speak her name out loud in less than a complimentary fashion, I'll further assume that you're tired of living in the state of Georgia. Are you following me, Dawes?"

"I hear you fine, but you're still kissin' kin to a donkey if you believe that girl's telling you the truth." He glanced longingly toward the ground below, then sidled down, fingers still wrapped around the railing. "I'll keep my trap shut about it, though. That good enough for you?"

Don't let him set you off, Kincaid. Just . . . don't. "Before we part company, Mr. Dawes, there *is* one other piece of information you can share." He waited until Dawes was wound up tighter than a buggy spring. "You can tell me what you were doing out at Rose Hill yesterday afternoon."

37

"If you make another mistake, I'll see to it that you rot in a stinking jail cell for the rest of your life."

"I didn't make no mistake. *You* supplied the information, and I did the job all neat and tidy-like. Ain't my fault there's lots of women what fit that description. So don't go blaming me now. Just pay me what you said, and we'll call it quits."

"I'll do a lot more than *blame* you, if you take that tone of voice with me again. And I'll pay you when you've earned it."

"You think you can do anything." Rufus's voice was sullen. He slid a glance across to the other man, wiped the back of his hand across his mouth, and stuffed his hands in his britches. "Why'd you get me outta jail, all up-front and legal-like, then? You want me to finish the job on that little gal or what?"

"Not . . . exactly."

The look on Crump's face gave Rufus the heebie-jeebies. He wished he could high-tail it out of the state and disappear. Crump had told the sheriff some fancy story 'bout Rufus being an employee and how Crump was willing to let bygones be bygones. But then he'd told Rufus they were taking the Tallahassee stage, and ordered him to come along and keep his mouth shut. Like a blamed fool Rufus had stuck around. This was a *Crump*. A body didn't just walk away when a Crump spoke up, and besides — he wanted his hundred dollars.

But they hadn't come to Tallahassee. When the stage stopped at a way-station down the road a bit, he and Crump had gotten off, mounted a pair of horses, and ridden into the woods. Crump might know where in tarnation they were — but Rufus was plumb lost.

"I've . . . made adjustments in my plans to compensate for your mistake," James was saying, still carrying on as though the Pritchard female's death was Rufus's fault. "Already results are falling into place." He flicked a piece of lint off the lapel of his fancy coat. "Even my sister-in-law's loyalty is wavering toward her children's companion . . . yes, everything will fit together nicely." His gaze trapped Rufus in a demonic stare. "And that brings us to *you*, Mr. Black."

"Whaddaya mean?" Rufus stepped back.

"This time, I need you to do a spot of kidnapping. I'll see that the . . . ah . . . 'little gal' is blamed, and that should tie up the loose ends very nicely." He lit up a hand-rolled cigar. "Even *better* than killing her off . . ."

"Kidnapping, huh? I don't know as I care to have any truck with a job like that." Rufus shook his head, backing away even further. "No sir, you find yourself some other poor sucker. Abduction ain't my line — way too risky. I ain't after sticking *my* head in no noose."

"You'll end up with your neck in a noose anyway, when I drop a few hints to the Pinks about the man who murdered Maisie Pritchard. And after I was so magnanimous, so charitable as to arrange for you to be set free, when all the while you were a cold-blooded killer of women. They'll hunt you down and have your head on a platter, Mr. Black. You might fancy yourself wily enough to double-cross me like you did Paxton — but you can't run far enough, or long enough, to escape from me." He paused, then added, "Or Pinkerton's."

"I can tell them Pinks a thing or two myself, about *you,* same's I did 'bout Paxton. He's in the calaboose now, thanks to me."

Crump laughed contemptuously. "The Pinks have been chasing Paxton for years. All they needed was concrete evidence — which *I* arranged for. You are nothing but a useful tool whose word holds up only because the authorities *wanted* to nail Paxton." His gaze raked Rufus from head to toe as though Rufus were a bug to be squashed. "Go ahead. Tell them what you dare about me. Who do you think they'll believe — a no-name hooligan . . . or a Crump?" He paused again, then added softly, "I'll pay you more, Rufus. Five hundred?"

He hunched his shoulders. "Who you want kidnapped, then?"

"A girl. Name's Joan. She's only eight, so quit your bellyaching. The job will be easy as plucking a ripe pear off the tree. Even a man of *your* limited imagination won't have any problem. Next time, I'll give you all the information. There's enough food in this old shack to keep you a couple of days, so you won't starve. And, Mr. Black? Think about running all you want — but don't delude yourself by thinking you can escape. If you try, the next place you'll be won't even be a scaffold. I'll hang you myself from the nearest tree, and leave your carcass for the vultures."

♦ ♦ ♦

Rose Hill
December 23, 1895

The unkempt detective ambled across her finest Aubusson carpet, no doubt leaving stains with every step of his disreputable-looking shoes. He looked, Georgina Crump decided in distaste, like a muddy hound who had successfully treed its quarry.

"I trust the smirk is an indication of good news," she remarked, carefully folding the week's telegrams into a neat stack.

325

"Your son spends most of his time hobnobbing at Glen Arven with the country club set, or visiting saloons. Sans Souci and Woodbine were the two night before last. But yesterday morning after he arranged for Rufus Black's release, the pair of them took the Tallahassee stage, and I couldn't follow without being spotted. Maybe he did us *both* a favor, since I wound up with a lead that turned out to be of considerable interest."

James had received her permission to secure Black's release, *not* accompany the ruffian on some rattle-trap public conveyance. Georgina hid her dismay. But while she was highly provoked with James for his behavior, she had nothing but contempt for low-life human beings who actually enjoyed spying on others. Especially when they became overly familiar in their manner. "I've told you before that I dislike guessing games, Mr. Dawes. I dislike even more the necessity which compels me to monitor my younger son's activities."

She opened her desk, slid the telegrams inside, then shut it with an emphatic snap. "But my family *must* be cared for, regardless of the unpleasant nature of the task." Her head lifted and she fixed an unswerving eye upon the abruptly still figure of Benjamin Dawes. "*Family,* Mr. Dawes — not paid informants. Do I make myself clear?"

"You make yourself perfectly clear, Miz

Crump. Yes, ma'am, you surely do. And since you're so fond of plain speaking, I'll point out a couple of things *you* haven't seemed to realize."

The upstart sauntered forward and planted his chapped hands on the desk, leaning over until his blue-veined nose was only inches from hers. "Number one — I've enough evidence, tucked away in places you'll never find, to blacken your precious family name in the eyes of every decent person within a hundred miles of here."

"Move away from me *at once*," Georgina ordered, her lips barely moving. How *dare* this — this *cretin* presume to threaten her!

A muscle jumped in Dawes's cheek and, for a crackling moment longer, he continued to challenge Georgina. Then, with a mocking bow, he wandered back across the room, stuffing his hands in his pockets. "The second piece of information *was* going to be a . . . gift. My way of reassuring you of my loyalty toward a long-term client?" He turned around, standing there as smug as a toad. "Now I might change my mind, being of such low esteem in your eyes, and all."

Georgina studied Benjamin Dawes in icy silence. "How much?" she asked finally, unwilling to completely disguise her curiosity.

"Not money." He shook his head. "Not money this time, Miz Crump. Just your signature on a piece of paper. It will need to say two things."

"One of which," Georgina interrupted acidly, "will include my personal guarantee of your continued . . . health and prosperity, I presume?"

"Neither of us is a fool," Dawes agreed with another supercilious smirk. "But it's the second which should really interest you." He paused for effect. "I'd like a twenty-five percent share of the $250,000 in gold I help a Miss Elizabeth Graham unearth, which her father stole back during the War. Oh yes — I think you know the young . . . lady . . . by another name — 'Granger,' isn't it?"

38

The Stuart Hotel

"She didn't strike me as a scheming temptress, Alexander." Eve watched her husband pace the hotel room, his expression thunderous. "In fact, I would have mentioned earlier — except you interrupted, then charged out the door —"

"Eve, I'm *not* in a good mood. If you've something to say, say it, and dinna bait me."

When the brogue thickened, Eve knew an explosion was imminent. "I'm sorry. I just wanted to tell you my impression of Elizabeth when I saw her with that greasy little detective. She didn't look as if she were plotting anything. Actually, she looked . . . troubled? Stunned?" She threw up her hands. "She was doing a good job of hiding it, and since she *always* looks small and fragile and lovely, I hesitate to add 'tragic' — but even Mrs. Endicott remarked on it when we left Levy's Mercantile. Alexander . . . I think she's as much of a victim as I was last year. Of course, Elizabeth is the kind of woman an efficient but gawky bluestocking like me hopes *is* a deceitful Jezebel. . . ."

Alexander finally responded to her blatant plea for reassurance. "God help Simon," he whispered, stopping in front of her to brush a light kiss on each of her eyelids, then her mouth. "She's affecting him like a certain 'gawky bluestocking' did me — she's driving him crackers."

Eve smiled against his mouth. "I thought that would jar you out of your black mood." Alexander straightened, a reluctant smile briefly lifting the corners of his mouth. Eve reached to smooth her fingers over the bushy moustache. "Alexander? Why is it so difficult for him to deal with Elizabeth? I know he used to make *me* a bit uncomfortable, but he was always courteous the few times he made his presence known."

"That, lass, is a matter between Simon, Elizabeth — and the Lord. I will tell you that in all the years I've worked with the man, he's never behaved like this toward a woman. If they're suspects, he stalks them like a tiger on the prowl, then goes for a swift clean kill, same as he does a man. But if they're helpless victims — like you, my love" — he tweaked a stray curl, tucking it behind her ear — "he goes all mush-brained. Remember that dog he rescued this past summer? The one he nursed back to health, then persuaded Mr. Sterns to take in?"

Eve nodded, remembering Simon's concern for the poor animal, his gentleness, his

330

enveloping *protectiveness.*

Alexander strode over to the window, glanced out. "He's always been like that. Seems to favor anyone or anything weaker, smaller, helpless. But he just can't seem to apply the same principle to his *own* weaknesses. If he'd just give up his guilt and bitterness . . ." Alex shrugged. "At any rate, he can't pigeonhole Elizabeth into his black-and-white world, so he lashes out in all directions. Lass . . . he'd cut off his arm before he'd hurt you — but all the same, when he arrives here, stay out of his way."

"You've been warning me for three hours now, Alexander. How many times do I have to repeat that I've no desire to have those green eyes of his whittling *me* down to the size of birdseed? And I might point out that the same goes for *you!*" Her own temper was short, given Alexander's mood and her dread of Simon's reaction to her presence. She began muttering bird species beneath her breath in a vain attempt to curb her tongue. *"Melanerpes erythrocephalus, Dryoco —"*

A quick single knock, followed by two light raps, interrupted. Alexander shot across the room, turned the lock, and Simon blew in like a cloud of smoke. Eve bit her cheek and lifted her chin. "Mr. Kincaid. How nice to see you again."

"Eve . . ."

Simon ignored her. Eve privately admitted

to relief. Not even Alexander at his most menacing emanated this man's cold, tightly controlled wrath when he was upset. And to say that he was upset to find her here was putting it mildly.

"If she compromises this case in any way, or finds herself in peril of her life —"

"Eve — or Elizabeth?" Alexander rapped out, his hands balling into fists. "Be careful, Simon. Neither of us has the time to indulge in a round of fisticuffs." He stepped right up to Simon. "But I'll no' be having you treat my wife as though she's done wrong. If it weren't for her, Sim — we'd no' have found out about Benjamin Dawes."

There was a long moment of pained silence. Eve sat unmoving, her gaze locked on Alexander. Even so, when Simon turned toward her, she could barely suppress a shudder.

Unfortunately, Simon was as observant as her husband. He froze in his tracks, and something very like a wince flitted across his face. "Sorry." The word was gruff, but sincere. "Mrs. MacKay, you shouldn't be here and you know it. But since you are, just . . . be careful, will you?"

"I will." Eve relaxed with a sigh. "I couldn't stand it if you and Alexander came to blows. I promise — have promised — to be very careful. But I — I —"

Alexander reached her side in two long

strides. "All right, lass. All right." His hand cupped her shoulder, and Eve reached back to grab his fingers. "I don't think anything else needs be said on the matter of your improper presence here. We've too much else to consider, and precious little time."

After a moment, Simon nodded, and the tense atmosphere in the room dissipated. He moved across the room to the window, making sure, Eve noted, to stay concealed behind the curtains. "It's time to bring in reinforcements," he announced. "You'll need to shadow Dawes most of the time now, Alex, and I'll do what I can with Horatio and James. We might have to pull in someone else. Sam Traynor out of Albany, perhaps. I can't risk exposing my true identity quite yet, and that limits the time I can legitimately be seen anywhere near a Crump who openly scorns all things equine." He turned, looking fierce and predatory. "We *still* have nothing solid to pin on any of the Crumps, but it shouldn't be long now. As for Elizabeth . . ."

Eve pounced on his hesitation. "You've tried and convicted her in your hearts already, haven't you?" she blurted, unable to contain herself. "Just because she took an assumed name and was seen talking to a suspicious man. Has it occurred to you how *ashamed* she must be of her family name? What it must have been like for her, growing up?" She intercepted the swift look that passed between the two men. "Yes, Mr. Kincaid, Alexander has told me, and you'll just have to put that in your pipe and smoke it! Neither of you has given the poor girl a chance to defend herself, and I think that it's the pair of *you* who ought to be ashamed."

"Lass, you misunderstand —"

"What I believe about Elizabeth Granger's guilt or innocence is *my* concern!" Simon shot back, his hard tone belying the torture shadowing his eyes. "But I will remind you, Mrs. MacKay, that I *am* the man who saved her life. Why didn't she at least tell *me* the truth? She lied to me, from the very beginning. . . . She talks about God as her Good Shepherd, trots out chapter and verse. Is she lying about that as well?" He slammed his palm against the wall. "Why did she have to deceive me?"

"Have you told her who *you* are?" Eve surged to her feet, almost shouting. "Elizabeth may have deceived you, but she's no more guilty than *you*, Simon Kincaid. What gives you the right to judge?"

Alexander wrapped both arms around her and pulled her back against him. "That's enough, Eve!" he barked, squeezing her tightly enough to choke off further words. "Both of you stop this pointless arguing. Elizabeth's 'deception' will have to be decided later. Later! Right now, it's the *Crumps* we're after — not Elizabeth Granger-Graham." He waited, breathing so hard Eve felt engulfed inside a bellows. "Simon? Are you listening, man?"

"Everyone in the hotel will be listening if you don't lower your voice," Simon observed mildly, the contrast of his level tone and Alexander's forceful blustering startling. "I'm listening, Alex. That's why I risked coming here in the middle of the day." He leaned back against the wall, arms crossed, one boot propped on the radiator. "So, talk."

"Ach, man! You'll be the death of me," Alexander muttered.

He gently placed Eve aside and, with slightly weakened knees, Eve sank onto the welcoming hardness of the chair seat. She kept her gaze riveted on her husband, praying he could confine his temper. And that she could confine *hers*, she added ruefully.

Against the wall, Simon stood, cold and silent as a tombstone.

"Last night, I was having dinner at the Mitchell House Hotel, with a couple of the locals," Alexander began, his diction lapsing into its customary Tidewater drawl. "One of them happened to mention that he was supposed to have met with James Crump for a game of billiards, only Crump had been delayed in Tallahassee and wasn't returning until close to eight, by stage. He wondered — as did I — why James hadn't used the family carriage. So . . . I made some excuse a little while later, and managed to beat the stage to the depot by five minutes."

He was watching Simon guardedly, but when Eve wrapped her hand around his, Alexander squeezed back. Warmth and reassurance flowed through his clasp even as he spoke the next chilling words.

"Well, I struck up a conversation with the station agent there, who told me it's unheard of for a Crump to utilize the stage. But he wasn't about to question Mr. James, especially when the young man wasn't alone. 'No?' I asked — and the agent then described the man with James. Medium height, with greasy light-colored hair . . . and I remembered how the stablehands had described the man who attacked you and Elizabeth at — Simon! No! Wait!"

Simon had exploded into action, fairly leaping across the room for the door.

Astonished, Eve barely had time to blink before Alexander jumped in front of her as *he* leaped to intercept Simon. She gasped as Simon threw her husband to the floor in a blur of soundless motion. *How had that happened?* Alexander was an expert at wrestling, and nobody had ever bested him. She dashed up from her chair, her temper igniting, but from his supine position on the floor, Alexander's voice stopped her cold.

"Simon, reassure Eve before you leave, at least. You've frightened her."

336

Simon pivoted on his heel, his hand already turning the doorknob. He stiffened, his gaze colliding with Eve's.

"I'm not frightened!" Eve stormed across the room and planted herself in front of the door. "I'm furious!"

Alexander propped himself on his elbows, but he didn't get to his feet. "Simon, don't even think it."

"Then tell her to move out of my way. *Now.*"

Alexander didn't have to tell her. Eve had been close enough to see the fury and fear glazing Simon's eyes into frozen green glass. She stepped aside, and he flowed into the hall. By the time Eve managed to close the door behind him, he had disappeared.

Alexander rose, dusting his hands on his trousers, an expression of disbelief lighting his face. "Now, if that's no' a ferlie wonder! I never would have thought. . . ."

Eve finally managed to tear her grip free of the doorknob and looked across at her husband, her heartbeat still drumming in her ears. "What? *What,* Alexander? How did he . . . why did you let him —"

"Lass . . . come here."

She obeyed, allowing him to hold her, comfort her, but pulled back so she could gaze up into his face. "Alexander, why?"

"I think I've just realized Simon's dilemma. He's in *love* with her," he murmured.

337

"Simon is in love with Elizabeth Granger — Graham — and he doesn't even know it." His hands caressed Eve's back, and at last she relaxed against his chest. Then Alexander spoke again, and she wanted to weep at the sorrowful gloom weighting his words.

"But when he finally does wake up to his feelings, I pray that Elizabeth is as innocent as both of you claim. Otherwise, I fear Simon's soul will be hardened beyond redemption."

39

What was he to do now?

Simon kept his horse to a trot while he maneuvered around the fancy carriages crowding Broad Street. People seemed to be *everywhere* — some walking briskly, others riding bicycles or rattling by in carriages. In fact, the whole town was bursting with energy and life. With the winter season in full swing, the festive holiday spirit was reflected on faces, in the sound of laughter and the jingle of harness bells.

And somewhere nearby lurked a killer. . . .

Simon swung onto the road leading out to Adelaide and kneed his mount to a gallop.

She might already be dead. God? What will I do?

Fifteen minutes later he pulled up outside the stable and tossed the reins to an astonished stablehand. "Walk him till he cools down. I rode him hard all the way from town." With that, Simon sprinted off toward the house.

A sober Luther answered his knock. "Miss Granger — where is she?" Simon demanded, barely remembering in time which name to use.

"I wouldn't know, Mr. Kincaid. Ah . . . the family has gone out to Rose Hill for the day." He paused, looking uncomfortable.

"What is it, Luther?" Simon asked, his voice very quiet. "Did Miss Granger accompany them, then?"

"Ah . . . no suh." Visibly agitated now, the butler glanced around, then stepped outside and shut the door behind him. "Mr. Kincaid . . . they done let her go. They *fired* Miss Granger. Give her twenty-four hours to be out of the house. She's to be gone by the time they return this evenin'. And it's *Christmas!*"

At least she's alive! "Where is she? Has she already left? When did this happen?"

"I'll ask the upstairs maid," Luther offered, his manner stiffly formal again. "I'll show you to the parlor, Mr. Kincaid."

Ten minutes dragged by. Simon was on the verge of ransacking the house when the doors were folded back, and Elizabeth walked into the room. Pale, remote as the moon, expressive eyes carefully blank — but *alive.*

"I — I don't have much time," she said, a slight stammer belying her calm composure. "I'm expected to be gone before the family returns from Rose Hill." She hesitated, her fingers nervously plucking at the ribbons of her shirtwaist. "Did you — was Mr. Dawes waiting?"

340

Now that Simon was confronting her, he didn't know how to proceed. He couldn't very well tell her that her life was in danger, not from Benjamin Dawes but from an unknown brigand. Above all, he wanted answers, he wanted to kiss her, he wanted to browbeat her into telling him the *truth*. He wanted to yell at her for offering him the first faint stirrings of hope he'd experienced in a decade — and then crushing it beneath her deceit. Above all, he wanted her *safe*.

In the end, he did his job. "I saw him. Don't worry — Benjamin Dawes won't trouble you further. Now . . . why didn't you tell me about William Soames?"

For a moment her face went slack, and she gaped at him as if he'd lost his senses. Then the confusion hardened to resolve. "Why should I?" she countered. "And why would it matter now?"

The tightness in his throat spread. "Answer me, Elizabeth."

"If I answer your questions, will you return the favor? Will you, for instance, tell me why an outsider who has only lived here a few months is demanding to know details of a three-year-old crime? Or why a man of no social standing is able to intimidate members of one of the most influential families in the state? Why a mere *horse trainer* takes it upon himself to —"

He reached her in two long strides. "Eliza-

beth . . . don't. Don't push. Not right now."
The impulse to spirit her away and stash her
someplace known only to him was fast erod-
ing his legendary control. Abruptly his hands
clenched. "About Dawes . . . he told me that
he'd arranged the meeting between you and
Soames. He wouldn't come right out and ac-
cuse you of his murder — but he left the possibility open for speculation." Simon
searched her mutinous face. "Elizabeth? I
know you didn't kill him. But I need to hear it
from you. What happened?" He hesitated,
then added roughly, "Please . . . tell me."

She heaved a deep sigh, then went over to
the window and idly fingered the rich bro-
cade of the draperies. "I might not have done
the deed, but for three years I've blamed myself, because I might have been able to stop
whoever *did*." She turned back to him, her
expression agonized.

"What do you mean?"

She opened her mouth, hesitated, then
shook her head. "I . . . don't know." Out in
the entryway, the Crumps' huge grandfather
clock ponderously sounded the hour. "I
should go. I told you . . . I have to be gone before the Crumps return."

"Why not stay and fight? You've done
nothing wrong," Simon pointed out. Then,
in spite of himself, "Do *they* know about your
involvement in William Soames's death?"

"No! Dear God, no!" Elizabeth burst out,

startling them both. They stared at each other, and Simon watched her hand creep up to cradle her necklace.

"Sit down and talk to me." He gestured to a chair opposite his. When Elizabeth still hesitated, he rose and stood over her. "Sit," he ordered quietly.

Something flashed behind her eyes. "Stop treating me as though I were a criminal." She sat down, tucking her feet beneath her gown and folding her hands in her lap. "I'm sitting."

Simon found her tart tone reassuring. It was her fear he dreaded. "Good. Let's get Soames out of the way. I'll still be able to drive you into town before the Crumps return — and we can discuss . . . other matters." *Like a greasy-haired, cosh-wielding killer.* "Where did you say you were going?"

"Ochlocknee," she murmured, looking dazed, probably from his tone of voice and meaningful look when he'd said "other matters."

Now, if he could *keep* her off balance. . . . "Hmm. Well, I'll explore that later. Tell me why you think *you're* responsible for Soames's death."

She stared at her clasped hands, the ceiling, the fringed lamp to Simon's right, and eventually an indeterminate spot over his left shoulder. "I was there," she finally admitted, her voice low.

After his chat with Dawes, Simon had already reached that conclusion on his own. He leaned forward. "Did you see the murderer, Elizabeth?"

She shook her head. "Of course not! If I had, I would have stayed and talked to the sheriff, regardless of the damage to my reputation." Her lips quivered. "Not that *that* matters any longer."

"Did you see anything, hear anything at all? Find something that would have helped the authorities?" *Anything that would implicate Benjamin Dawes, and through him — James Crump. . . .*

Elizabeth was regarding Simon with a look of keen interest. "Mr. Kincaid, who —"

"Was Soames still alive when you arrived? How did you manage to keep the murderer from seeing you?" Simon quickly inserted. *Careful, Kincaid.* Much more of that rapid-fire volley, and he might as well announce his real profession from the top of one of the Piney Woods towers. And yet — he *had* to know what happened, from Elizabeth's own mouth. "Was that the reason you didn't approach the Crumps three years ago? You didn't just run away, did you? You arrived at the stables, expecting to talk to Soames privately, and instead you heard — voices?"

She nodded, her eyes glued hopelessly to his face.

344

Sensing that Elizabeth wasn't yet able to talk about that day, he supplied the words, and hoped his hunch was accurate. "You didn't know what to do, since you were supposed to be meeting this man alone. Dawes told me Soames wouldn't agree to see anyone but you. So when you realized he wasn't alone, you —"

He was elated when she interrupted. "I . . . should have called out. Maybe I could have frightened the murderer away. . . ." Her voice trembled, and she drew a shaky breath. "I was afraid . . . after . . . that I might be murdered, too. I had no weapon, no way to stop him." She swallowed, and now Simon knew one of the reasons for the haunting shadows always present in her eyes. "I hid in a stall, and stayed there for . . . it seemed like hours. The man never returned. Then I — I realized I should have gone immediately to see if Mr. Soames was still alive." She stopped, closing her eyes.

"You did what you had to do, to stay alive," Simon stated flatly. "Listen to me. Are you listening?" He waited until her eyes opened. "There was absolutely nothing you could have done to prevent William Soames's murder, Elizabeth. Nothing. All you would have accomplished would have been to get *your* head bashed in as well. You have nothing to feel guilty about. Do you understand?"

Nothing to feel guilty about. Somewhere

345

deep in the soul Simon thought he had lost, something stirred and began to crumble. Not so long ago, Alex had said much the same thing to *him* . . . about Jake and Percy. *God,* he whispered beneath his breath, feeling as if a lightning bolt had hurled him against a brick wall. *God in heaven, what does it mean?* Was there a chance — however slim, however implausible — that Alex was right? That killing Jake and Percy *had* been an act of sheer self-defense — the only way Simon could have stayed alive?

But if Simon believed *that,* he would also have to believe that Alex was right about God as well.

He realized with a start that Elizabeth was perched, trembling, on the edge of her seat, one hand at her throat. Unable to restrain the sudden impulse, he reached out to touch her hand. Briefly his fingers closed over hers, then withdrew. He could not touch her again. Not here. Not now.

"Do you really believe that?" she asked, as if the course of the rest of her life hinged on the truth of his statement. "I — it took me longer to forgive myself than it did for me to accept *God's* forgiveness. But to hear someone else say it out loud . . ." She faltered, her voice catching. But a luminous smile began to spread, like a rainbow, in a slow arc across her face. "Again, Simon Kincaid . . . you show me how much God must love me, to send you —"

The accolade was too much. "Once and for all, I am *not* your blasted guardian angel!" Simon stalked behind the settee. Then he swirled and planted his hands on the antimacassar adorning the sofa's camel back, crumpling the flimsy lace. "If I've helped you overcome your misplaced guilt, I'm glad. But God turned His back on me two decades ago, and the only manifestation of Himself *I'm* ever likely to see is His judgment!"

Unless Alexander MacKay is right, a persistent voice whispered.

Elizabeth was shaking her head. "You're wrong. God never turns His back on anyone. Never. Human beings, now . . . they — we're different. We can all be weak and faithless . . . unreliable. I knew that practically from the cradle. But God — " she shook her head, her smile deepening. "Well . . . He always searches out His lost sheep, regardless of where we've strayed . . . or for how long!"

Feeling trapped — and touchy because of it — Simon was not amused. "Too bad I've known more of the God of judgment and wrath. And given the condition of the world, I find my view far more realistic than yours."

"On the contrary, given the condition of the world, I find *my* view the only hope of sanity."

Tension crackled in the air, but after a moment Simon relaxed and shook his head.

Only with Elizabeth . . . Here he was, having another theological debate instead of procuring vital information. Somehow he must discipline his unruly emotions, for both their sakes. He was standing in the middle of the Crumps' parlor, and like a raw recruit, was inches away from blurting out a declaration of love for a woman he *must* continue to treat as a suspect, regardless of his personal feelings.

How would Elizabeth feel when he *was* free to share his own deception?

Into the thickening pool of silence the butler's voice intruded like a clanging fire bell. "There's a call from Mr. James. He wants to know if Miss Granger has finished packing and is ready to leave Adelaide. What should I tell him?"

40

Elizabeth chanced a sidelong glance at the taciturn man guiding the horse and buggy down the drive. "Thank you for . . . persuading Luther to hand over my wages."

Simon shrugged. "You're welcome."

Elizabeth sat back with a sigh, deciding she would never understand Simon Kincaid. In the last hour, his mood had changed direction so many times, she was still reeling. Right now, for instance, he reflected the weather, which promised to turn thoroughly unpleasant on the next gust of wind.

They reached the square brick pillars at the end of the drive, and Simon turned onto the street toward town. The bleak gray sky and damp wind warned of impending rain; Elizabeth bit her lip, shivering inside the long woolen coat Josephine had given her the previous Christmas. Unshed tears clogged her throat as a wave of treacherous memories swept over her: Josephine, patting her shoulder as Elizabeth, nonplussed, stammered a thank-you for the extravagant gift; Josephine, changing before her very eyes as the older woman fluttered protectively around her children; Josephine, half-lifting a hand, opening her mouth — but then saying nothing in Elizabeth's defense when Horatio coldly ordered Elizabeth out of their home.

You can't trust people. Ever. Even Simon, whose baffling personality could not diffuse her hopeless longings, even more pronounced during this season of the year.

"Christmas is only two days away," she observed, half to herself.

Simon plainly wasn't interested in carrying on a conversation. "Joy to the world," he growled, directing the horse around a couple riding bicycles along the road.

They traveled in stiff silence. Elizabeth lapsed into dreary introspection, mulling over the defects in her character which had no doubt prompted her ultimate rejection by everyone she had ever cared for. If only she could achieve the same rapport with humans that she enjoyed with the horses. But the whimsical humor that normally sustained her fell flat. If she offered a carrot to Simon right now, his response would doubtless resemble Mosby's rather than the more tractable Strawberry's.

And yet . . . he *had* promised to protect her.

On either side of the road, piney glades were interspersed with occasional patches of raw, cleared earth where the foundations for new houses had been laid. Thomasville was growing by leaps and bounds . . . but like a fly in amber, Elizabeth was trapped in — and by — the past. On the other hand, she *could* reach out and risk reminding Simon of his promise. *But what if he spurns it . . . and me?*

"I don't understand you — I don't *know* who or what you are." Elizabeth didn't realize she had spoken the words aloud until Simon answered.

"I know. But right now, there's nothing I can say or do to —" He broke off, and the taut set of his mouth, his shoulders, conveyed his extreme frustration.

As explanations went, Simon's served only to further depress Elizabeth. The lump in her throat thickened. "I understand." She cleared her throat. "I can't trust you. You don't trust me. I've lied to you, and because of it, my every action must be questioned, evaluated. I can't convince you to trust me, anymore than I can convince you to believe in a loving Father rather than a vengeful God."

"Don't get sidetracked by religious issues again."

"I'm not sidetracking. Those 'issues' are part of my life — they're part of *me* — and since you can't accept that either, I think . . . I think it's best we end this here and now." She struggled against the desolation swamping her at the thought of losing Simon Kincaid, too, on a day already fraught with bitter partings. "I can't change the past. But I can trust God to take care of my future." She finally

351

looked directly at Simon, her heart twisting at the sight of his miserable face. "I *want* to trust you. If only I could —"

He tugged on the reins hard enough to send the horse's head rearing up in alarm. Instinctively, he calmed the animal, then jiggled the reins. He didn't speak again.

Moments later they pulled up at the depot. Down the tracks Elizabeth saw the billowing steam heralding the arrival of a train. Simon brought the buggy to a halt at the back of the building, away from the crowd of other wagons and carriages and milling people. He set the brake, then turned to Elizabeth. "You don't understand — and I can't tell you . . . yet. But Elizabeth . . . I need —"

"You don't have to tell me anything," Elizabeth interrupted, rushing the farewell, praying he would leave before she broke down completely. "And I understand better than you realize. The Crumps are a powerful family, with connections all over the state. You don't need to risk your own future any more than you already have. Everyone in Thomasville knows your extraordinary skill with horses by now, and I hope, after I leave, they'll forget all those rumors."

Simon jumped down and strode around to Elizabeth's side. Then he reached up, clamped his hands on her waist, and lifted her out of the buggy. "Do you know what happens to a woman who talks too much to a man whose mood is highly . . . unstable?" His hands were warm on her waist, holding her so she couldn't escape.

Elizabeth could only gape at him. "N-no," she stuttered.

His head lowered, and his mouth hovered inches from hers. "She finds herself kissed — very thoroughly. In spite of logic, common sense, or propriety."

Riotous color bloomed in Elizabeth's cheeks. She tried to speak, but couldn't find the words.

Gently, slowly he released her, propping her against the buggy until her scattered wits stiffened her watery limbs. "The desire confounds me near as much as I see it astonishes you." A muscle in his jaw twitched. "Well?"

"Astonishment," she finally managed, "doesn't begin to describe it. I can sense your . . . um . . . your vexation, with both the situation and with me. But I thought I was the only one who — oh!" Thoroughly discombobulated, she closed her eyes.

"Elizabeth . . ." he said on a sigh. He picked up her clenched hands, holding them between his. "You always take me by surprise. Open your eyes and look at me."

She had steeled herself for an impersonal, chilly parting, for the inevitable sense of isolation and aching loneliness that would follow. Instead, Elizabeth found herself swept into the bubbling lava of a volcano about to explode. She searched the stern face, wondering how she could ever have thought him detached. His green eyes were sizzling, and in the pewter gray December afternoon, even his dark hair seemed to smolder. "It's only fair," she murmured back. "You surprise me every time I see you."

A muscle at the corner of his cheek twitched. "I don't want to let you go," he muttered. "But I don't see any alternative." He pressed his lips to each palm, then stood there, staring down at her while his grip tightened almost painfully. "And much as I'd like to kiss you — I can't do that, either."

For a long moment they remained motionless. Heedless of its ramifications, Elizabeth committed to memory the rugged planes of Simon's face, the paradox of his fervent passion and his transcendent control, burning in the green eyes. She had never known anyone like Simon Kincaid. *When I saved your life — that day in the river . . . we were bound,* he had told her. If only . . .

"You shouldn't look at me like that," he murmured eventually, his voice gone deep and soft. He dropped her hands, and stepped back. "I'll bring your luggage. Go on and purchase your ticket."

Moving as if in a dream, she bought a one-way ticket to Ochlocknee, then watched as her battered trunk was trundled into the baggage compartment under Simon's supervision. He didn't glance her way again.

Elizabeth joined the clutch of passengers boarding the day coach, the silent sorrow gripping her heart. A hand, warm and strong, closed over her elbow as she prepared to mount the metal steps. Blinking hard, Elizabeth focused on Simon's face.

"You were right not to trust me," he said. "But as God is my witness . . . I wish you *could*. And I wish even more, that it was safe to trust *you*."

He turned, and Elizabeth picked up her skirts and boarded the train. They were halfway to Ochlocknee before the burning behind her eyes subsided, but the pain in her heart seared more hotly with each passing mile.

PART THREE

♦ ♦ ♦

Liberty

December 1895–May 1896

41

Rose Hill
December 26, 1895

Benjamin Dawes handed his hat and umbrella to the butler, a wooden-faced Negro who somehow always managed to make Dawes feel as if he were a ragpicker. Whole blasted family, *including* the servants, was rotten with pride. He deliberately scuffed his feet on the wide polished oak floorboards as he followed the butler down the hall.

It was a cold, ugly morning, and the elaborate pine boughs and clusters of holly decorating the foyer scraped his nerves even more raw. Dawes knew the entire clan had gathered together the previous day to celebrate Christmas, and he shuddered at the image of Georgina Crump playing the part of doting grandmother.

Today the brown recluse, as he privately referred to her, was in her greenhouse — another irritation. A driving rainstorm pelted the glass, distorting the view; he felt smothered by the profusion of hot-house greenery and the sound of the drumming rain.

Georgina, as usual, ignored him until the butler bowed himself out. Then she laid aside a pair of pruning shears and straightened.

"An unpleasant morning, Mr. Dawes. I trust the news you bring will brighten the day as much as my flowers here."

In her dove gray morning gown, relieved only by a bit of lace at the throat and sleeves, she reminded Dawes of a photograph he'd seen once of European royalty. A woman like this should be tending her gardens, pouring tea for her friends, reading to her grandchildren. She should *not* be dabbling in business matters.

"Mr. Dawes? Has the rain dampened your ability to speak?"

He'd rather be trapped in a bar between two drunks than confront Georgina Crump's regal disdain. "I'm here to report," he responded, then reached inside his pocket and pulled out a chewed cigar, knowing full well what would happen.

She didn't disappoint him. "Mr. Dawes!"

He looked up, his expression bland. "That's right. You'd prefer I not smoke. Well . . . frankly, I'd prefer to be somewhere other than your jungle room here. Ready to negotiate?"

He listened to the rain, holding the cigar poised at his mouth, while she struggled not to show her outrage. When she silently turned and left the room, he smiled to himself, regretfully tucking away the cigar. Nothing like a good smoke on a cold, rainy day. . . .

"Very well," she announced after leading him down the hall to the small room she had turned into an office. "I indulged your childish show of defiance. Do you feel vindicated, Mr. Dawes?"

"Yes, ma'am." He sketched a bow. "And I'm sure the lesson in humility was good for your soul as well."

Two spots of color deepened in the thin patrician face, but she refused to be goaded. "What have you learned?"

Dawes shifted uncomfortably, scratching his neck where the damp shirt collar was sticking. He hated rain, especially when he had to be out in it. Most folks tended to stay clear of him on rainy days. Most, that is, except the brown recluse here, looking down her snooty nose and silently daring him to persist in his needling. "The man Kincaid met at the Stuart is registered as Alexander MacKay. According to the clerk, MacKay's an agent for some big real estate developer up in Chicago who's interested in building a winter residence down here. MacKay's been snooping around town, taking a lot of notes, talking to all the locals. All up front and natural — if he's who he claims to be. The hotel clerk figures he wanted to pick Kincaid's brain about harness racing —"

"Horatio has not spoken of this Alexander

MacKay. I find it odd that such a man would not seek out my son's advice, don't you?"

Dawes resisted the obvious retort. Besides, the woman *did* have a point. "I'll keep digging."

"What of Kincaid?"

His armpits started sweating, but Dawes managed to answer without hesitation. "He warned me away from the companion. I haven't seen him since."

"I . . . see."

She was silent so long this time his skin began to crawl. He needed a smoke. When she spoke again, however, Dawes almost felt sorry for Elizabeth Graham.

"Elizabeth . . . I trusted her." Georgina Crump looked across the room at Dawes. "Tell me," she murmured, "about my son James."

"Uh . . . what about Miss Graham?"

"*I* will handle things from this point. Don't fret, Mr. Dawes. You'll be appropriately compensated. Now . . . my son?"

"Made his usual rounds to all your businesses here in Thomasville, and a couple in Boston and Quitman besides. Frequents the billiard parlors and hotels with his usual crowd." He named several prominent townsfolk, most of them young rapscallions like James. "Near as I can tell, he's not stirring up any more rumors or running off on his own, Mrs. Crump."

362

He slid her a calculating look from the corner of his eye. "Guess he doesn't have to, now that Horatio's sacked —"

"I will not discuss Elizabeth Graham with you." She walked across to the door and pressed a button on the wall. Without looking at him, she murmured, "You may go, Mr. Dawes."

A moment later Dawes was following the butler back down the hall. At the front door he accepted his umbrella and bowler, retrieved the bulging envelope stuffed inside the dome of his hat, and departed. Back at the hotel where he'd booked a room, he counted the money first, then read the instructions that had been folded around the money.

"Well, I'll be —" he swore to himself. Then he struck a match on the bottom of his shoe, lit up a fresh cigar, and touched the flame to the single sheet of paper.

♦ ♦ ♦

After the detective left, Georgina ordered a fire to be lit in the sitting room. She lingered there for over an hour, lost in thought, her gaze fixed upon the portrait of Helene. The crackling warmth of the fire slowly dispelled both the chill in the room and the chill in Georgina's soul.

Outside, the gloomy day darkened further as the rain intensified. She lifted her hand, brushing her fingers across the bottom of the canvas. Then she sat down behind her writing desk, pulled out several sheets of fresh stationery, and began to write.

♦ ♦ ♦

In the woods behind Rose Hill

James made his way through the dripping, thickly wooded forest, using only a small lantern. The rain had finally ended earlier that evening, but a wind had blown in from the northwest that had sent the temperature plummeting. He hunched his shoulders and ducked beneath the branches of a cluster of pines.

A shower of frigid drops splattered the brim of his hat and soaked the cashmere scarf around his neck. Muttering beneath his breath, James fought through the trees and into a small clearing. He dimmed the lantern immediately. Even though he had a perfect right to tramp through these woods at any hour he pleased, it would be foolish to draw unnecessary attention to himself.

Fortunately Rufus Black was waiting, playing solitaire with a soiled pack of dog-earred cards in the dim light of the lantern James had left there. Relieved, James shut the door. If the oaf had bolted, he would *not* have been pleased.

He looked down at the sullen man, who didn't bother to rise to his feet, and tugged out a piece of folded paper. "Here's a more detailed plan of my brother's house, showing you the girl's bedroom. Since she's the oldest, she sleeps alone now."

Black shoved aside the cards and casually opened the paper. "I been thinking some. With the companion still in the house, I don't see . . ."

"She's gone," James snapped, angry because this clod dared to question him. "But only as far as Ochlocknee. The plan will work perfectly. Stand up when I talk to you!" He kicked Black's foot.

Rufus rose with insolent slowness, casually tucking his thumbs inside the waistband of his trousers. "I wouldn't push too hard, if I was you," he commented, and James fought the urge to wipe the supercilious smirk off his face. "Told you I'd been thinking. Might be I'd get riled up. Might be I'd forget your 'orders' 'bout keeping the little shaver safe."

James tried to ignore the uneasy stab of fear at the threat. His mother would never forgive him if something happened to one of her precious grandchildren. "Just shut up and listen, then. I've come up with the perfect plan, and if you'll do exactly as I tell you, there won't be any problem." He lowered his voice and began to explain.

42

December 27, 1895

For a quarter of an hour now, Alex had listened to the sagacious observations of an elderly baggageman while they waited for the arrival of the Magnolia Special. Every so often, he glanced down the track, squinting against the brightness of a sky the color of his mother's flow blue china. "Should be along any moment now," he observed after a while.

"I 'specs so." The wiry colored man pushed back the brim of his cap. "Crump System trains has a reputation for running on time, moreso than *some* I could name."

"I'll leave you to get on with your work." Alex lifted a hand, then wandered off. He had no business being here, of course, but couldn't resist the overwhelming compulsion to have a look for himself at the operative assigned to bring Avery Paxton back to Denver. Adam Moreaux was his name, and right now Alex resented the unknown man more than he cared to admit. After all these years . . .

"He's as good as they come, Alex," Simon had promised, more than once. "He taught me all about stalking, remember?"

"Ach, man, how could I forget? You make him out to be a cross between Saint Paul and the greatest tracker since Charlie Siringo. Born to wealth, but raised by Indians . . . equally comfortable with tycoons or tinkers. . . ." Alex scowled at the sun. None of that mattered anyway; he had to stay in the background to avoid jeopardizing Simon. But there was no reason why he *couldn't* have himself a friendly stroll down the street and just happen to pass by the jail when Moreaux brought Paxton out.

Moments later the train arrived. Alex leaned against some barrels stacked against the side of the depot and watched the throngs of passengers disembark. The only description of Adam Moreaux he'd been able to wrest from Simon had been the promise that the operative would be impossible to miss. Seconds later, Alex jerked upright, his jaw dropping. *Sim, you sly dog, you!* And to think of all the times he'd roasted his friend about his lack of humor.

So Moreaux was . . . *noticeable*, was he? Bemused, Alex watched the Denver operative step lithely onto the platform, seemingly oblivious to the open stares of other passengers. Rustling murmurs of the curious rippled in widening circles as the tall man made his way across to the station agent's window. He moved like a great cat.

And he looked, Alex thought incredulously, like a performer in Buffalo Bill Cody's Wild West Show, dressed head to toe in fringed leather, right down to his knee-high moccasins. A jaunty feather pointed skyward from his wide-brimmed western-style hat. Beneath the hat, a neatly tied leather thong secured hair the color of pitch in a queue that fell halfway down his shoulders.

"Good afternoon," he spoke to the riveted station agent in a melting baritone voice. "I'm Operative Adam Moreaux, from Pinkerton's Denver office. I'd appreciate some directions to the county jail, if you can spare the time."

♦ ♦ ♦

Pastime Racetrack

In spite of his preoccupation, Simon won two of the four heats in which he raced that day, as well as placing in a third. But the familiar exhiliration, the sense of being where he was born to be — working with horses — paled in light of the consuming need to see Elizabeth. All afternoon, his gaze returned to the stands, where the entire Horatio Crump family held court, accepting the congratulations and respect of the crowd as if it were their due.

Between heats, Horatio came to the barn to talk with Simon. "They've never looked better," he admitted, standing well back

368

while Simon and Jefferson unhitched Mosby. "I'd like to thank you." He cleared his throat, looking more gaunt than usual, and unaccountably uncomfortable. "There's been some . . . unpleasantness, I know, but I'm hoping you'll stay on for the rest of the season."

Jefferson left, sulky in tow, and Simon busied himself with the temperamental stallion, running his hand over the lightly sweating flank. For some reason, he was finding it difficult to deceive Horatio in spite of what the man had done to Elizabeth, and the unaccustomed weakness made Simon angry. The man was a *Crump,* and a backstabbing coward at that. "I'll do what I can," he stated flatly. "I have some . . . other obligations."

Horatio's bony face flushed. "Um . . . I'd been meaning to give you your Christmas bonus . . . and if you'd like to take a few days off —" he broke off. "This is not a bribe, you understand." A sheepish grin twitched at the corners of his mouth. "All right, perhaps it was — but I certainly mean no offense."

Simon hooked a short lead line to Mosby's bridle and handed him over to Jefferson, whose carefully blank face told Simon the assistant had returned in time to hear Crump's offer. "I'll take tomorrow off, then. Jefferson, Mosby needs cooling down. Come on." He swiveled on his heel and stalked off without another word. *No offense!* Horatio Crump had dismissed Elizabeth without so much as blinking an eye — but he meant no offense.

For the rest of the afternoon, Simon avoided all contact with the Crumps.

♦ ♦ ♦

Benjamin Dawes waited until Horatio left the barn. "Mr. Crump? Could I have a word with you?"

They'd only met a few times, several years earlier, but the other man's face cleared almost instantly. "Dawes, isn't it? One of our private investigators?"

"Yessir." He kept his tone respectful. "I . . . if this weren't important, I wouldn't bother you on such a festive occasion." Looking about, he affected a nervous cough.

"What is it?"

Crump was beginning to look mildly alarmed, and Dawes had to suppress the inward gleeful chuckle. "Well . . . I have some news about your trainer, Simon Kincaid. I'm afraid you're not going to like it."

43

Ochlocknee

Though he traveled here on occasion, few people in Ochlocknee knew James Crump as anyone other than the proprietor of a certain club at the end of a back street. Even so, James had no trouble securing the addresses of all the respectable boardinghouses where a single young woman might find lodging for a reasonable price. After several fruitless inquiries, however, he was cursing Elizabeth, his mother's obsession for secrecy, and Simon Kincaid, who would *definitely* pay for interfering.

He was fed up with everyone telling him what to do, and it was going to stop, here and now. This time, not even Mother would be able to thwart his plans.

It was the middle of the afternoon before James ran Elizabeth down in a decrepit clapboard house on the edge of town; he barely managed to keep a smooth face and civil tongue for the landlady. When Elizabeth opened the door to her room, he shoved his way inside, locked the door, and pocketed the key.

"Hello, Elizabeth," he said. Triumph vibrated through the words. "I thought I'd stop by to wish you a belated Merry Christmas."

A quarter of an hour later James shut the door behind him, mission accomplished. A savage smile spread across his face as he eyed the delicate strands of a gold chain, now broken, his fingers idly stroking the charm. A lamb. *How . . . appropriate.*

He stuffed the necklace safely inside a hidden pocket, then gingerly rubbed his hand over the tender spot on his jaw. The little wildcat — how dare she strike him!

Soon, he reminded himself. After his trap was sprung, she would pay, like Kincaid, for trying to outwit a Crump. Nobody could stop him — and even his mother would finally have to admit that it was *James* who wielded the power in this family.

◆ ◆ ◆

Adelaide

Rufus had acquired a key to the kitchen door from James, along with the information that the entire family would be spending the day at Pastime, then dining with friends in town. Nonetheless, he prudently waited until just after the moon rose to slip inside the house.

The kitchen was deserted, doubtless due to the family's absence. He found the long nar-

372

row hall leading to the back servants' stairs, and climbed the steps without haste, marveling at the ease of his entry. This little caper had stuck in his craw from the start, even with the money James had promised to pay, but so far everything seemed to be falling in place.

He crept along the upstairs landing, his glance taking in the huge chandelier in the central foyer below. Ornate paintings covered the walls, and his nose twitched from the faint smell of evergreen, vanilla, and — Rufus paused, sniffing — cloves. The smell of cloves reminded him of his granny's house at Christmastime, when she'd stir up her special cider on the old wood cookstove.

Irritated with himself, Rufus hurried down the hall to the last room. He slipped inside, his eyes darting about the darkness. Fifteen minutes later, everything was set, and he settled himself on the windowsill to wait.

An hour later, when the family carriage clattered to a standstill below, he eased into the hiding place he'd prepared. Everything was ready; rope, gag, large duffle bag. He'd even grabbed one of the toys off the bed.

All he had to do now was wait.

44

By morning the bruises on her wrist had deepened to the color of overripe plums. The thin red welt on her neck was less obvious, Elizabeth decided, but it stung like the dickens. She sat on a rickety chair and stared into the cracked hand mirror, studying her appearance with macabre fascination. Her pale skin had always shown cuts and bruises more vividly than most.

An authoritative knock on the door froze her into immobility. She stared across the room, her mind blank. Seconds later, when the knock was repeated more forcefully, all she could do was frantically snatch up her shawl and hold it against her throat. Still, she didn't speak.

Silence descended. Elizabeth sat, stiff, afraid to take a deep breath — and without warning the door burst open, slamming back against the wall. Simon Kincaid exploded into the room in a soundless rush as deadly as the bullet from a gun, hands held out from his body like weapons at the ready. His fierce green gaze whipped the room in a single comprehensive sweep, and between one breath and the next, the air of violence dissipated. His eyes settled on Elizabeth.

"What did he do to you?"

She'd never heard that tone before and she hoped never to hear it again. "Simon?"

He crossed the room in the same soundless rush with which he had entered. "On her way outside to hang the laundry, your landlady told me I was the *second* gentlemen in as many days to inquire after you. It took very little encouragement to hear a description of your . . . cousin. What did James do to you, Elizabeth?"

As if in a dream, knowing the revelation was inevitable, she lowered the shawl, keeping her gaze fastened on Simon. His breath expelled in a hiss, and a look of naked rage leaped into his face.

Then he was beside her, lifting her to her feet, his touch gentle as his hands tilted her chin, brushed along the thin line of abraded skin. "*Elizabeth*, did he hurt you . . . in any other way?"

"No, no . . ." She swallowed convulsively, shaking her head. "It was very strange, actually. He was . . . angry, but he was . . . that is, he didn't even try to —" A flush suffused her cheeks, and she forced out the rest. "He grabbed me and then he jerked off my necklace. And then . . . he left. He just left —" she repeated in disbelief.

Simon's arms closed about her, pulling her hard against his chest. She felt his lips in her hair, heard him whispering broken, disjointed phrases that sounded impossibly like a prayer. "What am I to do?"

Paralyzed with shame and shyness, Elizabeth stood in his embrace, feeling about as responsive as a stick. Her mind crowded with questions, but sensations she was even less equipped to handle flooded her. *Simon.* His . . . solidity. The warmth of his embrace. The controlled strength of his hands. The earthy scent of him . . . of leather, of horses.

An unnerving, almost frightening *awareness* of his confused state of mind.

In some inexplicable manner, Elizabeth knew Simon needed her, but he was as shaken by that knowledge as she. He had unsettled and confused her, soothed and protected her; he reached out with one hand and pushed her away with the other. He kissed her, then he told her he couldn't trust her. *Well, Lord,* she decided somewhere in the befuddled cavern of her mind, *I don't know what to do, either.*

Suddenly she began to tremble. Her fingers clung to the supple leather of his vest. "Simon. Simon." Her throat closed, and the shaking intensified. He was *here,* really here. In this room, protecting her, shielding her, though she had never expected to see him again. He was here, and his presence dispelled in a single stroke the evil taint that lingered from James's presence. Until this moment, Elizabeth had not realized how much she had needed to be touched by someone who — who didn't despise her.

"Hold me," she managed to choke out. "Simon. Just . . . hold me."

"I will, little one. I will." He murmured her name again, and she felt his lips brushing her forehead, her ear. "It's all right. I'm here now. Shh . . . I'm here."

Simon waited in the drab parlor while Elizabeth tidied up. He was restless, his thoughts churning, cravenly relieved that the room was empty. All the other residents were out, and the friendly Mrs. Tilford was still hanging laundry. Through the drawn curtains in the parlor, Simon could see her stocky, no-nonsense frame, surrounded by flapping sheets and a dwindling pile in the basket at her feet. He forced himself to watch the prosaic activity, instead of dwelling on his fear.

The necklace. Somehow James planned to use that necklace to frame Elizabeth. Simon knew it in his bones. But how — and *when?*

Elizabeth appeared in the entrance to the room, looking collected in a plain burgundy gown with a high neck, the collar of which managed to conceal the angry red line on her neck. She had loosely gathered her hair at the base of her neck with a clasp, and the solemn look on her face made Simon want to gather her back into his arms and kiss the shadows from her eyes.

"Let's go for a walk," he said, and ushered her outside into the warm sunshine of the crisp winter morning.

He led her down a rutted dirt lane, then along a narrow path that wound its way through a field, and finally to the edge of the woods. Elizabeth didn't speak, not even to protest what might have seemed a cavalier abduction. Simon kept a firm grip on her elbow, and stopped only when he was confident of not being overheard. Struggling to remain calm, detached, he forced himself to release her and step back. "Now. Let's talk a little more about what happened."

Elizabeth heaved a sigh. "We both know nothing can be done. It's not worth your job, Simon."

"What makes you think so?" he bit out.

"I don't want anything to happen to you." She faltered when Simon muttered something beneath his breath.

"Happen to me? What about *you?*" he shot back in a deadly quiet voice. "How do you think I feel, seeing *this* —" He reached out, snagged her arm, and lifted it to wave her bruised wrist in front of her eyes. "You tried to hide this, I know. You didn't succeed."

Very gently he placed her arm at her side. Elizabeth didn't move a muscle. "That, I promise you, is just the beginning of what happens when arrogant bullies muck about in the lives of someone smaller and weaker."

"Is that how you see me? Small, weak, hopelessly provincial?"

Simon winced. "No," he ground out between clenched teeth. "That is not how *I* see you. That is how *James Crump* sees you. You've somehow managed — this past couple of years — to escape the *worst* he could do because of your position in his brother's household. Now, what happens the next time he catches you alone?" He was so terrified by the possibility that he wanted to shake her. "What if I'm not here to protect you?"

"But you *won't* be here. Your job — I never expected you to feel obligated. . . ."

The vulnerable set of her narrow shoulders struck Simon a blow straight to his gut. She looked so alone. In her mind, she *was* alone. "There's something I've got to tell you." The words escaped, forced and hurried. "Something I've been unable —" he stopped, tried again. "I haven't been entirely honest with you about myself, either."

"Simon, don't." She whirled about, fear and desperation glazing her eyes. "Don't —"

But he could no longer barricade himself against the overwhelming reality for another day. Not now. Especially now . . .

He reached out and pulled her to him. "Elizabeth, little one, I can't help this. I don't know how — or why . . ." He stopped her protest with his mouth, trying to tell her with his kiss the words he'd never spoken aloud to another human being. But when he lifted his head at last, dazed from the force of his emotions, the words spilled out. "I think I'm in love with you. I've never felt like this before — but I do know it's there, and it's real. Perhaps . . ." He squeezed his eyes shut, then opened them and lost himself in the dark pools of hers. With his hands framing her delicate face, he whispered, "Perhaps, God placed *you* in *my* life. To be *my* guardian angel."

Droplets of sweat broke out across his brow. It had been easier to watch his father die at the hands of Jake and Percy than to admit his feelings to this woman. "You've forced me to hope again. You, and my friend Alex. I . . . your faith in a loving God, when your entire life has been devoid of love — There's something else I must tell you, so there won't be any more deception between us."

Her hands came up and pressed against his lips. "No, Simon!" Her voice was strangled. "Don't."

If it hadn't been for the expression of incredulous wonder filling her face, Simon would have melted into the darkest hole in the woods and disappeared forever. But . . . what was the matter? She felt *something* for him — he could see it. But he also sensed the panic, the despair, as surely as he'd always sensed more about Elizabeth than he had anyone else. "Elizabeth." He kissed her trembling fingers, his voice soft. "What is it?"

"When I needed someone, when I needed *you* the most — you came." Her voice hoarsened, and he could see how difficult the words were for her to speak.

God, he screamed in his mind, *don't let her turn away.* He didn't deserve a woman like Elizabeth and he knew it. *But don't let her leave me now.* He waited, staring down into her face, feeling as if his insides were being skewered by a branding iron. *I'd rather You struck me dead, here and now, than —*

"I've learned," she whispered then, "not to be greedy, or question God's mercies and small gifts. Simon? You don't need to say any more, explain anything else to me. Just . . . hold me."

God's small mercies. The branding iron vanished, replaced by a relief as vast as the universe. As gentle and as calming as the gurgle of a finger-width brook beside a gigantic old cottonwood. It was as though, somehow, a Love that enfolded that vast universe had drifted inside Simon, filling his empty soul. He closed his eyes, and held Elizabeth.

45

Rose Hill

Georgina replaced the mouthpiece of the telephone, then sat staring at the handset. Her
hand was trembling, and she felt vaguely dizzy.
Groping blindly, her fingers fumbled for the
buzzer, and seconds later the housekeeper appeared.

"My eldest granddaughter . . . has been abducted, Mrs. Yancey. Please assemble the
entire staff at once, in the main hall. I'll . . .
be along to speak with everyone shortly."
She dismissed the shocked woman, then sat
for a few moments, lost in thought, before
she picked up the telephone again. After a
short conversation, she rose, her movements
slow, stiff. If Joan Aileen was harmed in any
way —

Georgina banished the possibility, lifted
her chin, and walked with measured poise
down the hall. On the way, she detoured by a
small room to which she had forbidden all entrance, even Mrs. Yancey and the butler,
Chester. If Elizabeth Graham wanted to play
vicious games, she would soon discover to

what lengths Georgina would go to protect her family.

Benjamin Dawes arrived several hours later, breathless and out of sorts. "This better be important. I was right in the middle of my breakfast."

Georgina waved aside the maid who had just laid a tray of refreshments down on the sideboard. "My eldest granddaughter Joan has been abducted from her home. By Elizabeth Graham. I want you to find them. At once!"

Dawes burst out laughing. "That's preposterous! Elizabeth Graham wouldn't hurt a fly!"

Georgina froze. The telegram she had been reading crumpled in her fingers. "You stupid, ignorant, boorish *twit!* You know *nothing* about Elizabeth Graham! You think you're so clever, snuffling around in hopes of lining your disgusting pockets with a share of that stolen gold." She whirled and stalked across the room to the fireplace. "Gold which Charles Graham — Elizabeth's *father!* — stole from my *husband*. Elizabeth Graham is a lying, cunning piece of work. And you, Mr. Dawes, are going to hunt her down like a rabid dog. You will bring her to me. *Find her.* Do you understand?"

After a long pause the detective nodded. "I'll find her," he agreed. "But you speak to me like that again, Miz Crump, and you can find yourself another flatfoot. I'm not one of your lackeys."

Georgina was staring up at the portrait of Helene, arms folded across her waist in a vain attempt to conceal the tremors. Not since her daughter died had she felt such all-consuming rage. "Just . . . find her."

◆ ◆ ◆

Adelaide

For hours now James had played the part of helpful uncle to his tearful nieces and nephews and consoled his devastated brother, Horatio. It was James who had contacted the local authorities and recommended that the family physician be summoned to sedate a hysterical Josephine.

It had been James who'd found Elizabeth's broken necklace on the floor of Joan's bedroom and had then explained in a sorrowful voice to the sheriff that Elizabeth doubtless had kidnapped Joan out of revenge. "And though it brings shame on my brother and his wife," he had confided, "I feel honor bound to warn you that Horatio was forced to fire her, due to Miss Granger's illicit relationship with his horse trainer."

He finally escaped from the bedlam to the guest cottage that had been his private quarters for the past few years, where he vented the wild laughter he'd contained. Then he began final preparations. *It won't be long now,*

384

Elizabeth. Still chuckling, he re-read the first note one last time: "Dearest Elizabeth, I cannot keep our secret from the world a moment longer. Meet me at our usual spot. Yours always, S.K."

Not as sickeningly sentimental as the one his foolish sister had penned all those years ago, but Elizabeth was bright enough to appreciate the delicious irony. James read the words one last time, in his mind matching them to the note he'd found in his sister's room all those years ago. He wished that he could see Elizabeth's face when she read his masterpiece.

But it was the response to the *second* note he had penned that filled James with even greater anticipation.

◆ ◆ ◆

Ochlocknee

Elizabeth wandered back to her room at Mrs. Tilford's boardinghouse, her heart grappling with unfamiliar joy — a bubbling euphoria singing through her veins. *Simon.* "Simon," she repeated out loud, just to hear the sound of his name.

He had promised to return as soon as possible, but he seemed determined to confront James in spite of Elizabeth's concern over his future as Horatio's trainer. "Don't worry about that," he'd told her, so forcefully Elizabeth had stifled further protest. "I'll explain

385

everything when I return. Just take care of yourself. Stay close to Mrs. Tilford and the other residents. I doubt if James will risk returning so soon, but if he does, remember to do exactly as I told you."

He'd held her at arm's length, looking hard and lethal . . . and loving. "I don't want to leave you, but I must." He kissed her and melted into the woods before Elizabeth opened her eyes.

She stopped now, gazing out over the brown, stubbly field to a ramshackle cluster of row houses, the leafless trees and bleak gray sky. She had never anticipated feeling . . . *happiness. Would You really do this, for me?* she asked. *I've always trusted* Your *love. Can I trust Simon's?*

There was no answer, but she smiled as she mounted the sagging steps of the front porch. If she chose to accept *Simon's* love, she would finally be able to admit that it was fully reciprocated.

"Miss Graham?"

Elizabeth blinked at Mrs. Tilford's reserved tone. She stood at the door, broom in one hand, her normally smiling face shuttered. Elizabeth stepped inside, concerned.

Mrs. Tilford picked up an envelope from a small table and slowly held it out. "This is for you. It was delivered by — by a woman decent folk hereabouts have no traffic with." Red spots dotted the worn cheeks. "You've been here such a short time, and I'd not like to pass hasty judgment, but — two gentlemen callers, in as many days? And now *this* . . ." She gestured toward the offending envelope. "Well, it does make a body wonder."

Elizabeth stared down at the white parchment, from which emanated the odor of cheap cologne. Elizabeth's name was neatly inscribed on the front, so there could be no mistake. "I don't know anybody here —" she began, and stopped. Given the circumstances, she didn't blame Mrs. Tilford a bit for her caution. She smiled at the troubled landlady. "I'd wonder about me, too! Would you prefer it if I moved out immediately?"

"Oh." Mrs. Tilford wiped her hands on her apron, looking uncomfortable. "Why, I don't know. It don't seem right, you being such a . . . *nice* young woman and all. It's just that . . . my other boarders —"

"It's quite all right, Mrs. Tilford. I don't mind. Truly. I can be ready to leave in the morning."

Mrs. Tilford studied her a moment. "You're most unusual," she declared, shaking her head. "Make me feel downright ashamed of myself."

"There's no need. Please don't." Elizabeth touched her arm. "You don't know me, but I promise you there's no reason for you to fret. You see" — her smile stretched until her cheeks ached — "for the first time, I have

387

someone waiting for me."

Elizabeth barely noticed the stupefied silence she left behind. *I won't be alone,* she repeated to herself as she entered her room, absently opening the envelope while she walked. *Simon will be there. He'll help. Lord? Isn't it a miracle?* Someone loved her, even knowing her background. . . .

She pulled out the folded sheet of paper, scanned the words — and her heart stopped beating. "So, unless you want the Crump brats to number *four* instead of five — you will destroy this note. You will talk to *no one.* And you will not be late."

46

Thomasville

Simon returned to his quarters at Adelaide late in the afternoon. He'd detoured by the drop-off site to leave Alex an urgent message and now, coldly determined, he planned to insure that neither James Crump nor his nefarious schemes would ever touch Elizabeth again. He almost missed the two pine needles jammed inside the door to his cottage, just to the left of the door handle. With a self-directed mental kick, Simon eased the door open, shutting it softly behind him. The room was in shadows. There was no sound, no sense of movement. "Alex?"

"Not this time," answered a drawling baritone voice Simon hadn't heard in four years. Seconds later Adam Moreaux appeared from Simon's darkened bedroom. "Last night MacKay sent a coded telegram to the Atlanta office. I turned Paxton over to Superintendent Jenkins and made it back down on a freight train an hour ago."

Simon silently considered the implications while he adjusted to Adam's unexpected presence. Taller than Simon, dressed all in black — what he once had laconically referred to as his "hunting clothes" — Adam Moreaux's strength and serenity offered a reassurance Simon had not experienced since their last meeting over four years earlier. He felt tense muscles relax, his festering rage against James Crump subsiding. If Alex was unavailable, there was no better man to have at his back than Adam Moreaux.

"It's good to see you, Panther," he admitted, running a hand around the back of his neck. "Even though there's little *good* about the situation here. Now . . . tell me what I need to know."

He gestured Adam over to the small sitting area in front of the fireplace. A thin strip of winter light streamed through a crack in the drawn curtains, allowing enough visibility without risking additional light from a lamp. Too restless to sit, Simon propped a shoulder against the mantel and watched his old friend.

"Benjamin Dawes left here an hour ago." Abruptly Adam turned to the faded tapestry sofa. In a swift movement that set the fringed leather on the arms of his buckskin waving, he knelt and reached beneath the sofas's tassled skirt, then stood. "He left you a . . . present. MacKay followed him out here and found it after Dawes left. He passed along the information to me."

Simon felt the skin on the back of his neck begin to tingle. He looked from Adam to the flat oblong box, tied with string, which had been hidden beneath the sofa. "How thoughtful of Mr. Dawes." He retrieved the box. "Did you —"

"A thousand dollars, in small bills, plus a 'signed agreement' between you and one Rupert Slade, in which you agree to fix a couple of the races next weekend. Are you acquainted with anyone named Rupert Slade?"

"He's the trainer for one of the winter residents, hails from Boston." Simon riffled through the bills. "He's something of a braggart, but I doubt if he's involved in this." He studied the *agreement,* and a muscle in his jaw twitched. "Just one more innocent victim."

"Like Elizabeth Graham?"

Simon tilted his head, studying the other man. "You must have had quite a chat with Alex."

"I like MacKay. A tad opinionated, perhaps something of a hot-tempered Scot . . . but I'm glad you've had him for a friend. He's a good operative — and a man of God."

"There's no doubt in my mind which of those two pleases you the most."

Adam smiled, unperturbed. "Dawes lives in a room at the City Hotel, near the depot. While you . . . ah . . . return his gift, I'll trot along to the courthouse to start proceedings on arrest warrants. Based on MacKay's assessment of the situation, your superintendent is sending along some extra men. They should be here by early evening."

"We've only sufficient grounds to indict Dawes for attempted extortion, and James Crump for assault," Simon snapped. "And nothing on Horatio." He pounded the mantel with his fist. "*Nothing!* I still have nothing on them, Adam."

"Easy, my friend. *You* might not . . . but you're not alone in this, remember? When I picked Paxton up at the jail the other day, I learned about one Rufus Black — now a *former* guest in Thomasville's jail. He's one of the men who sabotaged the bridge, under orders from Paxton. Guess, if you will, who 'arranged' for Rufus's signed confession — and subsequent release."

"Adam, I'm in no mood for guessing games."

"Hmm. So I see." Adam stretched, then fixed a serene but implacable gaze upon a smoldering Simon. "Now don't get your ruff up, Simon. You know better, with me."

He waited, and with a curt gesture of acknowledgment, Simon resumed his stance against the mantel, arms folded, eyes glittering. "Rufus Black?"

"Rufus decided upon reflection, I imagine, that he'd been trying to swim in a shark-infested ocean, instead of a country pond. So he talked to the sheriff before James sprung him from the jail. Seems Black was playing both ends against the middle, securing and selling information to Paxton while working for the Crumps. Simon, I'll tell you the rest later. Just . . . trust me." He pointed to the box Simon still held. "Right now, you need to make sure Dawes isn't sowing any more seeds of destruction."

"Very well." Simon re-tied the box and tossed it on the sofa. "Let me see to a few things and I'll be off. Where is Alex?"

"I told him to collect his wife and take the evening train back to Atlanta, now that I'm here to watch your back."

Simon lifted a brow. "He didn't offer any argument?"

"Not after I let slip the fact that Avery Paxton might be detained several days in the Fulton County Jail. Don't worry — he wouldn't have been nearly so amenable if I hadn't . . . insisted. Besides, you and Paxton are not his only concerns." He idly stroked the pearl handle of the bowie knife strapped to his waist. Then he smiled across at Simon. "Seems his wife woke up this morning feeling rather poorly. Seems she's been feeling rather poorly for about a week now and had hidden it from her husband."

Simon narrowed his gaze, for the moment completely speechless. He stared at Adam, whose smile broadened to a grin, though even in the dim light Simon could see the glint of compassion in his unusual amber-colored eyes. "She's pregnant, isn't she?" Simon concluded, seeing no need to dress it up. Adam Moreaux had little use for societal squeamishness.

"I've already begun praying for a healthy baby. Simon . . ." He paused, and Simon automatically tensed. Adam — being tentative? "I know you need to go, but I think you should tell me about Elizabeth Graham. There appears to be some uncertainty as to her guilt or innocence in —"

"She's innocent as far as Pinkerton's is concerned." Simon advanced on the other man. "She's a victim, Adam. She's had some troubles, and because of them she was working for the Crumps under an assumed name. But she is *not* part of our investigation. Leave her alone — and don't fight me on this one."

"Does she know who you are?"

"No." His hand curled into a fist. "No, she doesn't — but I'm going to tell her. I . . . have to."

"You don't have to explain, Simon." Adam's voice was level, steady. "You love her, don't you?"

"Yes." He took a deep breath. "And when this is over, I'm resigning from the Agency. I want to work with horses. I never knew, until these past weeks, how much I missed them. And I want to make my peace with God. Elizabeth . . ." Feeling as naked and vulnerable as a newborn, he had to turn away. "She's endured so much — far worse than I. Yet *her* faith in a loving God . . . it doesn't dim. Like yours and Alex's. I need . . . I need —"

All of a sudden Simon was engulfed in a bear hug that threatened to crush his rib cage. "Thank God!" Adam exclaimed, releasing his friend when Simon tensed. "Thank God. I've been praying for years that —" He hesitated, turning his head toward the window. "Someone's coming."

Simon had already moved toward the door, while Adam melted back into Simon's bedroom.

"Mr. Kincaid! Mr. Kincaid, you in there?" Jefferson yelled. Simon opened the door, and the wild-eyed stablehand burst into almost incoherent babbling. "Lawd save us, Mr. Kincaid! You's finally back. Lawd save us. What will we do? What will we do? Mr. Kincaid, last night someone done stole little Joan! Stole her right out of her bed! And they's saying — they's saying it was Miss *'Lizbeth* what done the deed!"

47

The abandoned sharecropper's shanty stood on the edge of a fallow field. Tin roof rusting, split logs warped and rotten, the structure appeared to be on the verge of collapse, deserted except for a thin plume of smoke streaming out of the crumbling chimney. There was no other sign of life.

Elizabeth stayed well within the cover of the woods, working her way around so that she could make her approach from the rear. The instructions James had given in the letter might very well be a trap, but until she knew for certain that Joan was *not* inside, she would have to take the chance. Gusts of winter-chilled winds buffeted the trees; above her, branches clacked together like dead men's bones, while the pines swayed in restless wailing shudders.

She moved closer, her gaze on the shanty's only window, covered by a tattered square of oilcloth. A bottom corner flapped with each new gust. She crept up until all that stood between her and the crude building was a tangled screen of dead shrubbery — sumac and brittle broom sedge. When a particularly strong blast of wind shrieked across the field, rattling the tin roof, she darted across the intervening twenty yards.

Crouched beneath the window, Elizabeth strained to listen while she struggled to steady her breathing. It was not yet four o'clock, the time she had been "ordered" to arrive — but if *she* had sneaked up early, so could James. Yet after several endless moments, the only sound she could distinguish from inside was the faint crackle and hiss of a fire. Cautiously, an inch at a time, Elizabeth raised her head until she could peek over the sill, through the inch-wide gap made by the ill-fitting curtain. She barely suppressed a gasp.

Joan *was* inside! Sitting on the bare floor, a dingy wool blanket wrapped about her thin shoulders. The blanket engulfed her entire body except for her feet, which, Elizabeth realized with a wrench, sported her best Sunday patent leather shoes, but no stockings.

Hot anger such as she had never known boiled up through Elizabeth. What kind of *barbarian* would kidnap a helpless little girl? Her furious gaze swept the room, then returned to Joan's abductor, who sat on the floor opposite the child, his back to the window. Even hunched over in a seated position, she recognized the thick shock of greasy blond hair. Revulsion and fear momentarily swamped the anger.

Then Joan spoke. "Hurry up! You're taking too long. Don't any of your cards match?"

"I ain't saying, and if you don't button your lip, I ain't playing no more, neither." His voice was surly as he added, "You *sure* you ain't never played rummy?"

"Mama says playing cards are a tool of the devil." Joan lifted her chin. Elizabeth almost moaned aloud at the trust shining from that solemn little face. "But it hasn't seemed bad, when we play. Do you want me to promise to lose the next time?"

"No!" He swept all the cards up, then stood, looming over Joan. "Come on," he ordered in a gruff tone. "I got to go check and see if your uncle's on his way yet. I'll be back in a bit."

Docile as a kitten, Joan followed him over to a narrow cot, allowing the blanket to slip to the floor. Just as meekly she sat down and put her hands behind her back, as if from habit. The man picked up a long rope, one end of which was already tied to the bed, and swiftly secured Joan's wrists with the other end. Then he wrapped the blanket around her again, tucking her in securely. Joan made no protest, but huddled on the floor beneath the coarse blanket.

For a fraction of a second, the man's fingers skimmed the tumble of light curls, and Elizabeth glimpsed a fleeting regret. The last time she had looked into those eyes they had glowed with feral suspicion and deadly intent . . . just before he slammed a blackjack against the side of her head at the edge of the paddock at Adelaide.

She closed her eyes, fighting nausea over the bizarre anomaly — a murderous villain who could still treat a child with kindness. The door of the shanty banged, and her eyes flew open. Joan was alone.

Elizabeth counted to twenty, then stuck her head inside the window. "Joan!" she whispered as loud as she dared. "Joan! Over here, at the window. It's Elizabeth!"

Joan looked up, obviously surprised to see her and more than a little uncertain. "Elizabeth! Why did you leave? Why are you *here?* Uncle James said you were going to steal me away, and so he brought me here to — to keep me safe."

Elizabeth wriggled through the window and dropped onto the floor in an inelegant heap of skirt and petticoats. "Ouch!" She rubbed her shoulder, then her scraped knees. "Joan . . . lambkin — I've come to take you *home* — not steal you away! I promise!" Even as she spoke, she had scrambled to her feet and dashed across the room to sweep Joan in a brief fierce hug. "You *know* me, Joan. How could you doubt me?"

Frantically she worked at the stiff knot, marveling at how loosely the man had tied it

— as if to prevent as much pain as possible. Tears stung her eyes, and the burning intensified when the rope gave at last, and Joan's thin arms wrapped around Elizabeth's neck, choking her in a feverish embrace. Then the blanket fell away, revealing a rumpled, long-sleeved nightgown visible beneath a man's filthy undershirt with all its buttons missing. The sleeves had been rolled up, but the hem hung well past Joan's knees.

"Elizabeth? Are you sure I can leave? Joe might not like it." The large brown eyes filled with confusion and doubt. "His name isn't really Joe — I heard Uncle James call him 'Rufus.' But he told me to call him 'Joe.' He said I remind him of his little sister. Elizabeth, why did he have to tie me? He said he had to, even though I promised I wouldn't move. And why did Uncle James say *you* wanted to —"

"Darling, I'll try to explain later. Right now we *must* leave." Rapidly she removed Joan's shoes, then her own walking shoes. After peeling off her thick cotton stockings, she tugged them up over Joan's bare legs. "They'll fall down, I know, but you'll be warmer," she explained while she crammed her bare feet back into her shoes, then helped Joan finish fastening her shoe straps.

"Hurry, darling. There isn't much time." Elizabeth dragged Joan to her feet, her gaze catching on the welcome sight of the girl's heavy winter coat, folded into a pillow at the end of the cot. She bundled the child into the coat, then led her over to the window. "Up you go." She hoisted Joan's slight body up and stuffed her through the opening. "When you drop to the ground, relax your knees and roll. Just like that day on the train, remember? I'll be right behind you."

Joan's expression was still uncertain. "But why can't we go through the door?"

"Don't talk, darling, all right? Just hurry!"

Seconds later they were scrambling for the shelter of the woods. "Run, Joan!" Elizabeth urged. She risked a quick backward glance. "Run!"

They fought through tangled underbrush and skirted a patch of swamp, not pausing until they reached a narrow ribbon of track, where Elizabeth stopped so they could catch their breath.

Joan didn't speak, but watched Elizabeth with dilated eyes, lips quivering. Her patent leather shoes were scratched, caked with dirt, and Elizabeth's stockings had bunched up around the ankles. Beneath the fine cashmere coat dangled a torn ruffle from her nightgown.

Elizabeth would never forget the wrenching tableau. She dropped to her knees so that her face was level with Joan's. "See the mark in that tree?" She pointed to the shallow gouge she had fashioned with a sharp stick.

Earlier, she had fretted over the time-consuming task, but now she thanked God for the inspiration. *James, this time you aren't going to win!* "I want you to stay on this path, and look for marks just like that one. This path leads to a road. When you come to the road, turn left. *Left,* lambkin. Hold up your left hand." Joan did so. "Your grandmother's house is at the end of that road. You'll be safe there, and I want you to run as fast as you can when you reach that road. If you have to rest, count to twenty, three times, then keep going. Promise me you'll keep going."

The little girl was still hesitant. "Is Joe a bad man, after all? What about Uncle James?" Tears welled. "Uncle James tried to tell me that you wanted to hurt me, but I didn't believe him."

Elizabeth grasped Joan's shoulders and squeezed. "I would give my life for you," she promised, her voice hoarse. "Joan, there's no time to explain. Later, I will —" She bit her lip, unwilling to make a promise she might not be able to keep.

A faint shout echoed in the distance. "Run!" Elizabeth commanded. "Run to your grandmother. You'll be safe there."

"What about you?"

"I'll . . . be right behind you. Go, now!"

With a last backward look of mingled fear and trust, Joan scampered down the path and disappeared.

Elizabeth waited, listening, then dashed back toward the shanty, eyes straining to see in the darkening woods. The clouds had blown away, leaving a pale sky the luminescent color of an opal. The moaning wind had died. Tall and silent in the hushed stillness of late afternoon, even the trees seemed to be waiting.

When she reached the shanty, there was no sign of Rufus. But Elizabeth could hear him, cursing a blue streak from somewhere on the other side of the building. She offered up a hasty prayer, then darted around the side of the shanty. Fifty yards away, his back to Elizabeth, Rufus was stabbing at the bushes which choked either side of the overgrown track.

She took a deep breath, then ran diagonally across the edge of the field, in plain view. When Rufus spotted her, he bellowed like an enraged buffalo.

Elizabeth whirled, leaped across a shallow ditch, and plunged headlong into the woods.

48

City Hotel
Thomasville

Benjamin Dawes, Simon decided during the long hours he waited for the detective, was thoroughly despicable. His hotel room more nearly resembled a flophouse in the fetid back streets of a large city than a room in a respectable hotel. As far as Simon was concerned, ascribing to Dawes the title of "private detective" insulted every legitimate flatfoot in the business.

Perched on a chair by the window, Simon dragged out his watch for the third time in the past half hour. What was Adam up to? It was past four o'clock. He ran his hand around the back of his shirt collar, irritated with himself for his obsession with Elizabeth. *Blast* Adam and his knowing cougar eyes!

"Now, don't sit there brooding while you wait, Simon," the fellow operative had counseled before they parted — Adam, accompanied by Jefferson, to the main house to introduce himself and find out what he could about Joan and Elizabeth; Simon back to town to wait for Benjamin Dawes. "God protects His children. And" — he'd held up his hand, warning Simon with a single penetrating look — "don't allow your fear for Elizabeth and your rage at James Crump to be vented on the likes of Dawes. He isn't worth it, my friend, and you know it." Suddenly the shrewd eyes began to twinkle. "And you know that I know that you know it."

Simon glanced out the window again, then settled onto the chair. He had also, for the past few hours, experimented with — why mince words? — with praying.

"It's been a long time, God," he muttered under his breath in an attempt to start *somewhere*. Hopefully the patience of the Almighty would prove more enduring than his own. "But I have a feeling I'm about to need —"

Scraping footsteps, followed by the rattle of a key, jerked Simon from his unaccustomed reverie. Old habits clicked instantly into place as he glided soundlessly behind the door. The moment Dawes turned to shut it, Simon was ready. Seconds later the stunned detective lay spread-eagled on the floor, with Simon's forearm pressed against his windpipe.

"Good afternoon, Mr. Dawes," he said. "I came to thank you for your generous gift."

The other man's eyes widened as fear replaced spitting anger. He tried to move, then began to choke when the pressure on his windpipe increased.

"You should be advised that I'm a little . . . miffed," Simon continued conversationally. "Also that I'm returning your package, contents intact, of course. Ah-ah, Dawes, I wouldn't try anything if I were you —" The threat hung, unfinished, in the rancid air.

The detective complied instantly. After a moment Simon eased the pressure, and Dawes began gagging, his weasel face suffused with color. "You got no call —" he wheezed. Coughing, he cleared his throat, then filled Simon's ears with a spate of curses and half-fearful pleas. "I'll explain, if you let me up!" he finally blurted.

Simon released him, feeling a pinprick of shame when Dawes scrambled up and flattened himself against the door. "Why —" he began, but Simon heard a rattle as Dawes fumbled with the doorknob at his back. This time Simon held his temper firmly in check, and merely stiff-armed the protesting Dawes over to the filthy, unmade bed and shoved him down. "Stay put," he advised, his voice deceptively mild.

Dawes struggled upright, peered into Simon's face, and finally gave up. Slump-shouldered, he wiped the back of his hand across his nose. "Whaddaya want to know?"

Simon picked up the box and tossed it on the bed. "There's too much money here for this to be your idea. Who paid you to set me up, and why?"

"Georgina Crump." He snorted at Simon's astonishment. "Thought it was someone else, did ya? Strikes me you're not a real popular fella hereabouts, Kincaid. Except maybe with Elizabeth . . . *Granger*. Oh, that's right, you know her real name, don't ya? What an innocent, misunderstood —"

"Don't push me, Dawes. In spite of my feelings right now, I really don't want to break your dirty neck." Simon dragged air into his lungs, flexed his shoulder muscles in an effort to relax. *I'd forgotten, Lord, how hard it can be to obey.*

I know, son . . . but trust Me. Simon froze, then slowly relaxed. In the rank, untidy room, he would have sworn in a court of law that he'd heard the Voice, felt the wash of loving affirmation spreading like sunlight through his soul. Unbelievable. He didn't deserve this, but God was responding to him as if nothing had ever happened. As if it hadn't been years since —

Simon looked down at Dawes. "Elizabeth *Graham* has nothing to do with this," he stated calmly. "What is it now? If there's something in your pockets, like a weapon, feel free to pull it out."

"Just wanted a smoke," Dawes grumbled. He tugged out a half-finished cigar, along with a crumbled piece of paper. "And *this*."

407

He flicked the paper onto the rumpled covers of the bed. "Read it, chump, and then tell me something I don't know about poor little Elizabeth Graham."

Simon scowled as he picked up the scrap of paper and read it. Rage stirred, then subsided. "I presume I'm the 'S.K.' Where did you find this?"

Dawes lit his cigar and blew a foul stream of smoke upward. "In her room in Ochlocknee. Anything else you want . . . besides Elizabeth Graham, I mean?"

"What I *expect* is for you to keep a civil tongue in your head. I've about had my fill of your lewd innuendos, and I've *sure* had a bellyful of your boorishness." Simon stepped closer, looking down as he ripped the paper to confetti-sized pieces and threw them in the detective's face. "Anyone who's learned his letters can pen a note. And any slug whose palm is greased well enough can plant 'evidence' to frame the innocent." His hand shot out, but instead of throttling Dawes, Simon grabbed the box full of money and shoved it under the other man's nose. "Or have you forgotten this?"

"So? What's it to you, anyway? You're just a no-account horse trainer."

"Humor me!" Simon retorted. "What *else* have you been paid to do for the Crumps? Is Georgina the only one who's paid? Remember — I have *no* use for liars."

"Why should I tell *you* anything?" Dawes muttered. When Simon made a threatening move, Dawes threw up his hands and scuttled crablike to the other side of the bed. "All right, all right! It was just the brown recluse — Georgina! She even had me spying on James, her own son! You're welcome to trot right on out there and verify it if you care to face her. Myself, I'd as soon tangle with a wounded wolverine."

"Georgina Crump. . . ." Simon echoed, still grappling with Dawes's revelation. He cast about in his memory for everything he'd learned about the eccentric elderly woman. A muscle in his cheek twitched. "You called her a 'brown recluse' — one of the most poisonous spiders in the South. Why?"

Dawes shot him an incredulous look. "If you're ever stupid enough to poke your snooker around her empire, you'll find out."

"From what I hear, she hasn't appeared in public in a decade," Simon mused aloud, ticking off the scant pieces of information he and Alex had gleaned. "Not since her husband died. Loves horticulture; Rose Hill was a showplace when Horatio, Sr., was alive, but in the past —" He paused, as pieces evolved to form a chilling hypothesis. "She had private telephone *and* telegraph lines installed; employs a private cadre of messenger boys." *God? Help me here . . . what does it mean? She's a cultured, very wealthy* woman. . . . "Obsessed with family."

At that moment Dawes made a frantic dash toward a scarred washstand in the corner of the room. Simon catapulted across the bed, felling the little rat as he clawed at a drawer in the washstand. Lips compressed, Simon yanked down the tasseled drapery tiebacks and fashioned them into a rope to bind Dawes's hands and ankles. Then he stood, breathing hard, fists planted on his hips, and waited. Dawes glowered at him — bested, at least for the moment, Simon hoped.

Calm returned slowly. He took a deep cleansing breath, for just a moment closing his eyes to better sense the warm Presence. *Sorry. It* has *been . . . a long time.*

"What else has Georgina paid you to do?" he asked Dawes when his pulse was restored to normal. "You've spied on James, and you planted money in my quarters — the intention being to get rid of me?" He waited until Dawes gave a reluctant nod. "And it was *Georgina's* idea — not Horatio's?"

"I told you so, didn't I?"

"Hmm. So you did." Simon stroked his chin thoughtfully. "Now . . . I know why *I'd* spy on James — but perhaps you'd better tell me why his own mother would do a thing like that."

Dawes grumbled something beneath his breath, then shrugged. "She . . . didn't trust him. He's a wild one, that James, likes to strut his family's power. He's been in trouble a time or two, and she's had to pay off some folks." His gaze narrowed. "And that's all you get outta me, Kincaid, no matter what fancy stunt you pull. You might be a fair hand in a fight, but I'll take a beating over what would happen if *she* got wind of this."

Simon scooped up the box holding the bills. "I might be tempted to . . . ah . . . 'manufacture' some evidence of my own," he pointed out.

Dawes spent a few more futile moments spewing curses and jerking on his bonds while Simon drew up a chair, then folded his arms as if prepared to wait indefinitely. Dawes quickly gave up. "Beats me why some no-name horse trainer thinks he can tangle with the Crumps," he groused. "Come on, let me up, and I'll tell you whatever you've a mind to know. Not that it'll do you much good." A crafty gleam appeared in his eye, then faded. "I'd have tried to get the goods on them myself a couple of years ago, if I hadn't figured I'd end up like Wade Lomax."

Simon went very still. "What do you know about Lomax?" Mentally he replayed that long-ago day, outside Sumner, listening to the nervous chairman of the bankrupt railroad who had claimed the Crumps were out to ruin him. He'd killed himself . . . or had he?

Dawes shrugged. "Nothing."

Simon tugged out his watch, suppressed a

stab of concern, then looked back at the crusty detective. "What do you know about Wade Lomax?" he repeated, softly.

Dawes spewed forth a volley of words. "They're rotten, the lot of 'em! Think just because their name is 'Crump,' and they have as much money as Vanderbilt himself, they can do whatever they please." He sniffed, and hunched his shoulder, wiping his nose.

Simon waited, arms still folded, gaze locked on the sweating man.

"I'd been looking for information for Eliz — for Miss Graham," Dawes corrected hastily, "but after Soames's murder, she took off. I started doing a few odd jobs for Horatio. Small-time stuff — getting the goods on employees, sniffing around rivals for information the Crumps could use —"

"Did you ever plant evidence like you tried to do to me?"

"A time or two . . . for Miz Crump. By that time, it was my neck or theirs." He studied Simon for a minute. "She's the real power, Kincaid, not Horatio. He's too much of a sissy-pants. Doesn't have a clue it's his mama who runs things."

Simon wasn't entirely convinced. "And Lomax?"

Dawes looked down at the floor. "He was an old fool, and a coward. If he'd had some starch, he'd have fought back, instead of putting a gun to his own head. Listen,

Kincaid, how about you and me cutting a deal? With your fighting skills and my brains, we'd make a fair team. . . ." He wriggled on the floor, looking wrinkled and pathetic.

Pathetic as a coiled copperhead, Simon amended silently. He took a deep breath, then walked over to Dawes. "Benjamin Dawes, I'm placing you under arrest — for extortion, attempted extortion, and accessory to murder. I'm not really a horse trainer. I'm an undercover operative for Pinkerton's National Detective Agency, and Mr. Dawes — *you're* in more trouble than an alley cat in a swamp full of alligators."

49

Two hard raps sounded on the door, which opened almost simultaneously. Adam stepped inside, pocketed the skeleton key, and eyed the scene briefly before turning to shut the door. "Looks like everything is under control. Good. Simon" — he hesitated, then finished quietly — "we need to telegraph Superintendent Jenkins. I've been talking with Horatio Crump."

Dread congealed in the pit of Simon's stomach. When it came to the art of persuasion, Adam was incomparable. "What did you find out?" He wasn't sure he wanted to know.

"It was more what he inferred, actually." Adam cocked an inquiring glance at Dawes. "Give you a spot of trouble, did he? I trust you remembered what I said?"

"Adam —" Simon bit off an impatient retort. Dawes was gawking as if Adam had burst through the door, screaming a war whoop and waving a tomahawk dripping with blood.

Adam's mouth quirked in a wry smile, but the amber eyes watched Simon with searching intensity. He casually unsheathed his bowie knife and began flipping it, end over end, a breathtaking skill in which Adam engaged to relax. Every movement of his arm stretched the supple fabric of his thin buckskin shirt and set the leather fringes to dancing.

Dawes gulped audibly, but Simon knew his friend. His spine prickled in warning. "What is it? Adam . . ."

Adam grimaced, and in a movement too rapid for the eye to follow, the knife disappeared back in its sheath. "Sorry. Old habits. Simon, Horatio Crump is not our man, even though I think he *is* aware of . . . certain criminal activities —" He broke off, eyeing Simon. "You know, don't you?" He glanced down at the man on the floor. "Dawes tell you?"

Simon nodded. "It's Georgina. And little brother James. That's about all I've verified at this point." He couldn't help it; he had to ask. "Elizabeth?" He was praying — as fervently as he'd ever prayed in his life — and at last believing that God would answer.

Dawes stirred. "Both of you are Pinks, huh?" His wary eye surveyed the unlikely duo looming above him. "Thought you'd give up on the Crumps by now. But it's your funeral — the brown recluse is out for blood. Like I told you, her daughter and El— uh, *Miss Graham's* old man were playing footsy. From what I've heard, the whole county knew it,

415

even if they weren't standing in line to tell about it. When Graham's son took a notion to avenge his mother's honor by killing his old man, it was all over. After that, even the Crumps didn't have the clout to force some poor sucker to marry their daughter."

"Until they bribed a sharecropper desperate for a way out of the quicksand of endless debt," Adam put in. "Horatio told me that his mother never recovered from the shame. And when Helene died in childbirth eighteen months later . . ."

All of a sudden, feeling mule-kicked, Simon whirled, hauled Dawes to his feet, and held him dangling six inches above the floor. *"You just came from Ochlocknee,"* he grated out, the terrifying knowledge charging him with an almost supernatural strength. "You were in Elizabeth's room. *What did you do to her, you low-down snake?* Georgina sent you over there to plant some more evidence, didn't she? What else besides a trashy note? Was that her way of getting even for what Elizabeth's father did to Helene?" *Elizabeth!*

"Simon . . ." Adam's tone placated . . . warned.

"Where's Elizabeth?"

"Simon, you're choking him. Simon, let him go." Firm hands gripped his shoulders, calming, reassuring.

Simon obeyed mindlessly, and the purple-faced Dawes fell writhing to the ground.

Adam used his knife to cut the gasping detective free, then helped him onto the bed. All Simon could do was stare into a future where the joy of heaven had plummeted to a bottomless black pit.

"Answer Mr. Kincaid's question now, my good man," Adam encouraged Dawes, his voice as implacable as it was serene, "or I'll be forced to let him have at you again."

"She weren't there!" Dawes sputtered, coughing a little. "I tell you, she weren't there! I even asked the landlady, but all she told me was some floozy delivered that letter." He shrank back as Simon turned. "I'm not lying! It wasn't me, Kincaid. I swear it!"

"She's not in Ochlocknee," Simon repeated through stiff lips. "And she's not at Adelaide." He and Adam stared at each other.

"I'll see to Mr. Dawes, and then have a chat with the sheriff," Adam announced. "The backup from Atlanta should be here within the hour." He hesitated. "Simon, have a care. I know you."

"Not anymore, you don't," Simon returned, and even Adam stepped back. "Bring deputies and the backup men to Rose Hill. The sheriff can provide directions."

His horse, whipped to a breakneck gallop, was a mile down the Tallahassee road before Simon remembered to breathe.

50

Rose Hill

A small door at the back of the west wing, almost hidden between two gigantic hydran-
geas, appeared to be Elizabeth's safest entry
into Georgina Crump's imposing Greek Re-
vival mansion. The two wings flanking either
side — added at some point over the years —
stretched out like massive arms waiting to
crush unwary intruders. Elizabeth suppressed
a shudder and ordered her overactive imagination to hush up.

Blood-red tendrils streaked the late afternoon sky. She knew she shouldn't linger.
Even so, she stayed crouched behind a hedge
of boxwoods, catching her breath while she
watched the house. And thought.

Ten minutes earlier, a lathered horse bearing a hatless, stone-faced James had cantered
past Elizabeth's hiding place. Horrified,
she'd watched him dismount at the front
door, throw the reins to a cowering boy, and
disappear inside the house.

She had escaped from Rufus, but James's
ill-timed appearance stymied her plan to ap-

peal to Georgina. The proud matriarch might be willing to shelter her from Joan's abductor, especially with Joan to corroborate Elizabeth's story. But Georgina would *never* believe that her younger son had masterminded the evil scheme, with James himself present.

Somewhere out of sight, the faint sound of raised voices rang out in the cool stillness of twilight. Anger? Surprise? *Joan!* Elizabeth concluded in buoyant relief, and she almost dashed out into the open before caution prevailed. Under the circumstances, Joan's safe return did not automatically insure *Elizabeth's* safety.

For several moments longer she waited and listened, sifting through her options. In the end, slipping inside the house through that small door still offered the most prudent solution. Once Joan's safety could be verified, Elizabeth would be able to address her own tenuous circumstance. If only she had been able to locate the gold!

Mouth dry, she peeked around the corner of the neatly trimmed hedge, then ran lightly across to the door. It opened easily, and Elizabeth slipped inside. The dark room appeared to be a jumbled storage room — thankfully deserted, at the moment — the only source of light a narrow window, whose view to the outside was completely obscured by shrubbery. Elizabeth tiptoed across the floor, skirting barrels, boxes, and oddments of furniture. A second, larger door on the other side of the room opened into a hall, illuminated by a single wall sconce at the far end.

Heart hammering, feeling very much the trespasser, she quietly shut the door behind her and started down the hall. As she passed by a second door that stood slightly ajar, she heard James's angry voice, loud enough to carry down the hall.

Elizabeth reacted without forethought, bolting through the nearby doorway. Only when the latch clicked did she realize what she had done. She leaned her forehead against the cool panel until her racing pulse slowed and she could calm herself enough to remember that she wasn't in the barn at Pastime, fleeing from a murderer. *Only James Crump!* she reminded herself, panic rising once more. *Fiddle-faddle, Elizabeth! Stop behaving like a ninny!*

Slowly she straightened and turned, peering through the shadows. A small desk lamp provided the only light, but it was sufficient for Elizabeth to realize in fresh horror that she had stumbled into Georgina's private telegraph room.

Even the servants at Adelaide whispered fearfully about this room. *Nobody* — not even Horatio or James — was allowed here. Josephine's upstairs maid had once confided to Elizabeth that she'd heard how Miz Georgina actually *whipped* one of the messenger boys for sneaking a peek. "Did it herself, she did. Cold and clear-eyed and not a whit sorry to be doin' it."

Elizabeth shook her head. What rubbish! Georgina Crump might be a chilly, forbidding matriarch — but whipping somebody just for looking inside a room? And yet, several times in the past few years, Elizabeth *had* overheard snatches of uneasy gossip about Georgina Crump. She hadn't been to Thomasville in a decade. She refused to leave Rose Hill except for the annual sabbatical to North Georgia and her servants made the highest wages in south Georgia but were forbidden to leave the premises.

Elizabeth resolutely set aside her qualms about Georgina Crump. She had never felt comfortable around the woman, but the children loved her, and right now, Joan's safety was all that mattered. Besides, a daring solution had just burst inside her head with all the brilliance of a thousand suns.

She walked over to the long table where the telegraph key sat. She knew how to work the device. As a bookkeeper at the Jekyll Island Resort Hotel, Elizabeth had frequently taken a letter or bill down to the hotel's telegrapher, a kindly old gentleman who had passed on his half-century's worth of knowledge.

She could send a telegram to Simon. He would help her — he would protect her. *God?*

Oh, God, only You understand what that means to me . . . .

If possible, she would send a telegram to Sheriff Calhoun as well, even though Georgina would be furious. She amended that hasty thought and deliberately fastened an image of Simon in her heart. Taking a hesitant step forward, her gaze fell on a large accordian folder labeled "Incoming Telegrams," and for a handful of breaths, Elizabeth debated whether or not to riffle through Georgina's messages.

She couldn't do it. Thirty years earlier Charles Graham had betrayed the Crump family; and now, for almost two years Elizabeth had deceived them about her name. Regardless of Georgina's flaws, regardless of the evil nature of her younger son, Elizabeth could not sit in judgment without bringing a similar condemnation upon herself. "Forgive me," she whispered, pinpricks of shame needling her skin. The end could not, *could not* justify the means. Bad enough to be sneaking around inside the house without Georgina's knowledge and using her private telegraph key without permission. . . . But to snoop in her private correspondence —

Elizabeth thrust her hand down toward the keypad, and her coat sleeve brushed a telegram lying on the table. The slip of paper drifted to the floor, and she automatically bent to retrieve it, with the intention of putting it back exactly where it had been.

The words leaped out: "Searched E.G.'s room, Ochlocknee. Stop. Obtained sufficient evidence for you. Stop. B.D."

As if in a dream, Elizabeth replaced the telegram on the table. Her brain wouldn't function, couldn't grasp the reality of those condemning words. They whirled through her head, burning an indelible message — and a terrifying truth. She sank down onto the hard seat of a straightback chair by the keypad. *Searched E.G.'s room, Ochlocknee.*

For a long time, Elizabeth sat, stiff and still, while she forced her numbed brain to sort through all the evidence. There *could* be other people living in Ochlocknee with the initials "E. G." And any number of people with the initials "B. D." *might* be employed by Georgina Crump.

But in her heart Elizabeth knew better. A bitter smile barely lifted the corners of her mouth. For months she had agonized, wondering how the Crumps would feel when they found out how *she* had deceived *them*. Now she knew. What she didn't understand was Georgina's motivation for hiring someone to spy on Elizabeth. Of course, if the "B. D." *did* stand for Benjamin Dawes, Georgina must already know that the "G" in Elizabeth's name did *not* stand for "Granger." Alarm propelled her to her feet. If Mr. Dawes worked for Georgina —

Run, Elizabeth. Flee. Now!

She didn't question the Voice. Had not questioned its firm, loving authority in fifteen years. She spared a single yearning glance at the telegraph key and hurried back across the room. Hands trembling, she fumbled to open the door, hesitated, then slipped into the hall. Ran lightly down the polished floor. Reached for the brass knob of the door that led outside, to safety . . . to Simon. Somehow she must find —

"Stop!" Georgina advanced upon her, thin face unforgiving, eyes narrowed to colorless chips of ice. "Stop there, or I'll have you shot on sight like a rabid dog."

The words and the look on her face confirmed the telegraph's message: Any explanation Elizabeth attempted to make would achieve little. She steeled herself. She would have to try, because of Joan. Nothing mattered right now but the safety of an innocent child. Regardless of Georgina's . . . peculiarities, she would *not* harm her granddaughter.

James appeared in the hallway behind his mother. When he caught sight of Elizabeth, he stopped dead. Cold chills coursed through Elizabeth's veins, numbing her hands, her feet, freezing her in their wake. She might have been able to escape from the older woman, but James was fit, strong — and merciless. Never in her life had she known such debilitating fear, not even on that long-ago

424

day in Pastime Stables.

She was trapped. Utterly helpless in the presence of an evil she had refused to comprehend or acknowledge . . . until it was too late.

51

Although Georgina halted several feet away, the force of her anger beat against Elizabeth in unrelenting waves. Mesmerized, she watched the approach of the formidable woman.

"Where is my granddaughter?" she demanded, each measured word stabbing Elizabeth like a well-aimed ice pick. "You lying, deceitful *whelp!* Where is my granddaughter?"

Stunned, Elizabeth could only stare at her. "Joan . . . isn't here?" she whispered. Her knees were shaking, and a roaring in her ears made her dizzy. "Ask . . . James," she managed.

Too late. It was too late. *God, help Joan. Help me.* They would shout now — at each other . . . at *her.* Somehow she would have to muster the fortitude to weather their wrath. James would probably — no! *Don't think about it!* She must convince them to listen . . . for Joan's sake. *If You don't help me, Lord, I'll fail. For Joan . . . help me for Joan's sake.*

Flushed, disheveled, James shouldered his way around his mother. He reached Elizabeth and grabbed her arm, shaking her like a doll. "I should have finished you the other day." Triumph — and fear — blazed from his eyes. "But even *I* never dreamed you'd abduct my niece!" He shook her again.

"James!" Georgina reprimanded him sharply. "Control yourself. That can wait until we find my granddaughter."

They loomed over Elizabeth like a pair of snarling wolves, but within the clarity of terror came a startling realization: James was afraid of his mother! *Thank You.* "Mrs. Crump, I didn't do it. James hired a man to kidnap —"

James's hand closed around her throat, choking off the words. "Let me reason with her, Mother. Just for a few minutes. She won't tell any more lies after I'm through with her."

"Not yet. James!" In a swirl of moire and satin, Georgina moved between them and knocked her son's hand from Elizabeth's throat. "You're behaving like a common hooligan!" She stared down at Elizabeth, and in the feeble glow of the wall sconce, her eyes burned. "She will pay, my son. I will *make* her pay for every lie she's perpetrated against my family. And for the sins of her *father.* . . ."

"Her father? Mother, what are you talking about? Listen — you don't know her like I do. You don't know —"

"I know more than you ever will, and I'll take a strap to you if you ever speak to me in that tone again!" Georgina's erosive control seemed to feed James's as well.

Dark fury flared in his face as he straightened, his fists clenching and unclenching. Elizabeth flattened herself against the wall. Moisture gathered between her shoulder blades and on her forehead. *Fight!* she ordered herself, but it was no use. *You have to fight.* . . . Helplessly, she felt herself slipping into the passive, trancelike state she had so often retreated to as a child. *Don't yell at me, please . . . don't yell.* . . .

"You don't even know her real name!" Georgina spat, her elegant white hand slashing toward Elizabeth. "The daughter of *Charles Graham!*"

"Charles Graham?" James's mouth went slack. His gaze darted from his mother to Elizabeth. "Charles Graham's . . . daughter?"

"Don't mimic me like a mindless puppet! Yes, Charles Graham. He ruined my daughter, and now I'll ruin *his* — just as I ruined his *sons*. She was just a year-old brat at the time —" Georgina raked Elizabeth's quaking form with a look of undisguised hatred. "I must admit Benjamin Dawes earned his money this time. She's been living under your noses for over a year, and *you had no idea who she was!*"

Elizabeth lifted her hand in a feeble attempt to placate their wrath, but the motion was wasted.

The hatred had twisted Georgina's fine-boned face into a distorted mask; her fever-bright gaze scorched Elizabeth. "You're despicable. You worm your way into my son's family, manipulate the feelings of my grandchildren . . ." She stopped, her mouth working. "You're just like your father!"

"No." Elizabeth shook her head. "No, I — I didn't know, until I found the list of names on Mr. Soames . . . at Pastime Racetrack . . . that your husband and my father — I was looking for the gold . . . to give it back. I wanted to . . . atone. . . ."

Trapped in the nightmare of childhood terrors, she did not realize the fatal danger her stammered words had roused. James made a sudden movement, but Elizabeth — mesmerized by Georgina's wrath — scarcely noticed.

Her whispered phrases, broken and incoherent, served only to further inflame the older woman. "You wanted to atone for your father?" she mimicked harshly. "Do you think all that gold could restore my daughter's good name? Do you think mere *gold* could atone for her disgrace . . . and her death?"

"Mother —"

"Go and clean up!" she snapped without turning her head in James's direction. "And change your clothes. You're filthy, and I won't have it in my house." The clipped insult tipped James over the edge.

"Tell me about the gold, Mother!" he roared. *"Tell me!"*

As mother and son squared off like wolves fighting over a kill, Elizabeth threw open the door to the storage room and ran.

52

Evening shadows blurred the rough road leading to the shanty. Blind with angry determination, James whipped his horse on, forcing the spent animal to maintain a dangerous canter down the rutted lane. He didn't care. He was determined to take care of Rufus Black as expeditiously as possible, then make it back to Rose Hill in time to witness Elizabeth Graham's punishment at his mother's hands.

And then it would be *his* turn. He intended to make Elizabeth squirm, to make her beg, to make her submit. . . .

James knew the scenario well. Twice, as a child, he had been on the receiving end of his mother's wrath. After that, he'd learned. And he had vowed that no *woman* would ever best him again.

She had deceived him from the very beginning, but it wasn't just her clever little charade that enraged James. It was his bitter realization that it had been *Elizabeth* in the barn that day, three years ago at Pastime. The only reason James hadn't dragged her out of his mother's house and finished her off then and there was the certainty that *she*

431

hadn't known the identity of William Soames's killer. James planned to keep that knowledge from surfacing. Ever.

Elizabeth. Bloodlust poured through him in a rising torrent every time he remembered her infuriating indifference to his power. From the very first, she had spurned his advances, and no matter what he had tried over the past year — including yesterday, in Ochlocknee — he hadn't been able to break her. Even after foiling her attempt to escape from the house thirty minutes earlier, she had refused to beg. James had dragged her, thrashing and kicking, back down the hall and into the sitting room, demonstrating again his superior strength. Still, she refused to submit.

She hadn't even submitted to his mother.

James lifted the crop and whipped his horse's flank, pretending it was Elizabeth. She had been terrified; he had seen it in her face, those blue eyes drowning in fear; he'd felt it in her shuddering body. His hands clenched on the reins, remembering the exultant stab of exhiliration when he had held her, felt the fragility of her bones. She was a nobody. A helpless woman. He had the power to crush her. *And before this night was over . . . she* would *admit it.*

An overhanging branch scored his cheek, but James forced himself onward. Then the road curved abruptly and the winded horse stumbled, almost falling. Cursing, James sawed back on the reins, then kicked the snorting animal. Seconds later they burst from the tree-choked road into the edge of a field. On the far side, outlined in the fading glow of the sunset, was the shanty.

If it weren't for Rufus Black, James could have remained at the house and made his mother listen. *He* could have been meting out Elizabeth's punishment. This was all Black's fault. If the clod had done his job right, James wouldn't be forced to take drastic measures now. Bungling, inept, incompetent jackanapes! First, he killed the wrong woman; then, he couldn't even keep track of a child. As far as James was concerned, Rufus Black deserved his fate.

Just as William Soames had deserved his.

Anticipation curled inside, along with the fierce exultation of limitless power. He would make Elizabeth beg, too, just as William Soames had begged for mercy in the musty stall. First, however, he would deal with Black, who was waiting for his return. Waiting . . . tied and trussed like a bagged turkey.

James dismounted in front of the shanty, swiping the back of his hand over his face. The glove came away stained with blood from the branch that had whipped across his face. Suddenly he chuckled. When he opened the door of the shanty, he was still laughing.

◆ ◆ ◆

The faint outline of a rising moon, almost transparent against the pale sky, accompanied Simon as he raced down the mile-long drive to Rose Hill. In contrast, the western sky burned in livid red and orange hues as painful as a scream. He tried to concentrate on the wide road, its pathway obscured by vague, clutching shadows. He wouldn't help anyone if he took a header or forced a gallant animal to break its leg because of carelessness.

Don't let them hurt Elizabeth. She's been hurt so much. So much. The fragmented prayers tormented Simon's thoughts almost as much as the vision of the gentle woman at the mercy of James Crump. James — and Georgina. Why? Simon railed to himself. *Why* hadn't he picked up on the truth earlier? He should have jumped on Dawes's revelation the moment the man confessed to being in Ochlocknee. And he would have, if he wasn't a single-minded, obtuse blockhead with the mental acuity of a manure rake.

Simon didn't know how he would forgive himself if Elizabeth were harmed. He knew that a woman could be as capable of treachery, of blind ambition as any man. And nobody — male or female — was spared the tragic consequences.

I'll take care of Elizabeth. Quit crucifying yourself. Let forgiveness heal both of you, Simon.

"Justice would help more, Lord."

Don't forget what happened the last time you administered your brand of justice.

"I won't forget!" He shouted the words into the wind, then clamped his jaw so tightly his teeth hurt. On the whole, it had been easier when he ignored his conscience. And the Voice.

Easier, but harmful to your soul. And My kingdom. . . .

The horse galloped past two gigantic iron gates imbedded in a pair of brick pillars similar to the smaller pillars flanking the drive at Adelaide. With his hands and his voice, Simon slowed his mount, easing the animal to a trot as they approached the elegant white-columned mansion.

Warning feathered his subconscious instantly. Something was amiss here. Frowning, he drew to a halt and dismounted. Nobody darted forward to take the horse, much less question Simon's presence. No butler waited to greet him at the massive double doors.

With night coming on, lights were already ablaze through all the windows, but he saw not even a hint of movement. On the surface, at least, Rose Hill appeared to be deserted.

The back of Simon's neck burned like the scalding sunset, and he felt as though steel wires were tightening about his throat in ever smaller coils. He took a step, then froze, lis-

435

tening hard. Seconds later he heard it again: a faint whistling sound, borne aloft in the crisp clear air of twilight. It was followed immediately by a sharp crack, like the report of . . . a pistol?

Somewhere in the woods off to the right, several dogs shattered the eery silence further, their deep-throated barks frantic and demanding. *Must have treed their quarry.* Acting on pure instinct, Simon dived behind some nearby bushes, every sense alert, humming. Then, soundless and invisible as a tongue of drifting smoke, he made his way toward the rear of the mansion. The dogs quit barking, abruptly and completely. Into the waiting silence another high-pitched whine intruded, followed by the sharp crack — and a childish scream.

Simon didn't remember moving, but somehow he was in a clearing, rounding the western wing of the mansion. He felt disembodied, as if floating over the ground. Hazy impressions of elaborate hedges, thick-trunked trees, and acres of prickly rosebushes vanished when the cleared grounds behind the house leaped into view. Simon stopped dead, immobilized by sheer, mind-numbing horror. Elizabeth. *God. Dear God . . . Elizabeth!*

She stood between two thick wood posts, her body arched in agony, arms outstretched, suspended by taut cords to the posts. Across her shoulders, faint red trickles oozed through the back of her shredded shirtwaist. Two stolid men dressed in identical uniforms stood guard, mute and rigid as the posts. Elizabeth's face was turned away from Simon, her profile obscured by the tangled strands of an unraveling braid.

Scant paces behind Elizabeth, a third man held a bullwhip, whose wicked lash lay momentarily silent in snakelike coils at his feet. Next to the third man, her face a rictus of hatred — and shame — a frozen Georginia Crump stood motionless, staring in disbelief at her granddaughter Joan. Dirty and disheveled, blond curls tangled, tears streamed down the little girl's cheeks. A stylish royal blue dress coat with several missing buttons covered what appeared to be a nightgown, and she looked as though she'd been rolling in a pile of muddy leaves. Eyes large and liquid as a spaniel's, she stared in horror at her grandmother, at the menacing whip, at Elizabeth.

When she spoke, her breathless treble voice floated across the yard with bell-like clarity. "Grandmother, why is that man hurting Elizabeth? She saved me from Joe . . . she told me to come here, that I would be safe with you. Why are you letting him hurt her?"

A spasm that might have been regret flickered in the ivory mask of Georgina's fine-boned face. Simon melted behind a gigantic sycamore, then a small shed, and some shrubs — step by silent step, moving in for the kill. His gaze never wavered from the monstrous scene. Like an unseen avenging angel, he heard — and recorded — every word.

"It's . . . necessary, child," Georgina finally answered with a sigh. Her hand half lifted toward Joan, then dropped. Even in the fading light, Simon saw that it was trembling. "Come . . . give your grandmother a kiss. I'm —" she stopped, her mouth working. "I've been so worried. . . ."

Joan took one hesitant step forward, her doubtful gaze flickering from Georgina to the shame-faced man holding the whip, and back to Elizabeth.

"Joan Aileen . . ."

Joan walked forward, allowing her grandmother to embrace her in a stiff one-armed hug. But even while she hugged her granddaughter, Simon marked the direction of her gaze. *She had no intention of freeing Elizabeth.* He continued to watch Georgina Crump with death in his heart.

After a thick, awkward pause, Joan wriggled free. "Grandmother?" she asked again, her face uplifted.

Georgina tore her gaze away from Elizabeth, and for the fraction of a second, her eyes closed. "Sometimes, one must do . . . things" — she swallowed convulsively —

438

"things which appear . . . unpleasant." Her chin lifted, and even from twenty feet away, Simon could see the autocratic mantle fall back into place. "Joan, never, ever forget that your family is more important than anyone or anything. Family —"

"Elizabeth is family."

"Elizabeth is *not* family!" That pronouncement made, Georgina turned and gestured impatiently. A short colored woman sidled over, tears brimming in her eyes. She avoided Georgina's gaze.

"Take my granddaughter inside, Frannie," Georgina ordered. "Bathe and feed her, and instruct Chester to call Horatio."

"But, Grandmother, what about Elizabeth?"

"Frannie?"

The servant wrapped a comforting arm about Joan and began urging her toward the house. "Come along, Miss Joan. I'll run you a nice hot bath, then we'll see what we can scare up in the kitchen. . . ."

Joan allowed herself to be herded along — but all the way up to the door, her head was twisted around toward Elizabeth.

Simon waited until the child was safely inside. He stepped into the open as Georgina gestured for her flunky to continue.

"Put that whip down at once!" The hard command rang out like the crack of the whip. Moving carefully, every muscle tensed, Simon glided across the yard, his gaze fixed on the man holding the bullwhip. "Put it down — now," he repeated and, with a thud, the whip collapsed into the dirt.

"I . . . didn't want to do it. She made me. . . ." Sweat glistened on the terrified man's forehead. Simon jerked his chin once, and the erstwhile executioner fled around the corner of the house.

"How dare you!" Georgina screamed. "Jones! Peavy! Don't just stand there like idiots! Remove this — this intruder at once. *At once,* do you hear!"

Simon did not acknowledge Georgina's demand by even the flicker of an eyelash, but turned to the two men standing guard. Georgina Crump wielded a despot's authority — but in a physical confrontation, the guards presented a far more immediate threat. Simon didn't so much as glance at Elizabeth. Right now . . . he couldn't risk it.

"You know this is wrong," he declared, a countering authority ringing in the words, *demanding* the guards' attention. "Wrong and evil. Cut her down."

The stocky man closest to Simon flushed suddenly, his fleshy cheeks quivering. He glanced across to the other guard, then toward the corner of the house where the third man had disappeared.

Simon took a step forward.

The first man broke, backing away with

440

uplifted hands and wild eyes. The second guard, a rough-looking bruiser with a cruel mouth and thick arms, sneered, moving toward Elizabeth.

"I wouldn't if I were you," Simon repeated, shifting slightly. "Please. I don't want to hurt you. Let her go."

"*Peavy!* Seize him!"

Oh, God . . . don't let me kill him. I don't want to kill again. . . . But Simon knew he wouldn't be able to stop himself if the man attacked. The woman he loved more than his own life had just lifted her head, whispered his name — and Simon had glimpsed her face.

53

"Simon." Elizabeth tried to smile, failed. "Told you . . . guardian angel. . . ." she whispered through a scarlet and black vortex of blinding pain. God had answered her prayers — both of them. She hadn't screamed, and Simon had come.

"Hold on, little one." She heard him speak as if from a great distance, his voice both soft as a sigh, yet harder, more unyielding than — Pain spun her back toward the void again, splintering her thoughts.

She fought oblivion, knowing with the instinct of love that Simon was in a killing rage, because of her — and only *she* could draw him back. "Don't . . ." she managed, the effort to force coherent words past numb lips so great that her locked knees finally gave way.

Above her, Elizabeth sensed a flurry of motion, swirling currents of air; heard muffled thuds, a distant moan. White-hot needles of pain scourged her back, but Elizabeth straightened again. "Simon," she sobbed, gasping. "No . . . don't . . ." *Lord, guide him. . . . Don't let him . . . he won't be able to live*

442

with himself if . . .

"It's all right, Elizabeth. I didn't kill him. Shh . . . hold on. Hold on. . . ."

First one arm, then the other dropped free, flopping uselessly. Then someone was laying her down . . . very gently. Still, the pain screamed through her with such intensity that for a few moments she was aware of nothing.

She drifted back slowly, the ebb and flow of voices in her ears. One of them was cold, filled with rage . . . a woman's voice? The other . . . Elizabeth tried to tune her ears to the unwavering solidity of *that* voice. Strong . . . firm . . . controlled. A man's voice — Simon's? Simon had saved her. Again.

Elizabeth vaguely realized that she was lying on her side, her cheek resting against some kind of fabric. The voices focused more sharply, words becoming distinct.

". . . no right to interfere! I won't let you interfere! Her father destroyed my daughter's life, and now I'm going to destroy hers!"

"She saved your grandchildren from dying in unspeakable torment. She's spent the last six years of her life trying to —"

"She's a *liar*, just like her father!"

"No, Mrs. Crump. She is *nothing* like her father. Come now, give me the whip."

"I'll have you arrested! There are a dozen men here, just waiting for my order to shoot you down."

No . . . Simon! He didn't seem to comprehend the ungovernable extent of Georgina's power, or James's — *James!* Where was James? She tried to turn her head, to warn Simon, but her strength had deserted her, and her limbs refused to budge. Panic swamped her, pain blinded her — but Simon's voice never wavered.

". . . and they aren't going to interfere." His tone was confident, utterly convincing. "*Nobody* wants any part of your vindictive revenge."

"My employees will not defy me! *You* can't stop me. I'll do it *myself!*"

Simon's voice altered. "Mrs. Crump — *no.* Don't lift that whip, or we'll both regret it!"

Fear roared through Elizabeth in a cataract. Somehow she was rolling, her hands pressing against the cool dirt. She tried to stand, had to stand. She could not bear —

The hiss of the bullwhip's lash propelled her to her knees, shaking uncontrollably. Her head lifted, and through the tangled screen of hair, her hazy vision found Simon, focused on him. He was standing next to Georgina Crump . . . embracing her? But Georgina's face mirrored alarm — and pain. With one hand, Simon held the woman's arms behind her back. With his free hand, he yanked the bullwhip from her and hurled it into the dirt.

"Georgina Crump, I'm placing you under arrest!" He waited for the space of a heartbeat, then released her and stepped back.

The pronouncement was so unexpected that both Georgina and Elizabeth froze.

"Don't be absurd!" Georgina finally spat. "You have no authority here. You're nothing but . . . a nameless *menial*. When my sons arrive, they'll have you strung from the nearest tree, and nobody will lift a finger to stop them."

For some reason a bolt of dread surged through Elizabeth. "Simon?" she tried to whisper. She blinked, trying to see him more clearly, but the black and scarlet vortex was spinning toward her again, inexorably sucking her into its maw.

There was no mistaking the voice, however. "I do have the authority," he refuted flatly, "as an undercover operative for Pinkerton's National Detective Agency. There's a posse of operatives and deputies on the way to Rose Hill, Mrs. Crump, with warrants for your and your son James's arrest. I suggest you cooperate."

"Wh-at?" Georgina's face paled, but Elizabeth barely noticed.

An undercover operative? Not a horse trainer? Elizabeth closed her eyes, her mind teetering on the brink of merciful oblivion.

Suddenly the world erupted in a cacophany of noise and movement — angry voices, barking dogs, and the restless stamping of many horses' hooves. A swarm of darkly clad men, some wearing badges, spilled into the yard through the back doors of the house and from around both corners. Herded in front of them like mindless cattle, Georgina's uniformed cadre of messengers and guards signaled their surrender with uplifted arms.

Warm hands, infinitely gentle, touched her. "Elizabeth?"

Puzzled, she tried to focus on Simon's blurred face. He was so close — "Did . . . I faint?" She tried to move, but firm hands pressed her back. "Simon?"

"Yes, Elizabeth, I'm here. Just lie still."

"You saved me . . . again. I —"

"Not soon enough . . . you're hurt."

She tried a smile. "Always . . . you rescue. Bad habit . . . for a horse tra—" Then she remembered, and the fragile smile faded. "You said . . . you said you were —"

"Yes. I did . . . and I am." His fingers brushed her face, smoothing away tangled strands of hair. They paused at her numb, swollen lip. "You're bleeding here. You've bitten yourself — please don't look at me like that!" He cupped her face, his expression agonized. "Elizabeth . . . I love you. As God is my witness, that part of it was never a lie. Tell me you believe me."

"Simon, take it easy. She's in a fair amount of pain," a mellow baritone voice intruded, liquid with compassion.

"Georgina had her *whipped,* Adam. Had her tied to those posts . . . and whipped!" Simon's savage response belied his gentleness as he laid Elizabeth down, careful not to touch her back. "I want that woman in jail, tonight. No bail. The same for James, or I won't answer for the consequences. Have you found him?"

"We . . . ah . . . met on the road. He tried to escape, but his horse was spent. Don't worry, Simon. Take care of your woman, and I'll handle the Crumps," said the mellow-voiced man Simon had called Adam. "And, Simon, if she knows who you are, give her time. Give *God* time to work His healing in both of you."

Elizabeth tried to concentrate on the words, tried to make out the blurred features of the man holding her as if she were a priceless treasure, instead of a limp bundle of bloodied rags and bones. Had he really told her that he loved her? Or had she been deluded by pain? ". . . love . . . *you.*" For some reason, it was important that he know. She swallowed, trying to force her thick tongue to shape the words she desperately needed to utter. "Simon?"

"Shh. Shh, love. I'm here. Everything will work out, Elizabeth. Trust me."

It was as if another lash had flicked across her burning back. Trust him? But . . . who was he? Her hand jerked free, uncoordinated and weak. "How?" The black and scarlet in-

447

tensified, building . . . swirling closer. "Simon?" She felt the blackness hovering over her now. Panicky, she fought its cloying shroud. "I love you . . . but, I'm afraid. Don't leave me. . . ."

"Never."

The promise followed Elizabeth as she tumbled headlong into unconsciousness.

♦ ♦ ♦

Thomasville
Three days later

She was sitting in a chair by the window, wrapped in a thick quilt, when Simon walked into the room. Hard pellets of sleet rattled the windowpane, and beneath the quilt her hands clenched into tight fists, her heartbeat echoing the drumming tattoo of the frozen rain.

"You're looking better today. How's the pain?"

"It's subsided to more of a growl than a roar." She watched the green eyes light with tenderness and amusement. But there was no hint of a smile, and his guarded manner was still evident. "Dr. and Mrs. Arbuckle insist that I stay here, but" — she swallowed hard, struggling to keep her voice level — "I've decided it would be best if I left. I . . . don't want to be any more of a burden, and I — I can't go back to the Crumps, so— " She faltered to a stop.

"You're leaving me as well, aren't you?" Simon asked, the quiet voice stripped of any emotion.

He strode across the room, dropping down by her chair to balance on the balls of his feet in front of her. "There's something I've been wanting to tell you." He gripped the chair arms and leaned forward, his gaze burning into hers. "I've resigned, Elizabeth. As of January first, I'll no longer be working for the Agency."

"Not — because of me, I hope." Her hand fought clear of the quilt, and she reached for his face. Then, remembering what she must say, she froze. She would have buried the hand beneath the quilt again, but Simon shifted and trapped it beneath his own before she could blink.

He carried her cold, trembling fingers to his cheek and held them there. "Not because of you," he murmured. "Because of *me*. I don't want to live in the shadows anymore, Elizabeth. I want to make my peace with God and recover something I thought I'd lost forever."

Elizabeth began to tremble. "I love you, Simon," she choked out. "Simon, I do love you. But I'm still — I can't —"

He pressed a kiss into each palm. "I know you love me. I can see it in your face. Elizabeth, God brought us together. Don't let your fear tear us apart."

"I don't want to," she whispered. "But I can't seem to help it. I don't understand why, when I know that I love you — and believe everything you're telling me — why am I still afraid?" She yanked her hands free and turned her head aside, covering her face. "For three days now, I've begged God to take away this fear, to help me . . . to show me what to do. But nothing helps."

She stopped, took a steadying breath, and forced herself to meet his gaze. "I love you, Simon Kincaid, but I don't know if I'll ever be able to trust you. It's not right — I'm not being fair to you and I — I" — her voice dropped to a whisper — "I'm very ashamed."

For a long moment Simon didn't move, though his eyes roamed over her like fingers, touching every feature as if committing them to memory. Then he rose in a single, effortless motion. "There's no need for shame or fear," he said. "But I can see now that there *does* need to be time and distance —" He hesitated, as though steeling himself.

Then his face hardened to the emotionless mask that chilled her soul. "So I'll give you both, Elizabeth. I'm going away. You won't be crowded, won't feel panicked into making a commitment you're not ready or willing to make." He looked down at her, and Elizabeth could only stare back in mute agony. "I love you, and so I'm willing to wait. But, Elizabeth . . . I *will* be back."

He leaned over, and his mouth closed over hers in a searing kiss that was both promise and good-bye. Then he turned and disappeared, as swiftly and silently as a puff of smoke.

54

Simon took the elevator up to the Pinkerton
offices in the Richmond and Danville railroad
building, grateful that he had not felt compelled, this time, to don collar and tie. The
past week had been a paradox — tedious, endless hours of writing reports, filling out forms,
rehashing the events of the preceding months
. . . and quiet hours of soul-searching, preparations for a new life, deep conversations with
Alexander — and Eve, when she wasn't sick
from her pregnancy. *Indisposed,* Simon reminded himself. He had promised Alexander,
out of deference to his wife, to be circumspect
when speaking of the "blessed event."

It was a small thing to ask, to Simon's way
of thinking. If he hadn't had such good
friends to nurture the rediscovery of his faith,
he probably would have taken the first train
south and refused to budge from Elizabeth's
side.

The front desk clerk nodded but did not
speak. Superintendent Jenkins was in confer-

452

ence with a potential client, so Simon poked his head through Perry Sterns's door.

The deputy's thin face lit up with surprised pleasure. "Mr. Kincaid! I'd heard you planned to stop by today, before you left for — Montana, is it?"

Simon nodded. "I'm trying to catch a noon train to Chicago, but Mr. Jenkins promised to fill me in on the Crumps." He was too keyed up to sit, and instead wandered about the tidy, uncluttered office, wishing Jenkins would hurry up.

"I . . . um . . . heard you plan to purchase a farm? In Montana?"

"Out west, they're known as ranches. Operative Moreaux found the place. I'll be fixing it up, come spring, so by the time I return for the trial, I'll be able to offer —" He skidded to an abrupt halt, unable to voice aloud his dream.

Plowing a hand through his hair, Simon glanced again through the open blinds, into Mr. Jenkins's office next door. The superintendent was getting to his feet at last, extending his hand to a man wearing a neat pinstriped suit. The man donned his bowler. *It shouldn't be long, now.* Simon turned to Sterns, whose expression had reverted to an anxious frown. Simon suppressed a fleeting prick of remorse. Some things never changed. "So, do you still have that dog I rescued last year?"

A relieved smile spread across the other man's face. "Yes. Yes, indeed we do. My wife and I — well, we'll always be grateful. Ginger — that's what we named her, you know — Ginger's as sweet and loving a creature as I've ever known. Never growls or snaps, hardly ever barks, though to look at her you'd think her the most ferocious of watchdogs, she's so large and fiercesome in appearance —" He flushed, halting the voluble flow of words. "I, uh, beg your pardon, Mr. Kincaid."

"Not at all, Mr. Sterns. I'm glad to hear everything turned out well, for you *and* the dog." He spent several more minutes in light conversation, attempting to relax the deputy, not for the first time marveling inwardly at the change in himself. *You really* do *make a difference in a man's life, Lord.* . . .

Unruffled, the instant affirmative response hovered in the air, fading only when Mr. Jenkins strode into the room.

"Mr. Kincaid!" They shook hands. "MacKay told me he'd dangled a juicy carrot to entice you to stop by. Glad you could make it. You look well." The older man studied him for a moment, stroking his full white beard. "I find I'm both relieved — and regretful. We'll miss you hereabouts, son."

"Thanks." Simon glanced at the large wall clock behind Sterns's desk. "Um . . . I'm trying to catch a noon train."

Jenkins stared hard at Simon another moment, then abruptly broke into a deep-bellied laugh. "I suppose I'm not overly surprised," he murmured. "Both MacKay and Moreaux tried to tell me, but I confess at the time I didn't believe them." He shook his head. " 'Simon Kincaid's the *last* man on earth to succumb to a woman's charms,' I told 'em. You were too hard. Too dangerous, for some sweet little lady to tame."

Simon could feel heat creeping into his cheeks, but he couldn't take offense. Not any longer. "A man can change, sir," he murmured. "Any man, with the heart, and the will to, can change." *With God's help.* . . .

"Especially when there's a woman like Elizabeth Graham waiting in the wings?"

Just the mention of her name brought the terrible craving clawing its way to the surface. Simon prayed daily that God would heal Elizabeth's heart, as well as her body, so she would learn to trust him. He had known, since their parting six days ago, that he would have to wait, but he hadn't known then how difficult the discipline would be.

He crammed his hands deep in his pockets. "Tell me about the Crumps." He had intended the topic switch as a diversion, even though he *was* curious. But the consuming bloodthirst for vengeance had metamorphosed over the past days and nights spent with the MacKays, melting away in the wake of a new set of priorities. With the help of his friends — and his God — Simon had learned to pray for justice instead of retribution. Ahead lay the rigorous task of hammering out a new life in a new land, in the hope that faith and hard work would help him pass the lonely months until he returned to claim the woman he loved.

But why this niggling disquiet festering at the back of his mind?

"It's all fallen together quite satisfactorily," Jenkins was telling him. "James, of course, has been officially charged with two counts of murder — William Soames and Rufus Black. Also as an accessory before the fact, of the murder of some local whose name escapes me at the moment."

"Maisie Pritchard," Simon murmured.

"Ah, yes." Jenkins coughed, patting his pockets until he produced a pair of spectacles. "Mr. Sterns? Hand me the report, why don't you?" Sterns hurriedly complied, and the superintendent scanned the pages and continued, "Benjamin Dawes is still incarcerated in the Thomasville jail, primarily for his safety at this point. But it is James Crump's actions, more than those of his two minions — or even Georgina's, that have stirred up the scandal of the century down there, so to speak. After his arrest, his behavior was hostile, even belligerent. He gloated over the murders, and, according to Operative Traynor, he even went so far as to threaten the sheriff, the judge, and" — his mouth quirked in a wry smile — "Pinkerton's National Detective Agency — yourself in particular, Mr. Kincaid."

Somehow Simon wasn't surprised. He had wandered over to the window while Jenkins talked, gazing at Atlanta's bustling skyline. "MacKay told me the decision was made to transfer Mr. Crump to . . . more neutral surroundings until his trial. Albany, wasn't it?"

Jenkins nodded. "The latest development — which you wouldn't have heard, since it happened only yesterday evening — is that Georgina has suffered a mild stroke. I've talked with Horatio myself, at some length, over the course of the week, and no — I didn't feel inclined to apprise you of that. Don't try that look on me, son. I'm not impressed."

Simon held his peace. He was well aware that his feelings toward Horatio — because of Elizabeth — were prejudiced and far from objective.

"Apparently the judge, the sheriff, and the town's aldermen — minus Horatio, of course — have been discussing a rather . . . *unconventional* . . . solution to the problem of Georgina Crump."

"Hmpf! She belongs in jail with James," Simon observed, then could have kicked himself. So much for peace and forgiveness. His eye homed in on the soaring spire of the First

Presbyterian Church across the street.

"Kincaid . . . Simon!" Jenkins barked irritably. "Turn around when I'm talking to you, if you please."

"Sorry," Simon apologized meekly. He dropped down into an office chair, crossing his legs. From the corner of his eye, he caught Perry Sterns's bug-eyed astonishment and grimaced. Had he given the man *that* much grief these past few years? "What about Georgina?"

The superintendent subjected Simon to another slow perusal and, satisfied with what he saw, continued, "It was agreed that, due to Mrs. Crump's age — and current health condition — an acceptable substitution to incarceration would be house arrest, at least while waiting for her trial. With, of course, a few modifications — a twenty-four-hour guard, all telephone and telegraph lines removed, visitors and correspondence screened. For all intents and purposes, she'll remain a virtual prisoner at Rose Hill." He looked down at the thick sheaf of papers on Perry Sterns's desk. "According to this last report, she's recovering from the stroke, resting comfortably, but weak. Right now about all she can do is hector her nurse. Take it easy, son. The black widow won't be spinning any more deadly webs."

"Dawes called her the brown recluse," Simon mused. He stood, restless, regretting that he had agreed to give Elizabeth time. He hated to leave her, alone and vulnerable, even with James and Georgina under guard. *Sorry.* Perhaps it was not Elizabeth only who needed to learn to trust. . . .

Right now he felt stifled in the cramped office, with an almost compulsive need to reassure himself, one last time before he left, that she was *safe.* "Mr. Jenkins, I'd like to verify James Crump's status in the Albany jail." Simon spoke far too abruptly, he knew, and although Jenkins's mouth pursed a bit at the tone, he obliged.

"Ring the Albany jail on the telephone, Mr. Sterns." The superintendent inspected Simon almost indulgently. "Beats me why you don't haul the filly off to Montana with you, Mr. Kincaid. It's plain as the nose on my face what *your* feelings are. . . ." He coughed and changed the subject. "Um . . . did I tell you Horatio's been absolved of all wrongdoing? He's admitted to knowledge of his mother's unethical, ultimately illegal, business practices, but had been unable to persuade her to modify her actions. I gather he invited Miss Graham to recuperate at Adelaide, but she, of course, declined, since —"

"*What?*" Perry Sterns exclaimed.

Simon whipped around, his gaze glued to the assistant's horrified face. And all those niggling doubts of the past week detonated in an internal explosion that almost rocked him back on his heels.

"When? How?" Sterns sputtered, one hand half raised toward Simon, as if to fend him off. He listened in silence for another minute, his face ashen, then hung up and turned to face Simon. "Mr. Kincaid . . . he's escaped. James Crump has escaped — sometime between midnight and dawn this morning. He . . . he bribed the guards and —"

"He's going after Elizabeth." Simon stared at the slack-jawed man, not seeing him. Not seeing anything at all. *"He's going after Elizabeth!"*

"Sterns, hand me that telephone!" Jenkins shoved past Simon, picked up the instrument, and rapped out his instructions to the operator. While he waited, drumming his fingers on the desktop, he ordered Sterns to telegraph Thomasville. "And if guards haven't been posted, tell them to take care of it at once. Around the clock. I'll square it with the local authorities later."

"I've got to get back there," Simon managed, his throat so tight the words emerged in a harsh whisper. "Immediately . . . I have to leave immediately. He's there by now . . . it's been over twelve hours." *I never should have left her alone. If anything happens to Elizabeth. . . .*

"Mr. Kincaid . . . Simon, get hold of yourself, son! What's the matter with you? This is no time for panic!"

460

Jenkins's sharp reprimand brought Simon to his senses. "Sorry." He inhaled, let out his breath slowly. She wasn't dead yet . . . he'd know it, somehow, in his soul. *Oh, God — I'd feel it, wouldn't I?*

I'm watching over Elizabeth, Simon. But, be careful.

"I'm on my way to the depot," he told Jenkins. "Telegraph whatever information you learn, and have the dispatcher relay it to me en route."

The superintendent pondered a moment, still watching Simon. "Very well. But, Mr. Kincaid, remember — until the end of the month, you're a Pinkerton operative. Don't do anything you — any of us — would regret. Be careful. . . ."

Simon absorbed the uncanny echo, but its import was lost beneath the weight of his desperate need. At the door he turned. "If James Crump lays a finger on Elizabeth Graham, you might as well send an operative after *me.*" He faced down the older man. "And they can give Crump's cell to somebody else. *He* won't be needing it . . . not if he harms Elizabeth!"

55

In the woods near Adelaide

James paced the abandoned log smokehouse where he'd been hiding out for the past twenty-four hours. Though drafty, dirty, and uncomfortable, it was preferable to the Albany jail; he'd survived heinous indignities in that rancid, rat-infested cell only by imagining — in gratifying detail — what he planned to do to Elizabeth Graham, once he escaped.

In a fit of temper, he kicked the splintering log wall, longing to vent his rage with a round of blistering curses. But though Horatio would have long forgotten their boyhood hideout, James wasn't about to take any more chances of being captured. Not this time.

Escaping had been as easy as pie, but having to wait until dawn to catch a southbound freight had pushed both his patience and his luck to the limit. He'd jumped train in Ochlocknee to foil searchers, but by the time he made it to Thomasville the previous afternoon, guards had already been posted around the doc's house. At least the guards' presence there had saved him from a trip to

Adelaide to look for Elizabeth.

Now . . . how to get past the guards. He'd tried twice, and the last time, early this morning, he'd almost been spotted.

It was all *her* fault, all of it. She'd been obstructive from the start, all the way back to that episode with William Soames at Pastime Stables. If only he'd known *then*. . . .

It was late. Cold, too, but he barely noticed. Shards of silver-white beams from a full moon sliced down through the woods. James darted from tree to tree, avoiding the cold slivers of light, hiding in the darkest shadows until he reached the drive. He figured it was close to ten o'clock, which gave him almost an hour to reach his destination. The packed dirt driveway was deserted, but James approached it cautiously. Guards had been posted around the house and outbuildings — he'd watched them from under cover of the woods — but he doubted they'd be patroling the road, and the empty drive proved it.

Tonight. It would happen tonight — he could feel it — and the anticipation of triumph made him want to shout. Last night, after his second attempt to approach the doctor's house had been thwarted by a barking dog, he had hidden across the street and watched the guards' movements. Shortly after the piercing train whistle shrilled the arrival of the eleven o'clock Chicago Flyer, the

man posted at the back of the house had disappeared for almost five minutes.

Ahead, the two brick pillars loomed like
sentinels. One was illuminated by a blinding
moonbeam, so James made a dash for cover
behind the other, gloating inwardly at the
skill of his reconnoitering.

Ah . . . soon now. Soon he'd have his revenge —

There was no warning. Something struck
him in the back, low and hard, hurling him
face first to the ground.

♦ ♦ ♦

Consumed by rage, Simon laid hold of the
dazed James, flipped him over, and delivered
a punishing right hook to his jaw. "*That's* for
assaulting Elizabeth!" he growled, and
hauled the other man to his feet.

James exploded, ripping free in a frenzy of
movement, his face in the bright moonlight
distorted by hatred bordering on madness.
"I'll kill you, too!"

From an inner pocket of his jacket, he
yanked out a crooked length of cast iron and,
arms flailing, he charged. Both men crashed
to the earth. A vicious blow to Simon's shoulder all but paralyzed his right arm. One-
handed, he struggled desperately, but James
managed two more crippling blows before Simon, in a burst of near superhuman strength,
threw the other man aside and surged to his
feet.

They squared off, circling each other, both men breathing hard. Simon divided his attention between James's face and the makeshift weapon still clutched in Crump's hand. It appeared to be a piece of pump handle, broken off some eight inches from the base.

James began to laugh, a harsh, grating sound that raised goosebumps on Simon's skin. "First you — then the girl!" he chanted, waving the handle, stalking Simon. "You can't stop me — *nobody* can stop me! I'm a *Crump!*"

"You're a murderer, a sniveling cowardly murderer!" Simon retorted, bloodlust flooding his veins, blocking the pain. "But you've killed your last victim, you lowdown, worthless vermin. Unless," he added, deliberately baiting, "your mother has another stroke, and dies. Then you'll have *her* death on your conscience. . . ."

With an inhuman howl, James lunged, swinging the pump handle in a violent arc. This time Simon was ready. Swiveling sideways, he slammed his hand down on the forearm holding the handle, while his out-thrust foot tripped James, who was already off balance. The handle dropped with a muffled thud as the other man hit the ground again. Simon followed him, and in a series of merciless blows, reduced the other man to a semiconscious lump of flesh.

Roaring filled his head, triumphant and

uncontrolled. He picked up the pump handle and hurled it away. Straddling James, knees pinning his arms, Simon stared down into the bloodied face of his mortal enemy. Only one thought remained: vindication. Their eyes met and Simon's hands closed around James's throat and began to squeeze.

"Was this what you planned for Elizabeth?" Simon ground out. "Just like you did to Rufus Black, lying trussed and helpless?" James's eyes flared wide, and Simon could smell his fear.

Simon . . . no . . . don't do this to Me.

"Or did you plan to bash in her head, like you did William Soames?" Simon squeezed harder. In the brutal white moonlight, James's face appeared mottled, but fear and hatred blazed unabated in his eyes.

Simon . . . remember Jake . . . and Percy.

"You deserve this! You *deserve* to die —"

But not by your hand, Simon.

The thought burst inside his head in a single piercing needle of blinding light. If he killed James Crump in the passion of outraged judgment, Simon would be as guilty of murder as James. He would catapult twenty years into the past, never to return, never to reclaim what he had so miraculously recovered.

With a hoarse cry Simon jerked his hands up and stared at them as if he'd never seen them before. Then he rolled off James and knelt, gasping, on the damp, chilled earth. By his side, James gagged and wheezed, fighting to draw air into his oxygen-deprived lungs.

Painfully, deliberately, Simon rolled James onto his side so he could breathe. "You might be a piece of swamp scum to me," he said, wiping a shaking hand across his own bloodied cheek, "but it will have to be up to a jury to decide whether you live or die." *I won't make that mistake again, Lord. Please . . . can You forgive me?*

Perhaps it was only a gentle breeze — or a remnant of half-crazed lunacy that had thrust him beyond the pale. But Simon *felt* the healing, life-giving Presence flow over and around him — supporting . . . loving. Forgiving. . . .

For the first time since he was a child, hot moisture stung the corners of his eyes. Swallowing over the lump in his throat, Simon pulled out the handcuffs the sheriff had loaned him and, satisfied that James was breathing freely, fastened his wrists behind his back.

"Let's go." He hefted the man to his feet. "For *both* our sakes, I think you'll be safer in a cell." He paused, then added quietly, "And this time . . . stay there."

Shoulders hunched, head down, James drew a shuddering breath. "My . . . mother," he mumbled, keeping his face averted. "Is she . . . will she be all right?"

Simon rummaged for a handkerchief, then used it to clear James's face of the worst of the dirt and blood. "She's resting comfortably. Don't worry."

They shuffled down the street toward town, Simon herding the vanquished James with an easy compassion he would have sworn was impossible twenty-four hours earlier . . . two *minutes* earlier.

I don't deserve Your love . . . Your forgiveness, Lord.

You're Mine, Simon . . . one of My flock. I'll never let you go, my son.

The rest of the way into town, Simon's step was a great deal lighter than it had been for, oh . . . he figured, at least twenty years.

Now to find the patience to wait while the Lord worked on Elizabeth.

56

Laurel Springs
May 1896

Elizabeth sat back on her heels, catching her breath while she surveyed the results of her day's labor. The smell of rich black earth filled her nostrils, and the afternoon sun beat pleasantly down on her shoulders and back. In front of her stretched a row of freshly planted beans, their flimsy stalks thrusting upward in brave defiance of a capricious, indifferent world.

Her hoe-dug furrows were comically crooked, she had to admit. With a rueful sigh, she tugged off a pair of frayed work gloves, then removed the old straw hat she wore to work the garden. If only the sun could warm her *inside* as well as out. Although spring had burst upon the earth in its unruly display of color and life, the stark barrenness of winter continued to chill the wasteland of Elizabeth's spirit.

In the distance a train whistle shrieked, announcing the arrival of Laurel Spring's only train of the day, the Blue Ridge Special, whistle-stopping its way from Atlanta to Chattanooga. The haunting sound never failed to tighten Elizabeth's throat. Would she ever be able to hear a train whistle without remembering the tragic circumstances of the preceding year?

As if it were yesterday, she recalled Horatio's awkward visit to the doctor's home, that next day when Elizabeth still lay in a pain-filled stupor. Turning his bowler round and round, hands trembling, he had apologized for his mother's inexcusable behavior. For his brother's perfidy and betrayal. If Elizabeth desired, she would be welcomed back at Adelaide with open arms. The children missed her, Josephine missed her. . . .

Simon had come in then. He'd taken one look at Elizabeth and escorted the shame-faced Horatio out of the room.

Simon. Blindly Elizabeth gathered her tools, but her hands were trembling, and she dropped the spade twice. Merciful Father, what was she going to do? "Why?" she whispered, lifting her face toward heaven, hearing the tortured uncertainty of a question voiced every hour of every one of the last hundred and fifty some days. How could she love someone — yet be afraid to trust that love? How could she not trust a man who understood her so well that he was willing to give her time? A man who had written her one short letter to reassure her of his love, then waited for her response? Was he still waiting?

The shy chipmunk she had befriended and dubbed Ebenezer darted out from his home in a jumbled outcropping of rock, at the base of a grove of sweetgums. Elizabeth dug in her pocket for the handful of crushed peanuts. "Here you are," she told Ebenezer. "Some more food for your horde. Now, can you tell me why I'm so afraid to trust Simon that I'm hiding up here, all alone, instead of writing to tell him to come and fetch me?"

Ebenezer's bright black eye honed in on the peanuts, but at least he listened while he stuffed his fattening jowls.

"I've never trusted anyone, as you know," Elizabeth tried next, dashing an impatient hand across her cheeks. If she ever made it through a day without weeping, she planned to bake herself a cake. "But then, I never thought I'd fall in love, either. I always thought I'd be alone, that God would provide all the comfort and companionship I'd need. Then God brought Simon, and I — I don't understand. . . ."

Her voice broke over the last words. Impatient, Elizabeth clamped her mouth shut and watched until Ebenezer's pouch was full, and the little creature scampered back to his den. Then she gathered the rest of her tools, concentrating on the mundane task until the protesting door slammed shut on her memories — and questions for which she had no answers.

She had only to survive the next minute. Then the next. By the end of each evening, when she dutifully bolted the door of her isolated bungalow, she could chalk up the triumph of having survived another day.

In one sense, living alone — unknown, friendless, beholden to nobody — had proved to be a triumph in itself. Elizabeth had been lonely all her life, but she had seldom *been* alone, and until she had hidden herself away in this isolated house in this lonely mountain town, she had never confronted head-on her secret fear of *being* alone.

Am I going to turn into a mirror image of Georgina Crump, Lord? An eccentric, emotionally crippled old woman who spends all her time cultivating her ragged vegetable garden?

Elizabeth's lips curved upward in the semblance of a smile at the irony of her improbable fancy. Well. That marked a milestone of sorts: she was actually smiling at the twisted humor of comparing herself to the bitter woman who had planned to destroy her.

Shaking her head, she rose stiffly, muscles protesting, then wandered back toward the tiny cottage she was renting until autumn. Come September, Mrs. MacCready would return from Memphis, where she had gone to nurse her youngest daughter through the confinement and birth of her first child. Elizabeth would —

From long practice she stopped the

thought mid-sentence. The future offered nothing, not any longer. No hope. No joy. No sense of purpose. She didn't know what to do about Simon, and she had no desire to continue the search for the missing gold, much less resume an impossible, wrong-headed quest for atonement. As far as Elizabeth was concerned, the gold could stay buried — just like her father. She had learned to survive without a family; she had learned to survive without acceptance, a sense of belonging.

If necessary, she would learn to survive without Simon.

Does that make me an emotional cripple, Lord? Even worse . . . if she believed God had brought Simon into her life, yet she still couldn't trust him, did that mean she wasn't trusting God either?

How would she *know?*

Once again, it all boiled down to a matter of trust. And the choice was up to Elizabeth alone.

She trudged back along the narrow path from the garden to a small, age-weathered shed. She had just hung her apron and hat on a nail when she heard the muffled thud of a horse's hooves. Mildly curious, Elizabeth walked around the corner to the front of the house — and stopped as if she had slammed into an invisible wall.

Simon Kincaid was climbing out of a dust-covered, dilapidated buggy. His clothing bore the same film of gray dust, and lines of strain were etched across the sun-browned planes of his bearded face. His eyes . . .

Elizabeth could not look away from the brilliant clarity of those eyes. That green gaze had haunted her sleep, her every waking thought. All the blood drained from her head, and for an instant she was afraid she was going to faint. Then she realized that the prickly sensation of dizziness and faint nausea was because she had forgotten to breathe. One hand went to her throat, as if she could somehow contain her leaping pulse.

Simon crossed the neatly swept path in front of the house, his stride smooth, determined. As if in a dream, Elizabeth watched him open the gate, watched him survey the cottage in a swift, comprehensive gaze, watched him keep walking until the panicked thought occurred that he was going to take her in his arms.

Instinctively she took a backward step, then another.

"Don't run," he said. "Please. Don't run away from me again, Elizabeth."

"I . . . no. I won't run," she stammered, her tongue thick and unresponsive. "You're here," she said stupidly.

He searched her face, a slow, penetrating study that sent a painful tide of red creeping up her throat, to her cheeks. "You have a smudge of dirt on your forehead and your

474

nose," he observed, and one of the hands held stiffly at his sides twitched, as though he had resisted touching her. "What have you been doing?"

The prosaic query, voiced in that deep, gentle tone, so disconcerted Elizabeth that she answered automatically. "I have a garden, behind the house. Today I planted four rows of pole beans."

"I see. The cottage . . . is it yours?"

His voice never lost its gentleness, and Elizabeth found herself responding, her thoughts too shattered to protest either his questions *or* his presence. "N— no. It belongs to Mrs. MacCready. Her husband died last year. She's letting me stay here until fall, because her daughter's with child . . . having a difficult confine—" The blush scalded its way to her hairline then, and she dropped her head in confusion. So accustomed had she grown to talking only with the animals, or to herself, that she had almost blurted out loud a topic reserved, in polite society, for women. Or so she had thought.

"Ah . . . there's a lot of that going around," Simon agreed. "I have a friend whose wife is due early this summer. Actually, you met her once. . . ." For the space of a blink, a warm light deepened the green eyes. "The birth of a child is a miracle, is it not?" he continued matter-of-factly, and Elizabeth flinched as if bee-stung. Simon kept right on talking. "But

475

then, any birth is a miracle. Babies. Horses. Dogs." He paused, then added, "Even sheep. All of them are gifts, would you agree? Gifts from God."

"Why are you talking like this?" Elizabeth blurted. She backed up another step, flinging a wild-eyed glance over her shoulder, toward the door. "Why did you come? You've come to say good-bye, haven't you? You're too kind to say it in a letter, though I wouldn't blame you —"

"Elizabeth . . ."

"Don't do this to me!" The months of self-doubt, of agonizing, exploded in a fire-storm of panicked words. "Go away. I cannot — *cannot* handle this pain, not when I have to look at you, listen to your voice. Know with every beat of my heart that it's over, and I'll be alone . . . again. I thought I could do it . . . thought I would *have* to learn to manage on my own. But now . . . to see you —"

Simon started forward and Elizabeth threw up her hands. "No! Please don't touch me." Her voice broke and, with a dry sob, she buried her face in her hands. "Dear God," she cried brokenly, "what have I done, that You're punishing me like this?"

"Oh, God isn't to blame," Simon refuted instantly. "*God* is not punishing you, Elizabeth. You're punishing *yourself*. Listen to me. *Listen.* Elizabeth, if you don't want me to touch you, then look at me and listen to what I have to say."

She shook her head until the untidy knot of her hair slipped sideways. Pins flew free and tumbled to the ground.

"Yes!" Simon snapped, though he lowered his voice in the next breath. "I love you, Elizabeth, and the last thing I ever wanted to do was to leave you alone this long. But last winter, you were hurt, confused, in shock — not only because of the Crumps but because I had to deceive you about my job as a Pinkerton operative."

He took a step forward, half-lifting his hand in a pleading gesture. "Don't you see? It would have been as much of a deception to force our relationship then. I wasn't going to do that. To you . . . or to me. But I can't stand what you're doing to yourself. What you're trying to do to *us*. You have to listen . . . please." He paused, then finished very quietly, "If you've decided in the last five months that you don't love me any longer, then turn around and walk away. Walk away, Elizabeth, and go back to your lonely existence. Be a hermit, if that's what you want. But don't make the mistake I did twenty years ago and walk away from God."

Walk away. All she had to do was turn around and walk away. She could lock herself in Mrs. MacCready's spartan little home and not risk having her heart broken a second time. She would be safe, free to pursue her "lonely existence."

"You haven't turned your back on God, have you?" Simon persisted.

Stung by his seeming ability to perceive her thoughts, Elizabeth stiffened her spine. "Of course not!" Then, because she sounded so defensive, she tried to explain, "I might not understand why He allows some things to happen, and I'm beginning to wonder why He continues to bother with me. But — but I still trust *Him*."

"You aren't too sure, though, are you?" Simon tilted his head and folded his arms across his chest. "So why don't you turn around, walk up that path, and slam the door in my face?"

The soft challenge stung, and she turned her back on him without thinking, wanting only to escape.

"But before you go, there's something I'd like to show you."

Was it her heart pounding in her ears — or did his voice sound strained? Even desperate? Elizabeth hesitated, then turned around. "What is it?" she asked, eyeing him suspiciously.

Simon unfolded his arms and dropped them to his sides, as if deliberately leaving himself vulnerable. "If you believe God can truly change a man's heart," he began slowly, hesitantly, "if you believe that one day the lamb *will* nestle securely within the mighty paws of the lion . . . then believe in my love for you. *Trust* me." After an intent perusal of her face, he turned toward the buggy. "Shadow," he called in a low voice. "Shadow, it's all right. You can come out now. Come on. . . ."

Elizabeth's heart swelled, choking her. A distinct bleat had answered Simon's call, and now a fleecy head popped up over the door of the buggy. Simon knelt, and the tiny animal tumbled out, all gangly legs and clumsy haste as it scampered into Simon's waiting arms.

He rose, holding the lamb, and turned back to Elizabeth. "She knows my voice, you see. And she trusts me." A pulse throbbed at his temple, and even through her own scalding tears, Elizabeth could see the love burning nakedly in his face. "She knows I'll take care of her, nurture her, protect her. She isn't afraid that I'll hurt her or abandon her." He choked and gently set the lamb down. "Elizabeth . . . ?"

Like the lamb, she ran into his embrace and felt his arms close around her. "I love you!" she promised in a breathless whisper. "I love you, Simon Kincaid . . . and — and I *trust* you, too! I didn't know how much, until —" His kiss ended the impassioned declaration.

Shadow butted her head against their legs, baaing indignantly. Reluctantly Simon broke away long enough to lean over and scoop up the little lamb.

A ripple of laughter escaped Elizabeth's lips as she stroked Shadow, snuggled between them. Overflowing with love — with trust — she lifted her gaze.

A smile like the breaking dawn was spreading across Simon's face.

Epilogue

Rocky Mountains, Colorado
August 1896

But what about Booker Rattray?

Adam Moreaux stretched out in the tall grasses of a mountain meadow, his head propped on Kat's belly. Beneath his ear the cougar's rumbling purr sounded more like a low-pitched growl, and Adam grinned, one hand lifting to scratch behind the dozing cat's ear.

"You make a softer pillow than a pound of goose down."

Kat's ear twitched, but she made no other response, and Adam's grin deepened. He wondered what Elizabeth Graham — *whoa! Kincaid, now* — would think of his companion. Simon had always given the cougar respect, but little affection, even though Kat had saved both his and Adam's hides on a few memorable occasions. Adam stroked the animal's huge paw, flopping limp as a wilted daisy now, claws sheathed. Such deadly power, concealed beneath such deceptive softness. Even after all these years, he mar-

veled at the unorthodox relationship he
shared with one of God's more savage creatures.

His thoughts returned to Simon and Elizabeth and their wedding the previous week.
"Elizabeth," he mused aloud now, "I've a
feeling you already know as well as I, that Simon and Kat are remarkably similar . . . but if
anyone can tame *Simon,* I think it's you."
Still vivid in his memory was the touching
tableau of the tame, half-grown lamb that
Elizabeth had insisted remain between herself and her groom as they spoke their vows.

"Trust me," she had promised the flabbergasted minister. "Shadow's presence has the
Lord's blessing. She'll behave."

Shadow had behaved, all right . . . until Simon had leaned over to kiss the bride. Remembering, Adam laughed out loud, and
Kat stirred, her long black-tipped tail twitching in annoyance. "Sorry." He soothed the
animal with a gentle hand. "It's a good thing
you weren't present. I have a feeling that, unlike Simon's, your and Shadow's relationship
would have been . . . brief."

A cloud slid across the sun and, with a regretful sigh, Adam rose. The newly wedded
couple were on their way to Simon's Montana ranch, where they planned to raise
horses and a houseful of little Kincaids.

"And they'll know of their parents' — and
God's — love for them, every day of their

482

lives," Elizabeth had vowed, her smiling eyes meeting those of her new husband.

Even now, the memory of Simon's reciprocal smile brought a lump to Adam's throat. So many years . . . for so many years he had prayed for his dark and dangerous friend. *Thank You.*

My pleasure. . . .

Adam nudged Kat with the toe of his knee-length moccasin. "Wake up, sleepyhead. I know you're a nocturnal creature and all that, but I've decided to make a brief run to Denver and check out the files on Booker Rattray. I know I've seen that name somewhere."

He had learned Elizabeth's background from Simon, and though the couple had agreed to set aside the mystery of the stolen gold, Adam's curiosity bone had been tickled. Charles Graham had been an adulterous thief and the Crumps — except for Horatio — extortionists and murderers.

So who *was* Booker Rattray?

◆ ◆ ◆

Denver, Colorado
Two days later

Sometimes a rapacious quest for neatly tied ends could land a man in a bushel of trouble. Adam tucked the bulging file beneath his arm, shut the heavy file drawer, and padded with noiseless tread back across the crowded room. Fortunately, despite his unorthodox clothes, nobody paid him any attention. He escaped down the hall to the tiny cubicle of a room he'd commandeered for his own whenever he was in town.

For hours he pored over the files, so immersed in his search that he scarcely noticed the passage of time. His hunch, unfortunately, was right on the mark. Booker Rattray appeared to be a scurrilous fellow with the dubious honor of a listing on both Pinkerton's *and* Wells Fargo's "Wanted" posters. His first arrest, according to a dog-eared Rogues' Gallery card, had taken place over twenty years earlier, in '72; his last-known whereabouts, in Cripple Creek, four years ago.

Hmm, Adam thought. *Interesting*. Suddenly he smiled, already composing a letter as he reached for his pen.

◆ ◆ ◆

"But let justice roll on like a river, righteousness like a never-failing stream!"

Amos 5:24